The Spark of Modernism

D1571389

ALSO BY THE EDITORS
AND FROM MCFARLAND

*Speculative Modernism: How Science Fiction,
Fantasy and Horror Conceived the Twentieth Century*
(William Gillard, James Reitter and Robert Stauffer, 2021)

The Spark of Modernism

*Twenty Speculative Stories and Writings
That Defined an Era, 1886–1939*

Edited by WILLIAM GILLARD,
JAMES REITTER *and* ROBERT STAUFFER

McFarland & Company, Inc., Publishers
Jefferson, North Carolina

Library of Congress Cataloguing-in-Publication Data

Names: Gillard, Bill (Professor), editor. | Reitter, James, 1973– editor. |
    Stauffer, Robert, 1965– editor.
Title: The spark of modernism : twenty speculative stories and writings that defined
    an era, 1886-1939 / edited by William Gillard, James Reitter and Robert Stauffer.
Description: Jefferson, North Carolina : McFarland & Company, Inc., Publishers, 2023 |
    Includes bibliographical references and index.
Identifiers: LCCN 2023016247 | ISBN 9781476691091 (paperback : acid free paper) ∞
    ISBN 9781476649467 (ebook)
Subjects: LCSH: Speculative fiction, American. | Short stories, American. | Speculative
    fiction, English. | Short stories, English. | LCGFT: Science fiction. | Fantasy fiction. |
    Horror fiction. | Short stories.
Classification: LCC PS648.S74 S63 2023 | DDC 823/.010808—dc23/eng/20230509
LC record available at https://lccn.loc.gov/2023016247

British Library cataloguing data are available

ISBN (print) 978-1-4766-9109-1
ISBN (ebook) 978-1-4766-4946-7

"Black God's Kiss"© 1934 by *Weird Tales*; reprinted by permission
of Don Congdon Associates, Inc.

Front cover illustration by Tithi Luadthong (Shutterstock)

Printed in the United States of America

*McFarland & Company, Inc., Publishers
    Box 611, Jefferson, North Carolina 28640
    www.mcfarlandpub.com*

Acknowledgments

Assembling this collection has been a joy for the three of us. Some of these wonderful stories and essays are well known; others have not been in print for many, many years. As editors, we waded through sometimes complex publication histories to find the earliest published versions of each text. Those are what we have chosen for this anthology, with three exceptions. First, "Rhythm of the Spheres" by A. Merritt was published by *Thrilling Wonder Stories* in 1936; that is the text we include here. That story was originally titled "The Last Poet and the Robots" and it was published as part of the collaborative novel *Cosmos* that was serialized from 1933 to 1935 in *Science Fiction Digest*. Second, William James's "What Pragmatism Means" was originally delivered as a lecture, and so we used its first publication in book form for this anthology. Finally, H.P. Lovecraft's "From Beyond" first appeared in *The Fantasy Fan* in 1934, but we include here the version published in *Weird Tales* in 1938. We would like to thank the literary estate of C. L. Moore for their permission to include "Black God's Kiss" in this collection.

The only changes we made to the texts from these original sources included (1) making all quotation marks follow the American style (double quotes first with single quotes within); (2) eliminating hyphens in words like "today," "tomorrow," and "tonight"; and (3) shrinking em dashes, where they were sometimes doubled or tripled, to just one dash. Otherwise, we retained original spellings and space breaks, and kept any original colloquialisms.

We would like to thank those who have labored to preserve these old texts both in digital and facsimile versions, particularly archive.org and the Hathi Trust. Preserving such ephemeral works of art provides an important link to the past, allowing readers to find works that would otherwise have been lost to the depredations of time. We would also like to thank librarians everywhere for their part in making accessible such foundational literary works. We would particularly like to thank Kelly Johnson and Ane Carriveau, librarians at the University of Wisconsin Oshkosh, who contributed their generous talents to this project.

Contents

Contents

Introduction

An average person living in the United States or the United Kingdom in 1886—if they could be transported more than five decades into their future—would hardly recognize the world of 1939. Automobiles had replaced horses. Airplanes had become ubiquitous. Generations had been ravaged by cataclysmic wars while colonial empires crumbled. Radio was the dominant carrier of culture, and film had become a massively popular art form. The worldwide economic depression was causing suffering and relocation on a grand scale. In literature, science fiction, fantasy, and horror were gaining a commercial foothold in popular culture. These genres provided a powerful response to the upheaval of the epoch. In many ways, they were the most reliably interesting and powerful responses to a world that seemed to be more and more strange with each passing day.

In our 2021 book *Speculative Modernism: How Science Fiction, Fantasy and Horror Conceived the 20th Century*, we presented the study of dozens of stories that demonstrate that a strong current of what became known as Modernist thinking was flowing through the often-ignored and forgotten genres of speculative fiction in both the United States and the United Kingdom. In this anthology, we offer a companion volume to that book: a collection of stories that best exemplify the radical changes in literature and culture that were occurring during the period 1886–1939. These stories—many of them forgotten, a few of them by well-known authors—are really fun to read. They are also fine examples of the anxieties prevalent in a world that was in the process of turning itself upside down. This anthology stands alone as a volume for readers curious about this era. It also serves as a teaching tool, especially when paired with our study of these stories and many others.

Our vision for this anthology has many elements. In a sea of anthologies that contain only horror or only fantasy or only science fiction, ours combines three speculative genres that truly have no well-defined boundaries. By looking at how fantasy, horror, and science fiction responded to the overwhelming forces of change during this era, a reader of this

1

anthology can get a more complete picture of the literary response to the seismic shifts across every aspect of life. We include brief introductions for each story that highlight the historical, cultural, and literary significance of the selection and its author. Our anthology is intended for a wide audience, including casual readers. When paired with *Speculative Modernism*, our anthology will be a useful and stimulating teaching resource for college classes but can operate just as well as a stand-alone collection both in and out of the classroom.

In assembling our anthology, we present a wide range of voices, from both the United States and the United Kingdom, all of whom have something interesting to say about the Modernist period from 1886 to 1939. We include men and women in horror, fantasy, and science fiction who push boundaries of all kinds. In many ways, they laid the groundwork for Ezra Pound, Virginia Woolf, Gertrude Stein, and all of the much more well-known Modernists who built upon ideas that originated in speculative fiction and brought them to the mainstream. Our anthology balances the three genres and includes stories from a wide range of both well-known and obscure writers. It is organized to match the thematic structure of *Speculative Modernism*. In that book, we studied seven themes that characterized the burgeoning Modernist movement in speculative fiction, and our anthology tracks with that structure.

We begin our book with social thinkers, including the nineteenth-century utopians, who were instrumental in building a speculative-fiction audience. These writers studied the way societies were organized and delved into the idea of social and individual perfectibility. We include here "Enoch Soames" by Max Beerbohm (1916) and "The Comet" by W.E.B. Du Bois (1920), two stories that tackle ideas about the individual's struggle for a place in society. The dreams of taming the wild frontiers instead of destroying them offered solutions to the terrors of the Modern era. The utopian society of the nineteenth century became something to flee.

Our next five narratives offer unique perspectives on the ghost, phantasmal, and vampire subgenres of horror fiction, stories that question the nature of life and death. "The Striding Place" by Gertrude Atherton (1896), "Haïta the Shepherd" by Ambrose Bierce (1891), "Luella Miller" by Mary E. Wilkins Freeman (1902), "The Ash-tree" by M.R. James (1904), and "The Bowmen" by Arthur Machen (1914) are stories that depicted the spiritual forces that the materialism of the period tended to deny and answered the call for originality posited by Olivia Howard Dunbar in "The Decay of the Ghost in Fiction" (1905). Stories like these adapted once-religious myths into something more concrete: warnings that can be useful in the temporal world as well as in the one hereafter. They are not just supernatural tales; they examine the horrors that humanity puts in its own way. These beings that exist somewhere between life and death can be seen as the bitter end of the institutions of the past that have wrought nothing but oppression and brutality.

We next turn our attention to the natural world, to once-pristine landscapes that had been ravaged by rapid industrialization. Speculative Modernists recognized that Earth could and would likely continue long after human extinction, that the end of humanity was an end but not *the* end. More stories arose, especially between the world wars, that depicted humanity willingly seeking its own end, looking for a quick and definitive surrender in its war against the non-human world. This anthology contains the short story "The Miracle of the Lily" (1928) by Clare Winger Harris, a story that exemplifies the Modernists' relationship with their blighted and benighted habitat. Harris's story wrestles with humanity's position to and in opposition with the non-human world.

In the new century, science not only discovered new worlds, but also reexamined the old ones in new ways. Mainstream Modernists struck down the failing institutions of society and religion; Speculative Modernists imagined what would replace them. "With the Night Mail" (1905) by Rudyard Kipling explores how the bureaucracies of the past century would develop with the opportunities science created, and how these new bureaucracies might transform every aspect of society. "From Beyond" (1934) by H.P. Lovecraft employs science's discoveries of realms that lie beyond human senses—like X-rays and ultraviolet light—and imagines the dangers that humanity has not yet experienced directly.

One undeniable aspect of Modernist experience is the transformation of day-to-day life by machines and the regimented, machine-like thinking that became ubiquitous during the period 1886–1939. Anxiety about developments in technology—especially instruments of war—consumed Modernist thinking. It was natural that machines and the wonders of the future became the subjects of Speculative Modernism. Technology took center stage, for better or worse, and matters of society and history sloughed off like scabs. This anthology includes the stories "The Machine Stops" (1909) by E.M. Forster and "Rust" (1939) by Joseph E. Kelleam. Forster is better known for his novels about the travails of his society, while Kelleam's "Rust" is a forgotten gem of science fiction. A. Merritt contributed "The Rhythm of the Spheres" to the serial collaborative novel *Cosmos* (1934) that showed how the human spirit would always win out over a directly antagonistic mechanical nightmare. These stories speak eloquently to the Modernist ambivalence about the rise of the Machine Age.

During the Speculative Modernist era, confidence in organized religions eroded steadily and dramatically. Many speculative writers of this era searched for something with which to replace the traditional idea of an all-powerful, all-loving creator. They created a mythology that looked both backward to a time before the building of worshipful institutions and forward to how the new sciences could be incorporated to find deeper meanings. They shaped a new kind of fantasy that saw the entire world—humanity's wars, troubles, and joys—as mere distraction from the broader mystical universe. These authors shone a light into the Dark Ages and brought back the mystical interests that were buried by those who sought out answers to the universe in more concrete terms. These writers rekindled interest in the medieval period as they recaptured and recast ideas that the industrial world dismissed as frivolous. An excerpt from Marie Corelli's *A Romance of Two Worlds* (1886), a chapter titled "The Electric Creed," explains how scientific discoveries could actually enhance rather than demystify our religious understanding of the universe. Evelyn Underhill chronicles the dark underbelly of crumbling religious institutions in "The Death of a Saint" (1904). William Hope Hodgson's "The Searcher of the End House" (1910) reminds readers that while so much has been discovered and explained, there is still a long way to go. The mystical forces introduced in all of these works exemplify the Speculative Modernist hopes and fears for humanity's collective future.

Finally, the dynamic forces of these times demanded a new kind of individual suited to thrive under rapidly changing circumstances. The final three selections in this anthology demonstrate that any optimism for the perfectibility of humanity has been irrevocably lost. Humans are what they have always been, and primal instincts are often a driving force and survival mechanism. However, these new protagonists take advantage of amoral perspectives, whether that be in precivilization or after the wreckage of institutions that provided social stability. Robert E. Howard's first speculative story, titled "Spear and Fang" (1925), and "Black God's Kiss" (1934) by C.L. Moore show a new kind of hero, one that turns inward to address what philosopher William James describes as "metaphysical disputes" in his lecture "What Pragmatism Means" (1907). The flaws of the individual mean absolutely nothing to the unimaginably cold, eternally indifferent universe. Freed of social and cultural restrictions, these characters do not carry the burden of responsibility for the universe's well-being. They are free in ways unimaginable to previous generations.

One of our aims for pairing *Speculative Modernism* with this anthology is to provide a potent teaching tool for university instructors who want to see the range of creative response in the speculative genres to the earthshaking forces of change during 1886–1939. We see this pair of books fitting into courses that study subjects as diverse as Modernism, speculative fiction in all of its forms, literature and film, Modernist philosophy, religious studies, cultural studies, history, and a host of other academic endeavors.

The stories you have in your hands right now have the power—even after all these years—to amaze, horrify, inspire, and shake you. We hope you enjoy the collection!

"The Comet"

by W.E.B. Du Bois*

W.E.B. Du Bois (1868–1963) is not usually known as a science-fiction writer. His most famous work, *The Souls of Black Folk* (1903), is regarded as one of the most influential and important works on African American culture. His role in the creation of National Association for the Advancement of Colored People (NAACP) spanned more than two decades, and his fight for equality among the races lasted until his death in 1963, just before the Civil Rights Act was passed. The story "The Comet" is the last work of prose in a book of essays called *Darkwater: Voices from Within the Veil* in 1920. This book created a stir among white reviewers; it also revealed a rift in the Black community by provoking and challenging white dominance in America rather than engaging with Booker T. Washington's talk of peace and conciliation. Du Bois' "The Comet" challenges racism and calls upon the marginalized to rise up against oppression by employing a major trope of Speculative Modernist fiction: an apocalyptic setting where all social institutions have been destroyed. The specter of capitalism and its racist tendencies still haunt the only two people left in a New York City destroyed by a passing comet. Even this devastation is not enough to cure the world of its ills. Du Bois never shied away from confronting the language of racism head on; a particular word used in this story might offend some readers, so please be warned.

* * * * *

He stood a moment on the steps of the bank, watching the human river that swirled down Broadway. Few noticed him. Few ever noticed him save in a way that stung. He was outside the world—"nothing!" as he said bitterly. Bits of the words of the walkers came to him.

"The comet?"

"The comet—"

*Du Bois, W.E.B. "The Comet." *Darkwater: Voices from Within the Veil*. Harcourt, Brace, and Howe, 1920, pp. 253–273.

Everybody was talking of it. Even the president, as he entered, smiled patronizingly at him, and asked:

"Well, Jim, are you scared?"

"No," said the messenger shortly.

"I thought we'd journeyed through the comet's tail once," broke in the junior clerk affably.

"Oh, that was Halley's," said the president; "this is a new comet, quite a stranger, they say—wonderful, wonderful! I saw it last night. Oh, by the way, Jim," turning again to the messenger, "I want you to go down into the lower vaults today."

The messenger followed the president silently. Of course, they wanted *him* to go down to the lower vaults. It was too dangerous for more valuable men. He smiled grimly and listened.

"Everything of value has been moved out since the water began to seep in," said the president; "but we miss two volumes of old records. Suppose you nose around down there,—it isn't very pleasant, I suppose."

"Not very," said the messenger, as he walked out.

"Well, Jim, the tail of the new comet hits us at noon this time," said the vault clerk, as he passed over the keys; but the messenger passed silently down the stairs. Down he went beneath Broadway, where the dim light filtered through the feet of hurrying men; down to the dark basement beneath; down into the blackness and silence beneath that lowest cavern. Here with his dark lantern he groped in the bowels of the earth, under the world.

He drew a long breath as he threw back the last great iron door and stepped into the fetid slime within. Here at last was peace, and he groped moodily forward. A great rat leaped past him and cobwebs crept across his face. He felt carefully around the room, shelf by shelf, on the muddied floor, and in crevice and corner. Nothing. Then he went back to the far end, where somehow the wall felt different. He sounded and pushed and pried. Nothing. He started away. Then something brought him back. He was sounding and working again when suddenly the whole black wall swung as on mighty hinges, and blackness yawned beyond. He peered in; it was evidently a secret vault—some hiding place of the old bank unknown in newer times. He entered hesitatingly. It was a long, narrow room with shelves, and at the far end, an old iron chest. On a high shelf lay the two missing volumes of records, and others. He put them carefully aside and stepped to the chest. It was old, strong, and rusty. He looked at the vast and old-fashioned lock and flashed his light on the hinges. They were deeply incrusted with rust. Looking about, he found a bit of iron and began to pry. The rust had eaten a hundred years, and it had gone deep. Slowly, wearily, the old lid lifted, and with a last, low groan lay bare its treasure—and he saw the dull sheen of gold!

"Boom!"

A low, grinding, reverberating crash struck upon his ear. He started up and looked about. All was black and still. He groped for his light and swung it about him. Then he knew! The great stone door had swung to. He forgot the gold and looked death squarely in the face. Then with a sigh he went methodically to work. The cold sweat stood on his forehead; but he searched, pounded, pushed, and worked until after what seemed endless hours his hand struck a cold bit of metal and the great door swung again harshly on its hinges, and then, striking against something soft and heavy, stopped. He had just room to squeeze through. There lay the body of the vault clerk, cold and stiff. He stared at it, and then felt sick and nauseated. The air seemed unaccountably foul, with a strong, peculiar odor. He stepped forward, clutched at the air, and fell fainting across the corpse.

He awoke with a sense of horror, leaped from the body, and groped up the stairs, calling to the guard. The watchman sat as if asleep, with the gate swinging free. With one glance at him the messenger hurried up to the sub-vault. In vain he called to the guards. His voice echoed and re-echoed weirdly. Up into the great basement he rushed. Here another guard lay prostrate on his face, cold and still. A fear arose in the messenger's heart. He dashed up to the cellar floor, up into the bank. The stillness of death lay everywhere and everywhere bowed, bent, and stretched the silent forms of men. The messenger paused and glanced about. He was not a man easily moved; but the sight was appalling! "Robbery and murder," he whispered slowly to himself as he saw the twisted, oozing mouth of the president where he lay half-buried on his desk. Then a new thought seized him: If they found him here alone—with all this money and all these dead men—what would his life be worth? He glanced about, tiptoed cautiously to a side door, and again looked behind. Quietly he turned the latch and stepped out into Wall Street.

How silent the street was! Not a soul was stirring, and yet it was high-noon—Wall Street? Broadway? He glanced almost wildly up and down, then across the street, and as he looked, a sickening horror froze in his limbs. With a choking cry of utter fright he lunged, leaned giddily against the cold building, and stared helplessly at the sight.

In the great stone doorway a hundred men and women and children lay crushed and twisted and jammed, forced into that great, gaping doorway like refuse in a can—as if in one wild, frantic rush to safety, they had crushed and ground themselves to death. Slowly the messenger crept along the walls, wetting his parched mouth and trying to comprehend, stilling the tremor in his limbs and the rising terror in his heart. He met a business man, silk-hatted and frock-coated, who had crept, too, along that smooth wall and stood now stone dead with wonder written on his lips.

The messenger turned his eyes hastily away and sought the curb. A woman leaned wearily against the signpost, her head bowed motionless on her lace and silken bosom. Before her stood a street car, silent, and within—but the messenger but glanced and hurried on. A grimy newsboy sat in the gutter with the "last edition" in his uplifted hand: "Danger!" screamed its black headlines. "Warnings wired around the world. The Comet's tail sweeps past us at noon. Deadly gases expected. Close doors and windows. Seek the cellar." The messenger read and staggered on. Far out from a window above, a girl lay with gasping face and sleevelets on her arms. On a store step sat a little, sweet-faced girl looking upward toward the skies, and in the carriage by her lay—but the messenger looked no longer. The cords gave way—the terror burst in his veins, and with one great, gasping cry he sprang desperately forward and ran,—ran as only the frightened run, shrieking and fighting the air until with one last wail of pain he sank on the grass of Madison Square and lay prone and still.

When he rose, he gave no glance at the still and silent forms on the benches, but, going to a fountain, bathed his face; then hiding himself in a corner away from the drama of death, he quietly gripped himself and thought the thing through: The comet had swept the earth and this was the end. Was everybody dead? He must search and see.

He knew that he must steady himself and keep calm, or he would go insane. First he must go to a restaurant. He walked up Fifth Avenue to a famous hostelry and entered its gorgeous, ghost-haunted halls. He beat back the nausea, and, seizing a tray from dead hands, hurried into the street and ate ravenously, hiding to keep out the sights.

"Yesterday, they would not have served me," he whispered, as he forced the food down.

Then he started up the street,—looking, peering, telephoning, ringing alarms; silent, silent all. Was nobody—nobody—he dared not think the thought and hurried on.

Suddenly he stopped still. He had forgotten. My God! How could he have forgotten? He must rush to the subway—then he almost laughed. No—a car; if he could find a Ford. He saw one. Gently he lifted off its burden, and took his place on the seat. He tested the throttle. There was gas. He glided off, shivering, and drove up the street. Everywhere stood, leaned, lounged, and lay the dead, in grim and awful silence. On he ran past an automobile, wrecked and overturned; past another, filled with a gay party whose smiles yet lingered on their death-struck lips; on past crowds and groups of cars, pausing by dead policemen; at 42nd Street he had to detour to Park Avenue to avoid the dead congestion. He came back on Fifth Avenue at 57th and flew past the Plaza and by the park with its hushed babies and silent throng, until as he was rushing past 72nd Street he heard a sharp cry, and saw a living form leaning wildly out an upper window. He gasped. The human voice sounded in his ears like the voice of God.

"Hello—hello—help, in God's name!" wailed the woman. "There's a dead girl in here and a man and—and see yonder dead men lying in the street and dead horses for the love of God go and bring the officers—" And the words trailed off into hysterical tears.

He wheeled the car in a sudden circle, running over the still body of a child and leaping on the curb. Then he rushed up the steps and tried the door and rang violently. There was a long pause, but at last the heavy door swung back. They stared a moment in silence. She had not noticed before that he was a Negro. He had not thought of her as white. She was a woman of perhaps twenty-five—rarely beautiful and richly gowned, with darkly-golden hair, and jewels. Yesterday, he thought with bitterness, she would scarcely have looked at him twice. He would have been dirt beneath her silken feet. She stared at him. Of all the sorts of men she had pictured as coming to her rescue she had not dreamed of one like him. Not that he was not human, but he dwelt in a world so far from hers, so infinitely far, that he seldom even entered her thought. Yet as she looked at him curiously he seemed quite commonplace and usual. He was a tall, dark workingman of the better class, with a sensitive face trained to stolidity and a poor man's clothes and hands. His face was soft and slow and his manner at once cold and nervous, like fires long banked, but not out.

So a moment each paused and gauged the other; then the thought of the dead world without rushed in and they started toward each other.

"What has happened?" she cried. "Tell me! Nothing stirs. All is silence! I see the dead strewn before my window as winnowed by the breath of God,—and see—" She dragged him through great, silken hangings to where, beneath the sheen of mahogany and silver, a little French maid lay stretched in quiet, everlasting sleep, and near her a butler lay prone in his livery.

The tears streamed down the woman's cheeks and she clung to his arm until the perfume of her breath swept his face and he felt the tremors racing through her body.

"I had been shut up in my dark room developing pictures of the comet which I took last night; when I came out—I saw the dead!"

"What has happened?" she cried again.

He answered slowly:

"Something—comet or devil—swept across the earth this morning and—many are dead!"

"Many? Very many?"

"I have searched and I have seen no other living soul but you."

She gasped and they stared at each other.

"My—father!" she whispered.

"Where is he?"

"He started for the office."

"Where is it?"

"In the Metropolitan Tower."

"Leave a note for him here and come."

Then he stopped.

"No," he said firmly—"first, we must go—to Harlem."

"Harlem!" she cried. Then she understood. She tapped her foot at first impatiently. She looked back and shuddered. Then she came resolutely down the steps.

"There's a swifter car in the garage in the court," she said.

"I don't know how to drive it," he said.

"I do," she answered.

In ten minutes they were flying to Harlem on the wind. The Stutz rose and raced like an airplane. They took the turn at 110th Street on two wheels and slipped with a shriek into 135th.

He was gone but a moment. Then he returned, and his face was gray. She did not look, but said:

"You have lost—somebody?"

"I have lost—everybody," he said, simply—"unless—"

He ran back and was gone several minutes—hours they seemed to her.

"Everybody," he said, and he walked slowly back with something film-like in his hand which he stuffed into his pocket.

"I'm afraid I was selfish," he said. But already the car was moving toward the park among the dark and lined dead of Harlem—the brown, still faces, the knotted hands, the homely garments, and the silence—the wild and haunting silence. Out of the park, and down Fifth Avenue they whirled. In and out among the dead they slipped and quivered, needing no sound of bell or horn, until the great, square Metropolitan Tower hove in sight. Gently he laid the dead elevator boy aside; the car shot upward. The door of the office stood open. On the threshold lay the stenographer, and, staring at her, sat the dead clerk. The inner office was empty, but a note lay on the desk, folded and addressed but unsent:

Dear Daughter:

I've gone for a hundred mile spin in Fred's new Mercedes. Shall not be back before dinner. I'll bring Fred with me.

J.B.H.

"Come," she cried nervously. "We must search the city."

Up and down, over and across, back again—on went that ghostly search. Everywhere was silence and death—death and silence! They hunted from Madison Square to Spuyten Duyvel; they rushed across the Williamsburg Bridge; they swept over Brooklyn; from the Battery and Morningside Heights they scanned the river. Silence, silence everywhere, and no human sign. Haggard and bedraggled they puffed a third time slowly down Broadway, under the broiling sun, and at last stopped. He sniffed the air. An odor—a smell—and with the shifting breeze a sickening stench filled their nostrils and brought its awful warning. The girl settled back helplessly in her seat.

"What can we do?" she cried.

It was his turn now to take the lead, and he did it quickly.

"The long distance telephone—the telegraph and the cable—night rockets and then—flight!"

She looked at him now with strength and confidence. He did not look like men, as she had always pictured men; but he acted like one and she was content. In fifteen minutes they were at the central telephone exchange. As they came to the door he stepped quickly before her and pressed her gently back as he closed it. She heard him moving to and fro, and knew his burdens—the poor, little burdens he bore. When she entered, he was alone in the room. The grim switchboard flashed its metallic face in cryptic, sphinxlike immobility. She seated herself on a stool and donned the bright earpiece. She looked at the mouthpiece. She had never looked at one so closely before. It was wide and black, pimpled with usage; inert; dead; almost sarcastic in its unfeeling curves. It looked—she beat back the thought—but it looked,—it persisted in looking like—she turned her head and found herself alone. One moment she was terrified; then she thanked him silently for his delicacy and turned resolutely, with a quick intaking of breath.

"Hello!" she called in low tones. She was calling to the world. The world *must* answer. Would the world *answer*? Was the world—

Silence!

She had spoken too low.

"Hello!" she cried, full-voiced.

She listened. Silence! Her heart beat quickly. She cried in clear, distinct, loud tones: "Hello—hello—hello!"

What was that whirring? Surely—no—was it the click of a receiver?

She bent close, she moved the pegs in the holes, and called and called, until her voice rose almost to a shriek, and her heart hammered. It was as if she had heard the last flicker of creation, and the evil was silence. Her voice dropped to a sob. She sat stupidly staring into the black and sarcastic mouthpiece, and the thought came again. Hope lay dead within her. Yes, the cable and the rockets remained; but the world—she could not frame the thought or say the word. It was too mighty—too terrible! She turned toward the door with a new fear in her heart. For the first time she seemed to realize that she was alone in the world with a stranger, with something more than a stranger,—with a man alien in blood and culture—unknown, perhaps unknowable. It was awful! She must escape—she must fly; he must not see her again. Who knew what awful thoughts—

She gathered her silken skirts deftly about her young, smooth limbs— listened, and glided into a side-hall. A moment she shrank back: the hall lay filled with dead women; then she leaped to the door and tore at it, with bleeding fingers, until it swung wide. She looked out. He was standing at the top of the alley,—silhouetted, tall and black, motionless. Was he looking at her or away? She did not know—she did not care. She simply leaped and ran—ran until she found herself alone amid the dead and the tall ramparts of towering buildings.

She stopped. She was alone. Alone! Alone on the streets—alone in the city—perhaps alone in the world! There crept in upon her the sense of deception—of creeping hands behind her back—of silent, moving things she could not see,—of voices hushed in fearsome conspiracy. She looked behind and sideways, started at strange sounds and heard still stranger, until every nerve within her stood sharp and quivering, stretched to scream at the barest touch. She whirled and flew back, whimpering like a child, until she found that narrow alley again and the dark, silent figure silhouetted at the top. She stopped and rested; then she walked silently toward him, looked at him timidly; but he said nothing as he handed her into the car. Her voice caught as she whispered:

"Not—that."

And he answered slowly: "No—not that!"

They climbed into the car. She bent forward on the wheel and sobbed, with great, dry, quivering sobs, as they flew toward the cable office on the east side, leaving the world of wealth and prosperity for the world of poverty and work. In the world behind them were death and silence, grave and grim, almost cynical, but always decent; here it was hideous. It clothed itself in every ghastly form of terror, struggle, hate, and suffering. It lay wreathed in crime and squalor, greed and lust. Only in its dread and awful silence was it like to death everywhere.

Yet as the two, flying and alone, looked upon the horror of the world, slowly, gradually, the sense of all-enveloping death deserted them. They seemed to move in a world silent and asleep,—not dead. They moved in quiet reverence, lest somehow they wake these sleeping forms who had, at last, found peace. They moved in some solemn, world-wide *Friedhof*, above which some mighty arm had waved its magic wand. All nature slept until—until, and quick with the same startling thought, they looked into each other's eyes—he, ashen, and she, crimson, with unspoken thought. To both, the vision of a mighty beauty—of vast, unspoken things, swelled in their souls; but they put it away.

Great, dark coils of wire came up from the earth and down from the sun and entered this low lair of witchery. The gathered lightnings of the world centered here, binding with beams of light the ends of the earth. The doors gaped on the gloom within. He paused on the threshold.

"Do you know the code?" she asked.

"I know the call for help—we used it formerly at the bank."

She hardly heard. She heard the lapping of the waters far below,—the dark and restless waters—the cold and luring waters, as they called. He stepped within. Slowly she walked to the wall, where the water called below, and stood and waited. Long she waited, and he did not come. Then with a start she saw him, too, standing beside the black waters. Slowly he removed his coat and stood there silently. She walked quickly to him and laid her hand on his arm. He did not start or look. The waters lapped on in luring, deadly rhythm. He pointed down to the waters, and said quietly:

"The world lies beneath the waters now—may I go?"

She looked into his stricken, tired face, and a great pity surged within her heart. She answered in a voice clear and calm, "No."

Upward they turned toward life again, and he seized the wheel. The world was darkening to twilight, and a great, gray pall was falling mercifully and gently on the sleeping dead. The ghastly glare of reality seemed replaced with the dream of some vast romance. The girl lay silently back, as the motor whizzed along, and looked half-consciously for the elf-queen to wave life into this dead world again. She forgot to wonder at the quickness with which he had learned to drive her car. It seemed natural. And then as they whirled and swung into Madison Square and at the door of the Metropolitan Tower she gave a low cry, and her eyes were great! Perhaps she had seen the elf-queen?

The man led her to the elevator of the tower and deftly they ascended. In her father's office they gathered rugs and chairs, and he wrote a note and laid it on the desk; then they ascended to the roof and he made her comfortable. For a while she rested and sank to dreamy somnolence, watching the worlds above and wondering. Below lay the dark shadows of the city and afar was the shining of the sea. She glanced at him timidly as he set food before her and took a shawl and wound her in it, touching her reverently, yet tenderly. She looked up at him with thankfulness in her eyes, eating what he served. He watched the city. She watched him. He seemed very human,—very near now.

"Have you had to work hard?" she asked softly.

"Always," he said.

"I have always been idle," she said. "I was rich."

"I was poor," he almost echoed.

"The rich and the poor are met together," she began, and he finished: "The Lord is the Maker of them all."

"Yes," she said slowly; "and how foolish our human distinctions seem—now," looking down to the great dead city stretched below, swimming in unlightened shadows.

"Yes—I was not—human, yesterday," he said.

She looked at him. "And your people were not my people," she said; "but today—" She paused. He was a man,—no more; but he was in some larger sense a gentleman,—sensitive, kindly, chivalrous, everything save his hands and—his face. Yet yesterday—

"Death, the leveler!" he muttered.

"And the revealer," she whispered gently, rising to her feet with great eyes. He turned away, and after fumbling a moment sent a rocket into the darkening air. It arose, shrieked, and flew up, a slim path of light, and, scattering its stars abroad, dropped on the city below. She scarcely noticed it. A vision of the world had risen before her. Slowly the mighty prophecy of her destiny overwhelmed her. Above the dead past hovered the Angel of Annunciation. She was no mere woman. She was neither high nor low, white nor black, rich nor poor. She was primal woman; mighty mother of all men to come and Bride of Life. She looked upon the man beside her and forgot all else but his manhood, his strong, vigorous manhood—his sorrow and sacrifice. She saw him glorified. He was no longer a thing apart, a creature below, a strange outcast of another clime and blood, but her Brother Humanity incarnate, Son of God and great All-Father of the race to be.

He did not glimpse the glory in her eyes, but stood looking outward toward the sea and sending rocket after rocket into the unanswering darkness. Dark-purple clouds lay banked and billowed in the west. Behind them and all around, the heavens glowed in dim, weird radiance that suffused the darkening world and made almost a minor music. Suddenly, as though gathered back in some vast hand, the great cloud-curtain fell away. Low on the horizon lay a long, white star mystic,—wonderful! And from it fled upward to the pole, like some wan bridal veil, a pale, wide sheet of flame that lighted all the world and dimmed the stars.

In fascinated silence the man gazed at the heavens and dropped his rockets to the floor. Memories of memories stirred to life in the dead recesses of his mind. The shackles seemed to rattle and fall from his soul. Up from the crass and crushing and cringing of his caste leaped the lone majesty of kings long dead. He arose within the shadows, tall, straight, and stern, with power in his eyes and ghostly scepters hovering to his grasp. It was as though some mighty Pharaoh lived again, or curled Assyrian lord. He turned and looked upon the lady, and found her gazing straight at him.

Silently, immovably, they saw each other face to face—eye to eye. Their souls lay naked to the night. It was not lust; it was not love—it was some vaster, mightier thing that needed neither touch of body nor thrill of soul. It was a thought divine, splendid.

Slowly, noiselessly, they moved toward each other—the heavens above, the seas around, the city grim and dead below. He loomed from out the velvet shadows vast and dark. Pearl-white and slender, she shone beneath the stars. She stretched her jeweled hands abroad. He lifted up his mighty arms, and they cried each to the other, almost with one voice, "The world is dead."

"Long live the—"

"Honk! Honk!" Hoarse and sharp the cry of a motor drifted clearly up from the silence below. They started backward with a cry and gazed upon each other with eyes that faltered and fell, with blood that boiled.

"Honk! Honk! Honk! Honk!" came the mad cry again, and almost from their feet a rocket blazed into the air and scattered its stars upon them. She covered her eyes with her hands, and her shoulders heaved. He dropped and bowed, groped blindly on his knees about the floor. A blue flame spluttered lazily after an age, and she heard the scream of an answering rocket as it flew.

Then they stood still as death, looking to opposite ends of the earth.

"Clang—crash—clang!"

The roar and ring of swift elevators shooting upward from below made the great tower tremble. A murmur and babel of voices swept in upon the night. All over the once dead city the lights blinked, flickered, and flamed; and then with a sudden clanging of doors the entrance to the platform was filled with men, and one with white and flying hair rushed to the girl and lifted her to his breast. "My daughter!" he sobbed.

Behind him hurried a younger, comelier man, carefully clad in motor costume, who bent above the girl with passionate solicitude and gazed into her staring eyes until they narrowed and dropped and her face flushed deeper and deeper crimson.

"Julia," he whispered; "my darling, I thought you were gone forever."

She looked up at him with strange, searching eyes.

"Fred," she murmured, almost vaguely, "is the world—gone?"

"Only New York," he answered; "it is terrible—awful! You know,— but you, how did you escape—how have you endured this horror? Are you well? Unharmed?"

"Unharmed!" she said.

"And this man here?" he asked, encircling her drooping form with one arm and turning toward the Negro. Suddenly he stiffened and his hand flew to his hip. "Why!" he snarled. "It's—a—nigger—Julia! Has he—has he dared—"

She lifted her head and looked at her late companion curiously and then dropped her eyes with a sigh.

"He has dared—all, to rescue me," she said quietly, "and I—thank him—much." But she did not look at him again. As the couple turned away, the father drew a roll of bills from his pockets.

"Here, my good fellow," he said, thrusting the money into the man's hands, "take that,—what's your name?"

"Jim Davis," came the answer, hollow-voiced.

"Well, Jim, I thank you. I've always liked your people. If you ever want a job, call on me." And they were gone.

The crowd poured up and out of the elevators, talking and whispering.

"Who was it?"

"Are they alive?"

"How many?"

"Two!"

"Who was saved?"

"A white girl and a nigger—there she goes."

"A nigger? Where is he? Let's lynch the damned—"

"Shut up—he's all right—he saved her."

"Saved hell! He had no business—"

"Here he comes."

Into the glare of the electric lights the colored man moved slowly, with the eyes of those that walk and sleep.

"Well, what do you think of that?" cried a bystander; "of all New York, just a white girl and a nigger!"

The colored man heard nothing. He stood silently beneath the glare of the light, gazing at the money in his hand and shrinking as he gazed; slowly he put his other hand into his pocket and brought out a baby's filmy cap, and gazed again. A woman mounted to the platform and looked about, shading her eyes. She was brown, small, and toil-worn, and in one arm lay the corpse of a dark baby. The crowd parted and her eyes fell on the colored man; with a cry she tottered toward him.

"Jim!"

He whirled and, with a sob of joy, caught her in his arms.

"Enoch Soames: A Memory of the Eighteen-nineties"

by Max Beerbohm*

Sir Max Beerbohm was a caricaturist, essayist, short story writer, and novelist. In addition to "Enoch Soames," Beerbohm is best known for his novel *Zuleika Dobson*, which is a satire of life at Oxford University. He was a major figure in the turn-of-the-century cultural scene in London, and his biting satires—both in essays and in caricature—exposed the pretense and hypocrisy of the social world. Known as a *bon vivant* and man about town as the drama critic for the *Saturday Review* (London) from 1898 through 1910, he was the image of a Victorian fop: impeccably dressed, a man of leisure with refined, aristocratic taste. Beerbohm's most enduring character is the opposite of all of that: Enoch Soames is a poet of undetectable talent whose main desire is to be remembered through his execrable poetry. "Enoch Soames" lampoons the idea of the poet as a special kind of genius, taking to task those preening dandies who write with an eye toward posterity. The story also takes on social engineers in the vein of Edward Bellamy and H.G. Wells by presenting the London of 1997—one hundred years following the events of the story—as a comical utopian fiasco. The Prince of Darkness, himself, is demystified and becomes just another creature of the Modernist world: self-interested, exploitive, and crass in this speculative fiction gem that brings Modernist sensibilities to a tale as old as Genesis.

* * * * *

When a book about the literature of the eighteen-nineties was given by Mr. Holbrook Jackson to the world, I looked eagerly in the index for Soames, Enoch. It was as I feared: he was not there. But everybody else was. Many writers whom I had quite forgotten, or remembered but faintly, lived again for me, they and their work, in Mr. Holbrook Jackson's pages.

*Beerbohm, Max. "Enoch Soames." *The Century Magazine* 92, May 1916, pp. 1–19.

The book was as thorough as it was brilliantly written. And thus the omission found by me was an all the deadlier record of poor Soames's failure to impress himself on his decade.

I dare say I am the only person who noticed the omission. Soames had failed so piteously as all that! Nor is there a counterpoise in the thought that if he had had some measure of success he might have passed, like those others, out of my mind, to return only at the historian's beck. It is true that had his gifts, such as they were, been acknowledged in his lifetime, he would never have made the bargain I saw him make—that strange bargain whose results have kept him always in the foreground of my memory. But it is from those very results that the full piteousness of him glares out.

Not my compassion, however, impels me to write of him. For his sake, poor fellow, I should be inclined to keep my pen out of the ink. It is ill to deride the dead. And how can I write about Enoch Soames without making him ridiculous? Or, rather, how am I to hush up the horrid fact that he *was* ridiculous? I shall not be able to do that. Yet, sooner or later, write about him I must. You will see in due course that I have no option. And I may as well get the thing done now.

* * *

In the summer term of '93 a bolt from the blue flashed down on Oxford. It drove deep; it hurtlingly embedded itself in the soil. Dons and undergraduates stood around, rather pale, discussing nothing but it. Whence came it, this meteorite? From Paris. Its name? Will Rothenstein. Its aim? To do a series of twenty-four portraits in lithograph. These were to be published from the Bodley Head, London. The matter was urgent. Already the warden of A, and the master of B, and the Regius Professor of C had meekly "sat." Dignified and doddering old men who had never consented to sit to anyone could not withstand this dynamic little stranger. He did not sue; he invited: he did not invite; he commanded. He was twenty-one years old. He wore spectacles that flashed more than any other pair ever seen. He was a wit. He was brimful of ideas. He knew Whistler. He knew Daudet and the Goncourts. He knew everyone in Paris. He knew them all by heart. He was Paris in Oxford. It was whispered that, so soon as he had polished off his selection of dons, he was going to include a few undergraduates. It was a proud day for me when I—I was included. I liked Rothenstein not less than I feared him; and there arose between us a friendship that has grown ever warmer, and been more and more valued by me, with every passing year.

At the end of term he settled in, or, rather, meteoritically into, London. It was to him I owed my first knowledge of that forever-enchanting little world-in-itself, Chelsea, and my first acquaintance with Walter Sickert and other August elders who dwelt there. It was Rothenstein that took me to see, in Cambridge Street, Pimlico, a young man whose drawings were already famous among the few—Aubrey Beardsley by name. With Rothenstein I paid my first visit to the Bodley Head. By him I was inducted into another haunt of intellect and daring, the domino-room of the Café Royal.

There, on that October evening—there, in that exuberant vista of gilding and crimson velvet set amidst all those opposing mirrors and upholding caryatids, with fumes of tobacco ever rising to the painted and pagan ceiling, and with the hum of presumably cynical conversation broken into so sharply now and again by the clatter of dominoes shuffled on marble tables, I drew a deep breath and, "This indeed," said I to myself, "is life!" (Forgive me that theory. Remember the waging of even the South African War was not yet.)

It was the hour before dinner. We drank vermouth. Those who knew Rothenstein were pointing him out to those who knew him only by name. Men were constantly coming in through the swing-doors and wandering slowly up and down in search of vacant tables or of tables occupied by friends. One of these rovers interested me because I was sure he wanted to catch Rothenstein's eye. He had twice passed our table, with a hesitating look; but Rothenstein, in the thick of a disquisition on Puvis de Chavannes, had not seen him. He was a stooping, shambling person, rather tall, very pale, with longish and brownish hair. He had a thin, vague beard, or, rather, he had a chin on which a large number of hairs weakly curled and clustered to cover its retreat. He was an odd-looking person; but in the nineties odd apparitions were more frequent, I think, than they are now. The young writers of that era—and I was sure this man was a writer—strove earnestly to be distinct in aspect. This man had striven unsuccessfully. He wore a soft black hat of clerical kind, but of Bohemian intention, and a gray waterproof cape which, perhaps because it was waterproof, failed to be romantic. I decided that "dim" was the *mot juste* for him. I had already essayed to write, and was immensely keen on the *mot juste*, that Holy Grail of the period.

The dim man was now again approaching our table, and this time he made up his mind to pause in front of it.

"You don't remember me," he said in a toneless voice.

Rothenstein brightly focused him.

"Yes, I do," he replied after a moment, with pride rather than effusion—pride in a retentive memory. "Edwin Soames."

"Enoch Soames," said Enoch.

"Enoch Soames," repeated Rothenstein in a tone implying that it was enough to have hit on the surname. "We met in Paris a few times when you were living there. We met at the Café Groche."

And I came to your studio once."

"Oh, yes; I was sorry I was out."

"But you were in. You showed me some of your paintings, you know. I hear you're in Chelsea now."

"Yes."

I almost wondered that Mr. Soames did not, after this monosyllable, pass along. He stood patiently there, rather like a dumb animal, rather like a donkey looking over a gate. A sad figure, his. It occurred to me that "hungry" was perhaps the *mot juste* for him; but—hungry for what? He looked as if he had little appetite for anything. I was sorry for him; and Rothenstein, though he had not invited him to Chelsea, did ask him to sit down and have something to drink.

Seated, he was more self-assertive. He flung back the wings of his cape with a gesture which, had not those wings been waterproof, might have seemed to hurl defiance at things in general. And he ordered an absinthe. "*Je me tiens toujours fidèle,*" he told Rothenstein, "*à la sorcière glauque.*"

"It is bad for you," said Rothenstein, dryly.

"Nothing is bad for one," answered Soames. "*Dans ce monde il n'y a ni bien ni mal.*"

"Nothing good and nothing bad? How do you mean?"

"I explained it all in the preface to 'Negations.'"

"'Negations'?"

"Yes, I gave you a copy of it."

"Oh, yes, of course. But, did you explain, for instance, that there was no such thing as bad or good grammar?"

"N-no," said Soames. "Of course in art there is the good and the evil. But in life—no." He was rolling a cigarette. He had weak, white hands, not well washed, and with finger-tips much stained with nicotine. "In life there are illusions of good and evil, but"—his voice trailed away to a murmur in which the words "*vieux jeu*" and "rococo" were faintly audible. I think he felt he was not doing himself justice, and feared that Rothenstein was going to point out fallacies. Anyhow, he cleared his throat and said, "*Parlons d'autre chose.*"

It occurs to you that he was a fool? It didn't to me. I was young, and had not the clarity of judgment that Rothenstein already had. Soames was quite five or six years older than either of us. Also—he had written a book. It was wonderful to have written a book.

If Rothenstein had not been there, I should have revered Soames. Even as it was, I respected him. And I was very near indeed to reverence when he said he had another book coming out soon. I asked if I might ask what kind of book it was to be.

"My poems," he answered. Rothenstein asked if this was to be the title of the book. The poet meditated on this suggestion, but said he rather thought of giving the book no title at all. "If a book is good in itself—" he murmured, and waved his cigarette.

Rothenstein objected that absence of title might be bad for the sale of a book.

"If," he urged, "I went into a bookseller's and said simply, 'Have you got?' or, 'Have you a copy of?' how would they know what I wanted?"

"Oh, of course I should have my name on the cover," Soames answered earnestly. "And I rather want," he added, looking hard at Rothenstein, "to have a drawing of myself as frontispiece." Rothenstein admitted that this was a capital idea, and mentioned that he was going into the country and would be there for some time. He then looked at his watch, exclaimed at the hour, paid the waiter, and went away with me to dinner. Soames remained at his post of fidelity to the glaucous witch.

"Why were you so determined not to draw him?" I asked.

"Draw him? Him? How can one draw a man who doesn't exist?"

"He is dim," I admitted. But my *mot juste* fell flat. Rothenstein repeated that Soames was non-existent.

Still, Soames had written a book. I asked if Rothenstein had read "Negations." He said he had looked into it, "but," he added crisply, "I don't profess to know anything about writing." A reservation very characteristic of the period! Painters would not then allow that anyone outside their own order had a right to any opinion about painting. This law (graven on the tablets brought down by Whistler from the summit of Fuji-yama) imposed certain limitations. If other arts than painting were not utterly unintelligible to all but the men who practiced them, the law tottered—the Monroe Doctrine, as it were, did not hold good. Therefore no painter would offer an opinion of a book without warning you at any rate that his opinion was worthless. No one is a better judge of literature than Rothenstein; but it wouldn't have done to tell him so in those days, and I knew that I must form an unaided judgment of "Negations."

Not to buy a book of which I had met the author face to face would have been for me in those days an impossible act of self-denial. When I returned to Oxford for the Christmas term I had duly secured "Negations." I used to keep it lying carelessly on the table in my room, and whenever a friend took it up and asked what it was about, I would say: "Oh, it's rather a remarkable book. It's by a man whom I know." Just "what it was about" I never was able to say. Head or tail was just what I hadn't made of that slim, green volume. I found in the preface no clue to the labyrinth of contents, and in that labyrinth nothing to explain the preface.

> Lean near to life. Lean very near—nearer.
>
> Life is web and therein nor warp nor woof is, but web only.

It is for this I am Catholick in church and in thought, yet do let swift Mood
weave there what the shuttle of Mood wills.

These were the opening phrases of the preface, but those which followed were less easy to understand. Then came "Stark: *A Conte*," about a
midinette who, so far as I could gather, murdered, or was about to murder, a *mannequin*. It was rather like a story by Catulle Mendès in which the
translator had either skipped or cut out every alternate sentence. Next, a
dialogue between Pan and St. Ursula, lacking, I rather thought, in "snap."
Next, some aphorisms (entitled αφοριαματα). Throughout, in fact, there
was a great variety of form, and the forms had evidently been wrought
with much care. It was rather the substance that eluded me. Was there,
I wondered, any substance at all? It did now occur to me: suppose Enoch
Soames was a fool! Up cropped a rival hypothesis: suppose *I* was! I inclined
to give Soames the benefit of the doubt. I had read "L'Après-midi d'un
faune" without extracting a glimmer of meaning; yet Mallarmé, of course,
was a master. How was I to know that Soames wasn't another? There was
a sort of music in his prose, not indeed, arresting, but perhaps, I thought,
haunting, and laden, perhaps, with meanings as deep as Mallarmé's own. I
awaited his poems with an open mind.

And I looked forward to them with positive impatience after I had
had a second meeting with him. This was on an evening in January. Going
into the aforesaid domino-room, I had passed a table at which sat a pale
man with an open book before him. He had looked from his book to me,
and I looked back over my shoulder with a vague sense that I ought to
have recognized him. I returned to pay my respects. After exchanging a
few words, I said with a glance to the open book, "I see I am interrupting
you," and was about to pass on, but, "I prefer," Soames replied in his toneless voice, "to be interrupted," and I obeyed his gesture that I should sit
down.

I asked him if he often read here.

"Yes; things of this kind I read here," he answered, indicating the title
of his book—"The Poems of Shelley."

"Anything that you really"—and I was going to say "admire?" But I
cautiously left my sentence unfinished, and was glad that I had done so, for
he said with unwonted emphasis, "Anything second-rate."

I had read little of Shelley, but, "Of course," I murmured, "he's very
uneven."

"I should have thought evenness was just what was wrong with him. A
deadly evenness. That's why I read him here. The noise of this place breaks
the rhythm. He's tolerable here." Soames took up the book and glanced
through the pages. He laughed. Soames's laugh was a short, single, and
mirthless sound from the throat, unaccompanied by any movement of the

face or brightening of the eyes. "What a period!" he uttered, laying the book down. And, "What a country!" he added.

I asked rather nervously if he didn't think Keats had more or less held his own against the drawbacks of time and place. He admitted that there were "passages in Keats," but did not specify them. Of "the older men," as he called them, he seemed to like only Milton. "Milton," he said, "wasn't sentimental." Also, "Milton had a dark insight." And again, "I can always read Milton in the reading-room."

"The reading-room?"

"Of the British Museum. I go there every day."

"You do? I've only been there once. I'm afraid I found it rather a depressing place. It—it seemed to sap one's vitality."

"It does. That's why I go there. The lower one's vitality, the more sensitive one is to great art. I live near the museum. I have rooms in Dyott Street."

"And you go round to the reading-room to read Milton?"

"Usually Milton." He looked at me. "It was Milton," he certificatively added, "who converted me to diabolism."

"Diabolism? Oh, yes? Really?" said I, with that vague discomfort and that intense desire to be polite which one feels when a man speaks of his own religion. "You—worship the devil?"

Soames shook his head.

"It's not exactly worship," he qualified, sipping his absinthe. "It's more a matter of trusting and encouraging."

"I see, yes. I had rather gathered from the preface to 'Negations' that you were a—a Catholic."

"*Je l'étais à cette époque.* In fact, I still am. I am a Catholic diabolist."

But this profession he made in an almost cursory tone. I could see that what was upmost in his mind was the fact that I had read "Negations." His pale eyes had for the first time gleamed. I felt as one who is about to be examined *viva voce* on the very subject in which he is shakiest. I hastily asked him how soon his poems were to be published.

"Next week," he told me.

"And are they to be published without a title?"

"No. I found a title at last. But I sha'n't tell you what it is," as though I had been so impertinent as to inquire. "I am not sure that it wholly satisfies me. But it is the best I can find. It suggests something of the quality of the poems—strange growths, natural and wild, yet exquisite," he added, "and many-hued, and full of poisons."

I asked him what he thought of Baudelaire. He uttered the snort that was his laugh, and, "Baudelaire," he said, "was a *bourgeois malgré lui*." France had had only one poet—Villon; "and two thirds of Villon were sheer journalism." Verlaine was "an *épicier malgré lui*." Altogether, rather to my surprise, he rated French literature lower than English. There were "passages" in Villiers de l'Isle-Adam. But, "I," he summed up, "owe nothing to France." He nodded at me. "You'll see," he predicted.

I did not, when the time came, quite see that. I thought the author of "Fungoids" did, unconsciously of course, owe something to the young Parisian decadents or to the young English ones who owed something to *them*. I still think so. The little book, bought by me in Oxford, lies before me as I write. Its pale-gray buckram cover and silver lettering have not worn well. Nor have its contents. Through these, with a melancholy interest, I have again been looking. They are not much. But at the time of their publication I had a vague suspicion that they *might* be. I suppose it is my capacity for faith, not poor Soames's work, that is weaker than it once was.

TO A YOUNG WOMAN

Thou art, who hast not been!
    Pale tunes irresolute
    And traceries of old sounds
    Blown from a rotted flute
Mingle with noise of cymbals rouged with rust,
Nor not strange forms and epicene
    Lie bleeding in the dust,
    Being wounded with wounds.
    For this it is
    That in thy counterpart
    Of age-long mockeries
Thou hast not been nor art!

There seemed to me a certain inconsistency as between the first and last lines of this. I tried, with bent brows, to resolve the discord. But I did not take my failure as wholly incompatible with a meaning in Soames's mind. Might it not rather indicate the depth of his meaning? As for the craftsmanship, "rouged with rust" seemed to me a fine stroke, and "nor not" instead of "and" had a curious felicity. I wondered who the "young woman" was and what she had made of it all. I sadly suspect that Soames could not have made more of it than she. Yet even now, if one doesn't try to make any sense at all of the poem, and reads it just for the sound, there is a certain grace of cadence. Soames was an artist, in so far as he was anything, poor fellow!

It seemed to me, when first I read "Fungoids," that, oddly enough, the diabolistic side of him was the best. Diabolism seemed to be a cheerful, even a wholesome influence in his life.

NOCTURNE

Round and round the shutter'd Square
I strolled with the Devil's arm in mine.

> No sound but the scrape of his hoofs was there
> And the ring of his laughter and mine.
> > We had drunk black wine.
> *I scream'd, "I will race you, Master!"*
> *"What matter," he shriek'd, "to-night*
> *Which of us runs the faster?*
> *There is nothing to fear to-night*
> > *In the foul moon's light!"*
> Then I look'd him in the eyes
> And I laugh'd full shrill at the lie he told
> And the gnawing fear he would fain disguise.
> It was true, what I'd time and again been told:
> > He was old—old.

There was, I felt, quite a swing about that first stanza—a joyous and rollicking note of comradeship. The second was slightly hysterical, perhaps. But I liked the third, it was so bracingly unorthodox, even according to the tenets of Soames's peculiar sect in the faith. Not much "trusting and encouraging" here! Soames triumphantly exposing the devil as a liar, and laughing "full shrill," cut a quite heartening figure, I thought, then! Now, in the light of what befell, none of his other poems depresses me so much as "Nocturne."

I looked out for what the metropolitan reviewers would have to say. They seemed to fall into two classes: those who had little to say and those who had nothing. The second class was the larger, and the words of the first were cold; insomuch that

Strikes a note of modernity.... These tripping numbers.
—"The Preston Telegraph."

was the only lure offered in advertisements by Soames's publisher. I had hoped that when next I met the poet I could congratulate him on having made a stir, for I fancied he was not so sure of his intrinsic greatness as he seemed. I was but able to say, rather coarsely, when next I did see him, that I hoped "Fungoids" was "selling splendidly." He looked at me across his glass of absinthe and asked if I had bought a copy. His publisher had told him that three had been sold. I laughed, as at a jest.

"You don't suppose I *care*, do you?" he said, with something like a snarl. I disclaimed the notion. He added that he was not a tradesman. I said mildly that I wasn't, either, and murmured that an artist who gave truly new and great things to the world had always to wait long for recognition. He said he cared not a sou for recognition. I agreed that the act of creation was its own reward.

His moroseness might have alienated me if I had regarded myself as a nobody. But ah! hadn't both John Lane and Aubrey Beardsley suggested that I should write an essay for the great new venture that was afoot—"The Yellow Book"? And hadn't Henry Harland, as editor, accepted my essay?

And wasn't it to be in the very first number? At Oxford I was still *in statu pupillari*. In London I regarded myself as very much indeed a graduate now—one whom no Soames could ruffle. Partly to show off, partly in sheer good-will, I told Soames he ought to contribute to "The Yellow Book." He uttered from the throat a sound of scorn for that publication.

Nevertheless, I did, a day or two later, tentatively ask Harland if he knew anything of the work of a man called Enoch Soames. Harland paused in the midst of his characteristic stride around the room, threw up his hands toward the ceiling, and groaned aloud: he had often met "that absurd creature" in Paris, and this very morning had received some poems in manuscript from him.

"Has he *no* talent?" I asked.

"He has an income. He's all right." Harland was the most joyous of men and most generous of critics, and he hated to talk of anything about which he couldn't be enthusiastic. So I dropped the subject of Soames. The news that Soames had an income did take the edge off solicitude. I learned afterward that he was the son of an unsuccessful and deceased bookseller in Preston, but had inherited an annuity of three hundred pounds from a married aunt, and had no surviving relatives of any kind. Materially, then, he was "all right." But there was still a spiritual pathos about him, sharpened for me now by the possibility that even the praises of "The Preston Telegraph" might not have been forthcoming had he not been the son of a Preston man He had a sort of weak doggedness which I could not but admire. Neither he nor his work received the slightest encouragement; but he persisted in behaving as a personage: always he kept his dingy little flag flying. Wherever congregated the *jeunes féroces* of the arts, in whatever Soho restaurant they had just discovered, in whatever music-hall they were most frequently, there was Soames in the midst of them, or, rather, on the fringe of them, a dim, but inevitable, figure. He never sought to propitiate his fellow-writers, never bated a jot of his arrogance about his own work or of his contempt for theirs. To the painters he was respectful, even humble; but for the poets and prosaists of "The Yellow Book" and later of "The Savoy" he had never a word but of scorn. He wasn't resented. It didn't occur to anybody that he or his Catholic diabolism mattered. When, in the autumn of '96, he brought out (at his own expense, this time) a third book, his last book, nobody said a word for or against it. I meant, but forgot, to buy it. I never saw it, and am ashamed to say I don't even remember what it was called. But I did, at the time of its publication, say to Rothenstein that I thought poor old Soames was really a rather tragic figure, and that I believed he would literally die for want of recognition. Rothenstein scoffed. He said I was trying to get credit for a kind heart which I didn't possess; and perhaps this was so. But at the private view of the New English Art

Club, a few weeks later, I beheld a pastel portrait of "Enoch Soames, Esq." It was very like him, and very like Rothenstein to have done it. Soames was standing near it, in his soft hat and his waterproof cape, all through the afternoon. Anybody who knew him would have recognized the portrait at a glance, but nobody who didn't know him would have recognized the portrait from its bystander: it "existed" so much more than he; it was bound to. Also, it had not that expression of faint happiness which on that day was discernible, yes, in Soames's countenance. Fame had breathed on him. Twice again in the course of the month I went to the New English, and on both occasions Soames himself was on view there. Looking back, I regard the close of that exhibition as having been virtually the close of his career. He had felt the breath of Fame against his cheek—so late, for such a little while; and at its withdrawal he gave in, gave up, gave out. He, who had never looked strong or well, looked ghastly now—a shadow of the shade he had once been. He still frequented the domino-room, but having lost all wish to excite curiosity, he no longer read books there. "You read only at the museum now?" I asked, with attempted cheerfulness. He said he never went there now. "No absinthe there," he muttered. It was the sort of thing that in old days he would have said for effect; but it carried conviction now. Absinthe, erst but a point in the "personality" he had striven so hard to build up, was solace and necessity now. He no longer called it *"la sorcière glauque."* He had shed away all his French phrases. He had become a plain, unvarnished Preston man.

Failure, if it be a plain, unvarnished, complete failure, and even though it be a squalid failure, has always a certain dignity. I avoided Soames because he made me feel rather vulgar. John Lane had published, by this time, two little books of mine, and they had had a pleasant little success of esteem. I was a—slight, but definite—"personality." Frank Harris had engaged me to kick up my heels in "The Saturday Review," Alfred Harmsworth was letting me do likewise in "The Daily Mail." I was just what Soames wasn't. And he shamed my gloss. Had I known that he really and firmly believed in the greatness of what he as an artist had achieved, I might not have shunned him. No man who hasn't lost his vanity can be held to have altogether failed. Soames's dignity was an illusion of mine. One day, in the first week of June 1897, that illusion went. But on the evening of that day Soames went, too.

I had been out most of the morning and, as it was too late to reach home in time for luncheon, I sought the Vingtième. This little place—Restaurant du Vingtième Siècle, to give it its full title—had been discovered in '96 by the poets and prosaists, but had now been more or less abandoned in favor of some later find. I don't think it lived long enough to justify its name; but at that time there it still was, in Greek Street, a few doors from Soho Square, and almost opposite to that house where,

in the first years of the century, a little girl, and with her a boy named De
Quincey, made nightly encampment in darkness and hunger among dust
and rats and old legal parchments. The Vingtième was but a small white-
washed room, leading out into the street at one end and into a kitchen at
the other. The proprietor and cook was a Frenchman, known to us as Monsieur Vingtième; the waiters were his two daughters, Rose and Berthe; and
the food, according to faith, was good. The tables were so narrow and were
set so close together that there was space for twelve of them, six jutting
from each wall.

Only the two nearest to the door, as I went in, were occupied. On one
side sat a tall, flashy, rather Mephistophelian man whom I had seen from
time to time in the domino-room and elsewhere. On the other side sat
Soames. They made a queer contrast in that sunlit room, Soames sitting
haggard in that hat and cape, which nowhere at any season had I seen him
doff, and this other, this keenly vital man, at sight of whom I more than
ever wondered whether he were a diamond merchant, a conjurer, or the
head of a private detective agency. I was sure Soames didn't want my company; but I asked, as it would have seemed brutal not to, whether I might
join him, and took the chair opposite to his. He was smoking a cigarette,
with an untasted salmi of something on his plate and a half-empty bottle
of Sauterne before him, and he was quite silent. I said that the preparations
for the Jubilee made London impossible. (I rather liked them, really.) I pro-
fessed a wish to go right away till the whole thing was over. In vain did I
attune myself to his gloom. He seemed not to hear me or even to see me. I
felt that his behavior made me ridiculous in the eyes of the other man. The
gangway between the two rows of tables at the Vingtième was hardly more
than two feet wide (Rose and Berthe, in their ministrations, had always to
edge past each other, quarreling in whispers as they did so), and any one
at the table abreast of yours was virtually at yours. I thought our neighbor
was amused at my failure to interest Soames, and so, as I could not explain
to him that my insistence was merely charitable, I became silent. Without turning my head, I had him well within my range of vision. I hoped I
looked less vulgar than he in contrast with Soames. I was sure he was not
an Englishman, but what *was* his nationality? Though his jet-black hair
was *en brosse*, I did not think he was French. To Berthe, who waited on
him, he spoke French fluently, but with a hardly native idiom and accent. I
gathered that this was his first visit to the Vingtième; but Berthe was off-
hand in her manner to him: he had not made a good impression. His eyes
were handsome, but, like the Vingtième's tables, too narrow and set too
close together. His nose was predatory, and the points of his mustache,
waxed up behind his nostrils, gave a fixity to his smile. Decidedly, he was
sinister. And my sense of discomfort in his presence was intensified by

the scarlet waistcoat which tightly, and so unseasonably in June, sheathed his ample chest. This waistcoat wasn't wrong merely because of the heat, either. It was somehow all wrong in itself. It wouldn't have done on Christmas morning. It would have struck a jarring note at the first night of "Hernani." I was trying to account for its wrongness when Soames suddenly and strangely broke silence. "A hundred years hence!" he murmured, as in a trance.

"We shall not be here," I briskly, but fatuously, added.

"We shall not be here. No," he droned, "but the museum will still be just where it is. And the reading-room just where it is. And people will be able to go and read there." He inhaled sharply, and a spasm as of actual pain contorted his features.

I wondered what train of thought poor Soames had been following. He did not enlighten me when he said, after a long pause, "You think I haven't minded."

"Minded what, Soames?"

"Neglect. Failure."

"*Failure?*" I said heartily. "Failure?" I repeated vaguely. "Neglect—yes, perhaps; but that's quite another matter. Of course you haven't been—appreciated. But what, then? Any artist who—who gives—" What I wanted to say was, "Any artist who gives truly new and great things to the world has always to wait long for recognition"; but the flattery would not out: in the face of his misery—a misery so genuine and so unmasked—my lips would not say the words.

And then he said them for me. I flushed. "That's what you were going to say, isn't it?" he asked.

"How did you know?"

"It's what you said to me three years ago, when 'Fungoids' was published." I flushed the more. I need not have flushed at all. "It's the only important thing I ever heard you say," he continued. "And I've never forgotten it. It's a true thing. It's a horrible truth. But—d'you remember what I answered? I said, 'I don't care a sou for recognition.' And you believed me. You've gone on believing I'm above that sort of thing. You're shallow. What should *you* know of the feelings of a man like me? You imagine that a great artist's faith in himself and in the verdict of posterity is enough to keep him happy. You've never guessed at the bitterness and loneliness, the"—his voice broke; but presently he resumed, speaking with a force that I had never known in him. "Posterity! What use is it to *me*? A dead man doesn't know that people are visiting his grave, visiting his birthplace, putting up tablets to him, unveiling statues of him. A dead man can't read the books that are written about him. A hundred years hence! Think of it! If I could come back to life *then*—just for a few hours—and go to the reading-room and *read*! Or, better still, if I could be projected now, at this moment, into that future, into that reading-room, just for this one afternoon! I'd sell myself body and soul to the devil for that! Think of the pages and pages in the catalogue: 'Soames, Enoch' endlessly—endless editions, commentaries, prolegomena, biographies"—But here he was interrupted by a sudden loud crack of the chair at the next table. Our neighbor had half risen from his place. He was leaning toward us, apologetically intrusive.

"Excuse—permit me," he said softly. "I have been unable not to hear. Might I take a liberty? In this little restaurant-*sans-façon*—might I, as the phrase is, cut in?"

I could but signify our acquiescence. Berthe had appeared at the kitchen door, thinking the stranger wanted his bill. He waved her away with his cigar, and in another moment had seated himself beside me, commanding a full view of Soames.

"Though not an Englishman," he explained, "I know my London well, Mr. Soames. Your name and fame—Mr. Beerbohm's, too—very known to me. Your point is, who am *I*?" He glanced quickly over his shoulder, and in a lowered voice said, "I am the devil."

I couldn't help it; I laughed. I tried not to, I knew there was nothing to laugh at, my rudeness shamed me; but—I laughed with increasing volume. The devil's quiet dignity, the surprise and disgust of his raised eyebrows, did but the more dissolve me. I rocked to and fro; I lay back aching; I behaved deplorably.

"I am a gentleman, and," he said with intense emphasis, "I thought I was in the company of *gentlemen*."

"Don't!" I gasped faintly. "Oh, don't!"

"Curious, *nicht wahr*?" I heard him say to Soames. "There is a type of person to whom the very mention of my name is—oh, so awfully—funny! In your theaters the dullest *comédien* needs only to say 'The devil!' and right away they give him 'the loud laugh what speaks the vacant mind.' Is it not so?"

I had now just breath enough to offer my apologies. He accepted them, but coldly, and re-addressed himself to Soames.

"I am a man of business," he said, "and always I would put things through 'right now,' as they say in the States. You are a poet. *Les affaires*—you detest them. So be it. But with me you will deal, eh? What you have said just now gives me furiously to hope."

Soames had not moved except to light a fresh cigarette. He sat crouched forward, with his elbows squared on the table, and his head just above the level of his hands, staring up at the devil.

"Go on," he nodded. I had no remnant of laughter in me now.

"It will be the more pleasant, our little deal," the devil went on, "because you are—I mistake not?—a diabolist."

"A Catholic diabolist," said Soames.

The devil accepted the reservation genially.

"You wish," he resumed, "to visit now—this afternoon as-ever-is—the reading-room of the British Museum, yes? But of a hundred years hence, yes? *Parfaitement.* Time—an illusion. Past and future—they are as ever present as the present, or at any rate only what you call 'just round the corner.' I switch you on to any date. I project you—*pouf!* You wish to be in the reading-room just as it will be on the afternoon of June 3, 1997? You wish to find yourself standing in that room, just past the swing-doors, this very minute, yes? And to stay there till closing-time? Am I right?"

Soames nodded.

The devil looked at his watch. "Ten past two," he said. "Closing-time in summer same then as now—seven o'clock. That will give you almost five hours. At seven o'clock—*pouf!*—you find yourself again here, sitting at this table. I am dining tonight *dans le monde—dans le higlif.* That concludes my present visit to your great city. I come and fetch you here, Mr. Soames, on my way home."

"Home?" I echoed.

"Be it never so humble!" said the devil, lightly.

"All right," said Soames.

"Soames!" I entreated. But my friend moved not a muscle.

The devil had made as though to stretch forth his hand across the table, but he paused in his gesture.

"A hundred years hence, as now," he smiled, "no smoking allowed in the reading-room. You would better therefore—"

Soames removed the cigarette from his mouth and dropped it into his glass of Sauterne.

"Soames!" again I cried. "Can't you"—but the devil had now stretched forth his hand across the table. He brought it slowly down on the table-cloth. Soames's chair was empty. His cigarette floated sodden in his wine-glass. There was no other trace of him.

For a few moments the devil let his hand rest where it lay, gazing at me out of the corners of his eyes, vulgarly triumphant.

A shudder shook me. With an effort I controlled myself and rose from my chair. "Very clever," I said condescendingly. "But—'The Time Machine' is a delightful book, don't you think? So entirely original!"

"You are pleased to sneer," said the devil, who had also risen, "but it is one thing to write about an impossible machine; it is a quite other thing to be a supernatural power." All the same, I had scored.

Berthe had come forth at the sound of our rising. I explained to her that Mr. Soames had been called away, and that both he and I would be dining here. It was not until I was out in the open air that I began to feel giddy. I have but the haziest recollection of what I did, where I wandered, in the glaring sunshine of that endless afternoon. I remember the sound of carpenters' hammers all along Piccadilly and the bare chaotic look of the half-erected "stands." Was it in the Green Park or in Kensington Gardens or *where* was it that I sat on a chair beneath a tree, trying to read an evening paper? There was a phrase in the leading article that went on repeating itself in my fagged mind: "Little is hidden from this august Lady full of the garnered wisdom of sixty years of Sovereignty." I remember wildly conceiving a letter (to reach Windsor by an express messenger told to await answer): "Madam: Well knowing that your Majesty is full of the garnered wisdom of sixty years of Sovereignty, I venture to ask your advice in the following delicate matter. Mr. Enoch Soames, whose poems you may or may not know—" Was there *no* way of helping him, saving him? A bargain was a bargain, and I was the last man to aid or abet any one in wriggling out of a reasonable obligation. I wouldn't have lifted a little finger to save *Faust*. But poor Soames! Doomed to pay without respite an eternal price for nothing but a fruitless search and a bitter disillusioning.

Odd and uncanny it seemed to me that he, Soames, in the flesh, in the waterproof cape, was at this moment living in the last decade of the next century, poring over books not yet written, and seeing and seen by men not yet born. Uncannier and odder still that tonight and evermore he would be in hell. Assuredly, truth was stranger than fiction.

Endless that afternoon was. Almost I wished I had gone with Soames, not, indeed, to stay in the reading-room, but to sally forth for a brisk sight-seeing walk around a new London. I wandered restlessly out of the park I had sat in. Vainly I tried to imagine myself an ardent tourist from the eighteenth century. Intolerable was the strain of the slow-passing and empty minutes. Long before seven o'clock I was back at the Vingtième.

I sat there just where I had sat for luncheon. Air came in listlessly through the open door behind me. Now and again Rose or Berthe appeared for a moment. I had told them I would not order any dinner till Mr. Soames came. A hurdy-gurdy began to play, abruptly drowning the noise of a quarrel between some Frenchmen farther up the street. Whenever the tune was changed I heard the quarrel still raging. I had bought another evening paper on my way. I unfolded it. My eyes gazed ever away from it to the clock over the kitchen door.

Five minutes now to the hour! I remembered that clocks in restaurants are kept five minutes fast. I concentrated my eyes on the paper. I vowed I would not look away from it again. I held it upright, at its full width, close to my face, so that I had no view of anything but it. Rather a tremulous sheet? Only because of the draft, I told myself.

My arms gradually became stiff; they ached; but I could not drop them—now. I had a suspicion, I had a certainty. Well, what, then? What else had I come for? Yet I held tight that barrier of newspaper. Only the sound of Berthe's brisk footstep from the kitchen enabled me, forced me, to drop it, and to utter:

"What shall we have to eat, Soames?"

"Il est souffrant, ce pauvre Monsieur Soames?" asked Berthe.

"He's only—tired." I asked her to get some wine—Burgundy—and whatever food might be ready. Soames sat crouched forward against the table exactly as when last I had seen him. It was as though he had never moved—he who had moved so unimaginably far. Once or twice in the afternoon it had for an instant occurred to me that perhaps his journey was not to be fruitless, that perhaps we had all been wrong in our estimate of the works of Enoch Soames. That we had been horribly right was horribly clear from the look of him. But, "Don't be discouraged," I falteringly said. "Perhaps it's only that you—didn't leave enough time. Two, three centuries hence, perhaps—"

"Yes," his voice came; "I've thought of that."

"And now—now for the more immediate future! Where are you going to hide? How would it be if you caught the Paris express from Charing Cross? Almost an hour to spare. Don't go on to Paris. Stop at Calais. Live in Calais. He'd never think of looking for you in Calais."

"It's like my luck," he said, "to spend my last hours on earth with an ass." But I was not offended. "And a treacherous ass," he strangely added, tossing across to me a crumpled bit of paper which he had been holding in his hand. I glanced at the writing on it—some sort of gibberish, apparently. I laid it impatiently aside.

"Come, Soames, pull yourself together! This isn't a mere matter of life or death. It's a question of eternal torment, mind you! You don't mean to say you're going to wait limply here till the devil comes to fetch you."

"I can't do anything else. I've no choice."

"Come! This is 'trusting and encouraging' with a vengeance! This is diabolism run mad!" I filled his glass with wine. "Surely, now that you've *seen* the brute—"

"It's no good abusing him."

"You must admit there's nothing Miltonic about him, Soames."

"I don't say he's not rather different from what I expected."

"He's a vulgarian, he's a swell mobs-man, he's the sort of man who hangs about the corridors of trains going to the Riviera and steals ladies' jewel-cases. Imagine eternal torment presided over by *him*!"

"You don't suppose I look forward to it, do you?"

"Then why not slip quietly out of the way?"

Again and again I filled his glass, and always, mechanically, he emptied it; but the wine kindled no spark of enterprise in him. He did not eat, and I myself ate hardly at all. I did not in my heart believe that any dash for freedom could save him. The chase would be swift, the capture certain. But better anything than this passive, meek, miserable waiting. I told Soames that for the honor of the human race he ought to make some show of resistance. He asked what the human race had ever done for him. "Besides," he said, "can't you understand that I'm in his power? You saw him touch me, didn't you? There's an end of it. I've no will. I'm sealed."

I made a gesture of despair. He went on repeating the word "sealed." I began to realize that the wine had clouded his brain. No wonder! Foodless he had gone into futurity, foodless he still was. I urged him to eat, at any rate, some bread. It was maddening to think that he, who had so much to tell, might tell nothing. "How was it all," I asked, "yonder? Come, tell me your adventures!"

"They'd make first-rate 'copy,' wouldn't they?"

"I'm awfully sorry for you, Soames, and I make all possible allowances; but what earthly right have you to insinuate that I should make 'copy,' as you call it, out of you?"

The poor fellow pressed his hands to his forehead.

"I don't know," he said. "I had some reason, I know. I'll try to remember. He sat plunged in thought."

"That's right. Try to remember everything. Eat a little more bread. What did the reading-room look like?"

"Much as usual," he at length muttered.

"Many people there?"

"Usual sort of number."

"What did they look like?"

Soames tried to visualize them.

"They all," he presently remembered, "looked very like one another."

My mind took a fearsome leap.

"All dressed in sanitary woolen?"

"Yes, I think so. Grayish-yellowish stuff."

"A sort of uniform?" He nodded. "With a number on it perhaps—a number on a large disk of metal strapped round the left arm? D.K.F. 78,910—that sort of thing?" It was even so. "And all of them, men and women alike, looking very well cared for? Very Utopian, and smelling rather strongly of carbolic, and all of them quite hairless?" I was right every time. Soames was only not sure whether the men and women were hairless or shorn. "I hadn't time to look at them very closely," he explained.

"No, of course not. But—"

"They stared at *me*, I can tell you. I attracted a great deal of attention." At last he had done that! "I think I rather scared them. They moved away whenever I came near. They followed me about, at a distance, wherever I went. The men at the round desk in the middle seemed to have a sort of panic whenever I went to make inquiries."

"What did you do when you arrived?"

Well, he had gone straight to the catalogue, of course,—to the S volumes,—and had stood long before SN-SOF, unable to take this volume out of the shelf because his heart was beating so. At first, he said, he wasn't disappointed; he only thought there was some new arrangement. He went to the middle desk and asked where the catalogue of twentieth-century books was kept. He gathered that there was still only one catalogue. Again he looked up his name, stared at the three little pasted slips he had known so well. Then he went and sat down for a long time.

"And then," he droned, "I looked up the 'Dictionary of National Biography,' and some encyclopedias. I went back to the middle desk and asked what was the best modern book on late nineteenth-century literature. They told me Mr. T.K. Nupton's book was considered the best. I looked it up in the catalogue and filled in a form for it. It was brought to me. My name wasn't in the index, but—yes!" he said with a sudden change of tone, "that's what I'd forgotten. Where's that bit of paper? Give it me back."

I, too, had forgotten that cryptic screed. I found it fallen on the floor, and handed it to him.

He smoothed it out, nodding and smiling at me disagreeably.

"I found myself glancing through Nupton's book," he resumed. "Not very easy reading. Some sort of phonetic spelling. All the modern books I saw were phonetic."

"Then I don't want to hear any more, Soames, please."

"The proper names seemed all to be spelt in the old way. But for that I mightn't have noticed my own name."

"Your own name? Really? Soames, I'm *very* glad."

"And yours."

"No!"

"I thought I should find you waiting here tonight, so I took the trouble to copy out the passage. Read it."

I snatched the paper. Soames's handwriting was characteristically dim. It and the noisome spelling and my excitement made me all the slower to grasp what T.K. Nupton was driving at.

The document lies before me at this moment. Strange that the words I here copy out for you were copied out for me by poor Soames just eighty-two years hence!

From page 234 of "Inglish Littracher 1890–1900" bi T.K. Nupton, publishd bi th Stait, 1992.

Fr egzarmpl, a riter ov th time, naimed Max Beerbohm, hoo woz stil alive in th twentith senchri, rote a stauri in wich e pautraid an immajnari karrakter kauld "Enoch Soames"—a thurd-rait poit hoo beleevz imself a grate jeneus an maix a bargin with th Devvl in auder ter no wot posterriti thinx ov im! It iz a sumwot labud sattire, but not without vallu az showing hou seriusli the yung men ov th aiteen-ninetiz took themselvz. Nou that th littreri profeshn haz bin auganized az a departmnt of publik servis, our riters hav found their levvl an hav lernt ter doo their duti without thort ov th morro. "Th laibrer iz werthi ov hiz hire" an that iz aul. Thank hevvn we hav no Enoch Soameses amung us to-dai!

I found that by murmuring the words aloud (a device which I commend to my reader) I was able to master them little by little. The clearer they became, the greater was my bewilderment, my distress and horror. The whole thing was a nightmare. Afar, the great grisly background of what was in store for the poor dear art of letters; here, at the table, fixing on me a gaze that made me hot all over, the poor fellow whom—whom evidently—but no: whatever down-grade my character might take in coming years, I should never be such a brute as to—

Again I examined the screed. "Immajnari." But here Soames was, no more imaginary, alas! than I. And "labud"—what on earth was that? (To this day I have never made out that word.) "It's all very—baffling," I at length stammered.

Soames said nothing, but cruelly did not cease to look at me.

"Are you sure," I temporized, "quite sure you copied the thing out correctly?"

"Quite."

"Well, then, it's this wretched Nupton who must have made—must be going to make—some idiotic mistake. Look here Soames, you know me better than to suppose that I—After all, the name Max Beerbohm is not at all an uncommon one, and there must be several Enoch Soameses running around, or, rather, Enoch Soames is a name that might occur to any one writing a story. And I don't write stories; I'm an essayist, an observer, a recorder. I admit that it's an extraordinary coincidence. But you must see—"

"I see the whole thing," said Soames, quietly. And he added, with a touch of his old manner, but with more dignity than I had ever known in him, "Parlons d'autre chose."

I accepted that suggestion very promptly. I returned straight to the more immediate future. I spent most of the long evening in renewed appeals to Soames to come away and seek refuge somewhere. I remember saying at last that if indeed I was destined to write about him, the supposed "stauri" had better have at least a happy ending. Soames repeated those last three words in a tone of intense scorn.

"In life and in art," he said, "all that matters is an *inevitable* ending."

"But," I urged more hopefully than I felt, "an ending that can be avoided *isn't* inevitable."

"You aren't an artist," he rasped. "And you're so hopelessly not an artist that, so far from being able to imagine a thing and make it seem true, you're going to make even a true thing seem as if you'd made it up. You're a miserable bungler. And it's like my luck."

I protested that the miserable bungler was not I, was not going to be I, but T.K. Nupton; and we had a rather heated argument, in the thick of which it suddenly seemed to me that Soames saw he was in the wrong: he had quite physically cowered. But I wondered why—and now I guessed with a cold throb just why—he stared so past me. The bringer of that "inevitable ending" filled the doorway.

I managed to turn in my chair and to say, not without a semblance of lightness, "Aha, come in!" Dread was indeed rather blunted in me by his looking so absurdly like a villain in a melodrama. The sheen of his tilted hat and of his shirt-front, the repeated twists he was giving to his mustache, and most of all the magnificence of his sneer, gave token that he was there only to be foiled.

He was at our table in a stride. "I am sorry," he sneered witheringly, "to break up your pleasant party, but—"

"You don't; you complete it," I assured him. "Mr. Soames and I want to have a little talk with you. Won't you sit? Mr. Soames got nothing, frankly nothing, by his journey this afternoon. We don't wish to say that the whole thing was a swindle, a common swindle. On the contrary, we believe you meant well. But of course the bargain, such as it was, is off."

The devil gave no verbal answer. He merely looked at Soames and pointed with rigid forefinger to the door. Soames was wretchedly rising from his chair when, with a desperate, quick gesture, I swept together two dinner-knives that were on the table, and laid their blades across each other. The devil stepped sharp back against the table behind him, averting his face and shuddering.

"You are not superstitious!" he hissed.

"Not at all," I smiled.

"Soames," he said as to an underling, but without turning his face, "put those knives straight!"

With an inhibitive gesture to my friend, "Mr. Soames," I said emphatically to the devil, "is a *Catholic* diabolist"; but my poor friend did the devil's bidding, not mine; and now, with his master's eyes again fixed on him, he arose, he shuffled past me. I tried to speak. It was he that spoke. "Try," was the prayer he threw back at me as the devil pushed him roughly out through the door—"*try* to make them know that I did exist!"

In another instant I, too, was through that door. I stood staring all ways, up the street, across it, down it. There was moonlight and lamplight, but there was not Soames nor that other.

Dazed, I stood there. Dazed, I turned back at length into the little room, and I suppose I paid Berthe or Rose for my dinner and luncheon and for Soames's; I hope so, for I never went to the Vingtième again. Ever since that night I have avoided Greek Street altogether. And for years I did not set foot even in Soho Square, because on that same night it was there that I paced and loitered, long and long, with some such dull sense of hope as a man has in not straying far from the place where he has lost something. "Round and round the shutter'd Square"—that line came back to me on my lonely beat, and with it the whole stanza, ringing in my brain and bearing in on me how tragically different from the happy scene imagined by him was the poet's actual experience of that prince in whom of all princes we should put not our trust!

But strange how the mind of an essayist, be it never so stricken, roves and ranges! I remember pausing before a wide door-step and wondering if perchance it was on this very one that the young De Quincey lay ill and faint while poor Ann flew as fast as her feet would carry her to Oxford Street, the "stony-hearted stepmother" of them both, and came back bearing that "glass of port wine and spices" but for which he might, so he thought, actually have died. Was this the very door-step that the old De Quincey used to revisit in homage? I pondered Ann's fate, the cause of her sudden vanishing from the ken of her boyfriend; and presently I blamed myself for letting the past override the present. Poor vanished Soames!

And for myself, too, I began to be troubled. What had I better do? Would there be a hue and cry—"Mysterious Disappearance of an Author," and all that? He had last been seen lunching and dining in my company. Hadn't I better get a hansom and drive straight to Scotland Yard? They would think I was a lunatic. After all, I reassured myself, London was a very large place, and one very dim figure might easily drop out of it unobserved, now especially, in the blinding glare of the near Jubilee. Better say nothing at all, I thought.

* * *

And I was right. Soames's disappearance made no stir at all. He was utterly forgotten before any one, so far as I am aware, noticed that he was no longer hanging around. Now and again some poet or prosaist may have said to another, "What has become of that man Soames?" but I never heard any such question asked. As for his landlady in Dyott Street, no doubt he had paid her weekly, and what possessions he may have had in his rooms were enough to save her from fretting. The solicitor through whom he was paid his annuity may be presumed to have made inquiries, but no echo of these resounded. There was something rather ghastly to me in the general unconsciousness that Soames had existed, and more than once I caught myself wondering whether Nupton, that babe unborn, were going to be right in thinking him a figment of my brain.

In that extract from Nupton's repulsive book there is one point which perhaps puzzles you. How is it that the author, though I have here mentioned him by name and have quoted the exact words he is going to write, is not going to grasp the obvious corollary that I have invented nothing? The answer can be only this: Nupton will not have read the later passages of this memoir. Such lack of thoroughness is a serious fault in any one who undertakes to do scholar's work. And I hope these words will meet the eye of some contemporary rival to Nupton and be the undoing of Nupton.

I like to think that sometime between 1992 and 1997 somebody will have looked up this memoir, and will have forced on the world his inevitable and startling conclusions. And I have reason for believing that this will be so. You realize that the reading-room into which Soames was projected by the devil was in all respects precisely as it will be on the afternoon of June 3, 1997. You realize, therefore, that on that afternoon, when it comes round, there the selfsame crowd will be, and there Soames will be, punctually, he and they doing precisely what they did before. Recall now Soames's account of the sensation he made. You may say that the mere difference of his costume was enough to make him sensational in that uniformed crowd. You wouldn't say so if you had ever seen him, and I assure you that in no period would Soames be anything but dim. The fact that people are going to stare at him and follow him around and seem afraid of him, can be explained only on the hypothesis that they will somehow have been prepared for his ghostly visitation. They will have been awfully waiting to see whether he really would come. And when he does come the effect will of course be—awful.

An authentic, guaranteed, proved ghost, but; only a ghost, alas! Only that. In his first visit Soames was a creature of flesh and blood, whereas the creatures among whom he was projected were but ghosts, I take it—solid, palpable, vocal, but unconscious and automatic ghosts, in a building that was itself an illusion. Next time that building and those creatures will be real. It is of Soames that there will be but the semblance. I wish I could think him destined to revisit the world actually, physically, consciously. I wish he had this one brief escape, this one small treat, to look forward to. I never forget him for long. He is where he is and forever. The more rigid moralists among you may say he has only himself to blame. For my part,

I think he has been very hardly used. It is well that vanity should be chastened; and Enoch Soames's vanity was, I admit, above the average, and called for special treatment. But there was no need for vindictiveness. You say he contracted to pay the price he is paying. Yes; but I maintain that he was induced to do so by fraud. Well informed in all things, the devil must have known that my friend would gain nothing by his visit to futurity. The whole thing was a very shabby trick. The more I think of it, the more detestable the devil seems to me.

Of him I have caught sight several times, here and there, since that day at the Vingtième. Only once, however, have I seen him at close quarters. This was a couple of years ago, in Paris. I was walking one afternoon along the rue d'Antin, and I saw him advancing from the opposite direction, overdressed as ever, and swinging an ebony cane and altogether behaving as though the whole pavement belonged to him. At thought of Enoch Soames and the myriads of other sufferers eternally in this brute's dominion, a great cold wrath filled me, and I drew myself up to my full height. But—well, one is so used to nodding and smiling in the street to anybody whom one knows that the action becomes almost independent of oneself; to prevent it requires a very sharp effort and great presence of mind. I was miserably aware, as I passed the devil, that I nodded and smiled to him. And my shame was the deeper and hotter because he, if you please, stared straight at me with the utmost haughtiness.

To be cut, deliberately cut, by *him*! I was, I still am, furious at having had that happen to me.

"The Striding Place"

by Gertrude Atherton*

Gertrude Atherton (1857–1948) was born and died in San Francisco, but she lived in New York, London, and Paris along the way, befriending several bright lights of the era, such as Oscar Wilde, the biographer William Sharpe, a young Winston Churchill, and Ambrose Bierce. All the while she was writing and publishing prolifically, most of her work very well received and often compared to that of Henry James and Edith Wharton. "The Striding Place" (1905) was one of the short stories contained in Atherton's collection of mostly supernatural stories, *The Bell in the Fog and Other Stories*, about which *The Oxford Magazine* said, "the value of her work lies in the fact that her clear analysis of ephemeral motives is always in relief against a suggestion of vast surrounding mysteries, of unintelligible powers that were, and are, and are to be." In contrast to the rush toward science and knowing that characterized the Victorian age, Atherton's stories edge toward a Modernist outlook in that they recognize the limits of humanity's ability to understand and master their world. The ending of "The Striding Place" shows that even what we think that we know about life and death is paltry compared to the vast, larger truths that lie just beyond the reach of human senses and reason.

* * * * *

Weigall, continental and detached, tired early of grouse-shooting. To stand propped against a sod fence while his host's workmen routed up the birds with long poles and drove them towards the waiting guns, made him feel himself a parody on the ancestors who had roamed the moors and forests of this West Riding of Yorkshire in hot pursuit of game worth the killing. But when in England in August he always accepted whatever proffered for the season, and invited his host to shoot pheasants on his estates in

---

*Atherton, Gertrude. "The Striding Place." *The Bell in the Fog*. MacMillan, 1905, pp. 57–72.

the South. The amusements of life, he argued, should be accepted with the same philosophy as its ills.

It had been a bad day. A heavy rain had made the moor so spongy that it fairly sprang beneath the feet. Whether or not the grouse had haunts of their own, wherein they were immune from rheumatism, the bag had been small. The women, too, were an unusually dull lot, with the exception of a new-minded debutante who bothered Weigall at dinner by demanding the verbal restoration of the vague paintings on the vaulted roof above them.

But it was no one of these things that sat on Weigall's mind as, when the other men went up to bed, he let himself out of the castle and sauntered down to the river. His intimate friend, the companion of his boyhood, the chum of his college days, his fellow-traveler in many lands, the man for whom he possessed stronger affection than for all men, had mysteriously disappeared two days ago, and his track might have sprung to the upper air for all trace he had left behind him. He had been a guest on the adjoining estate during the past week, shooting with the fervor of the true sportsman, making love in the intervals to Adeline Cavan, and apparently in the best of spirits. As far as was known there was nothing to lower his mental mercury, for his rent-roll was a large one, Miss Cavan blushed whenever he looked at her, and, being one of the best shots in England, he was never happier than in August. The suicide theory was preposterous, all agreed, and there was as little reason to believe him murdered. Nevertheless, he had walked out of March Abbey two nights ago without hat or overcoat, and had not been seen since.

The country was being patrolled night and day. A hundred keepers and workmen were beating the woods and poking the bogs on the moors, but as yet not so much as a handkerchief had been found.

Weigall did not believe for a moment that Wyatt Gifford was dead, and although it was impossible not to be affected by the general uneasiness, he was disposed to be more angry than frightened. At Cambridge Gifford had been an incorrigible practical joker, and by no means had outgrown the habit; it would be like him to cut across the country in his evening clothes, board a cattle-train, and amuse himself touching up the picture of the sensation in West Riding.

However, Weigall's affection for his friend was too deep to companion with tranquility in the present state of doubt, and, instead of going to bed early with the other men, he determined to walk until ready for sleep. He went down to the river and followed the path through the woods. There was no moon, but the stars sprinkled their cold light upon the pretty belt of water flowing placidly past wood and ruin, between green masses of overhanging rocks or sloping banks tangled with tree and shrub, leaping occasionally over stones with the harsh notes of an angry scold, to recover its equanimity the moment the way was clear again.

It was very dark in the depths where Weigall trod. He smiled as he recalled a remark of Gifford's: "An English wood is like a good many other things in life—very promising at a distance, but a hollow mockery when you get within. You see daylight on both sides, and the sun freckles the very bracken. Our woods need the night to make them seem what they ought to be—what they once were, before our ancestors' descendants demanded so much more money, in these so much more various days."

Weigall strolled along, smoking, and thinking of his friend, his pranks—many of which had done more credit to his imagination than this—and recalling conversations that had lasted the night through. Just before the end of the London season they had walked the streets one hot night after a party, discussing the various theories of the soul's destiny. That afternoon they had met at the coffin of a college friend whose mind had been a blank for the past three years. Some months previously they had called at the asylum to see him. His expression had been senile, his face imprinted with the record of debauchery. In death the face was placid, intelligent, without ignoble lineation—the face of the man they had known at college. Weigall and Gifford had had no time to comment there, and the afternoon and evening were full; but, coming forth from the house of festivity together, they had reverted almost at once to the topic.

"I cherish the theory," Gifford had said, "that the soul sometimes lingers in the body after death. During madness, of course, it is an impotent prisoner, albeit a conscious one. Fancy its agony, and its horror! What more natural than that, when the life-spark goes out, the tortured soul should take possession of the vacant skull and triumph once more for a few hours while old friends look their last? It has had time to repent while compelled to crouch and behold the result of its work, and it has shrived itself into a state of comparative purity. If I had my way, I should stay inside my bones until the coffin had gone into its niche, that I might obviate for my poor old comrade the tragic impersonality of death. And I should like to see justice done to it, as it were—to see it lowered among its ancestors with the ceremony and solemnity that are its due. I am afraid that if I dissevered myself too quickly, I should yield to curiosity and hasten to investigate the mysteries of space."

"You believe in the soul as an independent entity, then—that it and the vital principle are not one and the same?"

"Absolutely. The body and soul are twins, life comrades—sometimes friends, sometimes enemies, but always loyal in the last instance. Some day, when I am tired of the world, I shall go to India and become a mahatma, solely for the pleasure of receiving proof during life of this independent relationship."

"Suppose you were not sealed up properly, and returned after one of your astral flights to find your earthly part unfit for habitation? It is an experiment I don't think I should care to try, unless even juggling with soul and flesh had palled."

"That would not be an uninteresting predicament. I should rather enjoy experimenting with broken machinery."

The high wild roar of water smote suddenly upon Weigall's ear and checked his memories. He left the wood and walked out on the huge slippery stones which nearly close the River Wharfe at this point, and watched the waters boil down into the narrow pass with their furious untiring energy. The black quiet of the woods rose high on either side. The stars seemed colder and whiter just above. On either hand the perspective of the river might have run into a rayless cavern. There was no lonelier spot in England, nor one which had the right to claim so many ghosts, if ghosts there were.

Weigall was not a coward, but he recalled uncomfortably the tales of those that had been done to death in the Strid. Wordsworth's Boy of Egremond had been disposed of by the practical Whitaker; but countless others, more venturesome than wise, had gone down into that narrow boiling course, never to appear in the still pool a few yards beyond. Below the great rocks which form the walls of the Strid was believed to be a natural vault, on to whose shelves the dead were drawn. The spot had an ugly fascination. Weigall stood, visioning skeletons, uncoffined and green, the home of the eyeless things which had devoured all that had covered and filled that rattling symbol of man's mortality; then fell to wondering if anyone had attempted to leap the Strid of late. It was covered with slime; he had never seen it look so treacherous.

He shuddered and turned away, impelled, despite his manhood, to flee the spot. As he did so, something tossing in the foam below the fall—something as white, yet independent of it—caught his eye and arrested his step. Then he saw that it was describing a contrary motion to the rushing water—an upward backward motion. Weigall stood rigid, breathless; he fancied he heard the crackling of his hair. Was that a hand? It thrust itself still higher above the boiling foam, turned sidewise, and four frantic fingers were distinctly visible against the black rock beyond.

Weigall's superstitious terror left him. A man was there, struggling to free himself from the suction beneath the Strid, swept down, doubtless, but a moment before his arrival, perhaps as he stood with his back to the current.

He stepped as close to the edge as he dared. The hand doubled as if in imprecation, shaking savagely in the face of that force which leaves its creatures to immutable law; then spread wide again, clutching, expanding, crying for help as audibly as the human voice.

Weigall dashed to the nearest tree, dragged and twisted off a branch with his strong arms, and returned as swiftly to the Strid. The hand was in the same place, still gesticulating as wildly; the body was undoubtedly caught in the rocks below, perhaps already half-way along one of those hideous shelves. Weigall let himself down upon a lower rock, braced his shoulder against the mass beside him, then, leaning out over the water, thrust the branch into the hand. The fingers clutched it convulsively. Weigall tugged powerfully, his own feet dragged perilously near the edge. For a moment he produced no impression, then an arm shot above the waters.

The blood sprang to Weigall's head; he was choked with the impression that the Strid had him in her roaring hold, and he saw nothing. Then the mist cleared. The hand and arm were nearer, although the rest of the body was still concealed by the foam. Weigall peered out with distended eyes. The meagre light revealed in the cuffs links of a peculiar device. The fingers clutching the branch were as familiar.

Weigall forgot the slippery stones, the terrible death if he stepped too far. He pulled with passionate will and muscle. Memories flung themselves into the hot light of his brain, trooping rapidly upon each other's heels, as in the thought of the drowning. Most of the pleasures of his life, good and bad, were identified in some way with this friend. Scenes of college days, of travel, where they had deliberately sought adventure and stood between one another and death upon more occasions than one, of hours of delightful companionship among the treasures of art, and others in the pursuit of pleasure, flashed like the changing particles of a kaleidoscope. Weigall had loved several women; but he would have flouted in these moments the thought that he had ever loved any woman as he loved Wyatt Gifford. There were so many charming women in the world, and in the thirty-two years of his life he had never known another man to whom he had cared to give his intimate friendship.

He threw himself on his face. His wrists were cracking, the skin was torn from his hands. The fingers still gripped the stick. There was life in them yet.

Suddenly something gave way. The hand swung about, tearing the branch from Weigall's grasp. The body had been liberated and flung outward, though still submerged by the foam and spray.

Weigall scrambled to his feet and sprang along the rocks, knowing that the danger from suction was over and that Gifford must be carried straight to the quiet pool. Gifford was a fish in the water and could live under it longer than most men. If he survived this, it would not be the first time that his pluck and science had saved him from drowning.

Weigall reached the pool. A man in his evening clothes floated on it, his face turned towards a projecting rock over which his arm had fallen, upholding the body. The hand that had held the branch hung limply over the rock, its white reflection visible in the black water. Weigall plunged into the shallow pool, lifted Gifford in his arms and returned to the bank. He laid the body down and threw off his coat that he might be the freer to practice the methods of resuscitation. He was glad of the moment's respite. The valiant life in the man might have been exhausted in that last struggle. He had not dared to look at his face, to put his ear to the heart. The hesitation lasted but a moment. There was no time to lose.

He turned to his prostrate friend. As he did so, something strange and disagreeable smote his senses. For a half-moment he did not appreciate its nature. Then his teeth clacked together, his feet, his outstretched arms pointed towards the woods. But he sprang to the side of the man and bent down and peered into his face. There was no face.

"Haïta the Shepherd"

by Ambrose Bierce*

"Haïta the Shepherd," written by Ambrose Bierce (1842–1914) and first published in *The Wave* (January 24, 1891), is a curious short story that speaks to philosophy as much as it does to ethereal entities and humanity's relationship to them. An American writer and Civil War veteran, Bierce is primarily known for "An Occurrence at Owl Creek Bridge" (1890), the satirical *The Devil's Dictionary* (1911), and the widely anthologized "The Damned Thing" (1893), but it is Haïta, a common shepherd, who experiences the fickle nature of fate and free will and causes readers to evaluate their own perspective on the nature of the universe. This story also introduces the world to Hastur, a benign spirit that would have a larger significance in the H.P. Lovecraft and August Derleth Cthulhu mythos, eventually being identified as a Great Old One in stories by Lovecraft and Robert W. Chambers. Bierce's tale explores themes of isolationism, alienation, mysticism, and an evaluation of what is real and what is imagined. As Haïta discovers, there are certain things that will always be just out of reach.

* * * * *

In the heart of Haïta the illusions of learning and experience had not supplanted those of youth. His thoughts were pure and pleasant, for his life was simple and his soul devoid of ambition. He rose with the sun and went forth to pray at the shrine of Hastur, the god of shepherds, who heard and was pleased. After performance of this pious rite, Haïta unbarred the gate of the fold, and with a cheerful mind drove his flock afield, eating his morning meal of curds and oat-cake as he went, occasionally pausing to add a few berries, cold with dew, or to drink of the waters that came away from the hills to join the stream in the middle of the valley and be borne along with

---

*Bierce, Ambrose. "Haïta the Shepherd." *The Wave* VI, no. 38, 24 January 1891, p. 11.

it, he knew not whither. During the long summer day, as his sheep cropped the good grass which the gods had made to grow for them, or lay with their fore-legs doubled under their breasts and indolently chewed the cud, Haïta, reclining in the shadow of a tree or sitting upon a rock, played so sweet music upon his reed pipe that sometimes from the corner of his eye he got glimpses of the minor sylvan deities leaning forward out of the copse to hear; but if he looked at them directly they vanished. From this—for he must be thinking if he would not turn into one of his own sheep—he drew the solemn inference that happiness may come if not sought, but if looked for will never be seen; for next to the favor of Hastur, who never disclosed himself, Haïta most valued the friendly interest of his neighbors, the shy immortals of the wood and stream. At nightfall he drove his flock back to the fold, saw that the gate was secure, and retired to his cave for refreshment and for dreams.

So passed his life, one day like another, save when the storms uttered the wrath of an offended god. Then Haïta cowered in his cave, his face hidden in his hands, and prayed that he alone might be punished for his sins and the world saved from destruction. Sometimes when there was a great rain, and the stream came out of its banks, compelling him to urge his terrified flock to the uplands, he interceded for the people in the great cities which he had been told lay in the plain beyond the two blue hills which formed a gateway of his valley.

"It is kind of thee, O! Hastur," so he prayed, "to give me mountains so near to my dwelling and my fold, that I and my sheep can escape the angry torrents; but the rest of the world thou must thyself deliver in some way that I know not of, or I will no longer worship thee."

And Hastur, knowing that Haïta was a youth who kept his word, spared the cities and turned the waters into the sea.

So he had lived since he could remember. He could not rightly conceive any other mode of existence. The holy hermit who lived at the head of the valley, a full hour's journey away, from whom he had the tale of the great cities where dwelt people—poor souls!—who had no sheep, gave him no knowledge of that early time when, so he reasoned, he must have been small and helpless like a lamb.

It was through thinking on these mysteries and marvels and on that horrible change to silence and decay which he felt sure must sometime come to him as he had seen it come to so many of his flock—as it came to all living things except the birds—that Haïta first became conscious how miserable was his lot.

"It is necessary," he said, "that I know whence and how I came; for how can one perform his duties unless able to judge what they are by the way in which he was entrusted with them? And what contentment can I have when I know not how long it is to last? Perhaps before another sun I may be changed, and then what will become of the sheep? What, indeed, will have become of me?"

Pondering these things Haïta became melancholy and morose. He no longer spoke cheerfully to his flock, nor ran with alacrity to the shrine of Hastur. In every breeze he heard whispers of malign deities whose existence he now first observed. Every cloud was a portent signifying disaster, and the darkness was full of terrors. His reed pipe when applied to his lips gave out no melody but a dismal wail; the sylvan and riparian intelligences no longer thronged the thicket-side to listen, but fled from the sound, as he knew by the stirred leaves and bent flowers. He relaxed his vigilance and many of his sheep strayed away into the hills and were lost. Those that remained became lean and ill for lack of good pasturage, for he would not seek it for them, but conducted them day after day to the same spot through mere abstraction while puzzling about life and death—of immortality he knew nothing.

One day while indulging in the gloomiest reflections he suddenly sprang from the rock upon which he sat, and with a determined gesture of the right hand exclaimed: "I will no longer be a suppliant for knowledge which the gods withhold. Let them look to it that they do me no wrong. I will do my duty as best I can, and if I err, upon their own heads be it!"

Suddenly, as he spoke, a great brightness fell about him, causing him to look upward, thinking the sun had burst through a rift in the clouds; but there were no clouds. Hardly more than an arm's length away stood a beautiful maiden. So beautiful she was that the flowers about her feet folded their petals in despair and bent their heads in token of submission; so sweet her look that the humming birds thronged her eyes, thrusting their thirsty bills almost into them, and the wild bees were about her lips. And such was her radiance that the shadows of all objects fell divergent, turning as she moved.

Haïta was entranced. Rising, he knelt at her feet in adoration, and she laid her hand upon his head.

"Come," she said in a voice which had the music of all the bells of his flock—"come, thou art not to worship me, who am no goddess, but if thou art truthful and dutiful I will abide with thee."

Haïta seized her hand and, stammering his joy and gratitude, arose, and hand in hand they stood and smiled in one another's eyes. He gazed upon her with reverence and rapture. He said: "I pray thee, lovely maid, tell me thy name and whence thou comest."

At this she laid a warning finger on her lip and began to withdraw. Her beauty underwent a visible alteration that made him shudder, he knew not why, for still she was beautiful. The landscape was darkened by a giant shadow sweeping across the valley with the speed of a vulture. In the obscurity the maiden's figure grew dim and indistinct and her voice seemed to come from a distance, as she said, in a tone of sorrowful reproach: "Presumptuous and ungrateful man! must I then so soon leave thee? Would nothing do but thou must at once break the Eternal Compact?"

Inexpressibly grieved, Haïta fell upon his knees and implored her to remain—rose and sought her in the deepening darkness—ran in circles, calling to her aloud; but all in vain. She was no longer visible, but out of the gloom he heard her voice saying: "Nay, thou shalt not have me by seeking. Go to thy duty, faithless shepherd, or we never meet again."

Night had fallen; the wolves were howling in the hills and the terrified sheep crowding about his feet. In the demands of the hour he forgot his disappointment, drove his flock to the fold, and repairing to the place of worship, poured out his heart in gratitude to Hastur, then retired to his cave and slept.

When Haïta awoke the sun was high and shone in at his cave, illuminating it with a great glory. And there, beside him, sat the maiden! She smiled upon him with a smile that seemed the visible music of his pipe of reeds. He dared not speak, fearing to offend her as before, for he knew not what he would venture to say.

"Because," she said, "thou didst thy duty by the flock, and didst not forget to thank Hastur for staying the wolves of the night, I am come to thee again. Wilt thou have me for a companion?"

"Who would not have thee forever?" replied Haïta. "O! never again leave me until—until I—change and become silent and motionless."

Haïta had no word for death.

"I wish, indeed," he continued, "that thou wert of my own sex, that we might wrestle and run races and so never tire of being together."

At these words the maiden arose and passed out of the cave, and Haïta, springing from his couch of fragrant boughs to overtake and detain her, observed to his astonishment that the rain was falling and the stream in the middle of the valley had come out of its banks. The sheep were bleating in terror, for the rising waters had invaded their fold, and there was danger for the unknown cities of the distant plain.

It was many days before Haïta saw the maiden again. One day he was returning from the head of the valley, where he had gone with ewe's milk and oat cake and berries for the holy hermit, who was too old and feeble to provide himself with food.

"Poor old man!" he said aloud, as he trudged along homeward. "I will return tomorrow and bear him on my back to my own dwelling, where I can care for him. Doubtless it is for that that Hastur has reared me all these years, and gives me health and strength."

As he spoke, the maiden, clad all in glittering garments, met him in the path with a smile which took away his breath.

"I am come again," she said, "to dwell with thee if thou wilt now have me, for none else will. Thou mayest have learned wisdom and art willing to take me as I am, nor care to know."

Haïta threw himself at her feet. "Beautiful being," he cried, "if thou wilt but deign to accept all the devotion of my heart and soul—after Hastur be served—it is yours forever. But, alas! thou art capricious and wayward. Before tomorrow's sun I may lose thee again. Promise, I beseech thee, that however in my ignorance I may offend, thou wilt forgive and remain always with me."

Scarcely had he finished speaking when a troop of wolves sprang out of the hills and came racing toward him with fiery eyes and dreadful howls. The maiden again vanished and he turned and fled for his life. Nor did he stop until he was in the humble dwelling of the holy hermit, whence he had set out. Hastily barring the door against the wolves, he cast himself upon the ground and wept.

"My son," said the hermit from his couch of straw freshly gathered that morning by Haïta's hands, "it is not like thee to weep for wolves—tell me what sorrow has befallen thee, that age may minister to the hurts of youth with such balms as it hath of its wisdom."

Haïta told him all, how thrice he had met the radiant maid and thrice she had left him forlorn. He related minutely all that had passed between them, omitting no word of what had been said.

When he had ended, the holy hermit was a moment silent, then said: "My son, I have attended to thy story and I know the maiden. I have myself seen her, as have many. Know, then, that her name, which she would not even permit thee to inquire, is Happiness. Thou saidst well to her that she was capricious, for she imposes conditions that man cannot fulfil, and delinquency is punished by desertion. She cometh only when unsought, and will not be questioned. One manifestation of curiosity, one sign of doubt, one expression of misgiving, and she is away! How long didst thou have her at any time before she fled?"

"But a single instant," answered Haïta, blushing with shame at the confession. "Each time I drove her away in one moment."

"Unfortunate youth!" said the holy hermit, "but for thine indiscretion thou mightst have had her for two."

"Luella Miller"

by Mary E. Wilkins Freeman*

Horror fiction existed long before it was ever categorized into a specific genre. However, during the late nineteenth and early twentieth centuries, stories about ghosts, vampires, and doppelgängers became rather pervasive in magazines and novels. Mary E. Wilkins Freeman was part of this wave, publishing collections such as *The Wind in the Rosebush and Other Supernatural Ghost Stories* (1903). "Luella Miller," first published in *Everybody's Magazine* in December 1902, provides an interesting wrinkle to the traditional vampire narrative. Reminiscent of Charles Dickens's Miss Havisham (*Great Expectations*) and Nathaniel Hawthorne's Hepzibah Pyncheon (*The House of Seven Gables*), Luella Miller is a sort of energy vampire, sustaining herself in her old age by sapping the metaphysical vitality of those around her. There are no fangs, puncture marks, or blood-lust here—only the manipulations of a seemingly helpless and harmless old woman. Likewise, there is no obvious malignancy, a tone underscored in the final passage of the text by associating her with flowers that grow despite being surrounded by weeds. "Luella Miller" is one of those stories that turns genre expectations on their head, surprising readers by offering a different perspective. It forces readers to conceive of the familiar in a different way and subverts moral, ethical, spiritual, and scientific norms.

* * * * *

Close to the village street stood the one-story house in which Luella Miller, who had an evil name in the village, had dwelt. She had been dead for years, yet there were those in the village who, in spite of the clearer light which comes on a vantage-point from a long-past danger, half believed in the tale which they had heard from their childhood. In their hearts, although they scarcely would have owned it, was a survival of the wild

*Freeman, Mary E. Wilkins. "Luella Miller." *Everybody's Magazine* 7, no. 6, December 1902, pp. 553–560.

horror and frenzied fear of their ancestors who had dwelt in the same age with Luella Miller. Young people even would stare with a shudder at the old house as they passed, and children never played around it as was their wont around an untenanted building. Not a window in the old Miller house was broken: the panes reflected the morning sunlight in patches of emerald and blue, and the latch of the sagging front door was never lifted, although no bolt secured it. Since Luella Miller had been carried out of it, the house had had no tenant except one friendless old soul who had no choice between that and the far-off shelter of the open sky. This old woman, who had survived her kindred and friends, lived in the house one week, then one morning no smoke came out of the chimney, and a body of neighbors, a score strong, entered and found her dead in her bed. There were dark whispers as to the cause of her death, and there were those who testified to an expression of fear so exalted that it showed forth the state of the departing soul upon the dead face. The old woman had been hale and hearty when she entered the house, and in seven days she was dead; it seemed that she had fallen a victim to some uncanny power. The minister talked in the pulpit with covert severity against the sin of superstition, still the belief prevailed. Not a soul in the village but would have chosen the almshouse rather than that dwelling. No vagrant, if he heard the tale, would seek shelter beneath that old roof, unhallowed by nearly half a century of superstitious fear.

There was only one person in the village who had actually known Luella Miller. That person was a woman well over eighty, but a marvel of vitality and unextinct youth. Straight as an arrow, with the spring of one recently let loose from the bow of life, she moved about the streets, and she always went to church, rain or shine. She had never married, and had lived alone for years in a house across the road from Luella Miller's.

This woman had none of the garrulousness of age, but never in all her life had she ever held her tongue for any will save her own, and she never spared the truth when she essayed to present it. She it was who bore testimony to the life, evil, though possibly wittingly or designedly so, of Luella Miller, and to her personal appearance. When this old woman spoke— and she had the gift of description, although her thoughts were clothed in the rude vernacular of her native village—one could seem to see Luella Miller as she had really looked. According to this woman, Lydia Anderson by name, Luella Miller had been a beauty of a type rather unusual in New England. She had been a slight, pliant sort of creature, as ready with a strong yielding to fate and as unbreakable as a willow. She had glimmering lengths of straight, fair hair, which she wore softly looped round a long, lovely face. She had blue eyes full of soft pleading, little slender, clinging hands, and a wonderful grace of motion and attitude.

"Luella Miller used to sit in a way nobody else could if they sat up and studied a week of Sundays," said Lydia Anderson, "and it was a sight to see her walk. If one of them willows over there on the edge of the brook could start up and get its roots free of the ground, and move off, it would go just the way Luella Miller used to. She had a green shot silk she used to wear, too, and a hat with green ribbon streamers, and a lace veil blowing across her face and out sideways, and a green ribbon flyin' from her waist. That was what she came out bride in when she married Erastus Miller. Her name before she was married was Hill. There was always a sight of 'l's' in her name, married or single. Erastus Miller was good lookin', too, better lookin' than Luella. Sometimes I used to think that Luella wa'n't so handsome after all. Erastus just about worshiped her. I used to know him pretty well. He lived next door to me, and we went to school together. Folks used to say he was waitin' on me, but he wa'n't. I never thought he was except once or twice when he said things that some girls might have suspected meant somethin'. That was before Luella came here to teach the district school. It was funny how she came to get it, for folks said she hadn't any education, and that one of the big girls, Lottie Henderson, used to do all the teachin' for her, while she sat back and did embroidery work on a cambric pocket-handkerchief. Lottie Henderson was a real smart girl, a splendid scholar, and she just set her eyes by Luella, as all the girls did. Lottie would have made a real smart woman, but she died when Luella had been here about a year—just faded away and died: nobody knew what ailed her. She dragged herself to that schoolhouse and helped Luella teach till the very last minute. The committee all knew how Luella didn't do much of the work herself, but they winked at it. It wa'n't long after Lottie died that Erastus married her. I always thought he hurried it up because she wa'n't fit to teach. One of the big boys used to help her after Lottie died, but he hadn't much government, and the school didn't do very well, and Luella might have had to give it up, for the committee couldn't have shut their eyes to things much longer. The boy that helped her was a real honest, innocent sort of fellow, and he was a good scholar, too. Folks said he overstudied, and that was the reason he was took crazy the year after Luella married, but I don't know. And I don't know what made Erastus Miller go into consumption of the blood the year after he was married: consumption wa'n't in his family. He just grew weaker and weaker, and went almost bent double when he tried to wait on Luella, and he spoke feeble, like an old man. He worked terrible hard till the last trying to save up a little to leave Luella. I've seen him out in the worst storms on a wood-sled—he used to cut and sell wood—and he was hunched up on top lookin' more dead than alive. Once I couldn't stand it: I went over and helped him pitch some wood on the cart—I was always strong in my arms. I wouldn't stop for all he told me to, and I guess he was glad enough for the help. That was only a week before he died. He fell on the kitchen floor while he was gettin' breakfast. He always got the breakfast and let Luella lay abed. He did all the sweepin' and the washin' and the ironin' and most of the cookin'. He couldn't bear to have Luella lift her finger, and she let him do for her. She lived like a queen for all the work she did. She didn't even do her sewin'. She said it made her shoulder ache to sew, and poor Erastus's sister Lily used to do all her sewin'. She wa'n't able to, either; she was never strong in her back, but she did it beautifully. She had to, to suit Luella, she was so dreadful particular. I never saw anythin' like the fagottin' and hemstitchin' that Lily Miller did for Luella. She made all Luella's weddin' outfit, and that green silk dress, after Maria Babbit cut it. Maria she cut it for nothin', and she did a lot more cuttin' and fittin' for nothin' for Luella, too. Lily Miller went to live with Luella after Erastus died. She gave up her home, though she was real attached to it and wa'n't a mite afraid to stay alone. She rented it and she went to live with Luella right away after the funeral."

Then this old woman, Lydia Anderson, who remembered Luella Miller, would go on to relate the story of Lily Miller. It seemed that on the removal of Lily Miller to the house of her dead brother, to live with his widow, the village people first began to talk. This Lily Miller had been hardly past her first youth, and a most robust and blooming woman, rosy-cheeked, with curls of strong, black hair overshadowing round, candid temples and bright dark eyes. It was not six months after she had taken up her residence with her sister-in-law that her rosy color faded and her pretty curves became wan hollows. White shadows began to show in the black rings of her hair, and the light died out of her eyes, her features sharpened, and there were pathetic lines at her mouth, which yet wore always an expression of utter sweetness and even happiness. She was devoted to her sister; there was no doubt that she loved her with her whole heart, and was perfectly content in her service. It was her sole anxiety lest she should die and leave her alone.

"The way Lily Miller used to talk about Luella was enough to make you mad and enough to make you cry," said Lydia Anderson. "I've been in there sometimes toward the last when she was too feeble to cook and carried her some blanc-mange or custard—somethin' I thought she might relish, and she'd thank me, and when I asked her how she was, say she felt better than she did yesterday, and asked me if I didn't think she looked better, dreadful pitiful, and say poor Luella had an awful time takin' care of her and doin' the work—she wa'n't strong enough to do anythin'— when all the time Luella wa'n't liftin' her finger and poor Lily didn't get any care except what the neighbours gave her, and Luella eat up everythin' that was carried in for Lily. I had it real straight that she did. Luella used to just sit and cry and do nothin'. She did act real fond of Lily, and she pined away considerable, too. There was those that thought she'd go into a decline herself. But after Lily died, her Aunt Abby Mixter came, and then Luella picked up and grew as fat and rosy as ever. But poor Aunt Abby begun to droop just the way Lily had, and I guess somebody wrote to her married daughter, Mrs. Sam Abbot, who lived in Barre, for she wrote her mother that she must leave right away and come and make her a visit, but Aunt Abby wouldn't go. I can see her now. She was a real good-lookin' woman, tall and large, with a big, square face and a high forehead that looked of itself kind of benevolent and good. She just tended out on Luella as if she had been a baby, and when her married daughter sent for her she wouldn't stir one inch. She'd always thought a lot of her daughter, too, but she said Luella needed her and her married daughter didn't. Her daughter kept writin' and writin', but it didn't do any good. Finally she came, and when she saw how bad her mother looked, she broke down and cried and all but went on her knees to have her come away. She spoke her mind out to Luella, too. She told her that she'd killed her husband and everybody that had anythin' to do with her, and she'd thank her to leave her mother alone. Luella went into hysterics, and Aunt Abby was so frightened that she called me after her daughter went. Mrs. Sam Abbot she went away fairly cryin' out loud in the buggy, the neighbours heard her, and well she might, for she never saw her mother again alive. I went in that night when Aunt Abby called for me, standin' in the door with her little green-checked shawl over her head. I can see her now. 'Do come over here, Miss Anderson,' she sung out, kind of gasping for breath. I didn't stop for anythin'. I put over as fast as I could, and when I got there, there was Luella laughin' and cryin' all together, and Aunt Abby trying to hush her, and all the time she herself was white as a sheet and shakin' so she could hardly stand. 'For the land sakes, Mrs. Mixter,' says I, 'you look worse than she does. You ain't fit to be up out of your bed.'

"'Oh, there ain't anythin' the matter with me,' says she. Then she went on talkin' to Luella. 'There, there, don't, don't, poor little lamb,' says she. 'Aunt Abby is here. She ain't goin' away and leave you. Don't, poor little lamb.'

"'Do leave her with me, Mrs. Mixter, and you get back to bed,' says I, for Aunt Abby had been layin' down considerable lately, though somehow she contrived to do the work.

"'I'm well enough,' says she. 'Don't you think she had better have the doctor, Miss Anderson?'

"'The doctor,' says I, 'I think *you* had better have the doctor. I think you need him much worse than some folks I could mention.' And I looked right straight at Luella Miller laughin' and cryin' and goin' on as if she was the centre of all creation. All the time she was actin' so—seemed as if she was too sick to sense anythin'—she was keepin' a sharp lookout as to how we took it out of the corner of one eye. I see her. You could never cheat me about Luella Miller. Finally I got real mad and I run home and I got a bottle of valerian I had, and I poured some boilin' hot water on a handful of catnip, and I mixed up that catnip tea with most half a wineglass of valerian, and I went with it over to Luella's. I marched right up to Luella, a-holdin' out of that cup, all smokin'. 'Now,' says I, 'Luella Miller, *you swallar this!*'

"'What is—what is it, oh, what is it?' she sort of screeches out. Then she goes off a-laughin' enough to kill.

"'Poor lamb, poor little lamb,' says Aunt Abby, standin' over her, all kind of tottery, and tryin' to bathe her head with camphor.

"'*You swaller this right down,*' says I. And I didn't waste any ceremony. I just took hold of Luella Miller's chin and I tipped her head back, and I caught her mouth open with laughin', and I clapped that cup to her lips, and I fairly hollered at her: 'Swaller, swaller, swaller!' and she gulped it right down. She had to, and I guess it did her good. Anyhow, she stopped cryin' and laughin' and let me put her to bed, and she went to sleep like a baby inside of half an hour. That was more than poor Aunt Abby did. She lay awake all that night and I stayed with her, though she tried not to have me; said she wa'n't sick enough for watchers. But I stayed, and I made some good cornmeal gruel and I fed her a teaspoon every little while all night long. It seemed to me as if she was jest dyin' from bein' all wore out. In the mornin' as soon as it was light I run over to the Bisbees and sent Johnny Bisbee for the doctor. I told him to tell the doctor to hurry, and he come pretty quick. Poor Aunt Abby didn't seem to know much of anythin' when he got there. You couldn't hardly tell she breathed, she was so used up. When the doctor had gone, Luella came into the room lookin' like a baby in her ruffled nightgown. I can see her now. Her eyes were as blue and her face all pink and white like a blossom, and she looked at Aunt Abby in the bed sort of innocent and surprised. 'Why,' says she, 'Aunt Abby ain't got up yet?'

"'No, she ain't,' says I, pretty short.

"'I thought I didn't smell the coffee,' says Luella.

"'Coffee,' says I. 'I guess if you have coffee this mornin' you'll make it yourself.'

"'I never made the coffee in all my life,' says she, dreadful astonished. 'Erastus always made the coffee as long as he lived, and then Lily she made it, and then Aunt Abby made it. I don't believe I *can* make the coffee, Miss Anderson.'

"'You can make it or go without, jest as you please,' says I.

"'Ain't Aunt Abby goin' to get up?' says she.

"'I guess she won't get up,' says I, 'sick as she is.' I was gettin' madder and madder. There was somethin' about that little pink-and-white thing standin' there and talkin' about coffee, when she had killed so many better folks than she was, and had jest killed another, that made me feel 'most as if I wished somebody would up and kill her before she had a chance to do any more harm.

"'Is Aunt Abby sick?' says Luella, as if she was sort of aggrieved and injured.

"'Yes,' says I, 'she's sick, and she's goin' to die, and then you'll be left alone, and you'll have to do for yourself and wait on yourself, or do without things.' I don't know but I was sort of hard, but it was the truth, and if I was any harder than Luella Miller had been I'll give up. I ain't never been sorry that I said it. Well, Luella, she up and had hysterics again at that, and I jest let her have 'em. All I did was to bundle her into the room on the other side of the entry where Aunt Abby couldn't hear her, if she wa'n't past it—I don't know but she was—and set her down hard in a chair and told her not to come back into the other room, and she minded. She had her hysterics in there till she got tired. When she found out that nobody was comin' to coddle her and do for her she stopped. At least I suppose she did. I had all I could do with poor Aunt Abby tryin' to keep the breath of life in her. The doctor had told me that she was dreadful low, and give me some very strong medicine to give to her in drops real often, and told me real particular about the nourishment. Well, I did as he told me real faithful till she wa'n't able to swaller any longer. Then I had her daughter sent for. I had begun to realize that she wouldn't last any time at all. I hadn't realized it before, though I spoke to Luella the way I did. The doctor he came, and Mrs. Sam Abbot, but when she got there it was too late; her mother was dead. Aunt Abby's daughter just give one look at her mother layin' there, then she turned sort of sharp and sudden and looked at me.

"'Where is she?' says she, and I knew she meant Luella.

"'She's out in the kitchen,' says I. 'She's too nervous to see folks die. She's afraid it will make her sick.'

"The Doctor he speaks up then. He was a young man. Old Doctor Park had died the year before, and this was a young fellow just out of college. 'Mrs. Miller is not strong,' says he, kind of severe, 'and she is quite right in not agitating herself.'

"'You are another, young man; she's got her pretty claw on you,' thinks I, but I didn't say anythin' to him. I just said over to Mrs. Sam Abbot that Luella was in the kitchen, and Mrs. Sam Abbot she went out there, and I went, too, and I never heard anythin' like the way she talked to Luella Miller. I felt pretty hard to Luella myself, but this was more than I ever would have dared to say. Luella she was too scared to go into hysterics. She jest flopped. She seemed to jest shrink away to nothin' in that kitchen chair, with Mrs. Sam Abbot standin' over her and talkin' and tel-lin' her the truth. I guess the truth was most too much for her and no mis-take, because Luella presently actually did faint away, and there wa'n't any sham about it, the way I always suspected there was about them hysterics. She fainted dead away and we had to lay her flat on the floor, and the Doc-tor he came runnin' out and he said somethin' about a weak heart dread-ful fierce to Mrs. Sam Abbot, but she wa'n't a mite scared. She faced him jest as white as even Luella was layin' there lookin' like death and the Doc-tor feelin' of her pulse.

"'Weak heart,' says she, 'weak heart; weak fiddlesticks! There ain't nothin' weak about that woman. She's got strength enough to hang onto other folks till she kills 'em. Weak? It was my poor mother that was weak: this woman killed her as sure as if she had taken a knife to her.'

"But the Doctor he didn't pay much attention. He was bendin' over Luella layin' there with her yellow hair all streamin' and her pretty pink-and-white face all pale, and her blue eyes like stars gone out, and he was holdin' onto her hand and smoothin' her forehead, and tellin' me to get the brandy in Aunt Abby's room, and I was sure as I wanted to be that Luella had got somebody else to hang onto, now Aunt Abby was gone, and I thought of poor Erastus Miller, and I sort of pitied the poor young Doctor, led away by a pretty face, and I made up my mind I'd see what I could do.

"I waited till Aunt Abby had been dead and buried about a month, and the Doctor was goin' to see Luella steady and folks were beginnin' to talk; then one evenin', when I knew the Doctor had been called out of town and wouldn't be round, I went over to Luella's. I found her all dressed up in a blue muslin with white polka dots on it, and her hair curled jest as pretty, and there wa'n't a young girl in the place could compare with her. There was somethin' about Luella Miller seemed to draw the heart right out of you, but she didn't draw it out of me. She was settin' rocking in the chair by her sittin'-room window, and Maria Brown had gone home. Maria Brown had been in to help her, or rather to do the work, for Luella wa'n't helped when she didn't do anythin'. Maria Brown was real capable and she didn't have any ties; she wa'n't married, and lived alone, so she'd offered. I couldn't see why she should do the work any more than Luella; she wa'n't any too strong; but she seemed to think she could and Luella seemed to think so, too, so she went over and did all the work—washed, and ironed, and baked, while Luella sat and rocked. Maria didn't live long afterward. She began to fade away just the same fashion the others had. Well, she was warned, but she acted real mad when folks said anythin': said Luella was a poor, abused woman, too delicate to help herself, and they'd ought to be ashamed, and if she died helpin' them that couldn't help themselves she would—and she did.

"'I s'pose Maria has gone home,' says I to Luella, when I had gone in and sat down opposite her.

"'Yes, Maria went half an hour ago, after she had got supper and washed the dishes,' says Luella, in her pretty way.

"'I suppose she has got a lot of work to do in her own house tonight,' says I, kind of bitter, but that was all thrown away on Luella Miller. It seemed to her right that other folks that wa'n't any better able than she was herself should wait on her, and she couldn't get it through her head that anybody should think it *wa'n't* right.

"'Yes,' says Luella, real sweet and pretty, 'yes, she said she had to do her washin' tonight. She has let it go for a fortnight along of comin' over here.'

"'Why don't she stay home and do her washin' instead of comin' over here and doin' *your* work, when you are just as well able, and enough sight more so, than she is to do it?' says I.

"Then Luella she looked at me like a baby who has a rattle shook at it. She sort of laughed as innocent as you please. 'Oh, I can't do the work myself, Miss Anderson,' says she. 'I never did. Maria *has to* do it.'

"Then I spoke out: 'Has to do it!' says I. 'Has to do it!' She don't have to do it, either. Maria Brown has her own home and enough to live on. She ain't beholden to you to come over here and slave for you and kill herself.'

"Luella she jest set and stared at me for all the world like a doll-baby that was so abused that it was comin' to life.

"'Yes,' says I, 'she's killin' herself. She's goin' to die just the way Erastus did, and Lily, and your Aunt Abby. You're killin' her jest as you did them. I don't know what there is about you, but you seem to bring a curse,' says I. 'You kill everybody that is fool enough to care anythin' about you and do for you.'

"She stared at me and she was pretty pale.

"'And Maria ain't the only one you're goin' to kill,' says I. 'You're goin' to kill Doctor Malcom before you're done with him.'

"Then a red colour came flamin' all over her face. 'I ain't goin' to kill him, either,' says she, and she begun to cry.

"'Yes, you *be*!' says I. Then I spoke as I had never spoke before. You see, I felt it on account of Erastus. I told her that she hadn't any business to think of another man after she'd been married to one that had died for her: that she was a dreadful woman; and she was, that's true enough, but sometimes I have wondered lately if she knew it—if she wa'n't like a baby with scissors in its hand cuttin' everybody without knowin' what it was doin'.

"Luella she kept gettin' paler and paler, and she never took her eyes off my face. There was somethin' awful about the way she looked at me and never spoke one word. After awhile I quit talkin' and I went home. I watched that night, but her lamp went out before nine o'clock, and when Doctor Malcom came drivin' past and sort of slowed up he see there wa'n't any light and he drove along. I saw her sort of shy out of meetin' the next Sunday, too, so he shouldn't go home with her, and I begun to think mebbe she did have some conscience after all. It was only a week after that that Maria Brown died—sort of sudden at the last, though everybody had seen it was comin'. Well, then there was a good deal of feelin' and pretty dark whispers. Folks said the days of witchcraft had come again, and they were pretty shy of Luella. She acted sort of offish to the Doctor and he didn't go there, and there wa'n't anybody to do anythin' for her. I don't know how she *did* get along. I wouldn't go in there and offer to help her—not because I was afraid of dyin' like the rest, but I thought she was just as well able to do her own work as I was to do it for her, and I thought it was about time that she did it and stopped killin' other folks. But it wa'n't very long before folks began to say that Luella herself was goin' into a decline jest the way her husband, and Lily, and Aunt Abby and the others had, and I saw myself that she looked pretty bad. I used to see her goin' past from the store with a bundle as if she could hardly crawl, but I remembered how Erastus used to wait and 'tend when he couldn't hardly put one foot before the other, and I didn't go out to help her.

"But at last one afternoon I saw the Doctor come drivin' up like mad with his medicine chest, and Mrs. Babbit came in after supper and said that Luella was real sick.

"'I'd offer to go in and nurse her,' says she, 'but I've got my children to consider, and mebbe it ain't true what they say, but it's queer how many folks that have done for her have died.'

"I didn't say anythin', but I considered how she had been Erastus's wife and how he had set his eyes by her, and I made up my mind to go in the next mornin', unless she was better, and see what I could do; but the next mornin' I see her at the window, and pretty soon she came steppin' out as spry as you please, and a little while afterward Mrs. Babbit came in and told me that the Doctor had got a girl from out of town, a Sarah Jones, to come there, and she said she was pretty sure that the Doctor was goin' to marry Luella.

"I saw him kiss her in the door that night myself, and I knew it was true. The woman came that afternoon, and the way she flew around was a caution. I don't believe Luella had swept since Maria died. She swept and dusted, and washed and ironed; wet clothes and dusters and carpets were flyin' over there all day, and every time Luella set her foot out when the Doctor wa'n't there there was that Sarah Jones helpin' of her up and down the steps, as if she hadn't learned to walk.

"Well, everybody knew that Luella and the Doctor were goin' to be married, but it wa'n't long before they began to talk about his lookin' so poorly, jest as they had about the others; and they talked about Sarah Jones, too.

"Well, the Doctor did die, and he wanted to be married first, so as to leave what little he had to Luella, but he died before the minister could get there, and Sarah Jones died a week afterward.

"Well, that wound up everything for Luella Miller. Not another soul in the whole town would lift a finger for her. There got to be a sort of panic. Then she began to droop in good earnest. She used to have to go to the store herself, for Mrs. Babbit was afraid to let Tommy go for her, and I've seen her goin' past and stoppin' every two or three steps to rest. Well, I stood it as long as I could, but one day I see her comin' with her arms full and stoppin' to lean against the Babbit fence, and I run out and took her bundles and carried them to her house. Then I went home and never spoke one word to her though she called after me dreadful kind of pitiful. Well, that night I was taken sick with a chill, and I was sick as I wanted to be for two weeks. Mrs. Babbit had seen me run out to help Luella and she came in and told me I was goin' to die on account of it. I didn't know whether I was or not, but I considered I had done right by Erastus's wife.

"That last two weeks Luella she had a dreadful hard time, I guess. She was pretty sick, and as near as I could make out nobody dared go near her. I don't know as she was really needin' anythin' very much, for there was enough to eat in her house and it was warm weather, and she made out to cook a little flour gruel every day, I know, but I guess she had a hard time, she that had been so petted and done for all her life.

"When I got so I could go out, I went over there one morning. Mrs. Babbit had just come in to say she hadn't seen any smoke and she didn't know but it was somebody's duty to go in, but she couldn't help thinkin' of her children, and I got right up, though I hadn't been out of the house for two weeks, and I went in there, and Luella she was layin' on the bed, and she was dyin'.

"She lasted all that day and into the night. But I sat there after the new doctor had gone away. Nobody else dared to go there. It was about midnight that I left her for a minute to run home and get some medicine I had been takin', for I begun to feel rather bad.

"It was a full moon that night, and just as I started out of my door to cross the street back to Luella's, I stopped short, for I saw something."

Lydia Anderson at this juncture always said with a certain defiance that she did not expect to be believed, and then proceeded in a hushed voice:

"I saw what I saw, and I know I saw it, and I will swear on my death bed that I saw it. I saw Luella Miller and Erastus Miller, and Lily, and Aunt

Abby, and Maria, and the Doctor, and Sarah, all goin' out of her door, and all but Luella shone white in the moonlight, and they were all helpin' her along till she seemed to fairly fly in the midst of them. Then it all disappeared. I stood a minute with my heart poundin', then I went over there. I thought of goin' for Mrs. Babbit, but I thought she'd be afraid. So I went alone, though I knew what had happened. Luella was layin' real peaceful, dead on her bed."

This was the story that the old woman, Lydia Anderson, told, but the sequel was told by the people who survived her, and this is the tale which has become folklore in the village.

Lydia Anderson died when she was eighty-seven. She had continued wonderfully hale and hearty for one of her years until about two weeks before her death.

One bright moonlight evening she was sitting beside a window in her parlor when she made a sudden exclamation, and was out of the house and across the street before the neighbor who was taking care of her could stop her. She followed as fast as possible and found Lydia Anderson stretched on the ground before the door of Luella Miller's deserted house, and she was quite dead.

The next night there was a red gleam of fire athwart the moonlight and the old house of Luella Miller was burned to the ground. Nothing is now left of it except a few old cellar stones and a lilac bush, and in summer a helpless trail of morning glories among the weeds, which might be considered emblematic of Luella herself.

"The Ash-tree"

by M.R. James*

M. R. James (1862–1936) is known for two fields of endeavor: medieval-ism and ghost stories. As part of Cambridge University's tradition, James produced his ghost stories to be read aloud during the pre–Christmas weeks for the Chit-chat Club. His tales center on everything from haunted castles and ancient forests to ghost-filled photographs and books of spells, mak-ing them about his own antiquarian interests. "The Ash-tree" appeared in his first collection of these stories, *Ghost Stories of an Antiquary* (1904). Sev-eral more collections would follow over the next few decades. In the preface to his second collection, *More Ghost Stories of an Antiquary* (1911), James indicated that he preferred his ghost stories to have three elements: a famil-iar setting and time; the use of familiar rather than archaic speech patterns; and malign ghosts rather than helpful or friendly ones. He wanted his read-ers to feel like the events of the stories could really happen to them. "The Ash-tree" focuses on the aristocracy who mock the traditions and supersti-tions of times gone by without realizing that their time is done as well.

* * * * *

Everyone who has travelled over Eastern England knows the smaller country-houses with which it is studded—the rather dank little build-ings, usually in the Italian style, surrounded with parks of some eighty to a hundred acres. For me they have always had a very strong attrac-tion: with the grey paling of split oak, the noble trees, the meres with their reed-beds, and the line of distant woods. Then, I like the pillared portico—perhaps stuck on to a red-brick Queen Anne house which has been faced with stucco to bring it into line with the "Grecian" taste of the end of the eighteenth century; the hall inside, going up to the roof, which hall ought always to be provided with a gallery and a small organ. I like the library,

*James, M.R. "The Ash-tree." *Ghost-Stories of an Antiquary*, Edward Arnold, 1905, pp. 83–112.

too, where you may find anything from a Psalter of the thirteenth century to a Shakespeare quarto. I like the pictures, of course; and perhaps most of all I like fancying what life in such a house was when it was first built, and in the piping times of landlords' prosperity, and not least now, when, if money is not so plentiful, taste is more varied and life quite as interesting. I wish to have one of these houses, and enough money to keep it together and entertain my friends in it modestly.

But this is a digression. I have to tell you of a curious series of events which happened in such a house as I have tried to describe. It is Castringham Hall in Suffolk. I think a good deal has been done to the building since the period of my story, but the essential features I have sketched are still there—Italian portico, square block of white house, older inside than out, park with fringe of woods, and mere. The one feature that marked out the house from a score of others is gone. As you looked at it from the park, you saw on the right a great old ash-tree growing within half a dozen yards of the wall, and almost or quite touching the building with its branches. I suppose it had stood there ever since Castringham ceased to be a fortified place, and since the moat was filled in and the Elizabethan dwelling-house built. At any rate, it had well-nigh attained its full dimensions in the year 1690.

In that year the district in which the Hall is situated was the scene of a number of witch-trials. It will be long, I think, before we arrive at a just estimate of the amount of solid reason—if there was any—which lay at the root of the universal fear of witches in old times. Whether the persons accused of this offence really did imagine that they were possessed of unusual powers of any kind; or whether they had the will at least, if not the power, of doing mischief to their neighbors; or whether all the confessions, of which there are so many, were extorted by the mere cruelty of the witch-finders—these are questions which are not, I fancy, yet solved. And the present narrative gives me pause. I cannot altogether sweep it away as mere invention. The reader must judge for himself.

Castringham contributed a victim to the *auto-da-fé*. Mrs. Mothersole was her name, and she differed from the ordinary run of village witches only in being rather better off and in a more influential position. Efforts were made to save her by several reputable farmers of the parish. They did their best to testify to her character, and showed considerable anxiety as to the verdict of the jury.

But what seems to have been fatal to the woman was the evidence of the then proprietor of Castringham Hall—Sir Matthew Fell. He deposed to having watched her on three different occasions from his window, at the full of the moon, gathering sprigs "from the ash-tree near my house." She had climbed into the branches, clad only in her shift, and was cutting off small twigs with a peculiarly curved knife, and as she did so she seemed to be talking to herself. On each occasion Sir Matthew had done his best to capture the woman, but she had always taken alarm at some accidental noise he had made, and all he could see when he got down to the garden was a hare running across the park in the direction of the village.

On the third night he had been at the pains to follow at his best speed, and had gone straight to Mrs. Mothersole's house; but he had had to wait a quarter of an hour battering at her door, and then she had come out very cross, and apparently very sleepy, as if just out of bed; and he had no good explanation to offer of his visit.

Mainly on this evidence, though there was much more of a less striking and unusual kind from other parishioners, Mrs. Mothersole was found guilty and condemned to die. She was hanged a week after the trial, with five or six more unhappy creatures, at Bury St. Edmunds.

Sir Matthew Fell, then Deputy-Sheriff, was present at the execution. It was a damp, drizzly March morning when the cart made its way up the rough grass hill outside Northgate, where the gallows stood. The other victims were apathetic or broken down with misery; but Mrs. Mothersole was, as in life so in death, of a very different temper. Her "poysonous Rage," as a reporter of the time puts it, "did so work upon the Bystanders—yea, even upon the Hangman—that it was constantly affirmed of all that saw her that she presented the living Aspect of a mad Divell. Yet she offer'd no Resistance to the Officers of the Law; onely she looked upon those that laid Hands upon her with so direfull and venomous an Aspect that—as one of them afterwards assured me—the meer Thought of it preyed inwardly upon his Mind for six Months after."

However, all that she is reported to have said was the seemingly meaningless words: "There will be guests at the Hall." Which she repeated more than once in an undertone.

Sir Matthew Fell was not unimpressed by the bearing of the woman. He had some talk upon the matter with the Vicar of his parish, with whom he travelled home after the assize business was over. His evidence at the trial had not been very willingly given; he was not specially infected with the witch-finding mania, but he declared, then and afterwards, that he could not give any other account of the matter than that he had given, and that he could not possibly have been mistaken as to what he saw. The whole transaction had been repugnant to him, for he was a man who liked to be on pleasant terms with those about him; but he saw a duty to be done in this business, and he had done it. That seems to have been the gist of his sentiments, and the Vicar applauded it, as any reasonable man must have done.

A few weeks after, when the moon of May was at the full, Vicar and Squire met again in the park, and walked to the Hall together. Lady Fell was with her mother, who was dangerously ill, and Sir Matthew was alone at home; so the Vicar, Mr. Crome, was easily persuaded to take a late supper at the Hall.

Sir Matthew was not very good company this evening. The talk ran chiefly on family and parish matters, and, as luck would have it, Sir Matthew made a memorandum in writing of certain wishes or intentions of his regarding his estates, which afterwards proved exceedingly useful.

When Mr. Crome thought of starting for home, about half-past nine o'clock, Sir Matthew and he took a preliminary turn on the graveled walk at the back of the house. The only incident that struck Mr. Crome was this: they were in sight of the ash-tree which I described as growing near the windows of the building, when Sir Matthew stopped and said:

"What is that that runs up and down the stem of the ash? It is never a squirrel? They will all be in their nests by now."

The Vicar looked and saw the moving creature, but he could make nothing of its color in the moonlight. The sharp outline, however, seen for an instant, was imprinted on his brain, and he could have sworn, he said, though it sounded foolish, that, squirrel or not, it had more than four legs.

Still, not much was to be made of the momentary vision, and the two men parted. They may have met since then, but it was not for a score of years.

Next day Sir Matthew Fell was not downstairs at six in the morning, as was his custom, nor at seven, nor yet at eight. Hereupon the servants went and knocked at his chamber door. I need not prolong the description of their anxious listenings and renewed batterings on the panels. The door was opened at last from the outside, and they found their master dead and black. So much you have guessed. That there were any marks of violence did not at the moment appear; but the window was open.

One of the men went to fetch the parson, and then by his directions rode on to give notice to the coroner. Mr. Crome himself went as quick as he might to the Hall, and was shown to the room where the dead man lay. He has left some notes among his papers which show how genuine a respect and sorrow was felt for Sir Matthew, and there is also this passage, which I transcribe for the sake of the light it throws upon the course of events, and also upon the common beliefs of the time:

"There was not any the least Trace of an Entrance having been forc'd to the Chamber: but the Casement stood open, as my poor Friend would always have it in this Season. He had his Evening Drink of small Ale in a silver vessel of about a pint measure, and tonight had not drunk it out. This Drink was examined by the Physician from Bury, a Mr. Hodgkins, who could not, however, as he afterwards declar'd upon his Oath, before the Coroner's quest, discover that any matter of a venomous kind was present in it.

For, as was natural, in the great Swelling and Blackness of the Corpse, there was talk made among the Neighbours of Poyson. The Body was very much Disorder'd as it laid in the Bed, being twisted after so extream a sort as gave too probable Conjecture that my worthy Friend and Patron had expir'd in great Pain and Agony. And what is as yet unexplain'd, and to myself the Argument of some Horrid and Artfull Designe in the Perpetrators of this Barbarous Murther, was this, that the Women which were entrusted with the laying-out of the Corpse and washing it, being both sad Persons and very well Respected in their Mournfull Profession, came to me in a great Pain and Distress both of Mind and Body, saying, what was indeed confirmed upon the first View, that they had no sooner touch'd the Breast of the Corpse with their naked Hands than they were sensible of a more than ordinary violent Smart and Acheing in their Palms, which, with their whole Fore-arms, in no long time swell'd so immoderately, the Pain still continuing, that, as afterwards proved, during many weeks they were forc'd to lay by the exercise of their Calling; and yet no mark seen on the Skin.

"Upon hearing this, I sent for the Physician, who was still in the House, and we made as carefull a Proof as we were able by the Help of a small Magnifying Lens of Crystal of the condition of the Skinn on this Part of the Body: but could not detect with the Instrument we had any Matter of Importance beyond a couple of small Punctures or Pricks, which we then concluded were the Spotts by which the Poyson might be intro-duced, remembering that Ring of *Pope Borgia*, with other known Speci-mens of the Horrid Art of the Italian Poysoners of the last age.

"So much is to be said of the Symptoms seen on the Corpse. As to what I am to add, it is meerly my own Experiment, and to be left to Pos-terity to judge whether there be anything of Value therein. There was on the Table by the Beddside a Bible of the small size, in which my Friend—punctuall as in Matters of less Moment, so in this more weighty one—used nightly, and upon his First Rising, to read a sett Portion. And I taking it up—not without a Tear duly paid to him which from the Study of this poorer Adumbration was now pass'd to the contemplation of its great Originall—it came into my Thoughts, as at such moments of Helpless-ness we are prone to catch at any the least Glimmer that makes promise of Light, to make trial of that old and by many accounted Superstitious Prac-tice of drawing the *Sortes*: of which a Principall Instance, in the case of his late Sacred Majesty the Blessed Martyr King *Charles* and my Lord *Falk-land*, was now much talked of. I must needs admit that by my Trial not much Assistance was afforded me: yet, as the Cause and Origin of these Dreadfull Events may hereafter be search'd out, I set down the Results, in the case it may be found that they pointed the true Quarter of the Mischief to a quicker Intelligence than my own.

"I made, then, three trials, opening the Book and placing my Finger upon certain Words: which gave in the first these words, from Luke xiii. 7, *Cut it down*; in the second, Isaiah xiii. 20, *It shall never be inhabited*; and upon the third Experiment, Job xxxix. 30, *Her young ones also suck up blood*."

This is all that need be quoted from Mr. Crome's papers. Sir Matthew Fell was duly coffined and laid into the earth, and his funeral sermon, preached by Mr. Crome on the following Sunday, has been printed under the title of "The Unsearchable Way; or, England's Danger and the Malicious Dealings of Antichrist," it being the Vicar's view, as well as that most commonly held in the neighborhood, that the Squire was the victim of a recrudescence of the Popish Plot.

His son, Sir Matthew the second, succeeded to the title and estates. And so ends the first act of the Castringham tragedy. It is to be mentioned, though the fact is not surprising, that the new Baronet did not occupy the room in which his father had died. Nor, indeed, was it slept in by anyone but an occasional visitor during the whole of his occupation. He died in 1735, and I do not find that anything particular marked his reign, save a curiously constant mortality among his cattle and live-stock in general, which showed a tendency to increase slightly as time went on.

Those who are interested in the details will find a statistical account in a letter to the *Gentleman's Magazine* of 1772, which draws the facts from the Baronet's own papers. He put an end to it at last by a very simple expedient, that of shutting up all his beasts in sheds at night, and keeping no sheep in his park. For he had noticed that nothing was ever attacked that spent the night indoors. After that the disorder confined itself to wild birds, and beasts of chase. But as we have no good account of the symptoms, and as all-night watching was quite unproductive of any clue, I do not dwell on what the Suffolk farmers called the "Castringham sickness."

The second Sir Matthew died in 1735, as I said, and was duly succeeded by his son, Sir Richard. It was in his time that the great family pew was built out on the north side of the parish church. So large were the Squire's ideas that several of the graves on that unhallowed side of the building had to be disturbed to satisfy his requirements. Among them was that of Mrs. Mothersole, the position of which was accurately known, thanks to a note on a plan of the church and yard, both made by Mr. Crome.

A certain amount of interest was excited in the village when it was known that the famous witch, who was still remembered by a few, was to be exhumed. And the feeling of surprise, and indeed disquiet, was very strong when it was found that, though her coffin was fairly sound and unbroken, there was no trace whatever inside it of body, bones, or dust. Indeed, it is a curious phenomenon, for at the time of her burying no such things were dreamt of as resurrection-men, and it is difficult to conceive any rational motive for stealing a body otherwise than for the uses of the dissecting-room.

The incident revived for a time all the stories of witch-trials and of the exploits of the witches, dormant for forty years, and Sir Richard's orders that the coffin should be burnt were thought by a good many to be rather foolhardy, though they were duly carried out.

Sir Richard was a pestilent innovator, it is certain. Before his time the Hall had been a fine block of the mellowest red brick; but Sir Richard had travelled in Italy and become infected with the Italian taste, and, having more money than his predecessors, he determined to leave an Italian palace where he had found an English house. So stucco and ashlar masked the brick; some indifferent Roman marbles were planted about in the entrance-hall and gardens; a reproduction of the Sibyl's temple at Tivoli was erected on the opposite bank of the mere; and Castringham took on an entirely new, and, I must say, a less engaging, aspect. But it was much admired, and served as a model to a good many of the neighboring gentry in after-years.

* * *

One morning (it was in 1754) Sir Richard woke after a night of discomfort. It had been windy, and his chimney had smoked persistently, and yet it was so cold that he must keep up a fire. Also something had so rattled about the window that no man could get a moment's peace. Further, there was the prospect of several guests of position arriving in the course of the day, who would expect sport of some kind, and the inroads of the distemper (which continued among his game) had been lately so serious that he was afraid for his reputation as a game-preserver. But what really touched him most nearly was the other matter of his sleepless night. He could certainly not sleep in that room again.

That was the chief subject of his meditations at breakfast, and after it he began a systematic examination of the rooms to see which would suit his notions best. It was long before he found one. This had a window with an eastern aspect and that with a northern; this door the servants would be always passing, and he did not like the bedstead in that. No, he must have a room with a western look-out, so that the sun could not wake him early, and it must be out of the way of the business of the house. The housekeeper was at the end of her resources.

"Well, Sir Richard," she said, "you know that there is but one room like that in the house."

"Which may that be?" said Sir Richard.

"And that is Sir Matthew's—the West Chamber."

"Well, put me in there, for there I'll lie tonight," said her master. "Which way is it? Here, to be sure"; and he hurried off.

"Oh, Sir Richard, but no one has slept there these forty years. The air has hardly been changed since Sir Matthew died there."

Thus she spoke, and rustled after him.

"Come, open the door, Mrs. Chiddock. I'll see the chamber, at least."

So it was opened, and, indeed, the smell was very close and earthy. Sir Richard crossed to the window, and, impatiently, as was his wont, threw the shutters back, and flung open the casement. For this end of the house was one which the alterations had barely touched, grown up as it was with the great ash-tree, and being otherwise concealed from view.

"Air it, Mrs. Chiddock, all today, and move my bed-furniture in in the afternoon. Put the Bishop of Kilmore in my old room."

"Pray, Sir Richard," said a new voice, breaking in on this speech, "might I have the favour of a moment's interview?"

Sir Richard turned round and saw a man in black in the doorway, who bowed.

"I must ask your indulgence for this intrusion, Sir Richard. You will, perhaps, hardly remember me. My name is William Crome, and my grandfather was Vicar here in your grandfather's time."

"Well, sir," said Sir Richard, "the name of Crome is always a passport to Castringham. I am glad to renew a friendship of two generations' standing. In what can I serve you? for your hour of calling—and, if I do not mistake you, your bearing—shows you to be in some haste."

"That is no more than the truth, sir. I am riding from Norwich to Bury St. Edmunds with what haste I can make, and I have called in on my way to leave with you some papers which we have but just come upon in looking over what my grandfather left at his death. It is thought you may find some matters of family interest in them."

"You are mighty obliging, Mr. Crome, and, if you will be so good as to follow me to the parlour, and drink a glass of wine, we will take a first look at these same papers together. And you, Mrs. Chiddock, as I said, be about airing this chamber.... Yes, it is here my grandfather died.... Yes, the tree, perhaps, does make the place a little dampish.... No; I do not wish to listen to any more. Make no difficulties, I beg. You have your orders—go. Will you follow me, sir?"

They went to the study. The packet which young Mr. Crome had brought—he was then just become a Fellow of Clare Hall in Cambridge, I may say, and subsequently brought out a respectable edition of Polyænus—contained among other things the notes which the old Vicar had made upon the occasion of Sir Matthew Fell's death. And for the first time Sir Richard was confronted with the enigmatical *Sortes Biblicæ* which you have heard. They amused him a good deal.

"Well," he said, "my grandfather's Bible gave one prudent piece of advice—*Cut it down*. If that stands for the ash-tree, he may rest assured I shall not neglect it. Such a nest of catarrhs and agues was never seen."

The parlor contained the family books, which, pending the arrival of a collection which Sir Richard had made in Italy, and the building of a proper room to receive them, were not many in number.

Sir Richard looked up from the paper to the bookcase.

"I wonder," says he, "whether the old prophet is there yet? I fancy I see him."

Crossing the room, he took out a dumpy Bible, which, sure enough, bore on the flyleaf the inscription: "To Matthew Fell, from his Loving Godmother, Anne Aldous, 2 September, 1659."

"It would be no bad plan to test him again, Mr. Crome. I will wager we get a couple of names in the Chronicles. H'm! what have we here? 'Thou shalt seek me in the morning, and I shall not be.' Well, well! Your grandfather would have made a fine omen of that, hey? No more prophets for me! They are all in a tale. And now, Mr. Crome, I am infinitely obliged to you for your packet. You will, I fear, be impatient to get on. Pray allow me—another glass."

So with offers of hospitality, which were genuinely meant (for Sir Richard thought well of the young man's address and manner), they parted.

In the afternoon came the guests—the Bishop of Kilmore, Lady Mary Hervey, Sir William Kentfield, etc. Dinner at five, wine, cards, supper, and dispersal to bed.

Next morning Sir Richard is disinclined to take his gun with the rest. He talks with the Bishop of Kilmore. This prelate, unlike a good many of the Irish Bishops of his day, had visited his see, and, indeed, resided there for some considerable time. This morning, as the two were walking along the terrace and talking over the alterations and improvements in the house, the Bishop said, pointing to the window of the West Room:

"You could never get one of my Irish flock to occupy that room, Sir Richard."

"Why is that, my lord? It is, in fact, my own."

"Well, our Irish peasantry will always have it that it brings the worst of luck to sleep near an ash-tree, and you have a fine growth of ash not two yards from your chamber window. Perhaps," the Bishop went on, with a smile, "it has given you a touch of its quality already, for you do not seem, if I may say it, so much the fresher for your night's rest as your friends would like to see you."

"That, or something else, it is true, cost me my sleep from twelve to four, my lord. But the tree is to come down tomorrow, so I shall not hear much more from it."

"I applaud your determination. It can hardly be wholesome to have the air you breathe strained, as it were, through all that leafage."

"Your lordship is right there, I think. But I had not my window open last night. It was rather the noise that went on—no doubt from the twigs sweeping the glass—that kept me open-eyed."

"I think that can hardly be, Sir Richard. Here—you see it from this point. None of these nearest branches even can touch your casement unless there were a gale, and there was none of that last night. They miss the panes by a foot."

"No, sir, true. What, then, will it be, I wonder, that scratched and rustled so—ay, and covered the dust on my sill with lines and marks?"

At last they agreed that the rats must have come up through the ivy. That was the Bishop's idea, and Sir Richard jumped at it.

So the day passed quietly, and night came, and the party dispersed to their rooms, and wished Sir Richard a better night.

And now we are in his bedroom, with the light out and the Squire in bed. The room is over the kitchen, and the night outside still and warm, so the window stands open.

There is very little light about the bedstead, but there is a strange movement there; it seems as if Sir Richard were moving his head rapidly to and fro with only the slightest possible sound. And now you would guess, so deceptive is the half-darkness, that he had several heads, round and brownish, which move back and forward, even as low as his chest. It is a horrible illusion. Is it nothing more? There! something drops off the bed with a soft plump, like a kitten, and is out of the window in a flash; another—four—and after that there is quiet again.

"Thou shalt seek me in the morning, and I shall not be."

As with Sir Matthew, so with Sir Richard—dead and black in his bed!

A pale and silent party of guests and servants gathered under the window when the news was known. Italian poisoners, Popish emissaries, infected air—all these and more guesses were hazarded, and the Bishop of Kilmore looked at the tree, in the fork of whose lower boughs a white tom-cat was crouching, looking down the hollow which years had gnawed in the trunk. It was watching something inside the tree with great interest.

Suddenly it got up and craned over the hole. Then a bit of the edge on which it stood gave way, and it went slithering in. Everyone looked up at the noise of the fall.

It is known to most of us that a cat can cry; but few of us have heard, I hope, such a yell as came out of the trunk of the great ash. Two or three screams there were—the witnesses are not sure which—and then a slight and muffled noise of some commotion or struggling was all that came. But Lady Mary Hervey fainted outright, and the housekeeper stopped her ears and fled till she fell on the terrace.

The Bishop of Kilmore and Sir William Kentfield stayed. Yet even they were daunted, though it was only at the cry of a cat; and Sir William swallowed once or twice before he could say:

"There is something more than we know of in that tree, my lord. I am for an instant search."

And this was agreed upon. A ladder was brought, and one of the gardeners went up, and, looking down the hollow, could detect nothing but a few dim indications of something moving. They got a lantern, and let it down by a rope.

"We must get at the bottom of this. My life upon it, my lord, but the secret of these terrible deaths is there."

Up went the gardener again with the lantern, and let it down the hole cautiously. They saw the yellow light upon his face as he bent over, and saw his face struck with an incredulous terror and loathing before he cried out in a dreadful voice and fell back from the ladder—where, happily, he was caught by two of the men—letting the lantern fall inside the tree.

He was in a dead faint, and it was some time before any word could be got from him.

By then they had something else to look at. The lantern must have broken at the bottom, and the light in it caught upon dry leaves and rubbish that lay there, for in a few minutes a dense smoke began to come up, and then flame; and, to be short, the tree was in a blaze.

The bystanders made a ring at some yards' distance, and Sir William and the Bishop sent men to get what weapons and tools they could; for, clearly, whatever might be using the tree as its lair would be forced out by the fire.

So it was. First, at the fork, they saw a round body covered with fire—the size of a man's head—appear very suddenly, then seem to collapse and fall back. This, five or six times; then a similar ball leapt into the air and fell on the grass, where after a moment it lay still. The Bishop went as near as he dared to it, and saw—what but the remains of an enormous spider, veinous and seared! And, as the fire burned lower down, more terrible bodies like this began to break out from the trunk, and it was seen that these were covered with grayish hair.

All that day the ash burned, and until it fell to pieces the men stood about it, and from time to time killed the brutes as they darted out. At last there was a long interval when none appeared, and they cautiously closed in and examined the roots of the tree.

"They found," says the Bishop of Kilmore, "below it a rounded hollow place in the earth, wherein were two or three bodies of these creatures that had plainly been smothered by the smoke; and, what is to me more curious, at the side of this den, against the wall, was crouching the anatomy or skeleton of a human being, with the skin dried upon the bones, having some remains of black hair, which was pronounced by those that examined it to be undoubtedly the body of a woman, and clearly dead for a period of fifty years."

"The Bowmen"

by Arthur Machen*

Arthur Machen (1963–1947) was a Welsh writer best known for his supernatural fiction, especially his novel *The Great God Pan* (1890), which at first was branded as scandalous and then, three decades later, widely recognized as a classic. Throughout his adulthood, his fiction writing was not generating the income he needed, and so he found work as an actor and a journalist. When war broke out in Europe in 1914, the British public became keenly interested in the first British battle of the Great War, the Battle of Mons in Belgium. One month after the battle in which the outnumbered British forces had some success against the advancing German army, Machen's story "The Bowmen" appeared in London's *Evening News*. It looked like every other news article in that publication. There was short fiction elsewhere in the newspaper, but they were all marked as such; "The Bowmen" was not. The tale of supernatural archers assisting the British forces caught the imagination of the public, and soon the story was everywhere. Churches far and wide invited Machen to speak about the divine intervention that he had "witnessed." Journalists and editors asked to see evidence that the ghostly apparitions were real. By then, the story had spiraled out of Machen's control. Machen explained: "Letters come from all the ends of the earth to the Editor of *The Evening News* with theories, beliefs, explanations, suggestions. It is all somewhat wonderful; one can say that the whole affair is a psychological phenomenon of considerable interest." A bevy of imitators proceeded to write "first-hand accounts" of supernatural forces aligning themselves against the Germans, and these stories proved to be helpful to the British war effort by propping up support on the home front.

* * * * *

*Machen, Arthur. "The Bowmen." *The Evening News*, 29 September 1914, p. 3.

It was during the Retreat of the Eighty Thousand, and the authority of the censorship is sufficient excuse for not being more explicit. But it was on the most awful day of that awful time, on the day when ruin and disaster came so near that their shadow fell over London far away; and, without any certain news, the hearts of men failed within them and grew faint; as if the agony of their brothers in the battlefield had entered into their souls.

On this dreadful day, then, when three hundred thousand men in arms with all their artillery swelled like a flood against the little English company, there was one point above all other points in our battle line that was for a time in awful danger, not merely of defeat, but of utter annihilation. With the permission of the censorship and of the military experts, this corner may, perhaps, be described as a salient, and if this angle were crushed and broken, then the English force as a whole would be shattered, the Allied left would be turned, and Sedan would inevitably follow.

All the morning the German guns had thundered and shrieked against this corner and against the thousand or so of men who held it. The men joked at the shells and found funny names for them, and had bets about them, and greeted them with scraps of music-hall songs. But the shells came on and burst and tore good Englishmen limb from limb, and tore brother from brother, and as the heat of the day increased, so did the fury of that terrific cannonade. There was no help, it seemed. The English artillery was good, but there was not nearly enough of it; it was being steadily battered into scrap iron.

There comes a moment in a storm at sea when people say to one another, "It is at its worst; it can blow no harder," and then there is a blast ten times more fierce than any before it. So it was in these British trenches.

There were no stouter hearts in the whole world than the hearts of those men; but even they were appalled as this seven-times-heated hell of the German cannonade fell upon them and rent them and destroyed them. And at this very moment they saw from their trenches that a tremendous host was moving against their lines. Five hundred of the thousand remained, and as far as they could see the German infantry was pressing on against them, column upon column, a grey world of men, ten thousand of them, as it appeared afterwards.

There was no hope at all. They shook hands, some of them. One man improvised a new version of the battle-song, "Goodbye, goodbye to Tipperary," ending with "And we shan't get there." And they all went on firing steadily. The officers pointed out that such an opportunity for fancy shooting might never occur again, the Germans dropped line after line, the Tipperary humorist asked, "What price Sidney Street?" and the few machine guns did their best. But everybody knew it was of no use. The dead grey bodies lay in companies and battalions; but others came on and on and on, and they swarmed and stirred and advanced from beyond and beyond.

"World without end. Amen," said one of the British soldiers with some irrelevance as he took aim and fired. And then he remembered a queer vegetarian restaurant in London where he had once or twice eaten queer dishes of cutlets made of lentils and nuts that pretended to be steaks. On all the plates in this restaurant there was printed a figure of St. George in blue, with the motto, *"Adsit Anglis Sanctus Georgius"*—"may St. George be a present help to the English." This soldier happened to know Latin and other useless things, and now as he fired at his man in the grey advancing mass—300 yards away— he uttered the pious vegetarian motto. He went on firing to the end, and at last Bill on his right had to clout him cheerfully over the head to make him stop, pointing out as he did so that the King's ammunition cost money and was not lightly to be wasted in drilling funny patterns into dead Germans.

For as the Latin scholar uttered his invocation he felt something between a shudder and an electric shock pass through his body. The roar of the battle died down in his ears to a gentle murmur; instead of it, he says, he heard a great voice and a shout louder than a thunder-peal crying, "Array, array, array!"

His heart grew hot as a burning coal, it grew cold as ice within him, as it seemed to him that a tumult of voices answered to this summons. He heard, or seemed to hear thousands shouting: "St. George! St. George!"

"Ha! Messire, ha! sweet saint, grant us good deliverance!"

"St. George for merry England!"

"Harow! Harow! Monseigneur St. George, succour us!"

"Ha! St. George! Ha! St. George; a long bow and a strong bow."

"Knight of Heaven, aid us!"

And as the soldier heard these voices he saw before him, beyond the trench, a long line of shapes, with a shining about them. They were like men who drew the bow, and with another shout, their cloud of arrows flew singing and tingling through the air towards the German hosts.

* * *

The other men in the trench were firing all the while. They had no hope; but they aimed just as if they had been shooting at Bisley.

Suddenly one of them lifted up his voice in the plainest English.

"Gawd help us!" he bellowed to the man next to him, "but we're blooming marvels! Look at those gray … gentlemen, look at them! D'ye see them? They're not going down in dozens nor in 'undreds; it's thousands, it is. Look! look! there's a regiment gone while I'm talking to ye."

"Shut it!" the other soldier bellowed, taking aim, "what are ye gassing about?"

But he gulped with astonishment even as he spoke; for, indeed, the grey men were falling by the thousand. The English could hear the guttural scream of the German officers, the crackle of their revolvers as they shot the reluctant; and still line after line crashed to the earth.

* * *

All the while the Latin-bred soldier heard the cry:

"Harow! Harow! Monseigneur, dear saint, quick to our aid! St. George help us!"

The singing arrows darkened the air; the heathen horde melted from before them.

* * *

"More machine guns!" Bill yelled to Tom.

"Don't hear them," Tom yelled back; "but, thank God, anyway; they've got it in the neck."

In fact, there were ten thousand dead German soldiers left before that salient of the English army, and consequently there was no Sedan. In Germany, a country ruled by scientific principles, the Great General Staff decided that the contemptible English must have employed turpinite shells, as no wounds were discernible on the bodies of the dead German soldiers. But the man what knew what nuts tasted like when they called themselves steak knew also that St. George had brought his Agincourt bowmen to help the English.

"The Decay of the Ghost in Fiction"

by Olivia Howard Dunbar*

As a journalist and voice for feminism, Olivia Howard Dunbar (1873–1953) was a critic to be reckoned with, writing for such influential and popular publications like *The Dial* and *Harper's Magazine*. She also penned a few of her own stories about ghosts and the supernatural and defended fictions with those themes in her essay "The Decay of the Ghost in Fiction," published in 1905 as a response to criticisms of the modern ghost story. By the turn of the century, ghost stories had lost a bit of their stature, garnering a reputation as poorly written fiction that was riddled with cliché. Recognizing the evolution of the ghost story of Victorian England and the new voices emerging in speculative fiction, Dunbar argues for a re-imagining of the ghost and its motivations. She contends that the lack of ghost stories in the latter third of the nineteenth century is the result of an Anglo-Saxon scientific perspective. Despite understanding this, she argues that ghost stories are still intrinsically linked to the human condition. The authors of ghost fiction, Dunbar implores, must look back to the creativity and imagination in stories of ghosts in folklore and not settle for trite motivations such as reputation or revenge. The new century can breathe life back into a decaying form.

* * * * *

"For one, I cannot purge my mind of that forlorn faith."
—Andrew Lang

For approximately a generation, the ghost has been missing from fiction; after a disappearance so sudden and of such far-reaching implications that it is a matter of some amazement that those who profess to concern themselves with the phenomena of imaginative literature should have paid so little attention to it. It is a commonplace that ever since literature began,

---

*Dunbar, Olivia Howard. "The Decay of the Ghost in Fiction." *The Dial* XXXVIII, no. 455, 1 June 1905, pp. 377–380.

as well as considerably before that interesting period, what we call "the supernatural" has been a staple material of the tellers of tales. As there has always been a literature of love, so there has always been a literature of fear; and until the development of the present narrow and timorous popular taste, one had perhaps as strong an appeal as the other. Ghosts in their most literal acceptation—not as the more or less impersonal shades we have sometimes indifferently pictured them—have always been held an essential complement of tangible everyday life, inextricably bound up with religion, with love for the dead, with hunger for the unknown, with many of the most intimate and profound emotions; and their literary use has seemed, to the greater public, not only no less, but even more "realistic," than the modern exploitation of the commonplace.

Twenty-five years ago, even, the reader of magazine fiction was still able to shudder to his heart's content. Specters glided with the precision of long-established custom through the pages of the more conventional compendiums of light literature. The familiar paraphernalia of supernatural incident,—draughty chambers, tempestuous nights, blood-stains, wan-faced women,—were still in constant and elaborate requisition. And while there was a discreet dribbling of phantoms from week to week or from month to month, a magnificent convocation of the spectral tribe occurred annually. That is to say, a curious association of ideas connected the maximum of ghostly prevalence with Christmas, the season of popular rejoicing; and by way of making sure of these dismal but doubtless salutary companions, it was customary, as Mr. Anstey once remarked, "to commission a band of ingenious littérateurs to turn out batches of ready-made spectres for the Christmas annuals." The business of chilling the popular spine was taken with due seriousness and was all the more effectually brought about in that the "magazine ghost" as this source of popular refreshment was termed, was as stereotyped and conventional as the old-fashioned novel-heroine. Its looks, manner, haunts, companions, and alleged errands were those long since laid down by tradition; it evinced no sensational modern unexpectedness.

But suddenly, and it must surely have seemed mysteriously, the magazine ghost vanished; nor were its eerie footprints traced. Whether by a concerted action of magazine editors, or by a swift and complete paralysis of the contributors' imaginations, or by a profound alteration of popular sentiment, or by the operation of a principle presently to be suggested, the literature of the supernatural ceased to be produced. Can this have happened without protest, without comment, even? The subject is rich in its possibilities of speculation. For if the acceptance and enjoyment of ghost-lore imply a childish quality of mind, as one sometimes hears superior persons assert, then our rejection of them would argue that we are the wisest generation that ever lived. If, again, the reading or writing of such tales demand a freshness of imagination that in our little day has become desiccated, then our plight is pitiable indeed.

There is at hand, of course, an easy but superficial explanation to the effect that a prevalence of ghost-stories must depend upon a stout popular belief in ghosts; and that having lost the one, we must forego the other. The slightest reflection shows that this position is untenable. Not believe in ghosts? We believe in them with all our hearts. Never before, since spectral feet first crossed a man-made threshold, have ghosts been so squarely, openly, and enthusiastically believed in, so assiduously cultivated, as now. We have raised ghost-lore to the dusty dignity of a science. The invocation of the spirits of the dead, far from having its former suggestion of vulgar mystery, is one of the most reputable of practices, which men of learning carry on publicly, with stenographers conveniently at hand. There even flourishes a "Haunted House Committee," appointed and maintained by the foremost society for the promotion of ghosts, and this for the express purpose of encouraging the presence of the shyer and less aggressive specters in what seem their appropriate habitations,—of making them, as it were, feel at home. We believe in ghosts as sincerely as we believe in the very poor; and in similar fashion we endeavor to live among them, establish a cordial understanding, and write about them in our notebooks. Nor do we believe in them the less because, when on our learned behavior, we may refer to them as "phantasmogenetic agencies." Not believe in ghosts? They are our fetish. Let it never be imagined that ghost-stories have suffered decline because of our indifference to their subject-matter, "material" though our age is commonly held to be. By our very zest in their pursuit, we have possibly proved the reverse of Scott's mistaken theory that to see ghosts it is only necessary to believe in them,—to wish to see. Much truer is the proposition that the seer of ghosts commonly does not premeditate his vision; that specters manifest themselves by preference to "unimaginative people in perfect health."

No small share of the fascination exerted by the ancient and outgrown ghost of fiction was due to its invariable and satisfactory conformity to type. However frequent its intrusion, or however familiar, it was never suffered to deviate from its character, so deeply rooted in human consciousness, as a source of dread. It was the function of the ghost to be consistently unpleasant, and that function was relentlessly fulfilled. No one personal characteristic of the ghost as we know it in song or story or as we learn from the unimpeachable testimony of our friends' friends, can explain its unequalled power to arouse the emotion of fear. Distasteful as is the ghostly habit of reducing its unfleshly essence to a threadlike, infinitely ductile filament—like a bit of transsubstantial chewing-gum— in order sneakily to penetrate keyholes; disturbing as is its fashion of upsetting our gravely accepted "laws of nature"; intolerable as is its lack of vocal organs (for phantoms, with few exceptions, cannot or will not speak);—neither one nor all of these undesirable characteristics can completely solve the interesting riddle of its fear-compelling power. And it is undoubtedly almost as remarkable that having for centuries, in and out of fiction, maintained this consistent and extremely prevalent personality, the ghost should have dropped out of literature altogether. Now, how can this have been?

To go as far back as the early English folktales and ballads, when the wherefore of phantoms was even better understood than now, and when fiction more essentially took its origin from life, ghost-tales gained their grim effectiveness from the accuracy with which they reflected popular belief. The audiences of that simple day had not attained a sufficient refinement of imagination to delight in vague, casual, incoherent specters; every ghost had a name and date. What is more important is that there was no ghost that had not a reason for being. The ingenious notion that the spirits of the dead return from an allegedly peaceful Elysium simply to make themselves disagreeable, by way of easing their minds, had not yet suggested itself. On the contrary, the animistic trend of popular thought, which of course greatly favored the appearance of ghosts in general, assigned them likewise adequate and intelligible motives, among the chief of which were: to reveal treasure, to reunite happy lovers, to avenge a crime, and to serve as "a primitive telegraphic service for the conveyance of bad news." Ghosts were therefore not only the recognizable shades of the familiarly known dead; they were sinister symbols of crime, remorse, vengeance. If you shuddered at sight of them, it was for a better reason than weak nerves. Horror was not piled on horror, in early ghost-tales, merely to satisfy the artist's own sense of cumulative effect. Each detail had a powerful conventional significance, and the consequent power to arouse a strong primitive emotion. This system not only lent an artistic strength and symmetry to the early literature; it was intensely satisfactory to the Anglo-Saxon mind.

But inevitably, when the motives and the language of literature became more complex, the *rationale* of ghost-lore became affected. Phantoms began to lose their original force, fell into the habit of haunting from motives relatively unworthy. Evidences multiplied of their degeneration into a morbid and meddlesome tribe, with a sadly diminished sense of the fitting and the picturesque. Their visits were even concerned with the payment of debts, of strictly mortal contraction; and they lamentably lost caste by exhibiting themselves as the victims, rather than as the scourge, of conscience. A ghost has been known to go to the trouble of haunting a house for the mere purpose of ensuring the payment of a shilling,—an episode that might well permanently compromise the dignity of the entire spectral tribe. Likewise when they acquired the intrusive habit of giving evidence in trials, the original and forceful idea that ghosts were agents of retribution became seriously coarsened. Legally, the fact that the issue of many an actual trial has hinged on ghostly testimony is of extraordinary interest. So far as imaginative terror-literature is concerned, however, the introduction of this matter serves as a mixed and weakened motive, only.

During the later years of the ghost's popularity in literature, it will readily be seen that the greater number of the earliest ghost-motives were outgrown. It is some time, for instance, since the motive of recovering buried treasure through supernatural aid has been able to "carry," the custom of burying treasure having itself somewhat tamely died out. Far more incongruous, even, came to seem the supernatural reunion of lovers, as in the familiar case where the posthumous suitor reappears to bear his still living sweetheart back to the grave with him. Ghosts that are to be understood as the projections of the spirit at the moment of death have always been popular, it is true, but this motive is not in itself strong or picturesque enough to serve as the backbone of a corporate section of imaginative literature.

In short, the only ghost-motive that retained its strength, plausibility, and appeal to the Anglo-Saxon mind was the retribution-motive,—the idea that the ghost's function was to recall, expiate, or avenge a crime. This was impressive; it was terrifying; it had moral and religious significance; it was not subtle; it was susceptible of indefinitely repeated adjustment to time and place. It was the perfect, perhaps the only perfect, ghost-motive for English literature. So valorous is the Anglo-Saxon temper that it scorns or is ashamed to tremble at mere empty shadow-tales. It demands not only to be impressed; there must be an adequate basis for the impression. The clue to the whole matter is that the ghost must not be a wanton and irresponsible power. It must be a moral agent.

Unfortunately, the realization of this simple truth has never been complete. Only subconsciously has the public known what it wanted. As for the tellers of tales, they seem, in those latter days of the ghost's literary existence, to have remained in criminal ignorance of the vital principle of their business. The decay of the ghost in fiction occurred, not through any loss of human interest in the spectral world, but through an indolent misapprehension, on the part of the story-tellers, of the real character of the ghost as we Anglo-Saxons have conceived it. Thus it came about that the ghost, previous to its subsidence, was, as Mr. Lang truly observed, "a purposeless creature. He appears, nobody knows why; he has no message to deliver, no secret crime to conceal, no appointment to keep, no treasure to disclose, no commissions to be executed, and, as an almost invariable rule, he does not speak, even if you speak to him." And he adds that inquirers have therefore concluded that the ghost, generically, is "not all there,"—a dreary result of skepticism, indeed! At the same time, what direct and utilitarian folk could put up with a confirmedly inconsequent ghost, even for the creepy fascination of shuddering at his phantom footfall? And could there be, on the whole, a more perfect example of the operation of natural selection in art than that, the ghost of fiction becoming unmoral, superficial, and flabby, it was its pitilessly appropriate penalty to be dropped and apparently forgotten?

A small group of kindred volumes, which have appeared during the past year or so, now for the first time indicate that a perception of the true nature of the literary ghost is returning to the absent-minded craft. Stevenson had, it is true, an admirable perception of the terror-inspiring, and he did not make the mistake of being vague; but his was not the temperament that produces the perfect ghost-story. Mr. Henry James, in that masterpiece, "The Turn of the Screw," has shown that he can convey a sense of mystery and terror more skillfully than any of his contemporaries; but his work is probably too esoteric to stand as typical, and it remains true that the pattern ghost-tale must be writ large and obvious. If, as now appears, a half-dozen of the ablest writers of the day are realizing this, there is hope for the renaissance of the literary ghost. It has already been proved that the problem of its readjustment to our literature is not insuperable,—that the chambers of our untenanted imaginations stand ready and waiting to be haunted by wraiths that our logic can approve. There may indeed develop with time a regenerated ghost-literature well worth acquaintance; for, as an essayist of other times has somewhat grandiloquently observed, "Our inborn proneness to a love of the marvellous and unimaginable, which has originated in our imperfect acquaintance with the laws of nature and our own being, does not appear to suffer diminution as education and culture advance; for it is found to coexist with the highest intellectual development and the most refined critical temper."

"The Miracle of the Lily"

by Clare Winger Harris*

Clare Winger Harris (1891–1968) was one of the first women to publish under her own name in science-fiction magazines. Hugo Gernsback, founder of *Amazing Stories*, adored her work and published six of her twelve short stories, though he did admit that he was surprised a woman could write science fiction of this caliber. "The Miracle of the Lily" first appeared in *Amazing* in 1928 and was later collected in *Away from the Here and Now* (1947), which contains nearly all of her short stories. Perhaps because her body of work is not very large—her one novel is not a speculative work— she was not remembered very well by the historians of science fiction until her work was included in *Daughters of Earth: Feminist Science Fiction of the Twentieth Century* (2006). In the "The Miracle of the Lily," Harris challenges the idea that anything that can be done by science should be done, a challenge that finds its roots in Mary Shelley's *Frankenstein*. Harris's depiction of a blithe humanity curing its problems with insects by destroying all plant-life and replacing it with artificial nutrients questions what humanity will do for the sake of convenience, or, even worse, for the sake of survival.

* * * * *

I. The Passing of a Kingdom

Since the comparatively recent résumé of the ancient order of agriculture I, Nathano, have been asked to set down the extraordinary events of the past two thousand years, at the beginning of which time the supremacy of man, chief of the mammals, threatened to come to an untimely end.

Ever since the dawn of life upon this globe, life, which it seemed had

---

*Harris, Clare Winger. "The Miracle of the Lily." *Amazing Stories* 3, no. 1, April 1928, pp. 48–55.

crept from the slime of the sea, only two great types had been the rulers; the reptiles and the mammals. The former held undisputed sway for eons, but gave way eventually before the smaller, but intellectually superior mammals. Man himself, the supreme example of the ability of life to govern and control inanimate matter, was master of the world with apparently none to dispute his right. Yet, so blinded was he with pride over the continued exercise of his power on Earth over other lower types of mammals and the nearly extinct reptiles, that he failed to notice the slow but steady rise of another branch of life, different from his own; smaller, it is true, but no smaller than he had been in comparison with the mighty reptilian monsters that roamed the swamps in Mesozoic times.

These new enemies of man, though seldom attacking him personally, threatened his downfall by destroying his chief means of sustenance, so that by the close of the twentieth century, strange and daring projects were laid before the various governments of the world with an idea of fighting man's insect enemies to the finish. These pests were growing in size, multiplying so rapidly and destroying so much vegetation, that eventually no plants would be left to sustain human life. Humanity suddenly woke to the realization that it might suffer the fate of the nearly extinct reptiles. Would mankind be able to prevent the encroachment of the insects? And at last man *knew* that unless drastic measures were taken *at once*, a third great class of life was on the brink of terrestrial sovereignty.

Of course no great changes in development come suddenly. Slow evolutionary progress had brought us up to the point, where, with the application of outside pressure, we were ready to handle a situation, that, a century before, would have overwhelmed us.

I reproduce here in part a lecture delivered by a great American scientist, a talk which, sent by radio throughout the world, changed the destiny of mankind: but whether for good or for evil I will leave you to judge at the conclusion of this story.

"Only in comparatively recent times has man succeeded in conquering natural enemies; flood, storm, inclemency of climate, distance, and now we face an encroaching menace to the whole of humanity. Have we learned more and more of truth and of the laws that control matter only to succumb to the first real danger that threatens us with extermination? Surely, no matter what the cost, you will rally to the solution of our problem, and I believe, friends, that I have discovered the answer to the enigma.

"I know that many of you, like my friend Professor Fair, will believe my ideas too extreme, but I am convinced that unless you are willing to put behind you those notions which are old and not utilitarian, you cannot hope to cope with the present situation.

"Already, in the past few decades, you have realized the utter futility of encumbering yourselves with superfluous possessions that had no useful virtue, but which, for various sentimental reasons, you continued to hoard, thus lessening the degree of your life's efficiency by using for it time and attention that should have been applied to the practical work of life's accomplishments. You have given these things up slowly, but I am now going to ask you to relinquish the rest of them *quickly*; everything that interferes in any way with the immediate disposal of our enemies, the insects."

At this point, it seems that my worthy ancestor, Professor Fair, objected to the scientist's words, asserting that efficiency at the expense of some of the sentimental virtues was undesirable and not conducive to happiness, the real goal of man. The scientist, in his turn, argued that happiness was available only through a perfect adaptability to one's environment, and that efficiency *sans* love, mercy and the softer sentiments was the short cut to human bliss.

It took a number of years for the scientist to put over his scheme of salvation, but in the end he succeeded, not so much from the persuasiveness of his words, as because prompt action of some sort was necessary. There was not enough food to feed the people of the earth. Fruit and vegetables were becoming a thing of the past. Too much protein food in the form of meat and fish was injuring the race, and at last the people realized that, for fruits and vegetables, or their nutritive equivalent, they must turn from the field to the laboratory; from the farmer to the chemist. Synthetic food was the solution to the problem. There was no longer any use in planting and caring for food stuffs destined to become the nourishment of man's most deadly enemy.

The last planting took place in 2900, but there was no harvest, the voracious insects took every green shoot as soon as it appeared, and even trees, that had previously withstood the attacks of the huge insects, were by this time, stripped of every vestige of greenery.

The vegetable world suddenly ceased to exist. Over the barren plains which had been gradually filling with vast cities, man-made fires brought devastation to every living bit of greenery, so that in all the world there was no food for the insect pests.

II. Man or Insect?

> *Extract from the diary of Delfair, a descendant of Professor*
> *Fair, who had opposed the daring scientist.*

From the borders of the great state-city of Iowa, I was witness to the passing of one of the great kingdoms of earth—the vegetable, and I cannot find words to express the grief that overwhelms me as I write of its demise, for

I loved all growing things. Many of us realized that Earth was no longer beautiful; but if beauty meant death, better life in the sterility of the metropolis.

The viciousness of the thwarted insects was a menace that we had foreseen and yet failed to take into adequate account. On the city-state borderland, life is constantly imperiled by the attacks of well organized bodies of our dreaded foe.

(*Note:* The organization that now exists among the ants, bees and other insects, testifies to the possibility of the development of military tactics among them in the centuries to come.)

Robbed of their source of food, they have become emboldened to such an extent that they will take any risks to carry human beings away for food, and after one of their well organized raids, the toll of human life is appalling.

But the great chemical laboratories where our synthetic food is made, and our oxygen plants, we thought were impregnable to their attacks. In that we were mistaken.

Let me say briefly that since the destruction of all vegetation which furnished a part of the oxygen essential to human life, it became necessary to manufacture this gas artificially for general diffusion through the atmosphere.

I was flying to my work, which is in Oxygen Plant No. 21, when I noticed a peculiar thing on the upper speedway near Food Plant No. 3,439. Although it was night, the various levels of the state-city were illuminated as brightly as by day. A pleasure vehicle was going with prodigious speed westward. I looked after it in amazement. It was unquestionably the car of Eric, my co-worker at Oxygen Plant No. 21. I recognized the gay color of its body, but to verify my suspicions beyond the question of a doubt, I turned my volplane in pursuit and made out the familiar license number. What was Eric doing away from the plant before I had arrived to relieve him from duty?

In hot pursuit, I sped above the car to the very border of the state-city, wondering what unheard of errand took him to the land of the enemy, for the car came to a sudden stop at the edge of what had once been an agricultural area. Miles ahead of me stretched an enormous expanse of black sterility; at my back was the teeming metropolis, five levels high—if one counted the hangar-level, which did not cover the residence sections.

I had not long to wait, for almost immediately my friend appeared. What a sight he presented to my incredulous gaze! He was literally covered from head to foot with the two-inch ants, that next to the beetles, had proved the greatest menace in their attacks upon humanity. With wild incoherent cries he fled over the rock and stubble-burned earth.

As soon as my stunned senses permitted, I swooped down toward him to effect a rescue, but even as my plane touched the barren earth, I saw that I was too late, for he fell, borne down by the vicious attacks of his myriad foes. I knew it was useless for me to set foot upon the ground, for my fate would be that of Eric. I rose ten feet and seizing my poison-gas weapon, let its contents out upon the tiny black evil things that swarmed below. I did not bother with my mask, for I planned to rise immediately, and it was not a moment too soon. From across the waste-land, a dark cloud eclipsed the stars and I saw coming toward me a horde of flying ants interspersed with larger flying insects, all bent upon my annihilation. I now took my mask and prepared to turn more gas upon my pursuers, but alas, I had used every atom of it in my attack upon the non-flying ants! I had no recourse but flight, and to this I immediately resorted, knowing that I could outdistance my pursuers.

When I could no longer see them, I removed my gas mask. A suffocating sensation seized me. I could not breathe! How high had I flown in my endeavor to escape the flying ants? I leaned over the side of my plane, expecting to see the city far, far below me. What was my utter amazement when I discovered that I was scarcely a thousand feet high! It was not altitude that was depriving me of the life-giving oxygen.

A drop of three hundred feet showed me inert specks of humanity lying about the streets. Then I knew; *the oxygen plant was not in operation!* In another minute I had on my oxygen mask, which was attached to a small portable tank for emergency use, and I rushed for the vicinity of the plant. There I witnessed the first signs of life. Men equipped with oxygen masks, were trying to force entrance into the locked building. Being an employee, I possessed knowledge of the combination of the great lock, and I opened the door, only to be greeted by a swarm of ants that commenced a concerted attack upon us.

The floor seemed to be covered with a moving black rug, the corner nearest the door appearing to unravel as we entered, and it was but a few seconds before we were covered with the clinging, biting creatures, who fought with a supernatural energy born of despair. Two very active ants succeeded in getting under my helmet. The bite of their sharp mandibles and the effect of their poisonous formic acid became intolerable. Did I dare remove my mask while the air about me was foul with the gas discharged from the weapons of my allies? While I felt the attacks elsewhere upon my body gradually diminishing as the insects succumbed to the deadly fumes, the two upon my face waxed more vicious under the protection of my mask. One at each eye, they were trying to blind me. The pain was unbearable. Better the suffocating death-gas than the torture of lacerated eyes! Frantically I removed the head-gear and tore at the shiny black fiends. Strange to tell, I discovered that I could breathe near the vicinity of the great oxygen tanks, where enough oxygen lingered to support life at least temporarily. The two vicious insects, no longer protected by my gas-mask, scurried from me like rats from a sinking ship and disappeared behind the oxygen tanks.

This attack of our enemies, though unsuccessful on their part, was dire in its significance, for it had shown more cunning and ingenuity than anything that had ever preceded it. Heretofore, their onslaughts had been confined to direct attacks upon us personally or upon the synthetic-food laboratories, but in this last raid they had shown an amazing cleverness that portended future disaster, unless they were checked at once. It was obvious they had ingeniously planned to smother us by the suspension of work at the oxygen plant, knowing that they themselves could exist in an atmosphere containing a greater percentage of carbon-dioxide. Their scheme, then, was to raid our laboratories for food.

III. Lucanus the Last

A Continuation of Delfair's Account

Although it was evident that the cessation of all plant-life spelled inevitable doom for the insect inhabitants of Earth, their extermination did not follow as rapidly as one might have supposed. There were years of internecine warfare. The insects continued to thrive, though in decreasing numbers, upon stolen laboratory foods, bodies of human-beings and finally upon each other; at first capturing enemy species and at last even resorting to a cannibalistic procedure. Their rapacity grew in inverse proportion to their waning numbers, until the meeting of even an isolated insect might mean death, unless one were equipped with poison gas and prepared to use it upon a second's notice.

I am an old man now, though I have not yet lived quite two centuries, but I am happy in the knowledge that I have lived to see the last living insect which was held in captivity. It was an excellent specimen of the stag-beetle (*Lucanus*) and the years have testified that it was the sole survivor of a form of life that might have succeeded man upon this planet. This beetle was caught weeks after we had previously seen what was supposed to be the last living thing upon the globe, barring man and the sea-life. Untiring search for years has failed to reveal any more insects, so that at last man rests secure in the knowledge that he is monarch of all he surveys.

I have heard that long, long ago man used to gaze with a fearful fascination upon the reptilian creatures which he displaced, and just so did he view this lone specimen of a type of life that might have covered the face of the earth, but for man's ingenuity.

It was this unholy lure that drew me one day to view the captive beetle in his cage in district 404 at Universapolis. I was amazed at the size of the creature, for it looked larger than when I had seen it by television, but I reasoned that upon that occasion there had been no object near with which to compare its size. True, the broadcaster had announced its dimensions, but the statistics concretely given had failed to register a perfect realization of its prodigious proportions.

As I approached the cage, the creature was lying with its dorsal covering toward me and I judged it measured fourteen inches from one extremity to the other. Its smooth horny sheath gleamed in the bright artificial light. (It was confined on the third level.) As I stood there, mentally conjuring a picture of a world overrun with billions of such creatures as the one before me, the keeper approached the cage with a meal-portion of synthetic food. Although the food has no odor, the beetle sensed the man's approach, for it rose on its jointed legs and came toward us, its horn-like prongs moving threateningly; then apparently remembering its confinement, and the impotency of an attack, it subsided and quickly ate the food which had been placed within its prison.

The food consumed, it lifted itself to its hind legs, partially supported by a box, and turned its great eyes upon me. I had never been regarded with such utter malevolence before. The detestation was almost tangible and I shuddered involuntarily. As plainly as if he spoke, I knew that Lucanus was perfectly cognizant of the situation and in his gaze I read the concentrated hate of an entire defeated race.

I had no desire to gloat over his misfortune, rather a great pity toward him welled up within me. I pictured myself alone, the last of my kind, held up for ridicule before the swarming hordes of insects who had conquered my people, and I knew that life would no longer be worth the living.

Whether he sensed my pity or not I do not know, but he continued to survey me with unmitigated rage, as if he would convey to me the information that his was an implacable hatred that would outlast eternity.

Not long after this he died, and a world long since intolerant of ceremony, surprised itself by interring the beetle's remains in a golden casket, accompanied by much pomp and splendor.

I have lived many long years since that memorable event, and undoubtedly my days here are numbered, but I can pass on happily, convinced that in this sphere man's conquest of his environment is supreme.

IV. Efficiency Maximum

In a direct line of descent from Professor Fair and Delfair,
the author of the preceding chapter, comes Thanor
whose journal is given in this chapter.

Am I a true product of the year 2928? Sometimes I am convinced that I am hopelessly old-fashioned, an anachronism, that should have existed a thousand years ago. In no other way can I account for the dissatisfaction I feel in a world where efficiency has at last reached a maximum.

I am told that I spring from a line of ancestors who were not readily acclimated to changing conditions. I love beauty, yet I see none of it here. There are many who think our lofty buildings that tower two and three thousand feet into the air are beautiful, but while they are architectural splendors, they do not represent the kind of loveliness I crave. Only when I visit the sea do I feel any satisfaction for a certain yearning in my soul. The ocean alone shows the handiwork of God. The land bears evidence only of man.

As I read back through the diaries of my sentimental ancestors I find occasional glowing descriptions of the world that was; the world before the insects menaced human existence. Trees, plants and flowers brought delight into the lives of people as they wandered among them in vast open spaces, I am told, where the earth was soft beneath the feet, and flying creatures, called birds, sang among the greenery. True, I learn that many people had not enough to eat, and that uncontrollable passions governed them, but I do believe it must have been more interesting than this methodical, unemotional existence. I cannot understand why many people were poor, for I am told that Nature as manifested in the vegetable kingdom was very prolific; so much so that year after year quantities of food rotted on the ground. The fault, I find by my reading, was not with Nature but with man's economic system which is now perfect, though this perfection really brings few of us happiness, I think.

Now there is no waste; all is converted into food. Long ago man learned how to reduce all matter to its constituent elements, of which there are nearly a hundred in number, and from them to rebuild compounds for food. The old axiom that nothing is created or destroyed, but merely changed from one form to another, has stood the test of ages. Man, as the agent of God, has simply performed the miracle of transmutation himself instead of waiting for natural forces to accomplish it as in the old days.

At first humanity was horrified when it was decreed that it must relinquish its dead to the laboratory. For too many eons had man closely associated the soul and body, failing to comprehend the body as merely a material agent, through which the spirit functioned. When man knew at last of the eternal qualities of spirit, he ceased to regard the discarded body with reverential awe, and saw in it only the same molecular constituents which comprised all matter about him. He recognized only material basically the same as that of stone or metal; material to be reduced to its atomic elements and rebuilt into matter that would render service to living humanity; that portion of matter wherein spirit functions.

The drab monotony of life is appalling. Is it possible that man had reached his height a thousand years ago and should have been willing to resign Earth's sovereignty to a coming order of creatures destined to be man's worthy successor in the eons to come? It seems that life is interesting only when there is a struggle, a goal to be reached through an evolutionary process. Once the goal is attained, all progress ceases. The huge reptiles of preglacial ages rose to supremacy by virtue of their great size, and yet was it not the excessive bulk of those creatures that finally wiped them out of existence? Nature, it seems, avoids extremes. She allows the fantastic to develop for awhile and then wipes the slate clean for a new order of development. Is it not conceivable that man could destroy himself through excessive development of his nervous system, and give place for the future evolution of a comparatively simple form of life, such as the insects were at man's height of development? This, it seems to me, was the great plan; a scheme with which man dared to interfere and for which he is now paying by the boredom of existence.

The earth's population is decreasing so rapidly, that I fear another thousand years will see a lifeless planet hurtling through space. It seems to me that only a miracle will save us now.

V. The Year 3928

The Original Writer, Nathano, Resumes the Narrative.

My ancestor, Thanor, of ten centuries ago, according to the records he gave to my great grandfather, seems to voice the general despair of humanity which, bad enough in his times, has reached the *nth* power in my day. A soulless world is gradually dying from self-inflicted boredom.

As I have ascertained from the perusal of the journals of my forebears, even antedating the extermination of the insects, I come of a stock that clings with sentimental tenacity to the things that made life worthwhile in the old days. If the world at large knew of my emotional musings concerning past ages, it would scarcely tolerate me, but surrounded by my thought-insulator, I often indulge in what fancies I will, and such meditation, coupled with a love for a few ancient relics from the past, has led me to a most amazing discovery.

Several months ago I found among my family relics a golden receptacle two feet long, one and a half in width and one in depth, which I found, upon opening, to contain many tiny square compartments, each filled with minute objects of slightly varying size, texture and color.

"Not sand!" I exclaimed as I closely examined the little particles of matter.

Food? After eating some, I was convinced that their nutritive value was small in comparison with a similar quantity of the products of our laboratories. What were the mysterious objects?

Just as I was about to close the lid again, convinced that I had one over-sentimental ancestor, whose gift to posterity was absolutely useless, my pocket-radio buzzed and the voice of my friend, Stentor, the interplanetary broadcaster, issued from the tiny instrument.

"If you're going to be home this afternoon," said Stentor, "I'll skate over. I have some interesting news."

I consented, for I thought I would share my "find" with this friend whom I loved above all others, but before he arrived I had again hidden my golden chest, for I had decided to await the development of events before sharing its mysterious secret with another. It was well that I did this for Stentor was so filled with the importance of his own news that he could have given me little attention at first.

"Well, what is your interesting news?" I asked after he was comfortably seated in my adjustable chair.

"You'd never guess," he replied with irritating leisureliness.

"Does it pertain to Mars or Venus?" I queried. "What news of our neighbor planets?"

"You may know it has nothing to do with the self-satisfied Martians," answered the broadcaster, "but the Venusians have a very serious problem confronting them. It is in connection with the same old difficulty they have had ever since interplanetary radio was developed forty years ago. You remember, that, in their second communication with us, they told us of their continual warfare on insect pests that were destroying all vegetable food? Well, last night after general broadcasting had ceased, I was surprised to hear the voice of the Venusian broadcaster. He is suggesting that we get up a scientific expedition to Venus to help the natives of his unfortunate planet solve their insect problem as we did ours. He says the Martians turn a deaf ear to their plea for help, but he expects sympathy and assistance from Earth who has so recently solved these problems for herself."

I was dumbfounded at Stentor's news.

"But the Venusians are farther advanced mechanically than we," I objected, "though they are behind us in the natural sciences. They could much more easily solve the difficulties of space-flying than we could."

"That is true," agreed Stentor, "but if we are to render them material aid in freeing their world from devastating insects, we must get to Venus. The past four decades have proved that we can not help them merely by verbal instructions."

"Now, last night," Stentor continued, with warming enthusiasm, "Wanyana, the Venusian broadcaster, informed me that scientists on

Venus are developing interplanetary television. This, if successful, will prove highly beneficial in facilitating communication, and it may even do away with the necessity of interplanetary travel, which I think is centuries ahead of us yet."

"Television, though so common here on Earth and on Venus, has seemed an impossibility across the ethereal void," I said, "but if it becomes a reality, I believe it will be the Venusians who will take the initiative, though of course they will be helpless without our friendly cooperation. In return for the mechanical instructions they have given us from time to time, I think it no more than right that we should try to give them all the help possible in freeing their world, as ours has been freed, of the insects that threaten their very existence. Personally, therefore, I hope it can be done through radio and television rather than by personal excursions."

"I believe you are right," he admitted, "but I hope we can be of service to them soon. Ever since I have served in the capacity of official interplanetary broadcaster, I have liked the spirit of good-fellowship shown by the Venusians through their spokesman, Wanyana. The impression is favorable in contrast to the superciliousness of the inhabitants of Mars."

We conversed for some time, but at length he rose to take his leave. It was then I ventured to broach the subject that was uppermost in my thoughts.

"I want to show you something, Stentor," I said, going into an adjoining room for my precious box and returning shortly with it. "A relic from the days of an ancestor named Delfair, who lived at the time the last insect, a beetle, was kept in captivity. Judging from his personal account, Delfair was fully aware of the significance of the changing times in which he lived, and contrary to the majority of his contemporaries, possessed a sentimentality of soul that has proved an historical asset to future generations. Look, my friend, these he left to posterity!"

I deposited the heavy casket on a table between us and lifted the lid, revealing to Stentor the mystifying particles.

The face of Stentor was eloquent of astonishment. Not unnaturally his mind took somewhat the same route as mine had followed previously, though he added atomic-power-units to the list of possibilities. He shook his head in perplexity.

"Whatever they are, there must have been a real purpose behind their preservation," he said at last. "You say this old Delfair witnessed the passing of the insects? What sort of a fellow was he? Likely to be up to any tricks?"

"Not at all," I asserted rather indignantly, "he seemed a very serious minded chap; worked in an oxygen-plant and took an active part in the last warfare between men and insects."

Suddenly Stentor stooped over and scooped up some of the minute particles into the palm of his hand—and then he uttered a maniacal shriek and flung them into the air.

"Great God, man, do you know what they are?" he screamed, shaking violently.

"No, I do not," I replied quietly, with an attempt at dignity I did not feel.

"Insect eggs!" he cried, and shuddering with terror, he made for the door.

I caught him on the threshold and pulled him forcibly back into the room.

"Now see here," I said sternly, "not a word of this to anyone. Do you understand? I will test out your theory in every possible way but I want no public interference."

At first he was obstinate, but finally yielded to threats when supplications were impotent.

"I will test them," I said, "and will endeavor to keep hatchings under absolute control, should they prove to be what you suspect."

It was time for the evening broadcasting, so he left, promising to keep our secret and leaving me regretting that I had taken another into my confidence.

VI. The Miracle

For days following my unfortunate experience with Stentor, I experimented upon the tiny objects that had so terrified him. I subjected them to various tests for the purpose of ascertaining whether or not they bore evidence of life, whether in egg, pupa or larva stages of development. And to all my experiments, there was but one answer. No life was manifest. Yet I was not satisfied, for chemical tests showed that they were composed of organic matter. Here was an inexplicable enigma! Many times I was on the verge of consigning the entire contents of the chest to the flames. I seemed to see in my mind's eye the world again over-ridden with insects, and that calamity due to the indiscretions of one man! My next impulse was to turn over my problem to scientists, when a suspicion of the truth dawned upon me. These were seeds, the germs of plant-life, and they might grow. But alas, where? Over all the earth man has spread his artificial dominion. The state-city has been succeeded by what could be termed the nation-city, for one great floor of concrete or rock covers the country.

I resolved to try an experiment, the far-reaching influence of which I did not at that time suspect. Beneath the lowest level of the community edifice in which I dwell, I removed, by means of a small atomic excavator, a slab of concrete large enough to admit my body. I let myself down into the hole and felt my feet resting on a soft dark substance that I knew to be dirt. I hastily filled a box of this, and after replacing the concrete slab, returned to my room, where I proceeded to plant a variety of the seeds.

Being a product of an age when practically to wish for a thing in a material sense is to have it, I experienced the greatest impatience, while waiting for any evidence of plant-life to become manifest. Daily, yes hourly, I watched the soil for signs of a type of life long since departed from the earth, and was about convinced that the germ of life could not have survived the centuries, when a tiny blade of green proved to me that a miracle, more wonderful to me than the works of man through the ages, was taking place before my eyes. This was an enigma so complex and yet so simple, that one recognized in it a direct revelation of Nature.

Daily and weekly I watched in secret the botanical miracle. It was my one obsession. I was amazed at the fascination it held for me—a man who viewed the marvels of the thirty-fourth century with unemotional complacency. It showed me that Nature is manifest in the simple things which mankind has chosen to ignore.

Then one morning, when I awoke, a white blossom displayed its immaculate beauty and sent forth its delicate fragrance into the air. The lily, a symbol of new life, resurrection! I felt within me the stirring of strange emotions I had long believed dead in the bosom of man. But the message must not be for me alone. As of old, the lily would be the symbol of life for all!

With trembling hands, I carried my precious burden to a front window where it might be witnessed by all who passed by. The first day there were few who saw it, for only rarely do men and women walk; they usually ride in speeding vehicles of one kind or another, or employ electric skates, a delightful means of locomotion, which gives the body some exercise. The fourth city level, which is reserved for skaters and pedestrians, is kept in a smooth glass-like condition. And so it was only the occasional pedestrian, walking on the outer border of the fourth level, upon which my window faced, who first carried the news of the growing plant to the world, and it was not long before it was necessary for civic authorities to disperse the crowds that thronged to my window for a glimpse of a miracle in green and white.

When I showed my beautiful plant to Stentor, he was most profuse in his apology and came to my rooms every day to watch it unfold and develop, but the majority of people, long used to business-like efficiency, were intolerant of the sentimental emotions that swayed a small minority, and I was commanded to dispose of the lily. But a figurative seed had been planted in the human heart, a seed that could not be disposed of so readily, and this seed ripened and grew until it finally bore fruit.

VII. Ex Terreno

It is a very different picture of humanity that I paint ten years after the last entry in my diary. My new vocation is farming, but it is farming on a far more intensive scale than had been done two thousand years ago. Our crops never fail, for temperature and rainfall are regulated artificially. But we attribute our success principally to the total absence of insect pests. Our small agricultural areas dot the country like the parks of ancient days and supply us with a type of food, no more nourishing, but more appetizing than that produced in the laboratories. Truly we are living in a marvelous age! If the earth is ours completely, why may we not turn our thoughts toward the other planets in our solar-system? For the past ten or eleven years the Venusians have repeatedly urged us to come and assist them in their battle for life. I believe it is our duty to help them.

Tomorrow will be a great day for us and especially for Stentor, as the new interplanetary television is to be tested, and it is possible that for the first time in history, we shall see our neighbors in the infinity of space. Although the people of Venus were about a thousand years behind us in many respects, they have made wonderful progress with radio and television. We have been in radio communication with them for the last half century and they shared with us the joy of the establishment of our Eden. They have always been greatly interested in hearing Stentor tell the story of our subjugation of the insects that threatened to wipe us out of existence, for they have exactly that problem to solve now; judging from their reports, we fear that theirs is a losing battle. Tomorrow we shall converse face to face with the Venusians! It will be an event second in importance only to the first radio communications interchanged fifty years ago. Stentor's excitement exceeds that displayed at the time of the discovery of the seeds.

Well it is over and the experiment was a success, but alas for the revelation!

The great assembly halls all over the continent were packed with humanity eager to catch a first glimpse of the Venusians. Prior to the test, we sent our message of friendship and good will by radio, and received a reciprocal one from our interplanetary neighbors. Alas, we were ignorant at that time! Then the television receiving apparatus was put into operation, and we sat with breathless interest, our eyes intent upon the crystal screen before us. I sat near Stentor and noted the feverish ardor with which he watched for the first glimpse of Wanyana.

At first hazy mist-like specters seemed to glide across the screen. We knew these figures were not in correct perspective. Finally, one object gradually became more opaque, its outlines could be seen clearly. Then across that vast assemblage, as well as thousands of others throughout the world, there swept a wave of speechless horror, as its full significance burst upon mankind.

The figure that stood facing us was a huge six-legged beetle, not identical in every detail with our earthly enemies of past years, but unmistakably an insect of gigantic proportions! Of course it could not see us, for our broadcaster was not to appear until afterward, but it spoke, and we had to close our eyes to convince ourselves that it was the familiar voice of Wanyana, the leading Venusian radio broadcaster. Stentor grabbed my arm, uttered an inarticulate cry and would have fallen but for my timely support.

"Friends of Earth, as you call your world," began the object of horror, "this is a momentous occasion in the annals of the twin planets, and we are looking forward to seeing one of you, and preferably Stentor, for the first time, as you are now viewing one of us. We have listened many times, with interest, to your story of the insect pests which threatened to follow you as lords of your planet. As you have often heard us tell, we are likewise molested with insects. Our fight is a losing one, unless we can soon exterminate them."

Suddenly, the Venusian was joined by another being, a colossal ant, who bore in his fore-legs a tiny light-colored object which he handed to the beetle-announcer, who took it and held it forward for our closer inspection. It seemed to be a tiny ape, but was so small we could not ascertain for a certainty. We were convinced, however, that it was a mammalian creature, an "insect" pest of Venus. Yet in it we recognized rudimentary man as we know him on earth!

There was no question as to the direction in which sympathies instinctively turned, yet reason told us that our pity should be given to the intelligent reigning race who had risen to its present mental attainment through eons of time. By some quirk or freak of nature, way back in the beginning, life had developed in the form of insects instead of mammals. Or (the thought was repellent) had insects in the past succeeded in displacing mammals, as they might have done here on earth?

There was no more television that night. Stentor would not appear, so disturbed was he by the sight of the Venusians, but in the morning, he talked to them by radio and explained the very natural antipathy we experienced in seeing them or in having them see us.

Now they no longer urge us to construct ether-ships and go to help them dispose of their "insects." I think they are afraid of us, and their very fear has aroused in mankind an unholy desire to conquer them.

I am against it. Have we not had enough of war in the past? We have subdued our own world and should be content with that, instead of seeking new worlds to conquer. But life is too easy here. I can plainly see that. Much as he may seem to dislike it, man is not happy, unless he has some enemy to overcome, some difficulty to surmount.

Alas my greatest fears for man were groundless!

A short time ago, when I went out into my field to see how my crops were faring, I found a six-pronged beetle voraciously eating. No—man will not need to go to Venus to fight "insects."

"With the Night Mail"

by Rudyard Kipling*

Rudyard Kipling (1865–1936) has remained a mainstay of English liter-ature for his beloved children's books such as *The Jungle Book* (1894), made popular by the Disney movies of the same name, *The Just-So Stories* (1902), and his inspirational poetry such as "If" (1895). In recent years, his defense of imperialism, particularly as it is defined in the poem "The White Man's Bur-den" (1899), has cost him a great deal of his reputation. In 1905, though, he had a vision of how bureaucracy would supersede even the power of empire in his story, "With the Night Mail." He sets his story a century into the future and foresees a worldwide force of dirigibles whose main task is to deliver the mail, and how this simple task would become the network for world peace. Where H.G. Wells saw mostly chaos and war with the advent of aircraft, especially in his *War in the Air* (1907), Kipling saw a level of order that would overtake all of humanity's affairs. "With the Night Mail" describes the voy-age of one of these aircraft across the North Atlantic—a century earlier it would have been a tale of the sea; a century later an interplanetary trip.

* * * * *

At 21 o'clock of a gusty winter night I stood on the lower stages of the G.P.O. outward mail tower. My purpose was a run to Quebec in "postal packet 162 or such other as may be appointed": and the Postmaster-General himself countersigned the order. This talisman opened all doors, even those in the dispatching-caisson at the foot of the tower, where they were delivering the sorted Continental mail. The bags lay packed close as her-rings in the long gray underbodies which our G.P.O. still calls "coaches." Five such coaches were filled as I watched, and were shot up the guides to be locked on to their waiting packets three hundred feet nearer the stars.

From the dispatching-caisson I was conducted by a courteous and

*Kipling, Rudyard. "With the Night Mail." *McClure's Magazine* XXVI, no. 1, November 1905, pp. 23–35.

wonderfully learned official—Mr. L.L. Geary, Second Despatcher of the Western Route—to the Captains' Room (this wakes an echo of old romance), where the mail captains come on for their turn of duty. He introduces me to the Captain of "162"—Captain Purnall, and his relief, Captain Hodgson. The one is small and dark: the other large and red; but each has the brooding sheathed glance characteristic of eagles and aeronauts. You can see it in the pictures of our racing professionals, from L.V. Rautsch to little Ada Warrleigh—that fathomless abstraction of eyes habitually turned through naked space.

On the notice-board in the Captains' Room, the pulsing arrows of some twenty indicators register, degree by geographical degree, the progress of as many homeward-bound packets. The word "Cape" rises across the face of a dial; a gong strikes: the South African mid-weekly mail is in at the Highgate Receiving Towers. That is all. It reminds one comically of the traitorous little bell which in pigeon-fanciers' lofts notifies the return of a homer.

"Time for us to be on the move," says Captain Purnall, and we are shot up by the passenger-lift to the top of the dispatch-towers. "Our coach will lock on when it is filled and the clerks are aboard."

"No. 162" waits for us in Slip E of the topmost stage. The great curve of her back shines frostily under the lights, and some minute alteration of trim makes her rock a little in her holding-down clips.

Captain Purnall frowns and dives inside. Hissing softly, "162" comes to rest level as a rule. From her North Atlantic Winter nose-cap (worn bright as a diamond with boring through uncounted leagues of hail, snow and ice) to the inset of her three built-out propeller-shafts is some two hundred and forty feet. Her extreme diameter, carried well forward, is thirty-seven. Contrast this with the nine hundred by ninety-four of any crack liner and you will realize the power that must drive a hull through all weathers at more than twice the emergency-speed of the "Cyclonic"!

The eye detects no joint in her skin plating save the sweeping hair-crack of the bow-rudder—Magniac's rudder that assured us the dominion of the unstable air and left its inventor penniless and half-blind. It is calculated to Castelli's "gull-wing" curve. Raise a few feet of that all but invisible plate three-eighths of an inch and she will yaw five miles to port or starboard ere she is under control again. Give her full helm and she returns on her track like a whip-lash. Cant the whole forward—a touch on the wheel will suffice—and she sweeps at your good direction up or down. Open the full circle and she presents to the air a mushroom-head that will bring her up all standing within a half mile.

"Yes," says Captain Hodgson, answering my thought, "Castelli thought he'd discovered the secret of controlling aeroplanes when he'd only found out how to steer dirigible balloons. Magniac invented his rudder to help war-boats ram each other; and war went out of fashion and Magniac he went out of his mind because he said he couldn't serve his country any more. I wonder if any of us ever know what we're really doing."

"If you want to see the coach locked you'd better go aboard. It's due now," says Mr. Geary. I enter through the door amidships. There is nothing here for display. The inner skin of the gas-tanks comes down to within a foot or two of my head and turns over just short of the turn of the bilges. Liners and yachts disguise their tanks with decoration, but the G.P.O. serves them raw under a lick of gray official paint. The inner skin shuts off fifty feet of the bow and as much of the stern, but the bow-bulkhead is recessed for the lift-shunting apparatus as the stern is pierced for the shaft-tunnels. The engine-room lies almost amidships. Forward of it extending to the turn of the bow tanks is an aperture—a bottomless hatch at present—into which our coach will be locked. One looks down over the coamings three hundred feet to the dispatching-caisson whence voices boom upward. The light below is obscured to a sound of thunder, as the coach rises on its guides. It enlarges rapidly from a postage-stamp to a playing-card: to a punt and last a pontoon. The two clerks, its crew, do not even look up as it comes into place. The Quebec letters fly under their fingers and leap into the docketed racks, while both captains and Mr. Geary satisfy themselves that the coach is locked home. A clerk passes the way-bill over the hatch-coaming. Captain Purnall thumb-marks and passes it to Mr. Geary. Receipt has been given and taken. "Pleasant run," says Mr. Geary, and disappears through the door which a foot-high pneumatic compressor locks after him.

"A-ah!" sighs the compressor released. Our holding-down clips part with a tang. We are clear.

Captain Hodgson opens the great colloid underbody-porthole through which I watch million-lighted London slide eastward as the gale gets hold of us. The first of the low winter clouds cuts off the well-known view and darkens Middlesex. On the south edge of it I can see a packet's postal light plowing through the white fleece. For an instant she gleams like a star ere she drops toward the Highgate Receiving Towers. "The Bombay Mail," says Captain Hodgson, and looks at his watch. "She's forty minutes late."

"What's our level?" I ask.

"Four thousand. Aren't you coming up on the bridge?"

The bridge (let us ever bless the G.P.O. as a repository of ancientest tradition!) is represented by a view of Captain Hodgson's legs where he stands on the control platform that runs thwartships overhead. The bow colloid is unshuttered and Captain Purnall, one hand on the wheel, is feeling for a fair slant. The dial shows 4,300 feet.

"It's steep tonight," he mutters, as tier on tier of cloud drops under. "We generally pick up an easterly draught below three thousand at this time o' the year. I hate slathering through fluff."

"So does Van Cutsem. Look at him huntin' for a slant!" says Captain Hodgson. A fog-light breaks cloud a hundred fathoms below. The Antwerp Night Mail makes her signal and rises between two racing clouds far to port, her flanks blood-red in the glare of Sheerness Double Light. The gale will have us over the German ocean in half an hour, but Captain Purnall lets her go composedly—nosing to every point of the compass as she rises.

"Five thousand—six, six thousand eight hundred"—the dip-dial reads ere we find the easterly drift, heralded by a flurry of snow at the thousand-fathom level. Captain Purnall rings up the engines and keys down the governor on the switch before him. There is no sense in urging machinery when Æolus himself gives you good knots for nothing. We are away in earnest now—our nose notched home on our chosen star. At this level the lower clouds are laid out all neatly combed by the dry fingers of the East. Below that there is the strong westerly blow through which we rose. Overhead, a film of southerly drifting mist draws a theatrical gauze across the firmament. The moonlight turns the lower strata to silver without a stain except where our shadow underruns us. Bristol and Cardiff Double Lights (those stately inclined beams over Severnmouth) are dead ahead of us; for we keep the Southern Winter Route. Coventry Central, the pivot of the English system, stabs upward once in ten seconds its spear of diamond light to the north; and a point or two off our starboard bow The Leek, the great cloud-breaker of Saint David's Head, swings its unmistakable green beam twenty-five degrees each way. There must be half a mile of fluff over it in this weather, but it does not affect The Leek.

"Our planet's overlighted if anything," says Captain Purnall at the wheel, as Cardiff-Bristol slides under. "I remember the old days of common white verticals that 'ud show two or three thousand feet up in a mist, if you knew where to look for 'em. In really fluffy weather they might as well have been under your hat. One could get lost coming home then, an' have some fun. Now, it's like driving down Piccadilly."

He points to the pillars of light where the cloud-breakers bore through the cloud-floor. We see nothing of England's outlines: only a white pavement pierced in all directions by these manholes of variously colored fire—Holy Island's white and red—St. Bee's interrupted white, and so on as far as the eye can reach. Blessed be Sargent, Ahrens, and the Dubois brothers, who invented the cloud-breakers of the world whereby we travel in security!

"Are you going to lift for The Shamrock?" asks Captain Hodgson. Cork Light (green, fixed) enlarges as we rush to it. Captain Purnall nods. There is heavy traffic hereabouts—the bank beneath us is streaked with running fissures of flame where the Atlantic boats are hurrying London-wards just clear of the fluff. Mail-packets are supposed, under the Conference rules, to have the five-thousand-foot lanes to themselves, but the foreigner in a hurry is apt to take liberties with English air. "No. 162" lifts to a long-drawn wail of the breeze in the fore-flange of the rudder and we make Valencia (white, green, white) at a safe 7,000 feet, dipping our beam to an incoming Washington packet.

There is no cloud on the Atlantic, and faint streaks of cream round Dingle Bay show where the driven seas hammer the coast. A big S.A.T.A. liner (*Société Anonyme des Transports Aeriens*) is diving and lifting half a mile below us in search of some break in the solid west wind. Lower still lies a disabled Dane: she is telling the liner all about it in International. Our General Communication dial has caught her talk and begins to eaves-drop. Captain Hodgson makes a motion to shut it off but checks himself. "Perhaps you'd like to listen," he says.

"'Argol' of St. Thomas," the G.C. whispers. "Report owners three star-board shaft collar-bearings fused. Can make Flores as we are, but impossi-ble further. Shall we buy spares at Fayal?"

The liner acknowledges and recommends inverting the bearings. The "Argol" answers that she has already done so without effect, and begins to relieve her mind about cheap German enamels for collar-bearings. The Frenchman assents cordially, cries "*Courage, mon ami,*" and switches off.

Their lights sink under the curve of the ocean.

"That's one of Lundt & Bleamers's boats," says Captain Hodgson. "Serves 'em right for putting German compos in their thrust-blocks. *She* won't be in Fayal tonight! By the way, wouldn't you like to look round the engine-room?"

I have been waiting eagerly for this invitation and I follow Captain Hodgson from the control-platform, stooping low to avoid the bulge of the tanks. We know that Fleury's gas can lift anything, as the world-famous trials of '17 showed, but its almost indefinite powers of expansion neces-sitate vast tank room. Even in this thin air the lift-shunts are busy tak-ing out one-third of its normal lift, and still "162" must be checked by an occasional downdraw of the rudder or our flight would become a climb to the stars. Captain Purnall prefers an overlifted to an underlifted ship, but no two captains trim ship alike. "When *I* take the bridge," says Cap-tain Hodgson, "you'll see me shunt forty per cent. of the lift out of the gas and run her on the upper rudder. With a swoop upwards instead of a swoop downwards, *as* you say. Either way will do. It's only habit. Watch our dip-dial! Tim fetches her down once every thirty knots as regularly as breathing."

So is it shown on the dip-dial. For five or six minutes the arrow creeps from 6,700 to 7,300. There is the faint "szgee" of the rudder, and back slides the arrow to 6,500 on a falling slant of ten or fifteen knots.

"In heavy weather you jockey her with the screws as well," says Captain Hodgson, and, unclipping the jointed bar which divides the engine-room from the bare deck, he leads me on to the floor.

Here we find Fleury's Paradox of the Bulkheaded Vacuum—which we accept now without thought—literally in full blast. The three engines are H.T. &. T. assisted-vacuo Fleury turbines running from 3,000 to the Limit—that is to say, up to the point when the blades make the air "bell"—cut out a vacuum for themselves precisely as do over-driven marine propellers. "162's" Limit is low on account of the small size of her nine screws, which, though handier than the old colloid Thelussons, bell sooner. The midships engine, generally used as a reinforce, is not running; so the port and starboard turbine vacuum-chambers draw direct into the return-mains.

The turbines whistle reflectively. From the low-arched expansion-tanks on either side the valves descend pillarwise to the turbine-chests, and thence the obedient gas whirls through the spirals of blades with a force that would draw the teeth out of a power-saw. Behind, is its own pressure held in leash or spurred on by the lift-shunts; before it, the vacuum where Fleury's Ray dances in violet-green bands and whirled tourbillions of flame. The jointed U-tubes of the vacuum-chamber are pressure-tempered colloid (no glass would endure the strain for an instant) and a junior engineer with tinted spectacles watches the Ray intently. It is the very heart of the machine—a mystery to this day. Even Fleury who begat it and, unlike Magniac, died a multi-millionaire, could not explain how the restless little imp shuddering in the U-tube can in the fractional fraction of a second strike down the furious blast of gas into a chill grayish-green liquid that drains (you can hear it trickle) from the far end of the vacuum through the eduction-pipes and the mains back to the bilges. Here it returns to its gaseous, one had almost written sagacious, state and climbs to work afresh. Bilge-tank, upper tank, dorsal-tank, expansion-chamber, vacuum, main-return (as a liquid), and bilge-tank once more is the ordained cycle. Fleury's Ray sees to that; and the engineer with the tinted spectacles sees to Fleury's Ray. If a speck of oil, if even the natural grease of the human finger touch the hooded terminals, Fleury's Ray will wink and disappear and must be laboriously built up again. This means half a day's work for all hands and an expense of one hundred and seventy-odd pounds to the G.P.O. for radium-salts and such trifles.

"Now look at our thrust-collars. You won't find much German compo there. Full-jewelled, you see," says Captain Hodgson as the engineer shunts open the top of a cap. Our shaft-bearings are C. D.C. (Commercial Diamond Company) stones, ground with as much care as the lens of a telescope. They cost £37 apiece. So far we have not arrived at their term of life. These bearings came from "No. 97," which took them over from the old "Dominion of Light," which had them out of the wreck of the "Perseus" aeroplane in the years when men still flew kites over thorium engines.

They are a shining reproof to all low-grade German "ruby" enamels, so-called "boort" facings, and the dangerous and unsatisfactory alumina compounds which please dividend-hunting owners and turn skippers crazy.

The rudder-gear and the gas lift-shunt, seated side by side under the engine-room dials, are the only machines in visible motion. The former sighs from time to time as the oil plunger rises and falls half an inch. The latter, cased and guarded like the U-tube aft, exhibits another Fleury Ray, but inverted and more green than violet. Its function is to shunt the lift out of the gas, and this it will do without watching. That is all! A tiny pump-rod wheezing and whining to itself beside a sputtering green lamp. A hundred and fifty feet aft down the flat-topped tunnel of the tanks a violet light, restless and irresolute. Between the two, three white-painted turbine-trunks, like eel-baskets laid on their side, accentuate the empty perspectives. You can hear the trickle of the liquefied gas flowing from the vacuum into the bilge-tanks and the soft *gluck-glock* of gas-locks closing as Captain Purnall brings "162" down by the head. The hum of the turbines and the boom of the air on our skin is no more than a cotton-wool wrapping to the universal stillness. And we are running an eighteen-second mile.

I peer from the fore end of the engine-room over the hatch-coamings into the coach. The mail-clerks are sorting the Winnipeg, Calgary, and Medicine Hat bags: but there is a pack of cards ready on the table.

Suddenly a bell thrills; the engineers run to the turbine-valves and stand by; but the spectacled slave of the Ray in the U-tube never lifts his head. He must watch where he is. We are hard-braked and going astern; there is language from the control-platform.

"Tim's sparking badly about something," says the unruffled Captain Hodgson. "Let's look."

Captain Purnall is not the man we left half an hour ago, but the embodied authority of the G.P.O. Ahead of us floats an ancient, aluminum-patched, twin-screw tramp of the dingiest, with no more right to the 5,000 foot lanes than has a horse-cart to a town. She carries an obsolete "barbette" conning-tower—a six-foot affair with railed platform forward—and our warning beam plays on the top of it as a policeman's lantern flashes on the area sneak. Like a sneak-thief, too, emerges a shock-headed navigator in his shirt-sleeves. Captain Purnall wrenches open the colloid to talk with him man to man. There are times when Science does not satisfy.

"What under the stars are you doing here, you sky-scraping chimney-sweep?" he shouts as we two drift side by side. "Do you know this is a Mail-lane? You call yourself a sailor, sir? You ain't fit to peddle toy balloons to an Esquimaux. Your name and number! Report and get down!"

"I've been blown up once," the shock-headed man cries hoarsely as a dog barking. "I don't care two flips of a contact for anything *you* can do, Postey."

"Don't you, sir? But I'll make you care. I'll have you towed stern first to Disko and broke up. You can't recover insurance if you're broke for obstruction. Do you understand *that*?"

Then the stranger bellows: "Look at my propellers! There's been a wulli-wa down under that has knocked me into umbrella-frames! We've been blown up about forty thousand feet! We're all one conjuror's watch inside! My mate's arm's broke; my engineer's head's cut open; my Ray went out when the engines smashed; and ... and ... for pity's sake give me my height, Captain! We doubt we're dropping."

"Six thousand eight hundred. Can you hold it?" Captain Purnall overlooks all insults, and leans half out of the colloid, staring and snuffing. The stranger leaks pungently.

"We ought to blow back to St. John's with luck. We're trying to plug the fore-tank now, but she's simply whistling it away," her captain wails.

"She's sinking like a log," says Captain Purnall in an undertone. "Call up the Mark Boat, George." Our dip-dial shows that we abreast the tramp have dropped five hundred feet the last few minutes.

Captain Purnall presses a switch and our beam begins to swing through the night, twizzling spokes of light across infinity.

"That'll fetch something," he says, while Captain Hodgson watches the General Communicator. He has called up the Banks Mark Boat, a couple of hundred miles west, and is reporting the case.

"I'll stand by you," Captain Purnall roars to the lone figure on the conning-tower.

"Is it as bad as that?" comes the answer. "She isn't insured."

"Might have guessed as much," mutters Hodgson. "Owner's risk is the worst risk of all!"

"Can't I fetch St. John's—not even with this breeze?" the voice quavers.

"Stand by to abandon ship. Haven't you *any* lift in you, fore or aft?"

"Nothing but the midship tanks and they're none too tight. You see, my Ray gave out and—" he coughs in the reek of the escaping gas.

"You poor devil!" This does not reach our friend. "What does the Mark Boat say, George?"

"Wants to know if there's any danger to traffic. Says she's in a bit of weather herself and can't quit station. I've turned in a General Call, so even if they don't see our beam some one's bound to—or else we must. Shall I clear our slings? Hold on! Here we are! A Planet liner, too! She'll be up in a tick!"

"Tell her to get her slings ready," cries his brother captain. "There won't be much time to spare…. Tie up your mate," he roars to the tramp.

"My mate's all right. It's my engineer. He's gone crazy."

"Shunt the lift out of him with a spanner. Hurry!"

"But I can make land, if I've half a chance."

"You'll make the Atlantic in twenty minutes. You're less than fifty-eight hundred now. Get your log and papers."

A Planet liner, east bound, heaves up in a superb spiral and takes the air of us humming. Her underbody colloid is open and her transporter-slings hang down like tentacles. We shut off our beam as she adjusts herself—steering to a hair—over the tramp's conning-tower. The mate comes up, his arm strapped to his side, and stumbles into the cradle. A man with a ghastly scarlet head follows, shouting that he must go back and build up his Ray. The mate assures him that he will find a nice new Ray all ready in the liner's engine-room. The bandaged head goes up wagging excitedly. A youth and a woman follow. The liner cheers hollowly above us, and we see the passengers' faces at the saloon colloid.

"That's a good girl. What's the fool waiting for now?" says Captain Purnall.

The skipper comes up, still appealing to us to stand by and see him fetch St. John's. He dives below and returns—at which we little human beings in the void cheer louder than ever—with the ship's kitten. Up fly the liner's hissing slings; her underbody crashes home and she hurtles away again. The dial shows less than 3,000 feet.

The Mark Boat signals we must attend to the derelict, now whistling her death song, as she falls beneath us in long sick zigzags.

"Keep our beam on her and send out a general warning," says Captain Purnall, following her down.

There is no need. Not a liner in air but knows the meaning of that vertical beam and gives us and our quarry a wide berth.

"But she'll drown in the water, won't she?" I ask.

"I've known a derelict up-end and sift her engines out of herself and flicker round the Lower Lanes for three weeks on her forward tanks only.

We'll run no risks. Pith her, George, and look sharp. There's weather ahead."

Captain Hodgson opens the underbody colloid, swings the heavy pithing-iron out of its rack which in liners is generally cased as a settee, and at two hundred feet releases the catch. We hear the whir of the crescent-shaped arms opening as they descend. The derelict's forehead is punched in, starred across, and rent diagonally. She falls stern first, our beam upon her; slides like a lost soul down that pitiless ladder of light, and the Atlantic takes her.

"A filthy business," says Hodgson. "I wonder what it must have been like in the old days."

The thought had crossed my mind too. What if that wavering carcass had been filled with International-speaking men of all the International-ities, each one of them taught (*that* is the horror of it!) that after death he would very possibly go forever to unspeakable torment?

And not half a century since, we (one knows now that we are only our fathers re-enlarged upon the earth), *we*, I say, ripped and rammed and pithed to admiration.

Here Tim, from the control-platform, shouts that we are to get into our inflators and to bring him his at once.

We hurry into the heavy rubber suits—the engineers are already dressed—and inflate at the air-pump taps. G.P.O. inflaters are thrice as thick as a racing man's "heavies," and chafe abominably under the arm-pits. George takes the wheel until Tim has blown himself up to the extreme of rotundity. If you kicked him off the c. p. to the deck he would bounce back. But it is "162" that will do the kicking.

"The Mark Boat's mad—stark ravin' crazy," he snorts, returning to command. "She says there's a bad blow-out ahead and wants me to pull over to Greenland. I'll see her pithed first! We wasted an hour and a quarter over that dead duck down under and now I'm expected to go rubbin' my back all over the Pole. What does she think a postal packet's made of? Gummed silk? Tell her we're coming on straight."

George buckles him into the Frame and switches on the Direct Control. Now under Tim's left toe lies the port-engine Accelerator; under his left heel the Reverse, and so with the other foot. The lift-shunt stops stand out on the rim of the steering-wheel where the fingers of his left hand can play on them. At his right hand is the midships engine lever ready to be thrown into gear at a moment's notice. He leans forward in his belt, eyes glued to the colloid, and one ear cocked toward the General Communicator. Henceforth he is the strength and direction of "162," through whatever may befall.

The Banks Mark Boat is reeling out pages of Aerial Route Directions to the traffic at large. We are to secure all "loose objects"; hood up our Fleury Rays; and "on no account to attempt to clear snow from our conning-towers till the weather abates." Under-powered craft, we are told, can ascend to the limit of their lift, mail-packets to look out for them accordingly; the lanes westward are pitting very badly, "with frequent blow-outs, vortices, and laterals."

Still the clear dark holds up unblemished. The only warning is the electric skin-tension (I feel as though I were a lace-maker's pillow) and an irritability which the gibbering of the General Communicator increases almost to hysteria.

We have made eight thousand feet since we pithed the tramp and our turbines are giving us an honest two hundred and ten an hour.

Very far to the west an elongated blur of red, low down, shows us the Banks Mark Boat. There are specks of fire round her rising and falling—bewildered planets about an unstable sun—helpless shipping hanging on to her light for company's sake. No wonder she could not quit station.

She warns us to look out for the backwash of the bad vortex in which (her beam shows it) she is even now reeling.

The pits of gloom about us begin to fill with very faintly luminous films—wreathing and uneasy shapes. One forms itself into a globe of pale flame that waits shivering with eagerness as we sweep by. It leaps monstrously across the blackness, alights on the precise tip of our nose, pirouettes there an instant, and swings off. Our roaring bow sinks as though that light were lead—sinks and recovers to lurch and stumble again beneath the next blow-out. Tim's fingers on the lift-shunt strike chords of numbers—1:4:7:—2:4:6:—7:5:3; and so on; for he is running by his tanks only, lifting or lowering her against the uneasy air. All three engines are at work, the sooner we have skated over this thin ice the better. Higher we dare not go. The whole upper vault is charged with pale krypton vapors, which our skin friction may excite to unholy manifestations. Between the upper and the lower levels—5,000, and 7,000, hints the Mark Boat—we may perhaps bolt through if.... Our bow clothes itself in blue flame and falls like a sword. No human skill can keep pace with the changing tensions. A vortex has us by the beak and we dive down a two-thousand-foot slant at an angle (the dip-dial and my bouncing body record it) of thirty-five. Our turbines scream shrilly; the propellers cannot bite on the thin air; Tim shunts the lift out of five tanks at once and by sheer weight drives her bulletwise through the maelstrom till she cushions with a jar on an up-gust, three thousand feet below.

"*Now* we've done it," says George in my ear. "Our skin-friction that last slide, has played Old Harry with the tensions! Look out for laterals, Tim, she'll want lifting."

"I've got her," is the answer. "Come *up*, old woman."

She comes up nobly, but the laterals buffet her left and right like the pinions of angry angels. She is jolted off her chosen star twenty degrees to port or starboard, and cuffed into place again, only to be swung away and dropped into a new blow-out. We are never without a corposant grinning on our bows or rolling head over heels from nose to midships, and to the crackle of electricity round and within us is added once or twice the rattle of hail—hail that will never fall on any sea. Slow we must or we may break our back, pitch-poling.

"Air's a perfectly elastic fluid," roars George above the tumult. "About as elastic as a head sea off the Fastnet."

He is less than just to the good element. If one intrudes on the heavens when they are balancing their volt-accounts; if one disturbs the High Gods' market-rates by hurling steel hulls at ninety knots across tremblingly adjusted tensions, one must not complain of any rudeness in the reception. Tim met it with an unmoved countenance, one corner of his under lip caught up on a tooth, his eyes fleeting into the blackness twenty miles ahead, and the fierce sparks flying from his knuckles at every play of the hand. Now and again he shook his head to clear the sweat trickling from his eyebrows, and it was then that George, watching his chance, would slide down the life-rail and swab his face quickly with a big red handkerchief. I never imagined that a human being could so continuously labor and so collectedly think as did Tim through that Hell's half hour when the flurry was at its worst. We were dragged hither and yon by warm or frozen suctions, belched up on the tops of wulli-was, spun down by vortices and clubbed aside by laterals under a dizzying rush of stars, in the company of a drunken moon. I heard the rushing click of the midship engine lever sliding in and out, the low growl of the lift-shunts, and, louder than the yelling winds without, the scream of the bow-rudder gouging into any lull that promised hold for an instant. At last we began to claw up on a cant, bow-rudder and port-propeller together; only the nicest balancing of tanks saved us from spinning like the rifle-bullet of the old days.

"We've got to hitch to windward of that Mark Boat somehow," George cried.

"There's no windward," I protested feebly, where I swung shackled to a stanchion. "How can there be?"

He laughed—as we pitched into a thousand foot blow-out—that red man laughed beneath his inflated hood!

"Look!" he said. "We must clear those refugees with a high lift."

The Mark Boat was below and a little to the sou'west of us, fluctuating in the center of her distraught galaxy. The air was thick with moving lights at every level. I take it most of them were lying head to wind but, not being hydras, they failed. An under-tanked Moghrabi boat had risen to the limit of her lift and, finding no improvement, had dropped a couple of thousand. There she met a superb wulli-wa and was blown up spinning like a dead leaf. Instead of shutting off she went astern and, naturally, rebounded as from a wall almost into the Mark Boat, whose language (our G.C. took it in) was humanly simple.

"If they'd only ride it out quietly it 'ud be better," said George in a calm, as we climbed like a bat above them all. "But some skippers *will* navigate without lift. What does that Tad-boat think she is doing, Tim?"

"Playin' kiss in the ring," was Tim's unmoved reply. A Trans-Asiatic Direct liner had found a smooth and butted into it full power. But there was a vortex at the tail of that smooth, so the T.A.D. was flipped out like a pea from off a fingernail, braking madly as she fled down and all but over-ending.

"Now I hope she's satisfied," said Tim. "I'm glad I'm not a Mark Boat…. Do I want help?" The G.C. dial had caught his ear. "George, you may tell that gentleman with my love—love, remember, George—that I do not want help. Who *is* the officious sardine-tin?"

"Rimouski drogher on the lookout for a tow."

"Very kind of the Rimouski drogher. This postal packet isn't being towed at present."

"Those droghers will go anywhere on a chance of salvage," George explained. "We call 'em kittiwakes."

A long-beaked, bright steel ninety-footer floated at ease for one instant within hail of us, her slings coiled ready for rescues, and a single hand in her open tower. He was smoking. Surrendered to the insurrection of the airs through which we tore our way, he lay in absolute peace. I saw the smoke of his pipe ascend untroubled ere his boat dropped like a stone in a well.

We had just cleared the Mark Boat and her disorderly refugees when the storm ended as suddenly as it had begun. A shooting-star to northward filled the sky with the green blink of a meteorite dissipating itself in our atmosphere.

Said George: "That may iron out all the tensions." Even as he spoke, the conflicting winds came to rest; the levels filled; the laterals died out in long easy swells; the airways were smoothed before us. In less than three minutes the covey round the Mark Boat had shipped their power-lights and whirred away upon their businesses.

"What's happened?" I gasped. The nerve-storm within and the volt-tingle without had passed: my inflators weighed like lead.

"God he knows!" said Captain George soberly. "That old shooting-star's skin-friction has discharged the different levels. I've seen it happen before. Phew! What a relief!"

We dropped from twelve to six thousand and got rid of our clammy suits. Tim shut off and stepped out of the Frame. The Mark Boat was coming up behind us. He opened the colloid in that heavenly stillness and mopped his face.

"Hello, Williams!" he cried. "A degree or two out o' station, ain't you?"

"May be," was the answer. "I've had some company this evening."

"So I noticed. Wasn't that quite a little flurry?"

"I warned you. Why didn't you pull out round by Disko? The east-bound packets have."

"Me? Not till I'm running a Polar consumptives' Sanatorium boat! I was squinting through a colloid before you were out of your cradle, my son."

"I'd be the last man to deny it," the captain of the Mark Boat replies softly. "The way you handled her just now—I'm a pretty fair judge of traffic in a volt-flurry—it was a thousand revolutions beyond anything even I've ever seen."

Tim's back supples visibly to this oiling. Captain George on the c.p. winks and points to the portrait of a singularly attractive maiden pinned up on the telescope-bracket above the steering-wheel.

I see. Wholly and entirely do I see!

There is some talk overhead of "coming round to tea on Friday," a brief report of the derelict's fate, and Tim volunteers as he descends: "For an A.B.C. man young Williams is less of a high-tension fool than some.… Were you thinking of taking her on, George? Then I'll just have a look round that port-thrust—seems to me it's a trifle warm—and we'll fan along."

The Mark Boat hums off joyously and hangs herself up in her appointed eyrie. Here she will stay, a shutterless observatory; a life-boat station; a salvage tug; a court of ultimate appeal-cum-meteorological bureau for one thousand miles in all directions, till Wednesday next when her relief slides across the stars to take her buffeted place. Her black hull, double conning-tower, and ever-ready slings represent all that remains to the planet of that odd word authority. She is responsible only to the Aerial Board of Control—the A.B.C. of which Tim speaks so flippantly. But that semi-elected, semi-nominated body of a few score persons of both sexes, controls this planet. "Transportation is Civilization," our motto runs. Theoretically, we do what we please so long as we do not interfere with the traffic *and all it implies*. Practically, the A.B.C. confirms or annuls all international arrangements and, to judge from its last report, finds our tolerant, humorous, lazy little planet only too ready to lay the whole burden of private administration on its shoulder.

I discuss this with Tim, sipping maté on the c. p. while George fans her along over the white blur of the Banks in beautiful upward curves of fifty miles each. The dip-dial translates them on the tape in flowing freehand.

Tim gathers up a skein of it and surveys the last few feet, which record "162's" path through the volt-flurry.

"I haven't had a fever-chart like this to show up in five years," he says ruefully.

A postal packet's dip-dial records every yard of every run. The tapes then go to the A.B.C., which collates and makes composite photographs of them for the instruction of captains. Tim studies his irrevocable past, shaking his head.

"Hullo! Here's a fifteen-hundred-foot drop at eighty-five degrees! We must have been standing on our head then, George."

"You don't say so," George answers. "I fancied I noticed it at the time."

George may not have Captain Purnall's catlike swiftness, but he is all an artist to the tips of the broad fingers that play on the shunt-stops. The delicious flight-curves come away on the tape with never a waver. The Mark Boat's vertical spindle of light lies down to eastward, setting in the face of the following stars. Westward, where no planet should rise, the triple verticals of Trinity Bay (we keep still to the Southern route) make a low-lifting haze. We seem the only thing at rest under all the heavens; floating at ease till the earth's revolution shall turn up our landing-towers.

And minute by minute our silent clock gives us a sixteen-second mile.

"Some fine night," says Tim. "We'll be even with that clock's Master."

"He's coming now," says George. "I'm chasing the night already."

The stars ahead dim no more than if a film of mist had been drawn under unobserved, but the deep air-boom on our skin changes to a joyful shout.

"The dawn-gust," says Tim. "It'll go on to meet the Sun. Look! Look! There's the night being crammed back over our bow! Come to the aft colloid. I'll show you something."

The engine-room is hot and stuffy; the clerks in the coach are asleep, and the Slave of the Ray is near to follow them. Tim slides open the aft colloid and reveals the curve of the world—the ocean's deepest purple— edged with fuming and intolerable gold. Then the Sun rises and through the colloid strikes out our lamps. Tim scowls in his face.

"Squirrels in a cage," he mutters. "That's all we are. Squirrels in a cage! He's going twice as fast as us. Just you wait a few years, my shining friend and we'll take steps that will amaze you. *We'll* Joshua you!"

Yes, that is our dream: to turn all earth into the Vale of Ajalon at our pleasure. So far, we can drag out the dawn to twice its normal length in these latitudes. But some day—even on the Equator—we shall hold the Sun level in his full stride.

Now we look down on a sea thronged with heavy traffic. A big submersible breaks water suddenly. Another and another follow with a swash and a suck and a savage bubbling of relieved pressures. The deep-sea freighters are rising to lung up after the long night, and the leisurely ocean is all patterned with peacock's eyes of foam.

"We'll lung up, too," says Tim, and when we return to the c. p. George shuts off, the colloids are opened, and the fresh air sweeps her out. There is no hurry. The old contracts (they will be revised at the end of the year) allow twelve hours for a run which any packet can put behind her in ten. So we breakfast in the arms of an easterly slant which pushes us along at a languid twenty.

To enjoy life, and tobacco, begin both on a sunny morning half a mile or so above the dappled Atlantic cloud-belts and after a volt-flurry which has cleared and tempered your nerves. While we discussed the thickening traffic with the superiority that comes of having a high level to ourselves, we heard (and I for the first time) the morning hymn on a Hospital boat.

She was cloaked by a skein of raveled fluff beneath us and we caught the chant before she rose into the sunlight. *"Oh, ye Winds of God,"* sang the unseen voices: *"bless ye the Lord! Praise Him and magnify Him forever!"*

We slid off our caps and joined in. When our shadow fell across her great open platforms they looked up and stretched out their hands neighborly while they sang. We could see the doctors and the nurses and the white-button-like faces of the cot-patients. She passed slowly beneath us, heading northward, her hull, wet with the dews of the night, all ablaze in the sunshine. So took she the shadow of a cloud and vanished, her song continuing up. *Oh, ye holy and humble men of heart, bless ye the Lord! Praise Him and magnify Him forever.*

"She's a public lunger or she wouldn't have been singing the *Benedicite*; and she's a Greenlander or she wouldn't have snow-blinds over her colloids," said George at last. "She'll be bound for Frederikshavn or one of the Glacier sanatoriums for a month. If she was an accident ward she'd be hung up at the eight-thousand-foot level. Yes—consumptives."

"Funny how the new things are the old things. I've read in books," Tim answered, "that savages used to haul their sick and wounded up to the tops of hills because microbes were fewer there. We hoist 'em into sterilized air for a while. Same idea.

"How much do the doctors say we've added to the average life of a man?"

"Thirty years," says George with a twinkle in his eye. "Are you going to spend 'em all up here?"

"Flap along, then. Flap along. Who's hindering?" the senior captain laughed, as we went in.

We held a good lift to clear the coastwise and Continental shipping and we had need of it. Though our route is in no sense a populated one, there is a steady trickle of traffic this way along. We met Hudson Bay furriers out of the Great Preserve hurrying to make their departure from Bonavista with sable and black fox for the insatiable markets. We over-crossed Keewatin liners, small and cramped, but their captains, who see no land between Trepassy and Blanco, know what gold they bring back from West Africa. Trans-Asiatic Directs, we met, soberly ringing the world round the Fiftieth Meridian at an honest seventy knots; and white-painted Ackroyd & Hunt fruiters out of the south fled beneath us, their ventilated hulls whistling like Chinese kites. Their market is in the North among the northern sanatoria where you can smell their grapefruit and bananas across the cold snows. Argentine beef boats we sighted too, of enormous capacity and unlovely outline. They, too, feed the northern health stations in ice-bound ports where submersibles dare not rise.

Yellow-bellied ore-flats and Ungava petrol-tanks punted down leisurely out of the north like strings of unfrightened wild duck. It does not pay to "fly" minerals and oil a mile farther than is necessary; but the risks of transhipping to submersibles in the ice-pack off Nain or Hebron are so great that these heavy freighters fly down to Halifax direct and scent the air as they go. They are the biggest tramps aloft except the Athabasca grain tubs. But these last, now that the wheat is moved, are busy over the world's shoulder, timber-lifting in Siberia.

We held to the St. Lawrence (it is astonishing how the old water-ways still pull us children of the air), and followed his broad line of black between its drifting ice blocks, all down the Park that the wisdom of our fathers—but everyone knows the Quebec run.

We dropped to the Heights Receiving Towers twenty minutes ahead of time and there hung at ease till the Yokohama Intermediate Packet could pull out and give us our proper slip. It was curious to watch the action of the holding-down clips all along the frosty river front as the boats cleared or came to rest. A big Hamburger was leaving Pont Levis and the crew, unshipping the platform railings, began to sing "Elsinore"—the oldest of our chanteys. You know it of course:

> Mother Rugen's tea-house on the Baltic—
>   Forty couple waltzing on the floor!
> And you can watch my Ray,
> For I must go away
>   And dance with Ella Sweyn at Elsinore!

Then, while they sweated home the covering-plates:

Nor-Nor-Nor-Nor-
West from Sourabaya to the Baltic!
Ninety knot an hour to the Skaw!
Mother Rugen's tea-house on the Baltic
And a dance with Ella Sweyn at Elsinore!

The clips parted with a gesture of indignant dismissal, as though Quebec, glittering under her snows, were casting out these light and unworthy lovers. Our signal came from the Heights. Tim turned and floated up, but surely then it was with passionate appeal that the great arms flung open from our tower—or did I think so because on the upper staging a little hooded figure also opened her arms wide towards her father?

In ten seconds the coach with the clerks clashed down to the receiving-caisson; the hostlers displaced the engineers at the idle turbines, and Tim, prouder of this than all, introduced me to the maiden of the photograph on the shelf. "And by the way," said he to her, stepping forth in sunshine under the hat of civil life, "I saw young Williams in the Mark Boat. I've asked him to tea on Friday."

"From Beyond"

by H.P. Lovecraft*

H.P. Lovecraft (1890–1937) had one of the largest impacts on speculative fiction in the twentieth century. His work, particularly his Cthulhu
stories, has inspired a huge array of writers from Ramsey Campbell and
Stephen King to Victor LaValle and Matt Ruff, spanning all of the decades
since his death. Many of his stories, including "From Beyond," have been
adapted for radio, television, and movies, and his creations have inspired
comics, games, and all sorts of artwork. "From Beyond" was written in
1920, but did not appear until the June 1934 issue of *The Fantasy Fan*.
The main focus of this story is the scientific revelation of how ineffective
human sensory organs can be in gathering data about the universe. Tech-
nologies of the late-nineteenth and early-twentieth centuries—including
those used to discover X-rays, ultraviolet and infrared light, and trans-
mitting devices like radio and television—demonstrate over and over how
unable human senses are to perceive the depth of the universe and the
things that might dwell within it. In this story, Lovecraft reflects on how
much better off humanity is not knowing what lies in wait, not only in the
vastness of the cosmos, but also just around the corner.

* * * * *

Horrible beyond conception was the change which had taken place in
my best friend, Crawford Tillinghast. I had not seen him since that day, two
months and a half before, when he told me toward what goal his physical
and metaphysical researches were leading; when he had answered my awed
and almost frightened remonstrances by driving me from his laboratory
and his house in a burst of fanatical rage, I had known that he now remained
mostly shut in the attic laboratory with that accursed electrical machine,
eating little and excluding even the servants, but I had not thought that a

*Lovecraft, H.P. "From Beyond." *Weird Tales* 31, no. 2, February 1938, pp. 227–231.

brief period of ten weeks could so alter and disfigure any human creature. It is not pleasant to see a stout man suddenly grown thin, and it is even worse when the baggy skin becomes yellowed or grayed, the eyes sunken, circled, and uncannily glowing, the forehead veined and corrugated, and the hands tremulous and twitching. And if added to this there be a repellent unkemptness, a wild disorder of dress, a bushiness of dark hair white at the roots, and an unchecked growth of white beard on a face once clean-shaven, the cumulative effect is quite shocking. But such was the aspect of Crawford Tillinghast on the night his half-coherent message brought me to his door after my weeks of exile; such was the specter that trembled as it admitted me, candle in hand, and glanced furtively over its shoulder as if fearful of unseen things in the ancient, lonely house set back from Benevolent Street.

That Crawford Tillinghast should ever have studied science and philosophy was a mistake. These things should be left to the frigid and impersonal investigator for they offer two equally tragic alternatives to the man of feeling and action; despair, if he fail in his quest, and terrors unutterable and unimaginable if he succeed. Tillinghast had once been the prey of failure, solitary and melancholy; but now I knew, with nauseating fears of my own, that he was the prey of success. I had indeed warned him ten weeks before, when he burst forth with his tale of what he felt himself about to discover. He had been flushed and excited then, talking in a high and unnatural, though always pedantic, voice.

"What do we know," he had said, "of the world and the universe about us? Our means of receiving impressions are absurdly few, and our notions of surrounding objects infinitely narrow. We see things only as we are constructed to see them, and can gain no idea of their absolute nature. With five feeble senses we pretend to comprehend the boundlessly complex cosmos; yet other beings with wider, stronger, or different range of senses might not only see very differently the things we see, but might see and study whole worlds of matter, energy, and life which lie close at hand yet can never be detected with the senses we have. I have always believed that such strange, inaccessible worlds exist at our very elbows, *and now I believe I have found a way to break down the barriers.* I am not joking. Within twenty-four hours that machine near the table will generate waves acting on unrecognized sense-organs that exist in us as atrophied or rudimentary vestiges. Those waves will open up to us many vistas unknown to man, and several unknown to anything we consider organic life. We shall see that at which dogs howl in the dark, and that at which cats prick up their ears after midnight. We shall see these things, and other things which no breathing creature has yet seen. We shall overleap time, space, and dimensions, and without bodily motion peer to the bottom of creation."

When Tillinghast said these things I remonstrated, for I knew him well enough to be frightened rather than amused; but he was a fanatic, and drove me from the house. Now he was no less a fanatic, but his desire to speak had conquered his resentment, and he had written me imperatively in a hand I could scarcely recognize. As I entered the abode of the friend so suddenly metamorphosed to a shivering gargoyle, I became infected with the terror which seemed stalking in all the shadows. The words and beliefs expressed ten weeks before seemed bodied forth in the darkness beyond the small circle of candle light, and I sickened at the hollow, altered voice of my host. I wished the servants were about, and did not like it when he said they had all left three days previously. It seemed strange that old Gregory, at least, should desert his master without telling as tried a friend as I. It was he who had given me all the information I had of Tillinghast after I was repulsed in rage.

Yet I soon subordinated all my fears to my growing curiosity and fascination. Just what Crawford Tillinghast now wished of me I could only guess, but that he had some stupendous secret or discovery to impart, I could not doubt. Before I had protested at his unnatural pryings into the unthinkable; now that he had evidently succeeded to some degree I almost shared his spirit, terrible though the cost of victory appeared.

* * *

Up through the dark emptiness of the house I followed the bobbing candle in the hand of this shaking parody on man. The electricity seemed to be turned off, and when I asked my guide he said it was for a definite reason.

"It would be too much…. I would not dare," he continued to mutter. I especially noted his new habit of muttering, for it was not like him to talk to himself.

We entered the laboratory in the attic, and I observed that detestable electrical machine, glowing with a sickly, sinister violet luminosity. It was connected with a powerful chemical battery, but seemed to be receiving no current; for I recalled that in its experimental stage it had sputtered and purred when in action. In reply to my question Tillinghast mumbled that this permanent glow was not electrical in any sense that I could understand.

He now seated me near the machine, so that it was on my right, and turned a switch somewhere below the crowning cluster of glass bulbs. The usual sputtering began, turned to a whine, and terminated in a drone so soft as to suggest a return to silence. Meanwhile the luminosity increased, waned again, then assumed a pale, outré color or blend of colors which I could neither place nor describe. Tillinghast had been watching me, and noted my puzzled expression.

"Do you know what that is?" he whispered, "*That is ultra-violet.*" He chuckled oddly at my surprise. "You thought ultra-violet was invisible, and so it is—but you can see that and many other invisible things *now.*

"Listen to me! The waves from that thing are waking a thousand sleeping senses in us; senses which we inherit from eons of evolution from the state of detached electrons to the state of organic humanity. I have seen the *truth*, and I intend to show it to you. Do you wonder how it will seem? I will tell you."

Here Tillinghast seated himself directly opposite me, blowing out his candle and staring hideously into my eyes.

"Your existing sense-organs—ears first, I think—will pick up many of the impressions, for they are closely connected with the dormant organs. Then there will be others. You have heard of the pineal gland? I laugh at the shallow endocrinologist, fellow-dupe and fellow-parvenu of the Freudian. That gland is the great sense organ of organs—*I have found out*. It is like sight in the end, and transmits visual pictures to the brain. If you are normal, that is the way you ought to get most of it…. I mean get most of the evidence *from beyond*."

I looked about the immense attic room with the sloping south wall, dimly lit by rays which the everyday eye cannot see. The far corners were all shadows, and the whole place took on a hazy unreality which obscured its nature and invited the imagination to symbolism and phantasm. During the interval that Tillinghast was silent I fancied myself in some vast and incredible temple of long-dead gods; some vague edifice of innumerable black stone columns reaching up from a floor of damp slabs to a cloudy height beyond the range of my vision.

The picture was very vivid for a while, but gradually gave way to a more horrible conception; that of utter, absolute solitude in infinite, sightless, soundless space. There seemed to be a void, and nothing more, and I felt a childish fear which prompted me to draw from my hip pocket the revolver I always carried after dark since the night I was held up in East Providence. Then, from the farthermost regions of remoteness, the *sound* softly glided into existence. It was infinitely faint, subtly vibrant, and unmistakably musical, but held a quality of surpassing wildness which made its impact feel like a delicate torture of my whole body. I felt sensations like those one feels when accidentally scratching ground glass. Simultaneously there developed something like a cold draft, which apparently swept past me from the direction of the distant sound. As I waited breathlessly I perceived that both sound and wind were increasing; the effect being to give me an odd notion of myself as tied to a pair of rails in the path of a gigantic approaching locomotive.

I began to speak to Tillinghast, and as I did so all the unusual impressions abruptly vanished. I saw only the man, the glowing machine, and the dim apartment. Tillinghast was grinning repulsively at the revolver which I had almost unconsciously drawn, but from his expression I was sure he had seen and heard as much as I, if not a great deal more. I whispered what I had experienced and he bade me to remain as quiet and receptive as possible.

"Don't move," he cautioned, "for in these rays *we are able to be seen as well as to see*. I told you the servants left, but I didn't tell you *how*. It was that thick-witted house-keeper—who turned on the lights downstairs after I had warned her not to, and the wires picked up sympathetic vibrations. It must have been frightful—I could hear the screams up here in spite of all I was seeing and hearing from another direction, and later it was rather awful to find those empty heaps of clothes around the house. Mrs. Updike's clothes were close to the front hall switch—that's how I know she did it. It got them all. But so long as we don't move we're fairly safe. Remember we're dealing with a hideous world in which we are practically helpless.... *Keep still!*"

* * *

The combined shock of the revelation and of the abrupt command gave me a kind of paralysis, and in my terror my mind again opened to the impressions coming from what Tillinghast called "*beyond*." I was now in a vortex of sound and motion, with confused pictures before my eyes. I saw the blurred outlines of the room, but from some point in space there seemed to be pouring a seething column of unrecognizable shapes or clouds, penetrating the solid roof at a point ahead and to the right of me. Then I glimpsed the temple-like effect again, but this time the pillars reached up into an aerial ocean of light, which sent down one blinding beam along the path of the cloudy column I had seen before.

After that the scene was almost wholly kaleidoscopic, and in the jumble of sights, sounds, and unidentified sense-impressions I felt that I was about to dissolve or in some way lose the solid form. One definite flash I shall always remember. I seemed for an instant to behold a patch of strange night sky filled with shining, revolving spheres, and as it receded I saw that the glowing suns formed a constellation or galaxy of settled shape; this shape being the distorted face of Crawford Tillinghast. At another time I felt the huge animate things brushing past me and occasionally *walking or drifting through my supposedly solid body,* and thought I saw Tillinghast look at them as though his better trained senses could catch them visually. I recalled what he had said of the pineal gland, and wondered what he saw with this preternatural eye.

Suddenly I myself became possessed of a kind of augmented sight. Over and above the luminous and shadowy chaos arose a picture which, though vague, held the elements of consistency and permanence. It was indeed somewhat familiar, for the unusual part was superimposed upon the usual terrestrial scene much as a cinema view may be thrown upon the painted curtain of a theater. I saw the attic laboratory, the electrical machine, and the unsightly form of Tillinghast opposite me; but of all the space unoccupied by familiar objects not one particle was vacant. Indescribable shapes both alive and otherwise were mixed in disgusting disarray, and close to every known thing were whole worlds of alien, unknown entities. It likewise seemed that all the known things entered into the composition of other unknown things and vice versa.

Foremost among the living objects were inky, jellyfish monstrosities which flabbily quivered in harmony with the vibrations from the machine. They were present in loathsome profusion, and I saw to my horror that they *overlapped*; that they were semi-fluid and capable of passing through one another and through what we know as solids. These things were never still, but seemed ever floating about with some malignant purpose. Sometimes they appeared to devour one another, the attacker launching itself at its victim and instantaneously obliterating the latter from sight. Shudderingly I felt that I knew what had obliterated the unfortunate servants, and could not exclude the things from my mind as I strove to observe other properties of the newly visible world that lies unseen around us. But Tillinghast had been watching me and was speaking.

"You see them? You see them? You see the things that float and flop about you and through you every moment of your life? You see the creatures that form what men call the pure air and the blue sky? Have I not succeeded in breaking down the barrier; have I not shown you worlds that no other living men have seen?"

I heard his scream through the horrible chaos, and looked at the wild face thrust so offensively close to mine. His eyes were pits of flame, and they glared at me with what I now saw was overwhelming hatred. The machine droned detestably.

"You think those floundering things wiped out the servants? Fool, they are harmless! But the servants *are* gone, aren't they? You tried to stop me; you discouraged me when I needed every drop of encouragement I could get; you were afraid of the cosmic truth, you damned coward, but now I've got you! What swept up the servants? What made them scream so loud? ... Don't know, eh! You'll know soon enough. Look at me—listen to what I say—do you suppose there are really any such things as time and magnitude? Do you fancy there are such things as form or matter? I tell you, I have struck depths that your little brain can't picture. I have seen beyond the bounds of infinity and drawn down demons from the stars.... I have harnessed the shadows that stride from world to world to sow death and madness ... space belongs to me, do you hear? Things are hunting me now—the things that devour and dissolve—but I know how to elude them. It is you they will get, as they got the servants....

"Stirring, dear sir? I told you it was dangerous to move; I have saved you so far by telling you to keep still—saved you to see more sights and to listen to me. If you had moved, they would have been at you long ago. Don't worry, they won't *hurt* you. They didn't hurt the servants—it was the *seeing* that made the poor devils scream so. My pets are not pretty, for they come out of places where aesthetic standards are—*very different*. Disintegration is quite painless, I assure you—*but I want you to see them*. I almost saw them, but I knew how to stop.

"You are not curious? I always knew you were no scientist. Trembling, eh? Trembling with anxiety to see the ultimate things I have discovered. Why don't you move, then? Tired? Well, don't worry, my friend, *for they are coming....* Look, look, curse you, look ... it's just over your left shoulder...."

* * *

What remains to be told is very brief, and may be familiar to you from the newspaper accounts. The police heard a shot in the old Tillinghast house and found us there—Tillinghast dead and me unconscious. They arrested me because the revolver was in my hand, but released me in three hours, after they found it was apoplexy which had finished Tillinghast and saw that my shot had been directed at the noxious machine which now lay hopelessly shattered on the laboratory floor. I did not tell very much of what I had seen, for I feared the coroner would be skeptical; but from the evasive outline I did give, the doctor told me that I had undoubtedly been hypnotized by the vindictive and homicidal madman.

I wish I could believe that doctor. It would help my shaky nerves if I could dismiss what I now have to think of the air and the sky about and above me. I never feel alone or comfortable, and a hideous sense of pursuit sometimes comes chillingly on me when I am weary. What prevents me from believing the doctor is one simple fact—that the police never found the bodies of those servants whom they say Crawford Tillinghast murdered.

"The Machine Stops"

by E.M. Forster*

English writer E.M. Forster (1879–1970) is well known today not for his speculative fiction—of which there is only a little—but for his immensely popular novels that examine class differences and social mores among wide slices of English society. The novel that brought him his greatest commercial and critical success, *A Passage to India* (1924), is based on Forster's experience of living in India under British rule. "The Machine Stops" (1909) is a short story that first appeared in *The Oxford and Cambridge Review* in the middle of his most productive decade as a writer. It is a story that seems far, far ahead of its time, depicting a society whose individuals live in screen-mediated isolation as they engage in video conferencing, social media, and other aspects of what has become twenty-first-century internet life. All of human existence is mediated and determined by the machine at the heart of their communication; there is no human community outside of the machine. As the Industrial Age spawned the age of urbanization, this story showed readers that even living in close proximity to others does not necessarily cause a positive benefit for a community. In 1952, the story received perhaps the ultimate measure of immortality when Wally Wood adapted it into a profoundly bizarre comic for *Mad* magazine.

* * * * *

Part I. The Air-Ship

Imagine, if you can, a small room, hexagonal in shape, like the cell of a bee. It is lighted neither by window nor by lamp, yet it is filled with a soft radiance. There are no apertures for ventilation, yet the air is fresh. There are no musical instruments, and yet, at the moment that my meditation

*Forster, E.M. "The Machine Stops." *The Oxford and Cambridge Review* 8, 1909, pp. 83–122.

opens, this room is throbbing with melodious sounds. An arm-chair is in the center, by its side a reading-desk—that is all the furniture. And in the arm-chair there sits a swaddled lump of flesh—a woman, about five feet high, with a face as white as a fungus. It is to her that the little room belongs.

An electric bell rang.

The woman touched a switch and the music was silent.

"I suppose I must see who it is," she thought, and set her chair in motion. The chair, like the music, was worked by machinery and it rolled her to the other side of the room where the bell still rang importunately.

"Who is it?" she called. Her voice was irritable, for she had been interrupted often since the music began. She knew several thousand people, in certain directions human intercourse had advanced enormously.

But when she listened into the receiver, her white face wrinkled into smiles, and she said: "Very well. Let us talk, I will isolate myself. I do not expect anything important will happen for the next five minutes—for I can give you fully five minutes, Kuno. Then I must deliver my lecture on 'Music during the Australian Period.'"

She touched the isolation-knob, so that no one else could speak to her. Then she touched the lighting apparatus, and the little room was plunged into darkness.

"Be quick!" she called, her irritation returning. "Be quick, Kuno; here I am in the dark wasting my time."

But it was fully fifteen seconds before the round plate that she held in her hands began to glow. A faint blue light shot across it, darkening to purple, and presently she could see the image of her son, who lived on the other side of the earth, and he could see her. "Kuno, how slow you are."

He smiled gravely.

"I really believe you enjoy dawdling."

"I have called you before, mother, but you were always busy or isolated. I have something particular to say."

"What is it, dearest boy? Be quick. Why could you not send it by pneumatic post?"

"Because I prefer saying such a thing. I want—"

"Well?"

"I want you to come and see me."

Vashti watched his face in the blue plate.

"But I can see you!" she exclaimed. "What more do you want?"

"I want to see you not through the Machine," said Kuno. "I want to speak to you not through the wearisome Machine."

"Oh, hush!" said his mother, vaguely shocked. "You mustn't say anything against the Machine."

"Why not?"

"One mustn't."

"You talk as if a god had made the Machine," cried the other. "I believe that you pray to it when you are unhappy. Men made it, do not forget that. Great men, but men. The Machine is much, but it is not everything. I see something like you in this plate, but I do not see you. I hear something like you through this telephone, but I do not hear you. That is why I want you to come. Pay me a visit, so that we can meet face to face, and talk about the hopes that are in my mind."

She replied that she could scarcely spare the time for a visit.

"The air-ship barely takes two days to fly between me and you."

"I dislike air-ships."

"Why?"

"I dislike seeing the horrible brown earth, and the sea, and the stars when it is dark. I get no ideas in an air-ship."

"I do not get them anywhere else."

"What kind of ideas can the air give you?" He paused for an instant.

"Do you not know four big stars that form an oblong, and three stars close together in the middle of the oblong, and hanging from these stars, three other stars?"

"No, I do not. I dislike the stars. But did they give you an idea? How interesting; tell me."

"I had an idea that they were like a man."

"I do not understand."

"The four big stars are the man's shoulders and his knees. The three stars in the middle are like the belts that men wore once, and the three stars hanging are like a sword."

"A sword?"

"Men carried swords about with them, to kill animals and other men."

"It does not strike me as a very good idea, but it is certainly original. When did it come to you first?"

"In the air-ship—" He broke off, and she fancied that he looked sad. She could not be sure, for the Machine did not transmit *nuances* of expression. It only gave a general idea of people—an idea that was good enough for all practical purposes, Vashti thought. The imponderable bloom, declared by a discredited philosophy to be the actual essence of intercourse, was rightly ignored by the Machine, just as the imponderable bloom of the grape was ignored by the manufacturers of artificial fruit. Something "good enough" had long since been accepted by our race.

"The truth is," he continued, "that I want to see these stars again. They are curious stars. I want to see them not from the air-ship, but from the surface of the earth, as our ancestors did, thousands of years ago. I want to visit the surface of the earth."

She was shocked again.

"Mother, you must come, if only to explain to me what is the harm of visiting the surface of the earth."

"No harm," she replied, controlling herself. "But no advantage. The surface of the earth is only dust and mud, no life remains on it, and you would need a respirator, or the cold of the outer air would kill you. One dies immediately in the outer air."

"I know; of course I shall take all precautions."

"And besides—"

"Well?"

She considered, and chose her words with care. Her son had a queer temper, and she wished to dissuade him from the expedition.

"It is contrary to the spirit of the age," she asserted.

"Do you mean by that, contrary to the Machine?"

"In a sense, but—"

His image in the blue plate faded.

"Kuno!"

He had isolated himself.

For a moment Vashti felt lonely.

Then she generated the light, and the sight of her room, flooded with radiance and studded with electric buttons, revived her. There were buttons and switches everywhere—buttons to call for food, for music, for clothing. There was the hot-bath button, by pressure of which a basin of (imitation) marble rose out of the floor, filled to the brim with a warm deodorized liquid. There was the cold-bath button. There was the button that produced literature. And there were of course the buttons by which she communicated with her friends. The room, though it contained nothing, was in touch with all that she cared for in the world.

Vashti's next move was to turn off the isolation switch, and all the accumulations of the last three minutes burst upon her. The room was filled with the noise of bells, and speaking-tubes. What was the new food like? Could she recommend it? Has she had any ideas lately? Might one tell her one's own ideas? Would she make an engagement to visit the public nurseries at an early date?—say this day month.

To most of these questions she replied with irritation—a growing quality in that accelerated age. She said that the new food was horrible. That she could not visit the public nurseries through press of engagements. That she had no ideas of her own but had just been told one—that four stars and three in the middle were like a man: she doubted there was much in it. Then she switched off her correspondents, for it was time to deliver her lecture on Australian music.

The clumsy system of public gatherings had been long since abandoned;

neither Vashti nor her audience stirred from their rooms. Seated in her arm-chair she spoke, while they in their arm-chairs heard her, fairly well, and saw her, fairly well. She opened with a humorous account of music in the pre Mongolian epoch, and went on to describe the great outburst of song that followed the Chinese conquest. Remote and primeval as were the methods of I-San-So and the Brisbane school, she yet felt (she said) that study of them might repay the musician of today: they had freshness; they had, above all, ideas.

Her lecture, which lasted ten minutes, was well received, and at its conclusion she and many of her audience listened to a lecture on the sea; there were ideas to be got from the sea; the speaker had donned a respirator and visited it lately. Then she fed, talked to many friends, had a bath, talked again, and summoned her bed.

The bed was not to her liking. It was too large, and she had a feeling for a small bed. Complaint was useless, for beds were of the same dimension all over the world, and to have had an alternative size would have involved vast alterations in the Machine. Vashti isolated herself—it was necessary, for neither day nor night existed under the ground—and reviewed all that had happened since she had summoned the bed last. Ideas? Scarcely any. Events—was Kuno's invitation an event?

By her side, on the little reading-desk, was a survival from the ages of litter—one book. This was the Book of the Machine. In it were instructions against every possible contingency. If she was hot or cold or dyspeptic or at a loss for a word, she went to the book, and it told her which button to press. The Central Committee published it. In accordance with a growing habit, it was richly bound.

Sitting up in the bed, she took it reverently in her hands. She glanced round the glowing room as if someone might be watching her. Then, half ashamed, half joyful, she murmured "O Machine! O Machine!" and raised the volume to her lips. Thrice she kissed it, thrice inclined her head, thrice she felt the delirium of acquiescence. Her ritual performed, she turned to page 1367, which gave the times of the departure of the air-ships from the island in the Southern Hemisphere, under whose soil she lived, to the island in the northern hemisphere, whereunder lived her son.

She thought, "I have not the time."

She made the room dark and slept; she awoke and made the room light; she ate and exchanged ideas with her friends, and listened to music and attended lectures; she made the room dark and slept. Above her, beneath her, and around her, the Machine hummed eternally; she did not notice the noise, for she had been born with it in her ears. The earth, carrying her, hummed as it sped through silence, turning her now to the invisible sun, now to the invisible stars. She awoke and made the room light.

"Kuno!"

"I will not talk to you." he answered, "until you come."

"Have you been on the surface of the earth since we spoke last?"

His image faded.

Again she consulted the book. She became very nervous and lay back in her chair palpitating. Think of her as without teeth or hair. Presently she directed the chair to the wall, and pressed an unfamiliar button. The wall swung apart slowly. Through the opening she saw a tunnel that curved slightly, so that its goal was not visible. Should she go to see her son, here was the beginning of the journey.

Of course she knew all about the communication-system. There was nothing mysterious in it. She would summon a car and it would fly with her down the tunnel until it reached the lift that communicated with the air-ship station: the system had been in use for thousands of years, long before the universal establishment of the Machine. And of course she had studied the civilization that had immediately preceded her own—the civilization that had mistaken the functions of the system, and had used it for bringing people to things, instead of for bringing things to people. Those funny old days, when men went for change of air instead of changing the air in their rooms! And yet—she was frightened of the tunnel: she had not seen it since her last child was born. It curved—but not quite as she remembered; it was brilliant—but not quite as brilliant as a lecturer had suggested. Vashti was seized with the terrors of direct experience. She shrank back into the room, and the wall closed up again.

"Kuno," she said, "I cannot come to see you. I am not well."

Immediately an enormous apparatus fell on to her out of the ceiling, a thermometer was automatically inserted between her lips, a stethoscope was automatically laid upon her heart. She lay powerless. Cool pads soothed her forehead. Kuno had telegraphed to her doctor.

So the human passions still blundered up and down in the Machine. Vashti drank the medicine that the doctor projected into her mouth, and the machinery retired into the ceiling. The voice of Kuno was heard asking how she felt.

"Better." Then with irritation: "But why do you not come to me instead?"

"Because I cannot leave this place."

"Why?"

"Because, any moment, something tremendous may happen."

"Have you been on the surface of the earth yet?"

"Not yet."

"Then what is it?"

"I will not tell you through the Machine."

She resumed her life.

But she thought of Kuno as a baby, his birth, his removal to the public nurseries, her own visit to him there, his visits to her—visits which stopped when the Machine had assigned him a room on the other side of the earth. "Parents, duties of," said the book of the Machine, "cease at the moment of birth. P.422327483." True, but there was something special about Kuno—indeed there had been something special about all her children, and, after all, she must brave the journey if he desired it. And "something tremendous might happen." What did that mean? The nonsense of a youthful man, no doubt, but she must go. Again she pressed the unfamiliar button, again the wall swung back, and she saw the tunnel that curved out of sight. Clasping the Book, she rose, tottered on to the platform, and summoned the car. Her room closed behind her: the journey to the Northern Hemisphere had begun.

Of course it was perfectly easy. The car approached and in it she found arm-chairs exactly like her own. When she signaled, it stopped, and she tottered into the lift. One other passenger was in the lift, the first fellow creature she had seen face to face for months. Few travelled in these days, for, thanks to the advance of science, the earth was exactly alike all over. Rapid intercourse, from which the previous civilization had hoped so much, had ended by defeating itself. What was the good of going to Pekin when it was just like Shrewsbury? Why return to Shrewsbury when it would be just like Pekin? Men seldom moved their bodies; all unrest was concentrated in the soul.

The air-ship service was a relic from the former age. It was kept up, because it was easier to keep it up than to stop it or to diminish it, but it now far exceeded the wants of the population. Vessel after vessel would rise from the vomitories of Rye or of Christchurch (I use the antique names), would sail into the crowded sky, and would draw up at the wharves of the South—empty. So nicely adjusted was the system, so independent of meteorology, that the sky, whether calm or cloudy, resembled a vast kaleidoscope whereon the same patterns periodically recurred. The ship on which Vashti sailed started now at sunset, now at dawn. But always, as it passed above Rheims, it would neighbor the ship that served between Helsingfors and the Brazils, and, every third time it surmounted the Alps, the fleet of Palermo would cross its track behind. Night and day, wind and storm, tide and earthquake, impeded man no longer. He had harnessed Leviathan. All the old literature, with its praise of Nature, and its fear of Nature, rang false as the prattle of a child.

Yet as Vashti saw the vast flank of the ship, stained with exposure to the outer air, her horror of direct experience returned. It was not quite like the air-ship in the cinematophote. For one thing it smelt—not strongly or unpleasantly, but it did smell, and with her eyes shut she should have known that a new thing was close to her. Then she had to walk to it from the lift, had to submit to glances from the other passengers. The man in front dropped his Book—no great matter, but it disquieted them all. In the rooms, if the Book was dropped, the floor raised it mechanically, but the gangway to the air-ship was not so prepared, and the sacred volume lay motionless. They stopped—the thing was unforeseen—and the man, instead of picking up his property, felt the muscles of his arm to see how they had failed him. Then someone actually said with direct utterance: "We shall be late"—and they trooped on board, Vashti treading on the pages as she did so.

Inside, her anxiety increased. The arrangements were old-fashioned and rough. There was even a female attendant, to whom she would have to announce her wants during the voyage. Of course a revolving platform ran the length of the boat, but she was expected to walk from it to her cabin. Some cabins were better than others, and she did not get the best. She thought the attendant had been unfair, and spasms of rage shook her. The glass valves had closed, she could not go back. She saw, at the end of the vestibule, the lift in which she had ascended going quietly up and down, empty. Beneath those corridors of shining tiles were rooms, tier below tier, reaching far into the earth, and in each room there sat a human being, eating, or sleeping, or producing ideas. And buried deep in the hive was her own room. Vashti was afraid.

"O Machine!" she murmured, and caressed her Book, and was comforted.

Then the sides of the vestibule seemed to melt together, as do the passages that we see in dreams, the lift vanished, the Book that had been dropped slid to the left and vanished, polished tiles rushed by like a stream of water, there was a slight jar, and the air-ship, issuing from its tunnel, soared above the waters of a tropical ocean.

It was night. For a moment she saw the coast of Sumatra edged by the phosphorescence of waves, and crowned by lighthouses, still sending forth their disregarded beams. These also vanished, and only the stars distracted her. They were not motionless, but swayed to and fro above her head, thronging out of one skylight into another, as if the universe and not the air-ship was careening. And, as often happens on clear nights, they seemed now to be in perspective, now on a plane; now piled tier beyond tier into the infinite heavens, now concealing infinity, a roof limiting forever the visions of men. In either case they seemed intolerable. "Are we to travel in the dark?" called the passengers angrily, and the attendant, who had been careless, generated the light, and pulled down the blinds of pliable metal. When the air-ships had been built, the desire to look direct at things still lingered in the world. Hence the extraordinary number of skylights and windows, and the proportionate discomfort to those who were civilized and refined. Even in Vashti's cabin one star peeped through a flaw in the blind, and after a few hours' uneasy slumber, she was disturbed by an unfamiliar glow, which was the dawn.

Quick as the ship had sped westwards, the earth had rolled eastwards quicker still, and had dragged back Vashti and her companions towards the sun. Science could prolong the night, but only for a little, and those high hopes of neutralizing the earth's diurnal revolution had passed, together with hopes that were possibly higher. To "keep pace with the sun," or even to outstrip it, had been the aim of the civilization preceding this. Racing aeroplanes had been built for the purpose, capable of enormous speed, and steered by the greatest intellects of the epoch. Round the globe they went, round and round, westward, westward, round and round, amidst humanity's applause. In vain. The globe went eastward quicker still, horrible accidents occurred, and the Committee of the Machine, at the time rising into prominence, declared the pursuit illegal, unmechanical, and punishable by Homelessness.

Of Homelessness more will be said later.

Doubtless the Committee was right. Yet the attempt to "defeat the sun" aroused the last common interest that our race experienced about the heavenly bodies, or indeed about anything. It was the last time that men were compacted by thinking of a power outside the world. The sun had conquered, yet it was the end of his spiritual dominion. Dawn, midday, twilight, the zodiacal path, touched neither men's lives not their hearts, and science retreated into the ground, to concentrate herself upon problems that she was certain of solving.

So when Vashti found her cabin invaded by a rosy finger of light, she was annoyed, and tried to adjust the blind. But the blind flew up altogether, and she saw through the skylight small pink clouds, swaying against a background of blue, and as the sun crept higher, its radiance entered direct, brimming down the wall, like a golden sea. It rose and fell with the air-ship's motion, just as waves rise and fall, but it advanced steadily, as a tide advances. Unless she was careful, it would strike her face. A spasm of horror shook her and she rang for the attendant. The attendant too was horrified, but she could do nothing; it was not her place to mend the blind. She could only suggest that the lady should change her cabin, which she accordingly prepared to do.

People were almost exactly alike all over the world, but the attendant of the air-ship, perhaps owing to her exceptional duties, had grown a little out of the common. She had often to address passengers with direct speech, and this had given her a certain roughness and originality of manner. When Vashti swerved away from the sunbeams with a cry, she behaved barbarically—she put out her hand to steady her.

"How dare you!" exclaimed the passenger. "You forget yourself!"

The woman was confused, and apologized for not having let her fall. People never touched one another. The custom had become obsolete, owing to the Machine.

"Where are we now?" asked Vashti haughtily.

"We are over Asia," said the attendant, anxious to be polite.

"Asia?"

"You must excuse my common way of speaking. I have got into the habit of calling places over which I pass by their unmechanical names."

"Oh, I remember Asia. The Mongols came from it."

"Beneath us, in the open air, stood a city that was once called Simla."

"Have you ever heard of the Mongols and of the Brisbane school?"

"No."

"Brisbane also stood in the open air."

"Those mountains to the right—let me show you them." She pushed back a metal blind. The main chain of the Himalayas was revealed. "They were once called the Roof of the World, those mountains."

"What a foolish name!"

"You must remember that, before the dawn of civilisation, they seemed to be an impenetrable wall that touched the stars. It was supposed that no one but the gods could exist above their summits. How we have advanced, thanks to the Machine!"

"How we have advanced, thanks to the Machine!" said Vashti.

"How we have advanced, thanks to the Machine!" echoed the passenger who had dropped his Book the night before, and who was standing in the passage.

"And that white stuff in the cracks?—what is it?"

"I have forgotten its name."

"Cover the window, please. These mountains give me no ideas."

The northern aspect of the Himalayas was in deep shadow: on the Indian slope the sun had just prevailed. The forests had been destroyed during the literature epoch for the purpose of making newspaper-pulp, but the snows were awakening to their morning glory, and clouds still hung on the breasts of Kinchinjunga. In the plain were seen the ruins of cities, with diminished rivers creeping by their walls, and by the sides of these were sometimes the signs of vomitories, marking the cities of today. Over the whole prospect air-ships rushed, crossing the intercrossing with incredible *aplomb*, and rising nonchalantly when they desired to escape the perturbations of the lower atmosphere and to traverse the Roof of the World.

"We have indeed advanced, thanks to the Machine," repeated the attendant, and hid the Himalayas behind a metal blind.

The day dragged wearily forward. The passengers sat each in his cabin, avoiding one another with an almost physical repulsion and longing to be once more under the surface of the earth. There were eight or ten of them, mostly young males, sent out from the public nurseries to inhabit the rooms of those who had died in various parts of the earth. The man who had dropped his Book was on the homeward journey. He had been sent to Sumatra for the purpose of propagating the race. Vashti alone was travelling by her private will.

At midday she took a second glance at the earth. The air-ship was crossing another range of mountains, but she could see little, owing to clouds. Masses of black rock hovered below her, and merged indistinctly into grey. Their shapes were fantastic; one of them resembled a prostrate man.

"No ideas here," murmured Vashti, and hid the Caucasus behind a metal blind.

In the evening she looked again. They were crossing a golden sea, in which lay many small islands and one peninsula.

She repeated, "No ideas here," and hid Greece behind a metal blind.

Part II. The Mending Apparatus

By a vestibule, by a lift, by a tubular railway, by a platform, by a sliding door—by reversing all the steps of her departure did Vashti arrive at her son's room, which exactly resembled her own. She might well declare that the visit was superfluous. The buttons, the knobs, the reading-desk with the Book, the temperature, the atmosphere, the illumination—all were exactly the same. And if Kuno himself, flesh of her flesh, stood close beside her at last, what profit was there in that? She was too well bred to shake him by the hand.

Averting her eyes, she spoke as follows:

"Here I am. I have had the most terrible journey and greatly retarded the development of my soul. It is not worth it, Kuno, it is not worth it. My time is too precious. The sunlight almost touched me, and I have met with the rudest people. I can only stop a few minutes. Say what you want to say, and then I must return."

"I have been threatened with Homelessness," said Kuno.

She looked at him now.

"I have been threatened with Homelessness, and I could not tell you such a thing through the Machine."

Homelessness means death. The victim is exposed to the air, which kills him.

"I have been outside since I spoke to you last. The tremendous thing has happened, and they have discovered me."

"But why shouldn't you go outside?" she exclaimed, "It is perfectly legal, perfectly mechanical, to visit the surface of the earth. I have lately been to a lecture on the sea; there is no objection to that; one simply summons a respirator and gets an Egression-permit. It is not the kind of thing that spiritually minded people do, and I begged you not to do it, but there is no legal objection to it."

"I did not get an Egression-permit."

"Then how did you get out?"

"I found out a way of my own."

The phrase conveyed no meaning to her, and he had to repeat it.

"A way of your own?" she whispered. "But that would be wrong."

"Why?"

The question shocked her beyond measure.

"You are beginning to worship the Machine," he said coldly. "You think it irreligious of me to have found out a way of my own. It was just what the Committee thought, when they threatened me with Homelessness."

At this she grew angry. "I worship nothing!" she cried. "I am most advanced. I don't think you irreligious, for there is no such thing as religion left. All the fear and the superstition that existed once have been destroyed by the Machine. I only meant that to find out a way of your own was—Besides, there is no new way out."

"So it is always supposed."

"Except through the vomitories, for which one must have an Egression-permit, it is impossible to get out. The Book says so."

"Well, the Book's wrong, for I have been out on my feet."

For Kuno was possessed of a certain physical strength.

By these days it was a demerit to be muscular. Each infant was examined at birth, and all who promised undue strength were destroyed. Humanitarians may protest, but it would have been no true kindness to let an athlete live; he would never have been happy in that state of life to which the Machine had called him; he would have yearned for trees to climb, rivers to bathe in, meadows and hills against which he might measure his body. Man must be adapted to his surroundings, must he not? In the dawn of the world our weakly must be exposed on Mount Taygetus, in its twilight our strong will suffer euthanasia, that the Machine may progress, that the Machine may progress, that the Machine may progress eternally.

"You know that we have lost the sense of space." We say "space is annihilated," but we have annihilated not space, but the sense thereof. We have lost a part of ourselves. I determined to recover it, and I began by walking up and down the platform of the railway outside my room. Up and down, until I was tired, and so did recapture the meaning of "Near" and "Far." "Near" is a place to which I can get quickly *on my feet*, not a place to which the train or the air-ship will take me quickly. "Far" is a place to which I cannot get quickly on my feet; the vomitory is "far," though I could be there in thirty-eight seconds by summoning the train. Man is the measure. That was my first lesson. Man's feet are the measure for distance, his hands are the measure for ownership, his body is the measure for all that is lovable and desirable and strong. Then I went further: it was then that I called to you for the first time, and you would not come.

"This city, as you know, is built deep beneath the surface of the earth, with only the vomitories protruding. Having paced the platform outside my own room, I took the lift to the next platform and paced that also, and so with each in turn, until I came to the topmost, above which begins the earth. All the platforms were exactly alike, and all that I gained by visiting them was to develop my sense of space and my muscles. I think I should have been content with this—it is not a little thing,—but as I walked and brooded, it occurred to me that our cities had been built in the days when men still breathed the outer air, and that there had been ventilation shafts for the workmen. I could think of nothing but these ventilation shafts. Had they been destroyed by all the food-tubes and medicine-tubes and music-tubes that the Machine has evolved lately? Or did traces of them remain? One thing was certain. If I came upon them anywhere, it would be in the railway-tunnels of the topmost story. Everywhere else, all space was accounted for.

"I am telling my story quickly, but don't think that I was not a coward or that your answers never depressed me. It is not the proper thing, it is not mechanical, it is not decent to walk along a railway-tunnel. I did not fear that I might tread upon a live rail and be killed. I feared something far more intangible—doing what was not contemplated by the Machine. Then I said to myself, 'Man is the measure,' and I went, and after many visits I found an opening.

"The tunnels, of course, were lighted. Everything is light, artificial light; darkness is the exception. So when I saw a black gap in the tiles, I knew that it was an exception, and rejoiced. I put in my arm—I could put in no more at first—and waved it round and round in ecstasy. I loosened another tile, and put in my head, and shouted into the darkness: 'I am coming, I shall do it yet,' and my voice reverberated down endless passages. I seemed to hear the spirits of those dead workmen who had returned each evening to the starlight and to their wives, and all the generations who had lived in the open air called back to me, 'You will do it yet, you are coming.'"

He paused, and, absurd as he was, his last words moved her. For Kuno had lately asked to be a father, and his request had been refused by the Committee. His was not a type that the Machine desired to hand on.

"Then a train passed. It brushed by me, but I thrust my head and arms into the hole. I had done enough for one day, so I crawled back to the platform, went down in the lift, and summoned my bed. Ah what dreams! And again I called you, and again you refused."

She shook her head and said:

"Don't. Don't talk of these terrible things. You make me miserable. You are throwing civilisation away."

"But I had got back the sense of space and a man cannot rest then. I determined to get in at the hole and climb the shaft. And so I exercised my arms. Day after day I went through ridiculous movements, until my flesh ached, and I could hang by my hands and hold the pillow of my bed outstretched for many minutes. Then I summoned a respirator, and started.

"It was easy at first. The mortar had somehow rotted, and I soon pushed some more tiles in, and clambered after them into the darkness, and the spirits of the dead comforted me. I don't know what I mean by that. I just say what I felt. I felt, for the first time, that a protest had been lodged against corruption, and that even as the dead were comforting me, so I was comforting the unborn. I felt that humanity existed, and that it existed without clothes. How can I possibly explain this? It was naked, humanity seemed naked, and all these tubes and buttons and machineries neither came into the world with us, nor will they follow us out, nor do they matter supremely while we are here. Had I been strong, I would have torn off every garment I had, and gone out into the outer air unswaddled. But this is not for me, nor perhaps for my generation. I climbed with my respirator and my hygienic clothes and my dietetic tabloids! Better thus than not at all.

"There was a ladder, made of some primæval metal. The light from the railway fell upon its lowest rungs, and I saw that it led straight upwards out of the rubble at the bottom of the shaft. Perhaps our ancestors ran up and down it a dozen times daily, in their building. As I climbed, the rough edges cut through my gloves so that my hands bled. The light helped me for a little, and then came darkness and, worse still, silence which pierced my ears like a sword. The Machine hums! Did you know that? Its hum penetrates our blood, and may even guide our thoughts. Who knows! I was getting beyond its power. Then I thought: 'This silence means that I am doing wrong.' But I heard voices in the silence, and again they strengthened me." He laughed. "I had need of them. The next moment I cracked my head against something."

She sighed.

"I had reached one of those pneumatic stoppers that defend us from the outer air. You may have noticed them on the air-ship. Pitch dark, my feet on the rungs of an invisible ladder, my hands cut; I cannot explain how I lived through this part, but the voices still comforted me, and I felt for fastenings. The stopper, I suppose, was about eight feet across. I passed my hand over it as far as I could reach. It was perfectly smooth. I felt it almost to the centre. Not quite to the centre, for my arm was too short. Then the voice said: 'Jump. It is worth it. There may be a handle in the centre, and you may catch hold of it and so come to us your own way. And if there is no handle, so that you may fall and are dashed to pieces—it is still worth it: you will still come to us your own way.' So I jumped. There was a handle, and—"

He paused. Tears gathered in his mother's eyes. She knew that he was fated. If he did not die today he would die tomorrow. There was not room for such a person in the world. And with her pity disgust mingled. She was ashamed at having borne such a son, she who had always been so respectable and so full of ideas. Was he really the little boy to whom she had taught the use of his stops and buttons, and to whom she had given his first lessons in the Book? The very hair that disfigured his lip showed that he was reverting to some savage type. On atavism the Machine can have no mercy.

"There was a handle, and I did catch it. I hung tranced over the darkness and heard the hum of these workings as the last whisper in a dying dream. All the things I had cared about and all the people I had spoken to through tubes appeared infinitely little. Meanwhile the handle revolved. My weight had set something in motion and I span slowly, and then—

"I cannot describe it. I was lying with my face to the sunshine. Blood poured from my nose and ears and I heard a tremendous roaring. The stopper, with me clinging to it, had simply been blown out of the earth, and the air that we make down here was escaping through the vent into the air above. It burst up like a fountain. I crawled back to it—for the upper air hurts—and, as it were, I took great sips from the edge. My respirator had flown goodness knows where, my clothes were torn. I just lay with my lips close to the hole, and I sipped until the bleeding stopped. You can imagine nothing so curious. This hollow in the grass—I will speak of it in a minute,—the sun shining into it, not brilliantly but through marbled clouds,—the peace, the nonchalance, the sense of space, and, brushing my cheek, the roaring fountain of our artificial air! Soon I spied my respirator, bobbing up and down in the current high above my head, and higher still were many air-ships. But no one ever looks out of air-ships, and in any case they could not have picked me up. There I was, stranded. The sun shone a little way down the shaft, and revealed the topmost rung of the ladder, but it was hopeless trying to reach it. I should either have been tossed up again by the escape, or else have fallen in, and died. I could only lie on the grass, sipping and sipping, and from time to time glancing around me.

"I knew that I was in Wessex, for I had taken care to go to a lecture on the subject before starting. Wessex lies above the room in which we are talking now. It was once an important state. Its kings held all the southern coast from the Andredswald to Cornwall, while the Wansdyke protected them on the north, running over the high ground. The lecturer was only concerned with the rise of Wessex, so I do not know how long it remained an international power, nor would the knowledge have assisted me. To tell the truth I could do nothing but laugh, during this part. There was I, with a pneumatic stopper by my side and a respirator bobbing over my head, imprisoned, all three of us, in a grass-grown hollow that was edged with fern."

Then he grew grave again.

"Lucky for me that it was a hollow. For the air began to fall back into it and to fill it as water fills a bowl. I could crawl about. Presently I stood. I breathed a mixture, in which the air that hurts predominated whenever I tried to climb the sides. This was not so bad. I had not lost my tabloids and remained ridiculously cheerful, and as for the Machine, I forgot about it altogether. My one aim now was to get to the top, where the ferns were, and to view whatever objects lay beyond.

"I rushed the slope. The new air was still too bitter for me and I came rolling back, after a momentary vision of something grey. The sun grew very feeble, and I remembered that he was in Scorpio—I had been to a lecture on that too. If the sun is in Scorpio and you are in Wessex, it means that you must be as quick as you can, or it will get too dark. (This is the first bit of useful information I have ever got from a lecture, and I expect it will be the last.) It made me try frantically to breathe the new air, and to advance as far as I dared out of my pond. The hollow filled so slowly. At times I thought that the fountain played with less vigour. My respirator seemed to dance nearer the earth; the roar was decreasing."

He broke off.

"I don't think this is interesting you. The rest will interest you even less. There are no Ideas in it, and I wish that I had not troubled you to come. We are too different, mother."

She told him to continue.

"It was evening before I climbed the bank. The sun had very nearly slipped out of the sky by this time, and I could not get a good view. You, who have just crossed the Roof of the World, will not want to hear an account of the little hills that I saw—low colourless hills. But to me they were living and the turf that covered them was a skin, under which their muscles rippled, and I felt that those hills had called with incalculable force to men in the past, and that men had loved them. Now they sleep—perhaps for ever. They commune with humanity in dreams. Happy the man, happy the woman, who awakes the hills of Wessex. For though they sleep, they will never die."

His voice rose passionately.

"Cannot you see, cannot all your lecturers see, that it is we that are dying, and that down here the only thing that really lives is the Machine? We created the Machine, to do our will, but we cannot make it do our will now. It has robbed us of the sense of space and of the sense of touch, it has blurred every human relation and narrowed down love to a carnal act, it has paralysed our bodies and our wills, and now it compels us to worship it. The Machine develops—but not on our lines. The Machine proceeds—but not to our goal. We only exist as the blood corpuscles that course through its arteries, and if it could work without us, it would let us die. Oh, I have no remedy—or, at least, only one—to tell men again and again that I have seen the hills of Wessex as Ælfrid saw them when he overthrew the Danes.

"So the sun set. I forgot to mention that a belt of mist lay between my hill and other hills, and that it was the colour of pearl."

He broke off for the second time.

"Go on," said his mother wearily.

He shook his head.

"Go on. Nothing that you say can distress me now. I am hardened."

"I had meant to tell you the rest, but I cannot: I know that I cannot: good-bye."

Vashti stood irresolute. All her nerves were tingling with his blasphemies. But she was also inquisitive.

"This is unfair," she complained. "You have called me across the world to hear your story, and hear it I will. Tell me—as briefly as possible, for this is a disastrous waste of time—tell me how you returned to civilization."

"Oh—that!" he said, starting. "You would like to hear about civilisation. Certainly. Had I got to where my respirator fell down?"

"No—but I understand everything now. You put on your respirator, and managed to walk along the surface of the earth to a vomitory, and there your conduct was reported to the Central Committee."

"By no means."

He passed his hand over his forehead, as if dispelling some strong impression. Then, resuming his narrative, he warmed to it again.

"My respirator fell about sunset. I had mentioned that the fountain seemed feebler, had I not?"

"Yes."

"About sunset, it let the respirator fall. As I said, I had entirely for-gotten about the Machine, and I paid no great attention at the time, being occupied with other things. I had my pool of air, into which I could dip when the outer keenness became intolerable, and which would possibly remain for days, provided that no wind sprang up to disperse it. Not until it was too late did I realize what the stoppage of the escape implied. You see—the gap in the tunnel had been mended; the Mending Apparatus; the Mending Apparatus, was after me.

"One other warning I had, but I neglected it. The sky at night was clearer than it had been in the day, and the moon, which was about half the sky behind the sun, shone into the dell at moments quite brightly. I was in my usual place—on the boundary between the two atmospheres—when I thought I saw something dark move across the bottom of the dell, and vanish into the shaft. In my folly, I ran down. I bent over and listened, and I thought I heard a faint scraping noise in the depths.

"At this—but it was too late—I took alarm. I determined to put on my respirator and to walk right out of the dell. But my respirator had gone. I knew exactly where it had fallen—between the stopper and the aperture—and I could even feel the mark that it had made in the turf. It had gone, and I realised that something evil was at work, and I had better escape to the other air, and, if I must die, die running towards the cloud that had been the colour of a pearl. I never started. Out of the shaft—it is too horrible. A worm, a long white worm, had crawled out of the shaft and was gliding over the moonlit grass.

"I screamed. I did everything that I should not have done, I stamped upon the creature instead of flying from it, and it at once curled round the ankle. Then we fought. The worm let me run all over the dell, but edged up my leg as I ran. 'Help!' I cried. (That part is too awful. It belongs to the part that you will never know.) 'Help!' I cried. (Why cannot we suf-fer in silence?) 'Help!' I cried. Then my feet were wound together, I fell, I was dragged away from the dear ferns and the living hills, and past the great metal stopper (I can tell you this part), and I thought it might save me again if I caught hold of the handle. It also was enwrapped, it also. Oh, the whole dell was full of the things. They were searching it in all direc-tions, they were denuding it, and the white snouts of others peeped out of the hole, ready if needed. Everything that could be moved they brought—brushwood, bundles of fern, everything, and down we all went inter-twined into hell. The last things that I saw, ere the stopper closed after us, were certain stars, and I felt that a man of my sort lived in the sky. For I did fight, I fought till the very end, and it was only my head hitting against the ladder that quieted me. I woke up in this room. The worms had vanished. I was surrounded by artificial air, artificial light, artificial peace, and my friends were calling to me down speaking-tubes to know whether I had come across any new ideas lately."

Here his story ended. Discussion of it was impossible, and Vashti turned to go.

"It will end in Homelessness," she said quietly.

"I wish it would," retorted Kuno.

"The Machine has been most merciful."

"I prefer the mercy of God."

"By that superstitious phrase, do you mean that you could live in the outer air?"

"Yes."

"Have you ever seen, round the vomitories, the bones of those who were extruded after the Great Rebellion?"

"Yes."

"They were left where they perished for our edification. A few crawled away, but they perished, too—who can doubt it? And so with the Homeless of our own day. The surface of the earth supports life no longer."

"Indeed."

"Ferns and a little grass may survive, but all higher forms have perished. Has any air-ship detected them?"

"No."

"Has any lecturer dealt with them?"

"No."

"Then why this obstinacy?"

"Because I have seen them," he exploded.

"Seen *what*?"

"Because I have seen her in the twilight—because she came to my help when I called—because she, too, was entangled by the worms, and, luckier than I, was killed by one of them piercing her throat."

He was mad. Vashti departed, nor, in the troubles that followed, did she ever see his face again.

Part III. *The Homeless*

During the years that followed Kuno's escapade, two important developments took place in the Machine. On the surface they were revolutionary, but in either case men's minds had been prepared beforehand, and they did but express tendencies that were latent already.

The first of these was the abolition of respirators.

Advanced thinkers, like Vashti, had always held it foolish to visit the surface of the earth. Air-ships might be necessary, but what was the good of going out for mere curiosity and crawling along for a mile or two in a terrestrial motor? The habit was vulgar and perhaps faintly improper: it was unproductive of ideas, and had no connection with the habits that really mattered. So respirators were abolished, and with them, of course, the terrestrial motors, and except for a few lecturers, who complained that they were debarred access to their subject-matter, the development was accepted quietly. Those who still wanted to know what the earth was like had after all only to listen to some gramophone, or to look into some cinematophote. And even the lecturers acquiesced when they found that a lecture on the sea was none the less stimulating when compiled out of other lectures that had already been delivered on the same subject. "Beware of first-hand ideas!" exclaimed one of the most advanced of them. "First-hand ideas do not really exist. They are but the physical impressions produced by love and fear, and on this gross foundation who could erect a philosophy? Let your ideas be second-hand, and if possible tenth-hand, for then they will be far removed from that disturbing element—direct observation. Do not learn anything about this subject of mine—the French Revolution. Learn instead what I think that Enicharmon thought Urizen thought Gutch thought Ho-Yung thought Chi-Bo-Sing thought Lafcadio Hearn thought Carlyle thought Mirabeau said about the French Revolution. Through the medium of these eight great minds, the blood that was shed at Paris and the windows that were broken at Versailles will be clarified to an Idea which you may employ most profitably in your daily lives. But be sure that the intermediates are many and varied, for in history one authority exists to counteract another. Urizen must counteract the scepticism of Ho-Yung and Enicharmon, I must myself counteract the impetuosity of Gutch. You who listen to me are in a better position to judge about the French Revolution than I am. Your descendants will be even in a better position than you, for they will learn what you think I think, and yet another intermediate will be added to the chain. And in time"—his voice rose—"there will come a generation that has got beyond facts, beyond impressions, a generation absolutely colourless, a generation

    'seraphically free
    From taint of personality,'

which will see the French Revolution not as it happened, nor as they would like it to have happened, but as it would have happened, had it taken place in the days of the Machine."

Tremendous applause greeted this lecture, which did but voice a feeling already latent in the minds of men—a feeling that terrestrial facts must be ignored, and that the abolition of respirators was a positive gain. It was even suggested that air-ships should be abolished too. This was not done, because air-ships had somehow worked themselves into the Machine's system. But year by year they were used less, and mentioned less by thoughtful men.

The second great development was the re-establishment of religion.

This, too, had been voiced in the celebrated lecture. No one could mistake the reverent tone in which the peroration had concluded, and it awakened a responsive echo in the heart of each. Those who had long worshipped silently, now began to talk. They described the strange feeling of peace that came over them when they handled the Book of the Machine, the pleasure that it was to repeat certain numerals out of it, however little meaning those numerals conveyed to the outward ear, the ecstasy of touching a button, however unimportant, or of ringing an electric bell, however superfluously.

"The Machine," they exclaimed, "feeds us and clothes us and houses us; through it we speak to one another, through it we see one another, in it we have our being. The Machine is the friend of ideas and the enemy of superstition: the Machine is omnipotent, eternal; blessed is the Machine." And before long this allocution was printed on the first page of the Book, and in subsequent editions the ritual swelled into a complicated system of praise and prayer. The word "religion" was sedulously avoided, and in theory the Machine was still the creation and the implement of man. But in practice all, save a few retrogrades, worshipped it as divine. Nor was it worshipped in unity. One believer would be chiefly impressed by the blue optic plates, through which he saw other believers; another by the mending apparatus, which sinful Kuno had compared to worms; another by the lifts, another by the Book. And each would pray to this or to that, and ask it to intercede for him with the Machine as a whole. Persecution— that also was present. It did not break out, for reasons that will be set forward shortly. But it was latent, and all who did not accept the minimum known as "undenominational Mechanism" lived in danger of Homelessness, which means death, as we know.

To attribute these two great developments to the Central Committee, is to take a very narrow view of civilization. The Central Committee announced the developments, it is true, but they were no more the cause of them than were the Kings of the imperialistic period the cause of war. Rather did they yield to some invincible pressure, which came no one knew whither, and which, when gratified, was succeeded by some new pressure equally invincible. To such a state of affairs it is convenient to give the name of Progress. No one confessed the Machine was out of hand. Year by year it was served with increased efficiency and decreased intelligence. The better a man knew his own duties upon it, the less he understood the duties of his neighbor, and in all the world there was not one who understood the monster as a whole. Those master brains had perished. They had left full directions, it is true, and their successors had each of them mastered a portion of those directions. But Humanity, in its desire for comfort, had over-reached itself. It had exploited the riches of nature too far. Quietly and complacently, it was sinking into decadence, and Progress had come to mean the Progress of the Machine.

As for Vashti, her life went peacefully forward until the final disaster. She made her room dark and slept; she awoke and made the room light. She lectured and attended lectures. She exchanged ideas with her innumerable friends and believed she was growing more spiritual. At times a friend was granted Euthanasia, and left his or her room for the Homelessness that is beyond all human conception. Vashti did not much mind. After an unsuccessful lecture, she would sometimes ask for Euthanasia herself. But the death-rate was not permitted to exceed the birth-rate, and the Machine had hitherto refused it to her.

The troubles began quietly, long before she was conscious of them.

One day she was astonished at receiving a message from her son. They never communicated, having nothing in common, and she had only heard indirectly that he was still alive, and had been transferred from the northern hemisphere, where he had behaved so mischievously, to the southern—indeed, to a room not far from her own.

"Does he want me to visit him?" she thought. "Never again, never. And I have not the time."

No, it was madness of another kind.

He refused to visualize his face upon the blue plate, and speaking out of the darkness with solemnity said:

"The Machine stops."

"What do you say?"

"The Machine is stopping, I know it, I know the signs." She burst into a peal of laughter. He heard her and was angry, and they spoke no more.

"Can you imagine anything more absurd?" she cried to a friend. "A man who was my son believes that the Machine is stopping. It would be impious if it was not mad."

"The Machine is stopping?" her friend replied. "What does that mean? The phrase conveys nothing to me."

"Nor to me."

"He does not refer, I suppose, to the trouble there has been lately with the music?"

"Oh no, of course not. Let us talk about music."

"Have you complained to the authorities?"

"Yes, and they say it wants mending, and referred me to the Committee of the Mending Apparatus. I complained of those curious gasping sighs that disfigure the symphonies of the Brisbane school. They sound like some one in pain. The Committee of the Mending Apparatus say that it shall be remedied shortly."

Obscurely worried, she resumed her life. For one thing, the defect in the music irritated her. For another thing, she could not forget Kuno's speech. If he had known that the music was out of repair—he could not know it, for he detested music—if he had known that it was wrong, "the Machine stops" was exactly the venomous sort of remark he would have made. Of course he had made it at a venture, but the coincidence annoyed her, and she spoke with some petulance to the Committee of the Mending Apparatus.

They replied, as before, that the defect would be set right shortly.

"Shortly! At once!" she retorted. "Why should I be worried by imperfect music? Things are always put right at once. If you do not mend it at once, I shall complain to the Central Committee."

"No personal complaints are received by the Central Committee," the Committee of the Mending Apparatus replied.

"Through whom am I to make my complaint, then?"

"Through us."

"I complain then."

"Your complaint shall be forwarded in its turn."

"Have others complained?"

This question was unmechanical, and the Committee of the Mending Apparatus refused to answer it.

"It is too bad!" she exclaimed to another of her friends. "There never was such an unfortunate woman as myself. I can never be sure of my music now. It gets worse and worse each time I summon it."

"I too have my troubles," the friend replied. "Sometimes my ideas are interrupted by a slight jarring noise."

"What is it?"

"I do not know whether it is inside my head, or inside the wall."

"Complain, in either case."

"I have complained, and my complaint will be forwarded in its turn to the Central Committee."

Time passed, and they resented the defects no longer. The defects had not been remedied, but the human tissues in that latter day had become so subservient, that they readily adapted themselves to every caprice of the Machine. The sigh at the crisis of the Brisbane symphony no longer irritated Vashti; she accepted it as part of the melody. The jarring noise, whether in the head or in the wall, was no longer resented by her friend. And so with the moldy artificial fruit, so with the bath water that began to stink, so with the defective rhymes that the poetry machine had taken to emit. All were bitterly complained of at first, and then acquiesced in and forgotten. Things went from bad to worse unchallenged.

It was otherwise with the failure of the sleeping apparatus. That was a more serious stoppage. There came a day when over the whole world—in Sumatra, in Wessex, in the innumerable cities of Courland and Brazil—the beds, when summoned by their tired owners, failed to appear. It may seem a ludicrous matter, but from it we may date the collapse of humanity. The Committee responsible for the failure was assailed by complainants, whom it referred, as usual, to the Committee of the Mending Apparatus, who in its turn assured them that their complaints would be forwarded to the Central Committee. But the discontent grew, for mankind was not yet sufficiently adaptable to do without sleep.

"Some one is meddling with the Machine—" they began.

"Some one is trying to make himself king, to reintroduce the personal element."

"Punish that man with Homelessness."

"To the rescue! Avenge the Machine! Avenge the Machine!"

"War! Kill the man!"

But the Committee of the Mending Apparatus now came forward, and allayed the panic with well-chosen words. It confessed that the Mending Apparatus was itself in need of repair.

The effect of this frank confession was admirable.

"Of course," said a famous lecturer—he of the French Revolution, who gilded each new decay with splendor—"of course we shall not press our complaints now. The Mending Apparatus has treated us so well in the past that we all sympathise with it, and will wait patiently for its recovery. In its own good time it will resume its duties. Meanwhile let us do without our beds, our tabloids, our other little wants. Such, I feel sure, would be the wish of the Machine."

Thousands of miles away his audience applauded. The Machine still linked them. Under the seas, beneath the roots of the mountains, ran the wires through which they saw and heard, the enormous eyes and ears that were their heritage, and the hum of many workings clothed their thoughts in one garment of subserviency. Only the old and the sick remained ungrateful, for it was rumored that Euthanasia, too, was out of order, and that pain had reappeared among men.

It became difficult to read. A blight entered the atmosphere and dulled its luminosity. At times Vashti could scarcely see across her room. The air, too, was foul. Loud were the complaints, impotent the remedies, heroic the tone of the lecturer as he cried: "Courage! courage! What matter so long as the Machine goes on? To it the darkness and the light are one." And though things improved again after a time, the old brilliancy was never recaptured, and humanity never recovered from its entrance into twilight. There was an hysterical talk of "measures," of "provisional dictatorship," and the inhabitants of Sumatra were asked to familiarize themselves with the workings of the central power station, the said power station being situated in France. But for the most part panic reigned, and men spent their strength praying to their Books, tangible proofs of the Machine's omnipotence. There were gradations of terror—at times came rumors of hope—the Mending Apparatus was almost mended—the enemies of the Machine had been got under—new "nerve-centres" were evolving which would do the work even more magnificently than before. But there came a day when, without the slightest warning, without any previous hint of feebleness, the entire communication-system broke down, all over the world, and the world, as they understood it, ended.

Vashti was lecturing at the time and her earlier remarks had been punctuated with applause. As she proceeded the audience became silent, and at the conclusion there was no sound. Somewhat displeased, she called to a friend who was a specialist in sympathy. No sound: doubtless the friend was sleeping. And so with the next friend whom she tried to summon, and so with the next, until she remembered Kuno's cryptic remark, "The Machine stops."

The phrase still conveyed nothing. If Eternity was stopping it would of course be set going shortly.

For example, there was still a little light and air—the atmosphere had improved a few hours previously. There was still the Book, and while there was the Book there was security.

Then she broke down, for with the cessation of activity came an unexpected terror—silence.

She had never known silence, and the coming of it nearly killed her—it did kill many thousands of people outright. Ever since her birth she had been surrounded by the steady hum. It was to the ear what artificial air was to the lungs, and agonizing pains shot across her head. And scarcely knowing what she did, she stumbled forward and pressed the unfamiliar button, the one that opened the door of her cell.

Now the door of the cell worked on a simple hinge of its own. It was not connected with the central power station, dying far away in France. It opened, rousing immoderate hopes in Vashti, for she thought that the Machine had been mended. It opened, and she saw the dim tunnel that curved far away towards freedom. One look, and then she shrank back. For the tunnel was full of people—she was almost the last in that city to have taken alarm.

People at any time repelled her, and these were nightmares from her worst dreams. People were crawling about, people were screaming, whimpering, gasping for breath, touching each other, vanishing in the dark, and ever and anon being pushed off the platform on to the live rail. Some were fighting round the electric bells, trying to summon trains which could not be summoned. Others were yelling for Euthanasia or for respirators, or blaspheming the Machine. Others stood at the doors of their cells fearing, like herself, either to stop in them or to leave them. And behind all the uproar was silence—the silence which is the voice of the earth and of the generations who have gone.

No—it was worse than solitude. She closed the door again and sat down to wait for the end. The disintegration went on, accompanied by horrible cracks and rumbling. The valves that restrained the Medical Apparatus must have been weakened, for it ruptured and hung hideously from the ceiling. The floor heaved and fell and flung her from her chair. A tube oozed towards her serpent fashion. And at last the final horror approached—light began to ebb, and she knew that civilization's long day was closing.

She whirled round, praying to be saved from this, at any rate, kissing the Book, pressing button after button. The uproar outside was increasing, and even penetrated the wall. Slowly the brilliancy of her cell was dimmed, the reflections faded from the metal switches. Now she could not see the reading-stand, now not the Book, though she held it in her hand. Light followed the flight of sound, air was following light, and the original void returned to the cavern from which it had been so long excluded. Vashti continued to whirl, like the devotees of an earlier religion, screaming, praying, striking at the buttons with bleeding hands.

It was thus that she opened her prison and escaped—escaped in the spirit: at least so it seems to me, ere my meditation closes. That she escapes in the body—I cannot perceive that. She struck, by chance, the switch that released the door, and the rush of foul air on her skin, the loud throbbing whispers in her ears, told her that she was facing the tunnel again, and that tremendous platform on which she had seen men fighting. They were not fighting now. Only the whispers remained, and the little whimpering groans. They were dying by hundreds out in the dark.

She burst into tears.

Tears answered her.

They wept for humanity, those two, not for themselves. They could not bear that this should be the end. Ere silence was completed their hearts were opened, and they knew what had been important on the earth. Man, the flower of all flesh, the noblest of all creatures visible, man who had once made god in his image, and had mirrored his strength on the constellations, beautiful naked man was dying, strangled in the garments that he had woven. Century after century had he toiled, and here was his reward. Truly the garment had seemed heavenly at first, shot with colors of culture, sewn with the threads of self-denial. And heavenly it had been so long as it was a garment and no more, so long as man could shed it at will and live by the essence that is his soul, and the essence, equally divine, that is his body. The sin against the body—it was for that they wept in chief; the centuries of wrong against the muscles and the nerves, and those five portals by which we can alone apprehend—glossing it over with talk of evolution, until the body was white pap, the home of ideas as colorless, last sloshy stirrings of a spirit that had grasped the stars.

"Where are you?" she sobbed.

His voice in the darkness said, "Here."

"Is there any hope, Kuno?"

"None for us."

"Where are you?" She crawled towards him over the bodies of the dead. His blood spurted over her hands.

"Quicker," he gasped, "I am dying—but we touch, we talk, not through the Machine."

He kissed her.

"We have come back to our own. We die, but we have recaptured life, as it was in Wessex, when Ælfrid overthrew the Danes. We know what they know outside, they who dwelt in the cloud that is the colour of a pearl."

"But Kuno, is it true? Are there still men on the surface of the earth? Is this—this tunnel, this poisoned darkness—really not the end?"

He replied:

"I have seen them, spoken to them, loved them. They are hiding in the mist and the ferns until our civilisation stops. Today they are the Homeless—tomorrow—"

"Oh, tomorrow—some fool will start the Machine again, tomorrow."

"Never," said Kuno, "never. Humanity has learnt its lesson."

As he spoke, the whole city was broken like a honeycomb. An air-ship had sailed in through the vomitory into a ruined wharf. It crashed downwards, exploding as it went, rending gallery after gallery with its wings of steel. For a moment they saw the nations of the dead, and, ere they joined them, scraps of the untainted sky.

"Rust"

by Joseph E. Kelleam*

Joseph E. Kelleam (1913–1975) was born in Boswell, Oklahoma. He was a reliable, although not particularly prolific, contributor to the world of science fiction for most of his life, hitting his stride with a series of space travel/alien wars novels in the 1960s. His most enduring character is Jack Odin, who is based on Norse mythology and who does battle with villains in a landscape populated by mythic folk who would feel equally at home in a J.R.R. Tolkien novel. "Rust" appeared in the October 1939 issue of *Astounding*. This is Kelleam's first published story, and it has been translated into German and Italian and has appeared in several anthologies. Published at the dawn of the Atomic Age, the story stands as an indictment of humanity's inability to use their powerful inventions in the service of good. The mechanical protagonists of "Rust" wonder whether humanity is wise enough to handle ethically the fruits of its ingenuity. In a story where the machines did exactly what they were designed to do and with apocalyptic consequences, the answer is a resounding and tragic no.

* * * * *

The sun, rising over the hills, cast long shadows across the patches of snow and bathed the crumbling ruins in pale light. Had men been there they could have reckoned the month to be August. But men had gone, long since, and the sun had waned; and now, in this late period of the earth's age, the short spring was awakening.

Within the broken city, in a mighty-columned hall that still supported a part of a roof, life of a sort was stirring. Three grotesque creatures were moving, their limbs creaking dolefully.

X-120 faced the new day and the new spring with a feeling of exhilaration that nearly drove the age-old loneliness and emptiness from the

---

*Kelleam, Joseph E. "Rust." *Astounding* 24, no. 2, October 1939, pp. 134–140.

corroded metal of what might be called his brain. The sun was the source of his energy, even as it had been the source of the fleshy life before him; and with the sun's reappearance he felt new strength coursing through the wires and coils and gears of his complex body.

He and his companions were highly developed robots, the last ever to be made by the Earthmen. X-120 consisted of a globe of metal, eight feet in diameter, mounted upon four many-jointed legs. At the top of this globe was a protuberance like a kaiser's helmet which caught and stored his power from the rays of the sun.

From the "face" of the globe two ghostly quartz eyes bulged. The globe was divided by a heavy band of metal at its middle, and from this band, at each side, extended a long arm ending in a powerful claw. This claw was like the pincers of a lobster and had been built to shear through metal. Four long cables, which served as auxiliary arms, were drawn up like springs against the body.

X-120 stepped from the shadows of the broken hall into the ruined street. The sun's rays striking against his tarnished sides sent new strength coursing through his body. He had forgotten how many springs he had seen. Many generations of twisted oaks that grew among the ruins had sprung up and fallen since X-120 and his companions had been made. Countless hundreds of springs had flitted across the dying earth since the laughter and dreams and follies of men had ceased to disturb those crumbling walls.

"The sunlight is warm," called X-120. "Come out, G-3a and L-1716. I feel young again."

His companions lumbered into the sunlight. G-3a had lost one leg, and moved slowly and with difficulty. The steel of his body was nearly covered with red rust, and the copper and aluminum alloys that completed his make-up were pitted with deep stains of greenish black. L-1716 was not so badly tarnished, but he had lost one arm; and the four auxiliary cables were broken and dangled from his sides like trailing wires. Of the three X-120 was the best preserved. He still had the use of all his limbs, and here and there on his body shone the gleam of untarnished metal. His masters had made him well.

The crippled G-3a looked about him and whined like an old, old man. "It will surely rain," he shivered. "I cannot stand another rain."

"Nonsense," said L-1716, his broken arms, scraping along the ground as he moved, "there is not a cloud in the sky. Already I feel better."

G-3a looked about him in fear. "And are we all?" he questioned. "Last winter there were twelve."

X-120 had been thinking of the other nine, all that had been left of the countless horde that men had once fashioned. "The nine were to winter in the jade tower," he explained. "We will go there. Perhaps they do not think it is time to venture out."

"I cannot leave my work," grated G-3a. "There is so little time left. I have almost reached the goal." His whirring voice was raised to a pitch of triumph. "Soon I shall make living robots, even as men made us."

"The old story," sighed L-1716. "How long have we been working to make robots who will take our places? And what have we made? Usually nothing but lifeless blobs of steel. Sometimes we have fashioned mad things that had to be destroyed. But never in all the years have we made a single robot that resembled ourselves."

* * *

X-120 stood in the broken street, and the sunlight made a shimmering over his rust-dappled sides.

"That is where we have failed," he mused as he looked at his clawlike arms. "We have tried to make robots like ourselves. Men did not make us for life; they fashioned us for death." He waved his huge lobster claw in the air.

"What was this made for? Was it made for the shaping of other robots? Was it made to fashion anything? Blades like that were made for slaughter—nothing else."

"Even so," whined the crippled robot, "I have nearly succeeded. With help I can win."

"And have we ever refused to help?" snapped L-1716. "You are getting old, G-3a. All winter you have worked in that little dark room, never allowing us to enter."

There was a metallic cackle in G-3a's voice. "But I have nearly won. They said I wouldn't, but I have nearly won. I need help. One more operation. If it succeeds, the robots may yet rebuild the world."

Reluctantly X-120 followed the two back into the shadowy ruins. It was dark in there; but their round, glassy eyes had been made for both day and night.

"See," squeaked old G-3a, as he pointed to a metal skeleton upon the floor. "I have remade a robot from parts that I took from the scrap heap. It is perfect, all but the brain. Still, I believe this will work." He motioned to a gleaming object upon a littered table. It was a huge copper sphere with two black squares of a tarlike substance set into it. At the pole opposite from these squares was a protuberance no larger than a man's fist.

"This," said G-3a thoughtfully, "is the only perfect brain that I could find. You see, I am not trying to create something; I am merely rebuilding. Those"—he nodded to the black squares—"are the sensory organs. The visions from the eyes are flashed upon these as though they were screens. Beyond those eyes is the response mechanism, thousands and thousands of photo-electric cells. Men made it so that it would react mechanically to certain images. Movement, the simple avoidance of objects, the urge to kill, these are directed by the copper sphere.

"Beyond this"—he gestured to the bulge at the back of the brain—"is the thought mechanism. It is what made us different from other machines."

"It is very small," mocked X-120.

"So it is," replied G-3a. "I have heard that it was the reverse with the brains of men. But enough! See, this must fit into the body—so. The black squares rest behind the eyes. That wire brings energy to the brain, and those coils are connected to the power unit which operates the arms and legs. That wire goes to the balancing mechanism—" He droned on and on, explaining each part carefully. "And now," he finished, "someone must connect it. I cannot."

L-1716 stared at his one rusty claw with confusion. Then both he and G-3a were looking at X-120.

"I can only try," offered the robot. "But remember what I said. We were not fashioned to make anything; only to kill."

* * *

Clumsily he lifted the copper sphere and its cluster of wires from the table. He worked slowly and carefully. One by one the huge claws crimped the tiny wires together. The job was nearly finished. Then the great pincers, hovering so carefully above the last wire, came into contact with another. There was a flash as the power short-circuited. X-120 reeled back. The copper sphere melted and ran before their eyes.

X-120 huddled against the far wall. "It is as I said," he moaned; "we can build nothing. We were not made to work at anything. We were only made for one purpose, to kill." He looked at his bulky claws, and shook them as though he might cast them away."

"Do not take on so," pacified old G-3a. "Perhaps it is just as well. We are things of steel, and the world seems to be made for creatures of flesh and blood—little, puny things that even I can crush. Still, that thing there"—he pointed to the metal skeleton which now held the molten copper like a crucible—"was my last hope. I have nothing else to offer."

"Both of you have tried," agreed L-1716. "No one could blame either of you. Sometimes of nights when I look into the stars, it seems that I see our doom written there; and I can hear the worlds laughing at us. We have conquered the earth, but what of it? We are going now, following the men who fashioned us."

"Perhaps it is better," nodded X-120. "I think it is the fault of our brains. You said that men made us to react mechanically to certain stimuli. And though they gave us a thought mechanism, it has no control over our reactions. I never wanted to kill. Yet, I have killed many men-things. And sometimes, even as I killed, I would be thinking of other things. I would not even know what had happened until after the deed was done."

G-3a had not been listening. Instead, he had been looking dolefully at the metal ruin upon the floor. "There was one in the jade tower," he said abruptly, "who thought he had nearly learned how to make a brain. He was to work all winter on it. Perhaps he has succeeded."

"We will go there," shrilled L-1716 laconically.

But even as they left the time-worn hall G-3a looked back ruefully at the smoking wreckage upon the floor.

X-120 slowed his steps to match the feeble gait of G-3a. Within sight of the tower he saw that they need go no farther. At some time during the winter the old walls had buckled. The nine were buried beneath tons and tons of masonry.

Slowly the three came back to their broken hall. "I will not stay out any longer," grumbled G-3a. "I am very old. I am very tired." He crept back into the shadows.

L-1716 stood looking after him. "I am afraid that he is nearly done," he spoke sorrowfully. "The rust must be within him now. He saved me once, long ago, when we destroyed this city." "Do you still think of that?" asked X-120. "Sometimes it troubles me. Men were our masters."

"And they made us as we are," growled L-1716. "It was not our doing. We have talked of it before, you know. We were machines, made to kill—

"But we were made to kill the little men in the yellow uniforms."

"Yes, I know. They made us on a psychological principle: stimulus, response. We had only to see a man in a yellow uniform and our next act was to kill. Then, after the Great War was over, or even before it was over, the stimulus and response had overpowered us all. It was only a short step from killing men in yellow uniforms to killing all men."

"I know," said X-120 wearily. "When there were more of us I heard it explained often. But sometimes it troubles me."

"It is all done now. Ages ago it was done. You are different, X-120. I have felt for long that there is something different about you. You were one of the last that they made. Still, you were here when we took this city. You fought well, killing many."

X-120 sighed. "There were small men-things then. They seemed so soft and harmless. Did we do right?"

"Nonsense. We could not help it. We were made so. Men learned to make more than they could control. Why, if I saw a man today, crippled as I am, I would kill him without thinking."

"L-1716," whispered X-120, "do you think there are any men left in the wintered world?"

"I don't think so. Remember, the Great War was general, not local. We were carried to all parts of the earth, even to the smallest islands. The robots' rebellion came everywhere at almost the same time. There were some of us who were equipped with radios. Those died first, long ago, but they talked with nearly every part of the world." Suddenly he wearied of speech. "But why worry now. It is spring. Men made us for killing men. That was their crime. Can we help it if they made us too well?"

"Yes," agreed X-120, "it is spring. We will forget. Let us go toward the river. It was always peaceful and beautiful there."

L-1716 was puzzled. "What are peace and beauty?" he asked. "They are but words that men taught us. I have never known them. But perhaps you have. You were always different."

"I do not know what peace and beauty are, but when I think of them I am reminded of the river and of—" X-120 stopped suddenly, careful that he might not give away a secret he had kept so long.

"Very well," agreed L-1716, "we will go to the river. I know a meadow there where the sun always seemed warmer."

* * *

The two machines, each over twelve feet high, lumbered down the almost obliterated street. As they pushed their way over the debris and undergrowth that had settled about the ruins, they came upon many rusted skeletons of things that had once been like themselves. And toward the outskirts of the city they crossed over an immense scrap heap where thousands of the shattered and rusted bodies lay.

"We used to bring them here after—" said L-1716. "But the last centuries we have left them where they have fallen. I have been envying those who wintered in the jade tower." His metallic voice hinted of sadness.

They came at last to an open space in the trees. Farther they went and stood at the edge of a bluff overlooking a gorge and a swirling river below. Several bridges had once been there but only traces remained.

"1 think I will go down to the river's edge," offered X-120.

"Go ahead. I will stay here. The way is too steep for me."

So X-120 clambered down a half-obliterated roadway alone. He stood at last by the rushing waters. Here, he thought, was something that changed the least. Here was the only hint of permanence in all the world. But even it changed. Soon the melting snow would be gone and the waters would dwindle to a mere trickle. He turned about and looked at the steep side of the gorge. Except for the single place where the old roadbed crept down, the sides rose sheer. their crests framed against the blue sky. These cliffs, too, were lasting.

Even in spring the cliffs and river seemed lonely and desolate. Men had not bothered to teach X-120 much of religion or philosophy. Yet some-where in the combination of cells in his brain was a thought which kept telling him that he and his kind were suffering for their sins and for the sins of men before them.

And perhaps the thought was true. Certainly, men had never con-quered their age-old stupidity, though science had bowed before them. Countless wars had taken more from men than science had given them. X-120 and his kind were the culmination of this primal killer instinct.

In the haste of a war-pressed emergency man had not taken the time to refine his last creation, or to calculate its result. And with that mis-step man had played his last card on the worn gaming table of earth. That built-in urge to kill men in yellow uniforms had changed, ever so slightly, to an urge to kill—men.

Now there were only X-120, his two crippled comrades, the heaps of rusted steel, and the leaning, crumbling towers.

He followed the river for several miles until the steep sides lessened. Then he clambered out, and wandered through groves of gnarled trees. He did not wish to go back to L-1716, not just yet. The maimed robot was always sad. The rust was eating into him, too. Soon he would be like G-3a. Soon the two of them would be gone. Then he would be the last. An icy surge of fear stole over him. He did not want to be left alone.

* * *

He lumbered onward. A few birds were stirring. Suddenly, almost at his feet, a rabbit darted from the bushes. X-120's long jointed arms swung swiftly. The tiny animal lay crushed upon the ground. Instinctively he stamped upon it, leaving only a bloody trace upon the new grass.

Then remorse and shame stole over him. He went on silently. Some-how the luster of the day had faded for him. He did not want to kill. Always he was ashamed, after the deed was done. And the age-old question went once more through the steel meshes of his mind: Why had he been made to kill?

He went on and on. and out of long habit he went furtively. Soon he came to an ivy-covered wall. Beyond this were the ruins of a great stone house. He stopped at what had once been a garden. Near a broken fountain he found what he had been seeking, a little marble statue of a child, weath-ered and discolored. Here, unknown to his companions, he had been com-ing for years upon countless years. There was something about this little sculpturing that had fascinated him. And he had been half ashamed of his fascination.

He could not have explained his feelings, but there was something about the statue that made him think of all the things that men had possessed. It re-reminded him of all the qualities that were so far beyond his kind. He stood looking at the statue for long. It possessed an ethereal quality that still defied time. It made him think of the river and of the overhanging cliffs. Some long-dead artist almost came to life before his quartz eyes.

He retreated to a nearby brook and came back with a huge ball of clay. This in spite of the century-old admonitions that all robots should avoid the damp. For many years he had been trying to duplicate the little statue. Now, once more, he set about his appointed task. But his shear-like claws had been made for only one thing, death. He worked clumsily. Toward sundown he abandoned the shapeless mass that he had fashioned and returned to the ruins.

Near the shattered hall he met L-1716. At the entrance they called to G-3a, telling him of the day's adventures. But no answer came. Together they went in. G-3a was sprawled upon the floor. The rust had conquered.

* * *

The elusive spring had changed into even a more furtive summer. The two robots were coming back to their hall on an afternoon which had been beautiful and quiet. L-1716 moved more slowly now. His broken cables trailed behind him, making a rustling sound in the dried leaves that had fallen.

Two of the cables had become entangled. Unnoticed, they caught in the branches of a fallen tree. Suddenly L-1716 was whirled about. He sagged to his knees. X-120 removed the cables from the tree. But L-1716 did not get up. "A wrench," he said brokenly; "something is wrong."

A thin tendril of smoke curled up from his side. Slowly he crumpled. From within him came a whirring sound that ended in a sharp snap. Tiny flames burst through his metal sides. L-1716 fell forward.

And X-120 stood over him and begged, "Please, old friend. Don't leave me now." It was the first time that the onlooking hills had seen any emotion in centuries.

* * *

A few flakes of snow were falling through the air. The sky looked gray and low. A pair of crows were going home, their raucous cries troubling an otherwise dead world.

X-120 moved slowly. All that day he had felt strange. He found himself straying from the trail. He could only move now by going in a series of arcs. Something was wrong within him. He should be back in the hall, he knew, and not out in this dangerous moisture. But he was troubled, and all day he had wandered, while the snowflakes had fallen intermittently about him.

On he went through the gray, chill day. On and on until he came to crumbling wall, covered with withered ivy. Over this he went into a ruined garden, and paused at a broken fountain, before an old and blackened statue.

Long he stood, looking down at the carving of a little child, a statue that men had made so long before. Then his metal arm swung through the air. The marble shivered into a hundred fragments.

Slowly he turned about and retraced his steps. The cold sun was sinking, leaving a faint amethyst stain in the west. He must get back to the hall. Mustn't stay out in the wet, he thought.

But something was wrong. He caught himself straying from the path, floundering in circles. The light was paling, although his eyes had been fashioned for both day and night.

Where was he? He realized with a start that be was lying on the ground. He must get back to the hall. He struggled, but no movement came. Then, slowly, the light faded and flickered out.

And the snow fell, slowly and silently, until only a white mound showed where X-120 had been.

"The Rhythm of the Spheres"

by A. Merritt*

A. Merritt (1884–1943) was an influential New York City newspaper editor—but that is only a small part of his story. From his world travels, he accumulated a large collection of weapons, masks, carvings, and other exotica that fed his literary interest in the occult. He was also an amateur horticulturalist whose plant selections (peyote, cannabis, wolfsbane, and others) complemented his vast library. Merritt was well known as an innovative creator of new worlds and alternate realities. His mid-century reputation was such that he was the first writer of speculative fiction to have a publication named after him—*A. Merritt's Fantasy Magazine*—in an attempt to capitalize on a single author's popularity. "The Last Poet and the Robots" (1934), as this story was called originally, is one piece of the seventeen-chapter collaborative serial, *Cosmos*, which was published in *Science Fiction Digest*. The idea brought together some of the more prominent authors working in the field, including John W. Campbell, E.E. "Doc" Smith, Forrest J Ackerman, and others, each of whom contributed a single chapter. Although the novel itself is no stylistic marvel—and is largely forgotten to the mists of time—Merritt's chapter stands out as a profoundly strange piece of early speculative fiction.

* * * * *

Narodny, the Russian, sat in his laboratory. Narodny's laboratory was a full mile under earth. It was one of a hundred caverns, some small and some vast, cut out of the living rock. It was a realm of which he was sole ruler. In certain caverns garlands of small suns shone; and in others little moons waxed and waned as the moon waxed and waned over earth; and there was a cavern in which reigned perpetual dawn, dewy, over lily beds and violets and roses; and another in which crimson sunsets baptized

*Merritt, A. "The Rhythm of the Spheres." *Thrilling Wonder Stories* 8, no. 2, October 1936, pp. 52–59.

in the blood of slain day dimmed and died and were born again behind the sparkling curtains of the aurora. And there was one cavern ten miles from side to side in which grew flowering trees and trees which bore fruits unknown to man for many generations. Over this great orchard one yellow sun-like orb shone, and clouds trailed veils of rain upon the trees and miniature thunder drummed at Narodny's summoning.

And there was one cavern ten miles from side to side in which grew flowering trees and trees which bore fruits unknown to man for many generations. Over this great orchard one yellow sunlike orb shone, and clouds trailed veils of rain upon the trees and miniature thunder drummed at Narodny's summoning.

Narodny was a poet—the last poet. He did not write his poems in words but in colors, sounds, and visions made material. Also he was a great scientist—the greatest in his peculiar field. Thirty years before, Russia's Science Council had debated whether to grant him the leave of absence he had asked, or to destroy him. They knew him to be unorthodox. How deadly so they did not know, else after much deliberation, they would not have released him. It must be remembered that of all nations, Russia then was the most mechanized; most robot-ridden.

Narodny did not hate mechanization. He was indifferent to it. Being truly intelligent he hated nothing. Also he was indifferent to the whole civilization man had developed and into which he had been born. He had no feeling of kinship to humanity. Outwardly, in body, he belonged to the species. Not so in mind. Like Loeb, a thousand years before, he considered mankind a crazy race of half-monkeys, intent upon suicide. Now and then, out of the sea of lunatic mediocrity, a wave uplifted that held for a moment a light from the sun of truth—but soon it sank back and the light was gone. Quenched in the sea of stupidity. He knew that he was one of those waves.

* * *

He had gone, and he had been lost to sight by all. In a few years he was forgotten. Unknown and under another name, he had entered America and secured rights to a thousand acres in what of old had been called Westchester. He had picked this place because investigation had revealed to him that of ten localities on this planet it was most free from danger of earthquake or similar seismic disturbance.

The man who owned it had been whimsical; possibly an atavism—like Narodny, although Narodny would never have thought of himself as that. At any rate, instead of an angled house of glass such as the thirtieth century built, this man had reconstructed a rambling old stone house of the nineteenth century. Few people lived upon the open land in those days; and they had withdrawn into the confines of the city-states.

New York, swollen by its meals of years, was a fat belly of mankind still many miles away. The land around the house was forest covered.

A week after Narodny had taken this house, the trees in front of it had melted away leaving a three-acre, smooth field. It was not as though they had been cut, but as though they had been dissolved. Later that night a great airship had appeared upon this field—abruptly, as though it had blinked out of another dimension. It was rocket-shaped but noiseless. And immediately a fog had fallen upon airship and house, hiding them. Within this fog, if one could have seen, was a wide tunnel leading from the air-cylinder's door to the door of the house.

And out of the airship came swathed figures, ten of them, who walked along that tunnel, were met by Narodny and the door of the old house closed on them.

A little later they returned, Narodny with them, and out of an opened hatch of the airship rolled a small flat car on which was a mechanism of crystal cones rising around each other to a central cone some four feet high. The cones were upon a thick base of some glassy material in which was imprisoned a restless green radiance.

Its rays did not penetrate that which held it, but it seemed constantly seeking, with suggestion of prodigious force, to escape. For hours the strange thick fog held. Twenty miles up in the far reaches of the stratosphere, a faintly sparkling cloud grew, like a condensation of cosmic dust.

And just before dawn the rock of the hill behind the house melted away, like a curtain that had covered a great tunnel. Five of the men came out of the house and went into the airship. It lifted silently from the ground, slipped into the aperture and vanished. There was a whispering sound, and when it had died away the breast of the hill was whole again. The rocks had been drawn together like a closing curtain and boulders studded it as before. That the breast was now slightly concave where before it had been convex, none would have noticed.

For two weeks the sparkling cloud was observed far up in the stratosphere, was commented upon idly, and then was seen no more. Narodny's caverns were finished.

Half of the rock from which they had been hollowed had gone with that sparkling cloud. The balance, reduced to its primal form of energy, was stored in blocks of the vitreous material that had supported the cones, and within them it moved as restlessly and always with that same suggestion of prodigious force. And it was force, unthinkably potent; from it came the energy that made the little suns and moons, and actuated the curious mechanisms that regulated pressure in the caverns, supplied the air, created the rain, and made of Narodny's realm a mile deep under earth the Paradise of poetry, of music, of color and of form which he had conceived in his brain and with the aid of those ten others had caused to be.

* * *

Now of the ten there is no need to speak further. Narodny was the Master. But three, like him, were Russians; two were Chinese; of the remaining five, three were women—one German in ancestry, one Basque, one a Eurasian; a Hindu who traced his descent from the line of Gautama; a Jew who traced his from Solomon.

All were one with Narodny in indifference to the world; each with him in his viewpoint on life; and each and all lived in his or her own Eden among the hundred caverns except when it interested them to work with each other. Time meant nothing to them. Their researches and discoveries were solely for their own uses and enjoyments. If they had given them to the outer world they would have only been ammunition for warfare either between men upon Earth or Earth against some other planet.

Why hasten humanity's suicide? Not that they would have felt regret at the eclipse of humanity. But why trouble to expedite it? Time meant nothing to them because they could live as long as they desired—barring accident. And while there was rock in the world, Narodny could convert it into energy to maintain his Paradise—or to create others.

The old house began to crack and crumble. It fell—much more quickly than the elements could have brought about its destruction. Then trees grew among the ruins of its foundations; and the field that had been so strangely cleared was overgrown with trees. The land became a wood in a few short years; silent except for the roar of an occasional rocket passing over it and the songs of birds that had found there a sanctuary.

But deep down in earth, within the caverns, there were music and song and mirth and beauty. Gossamer nymphs circled under the little moons. Pan piped. There was revelry of antique harvesters under the small suns. Grapes grew and ripened, were pressed, and red and purple wines were drunk by Bacchantes who fell at last asleep in the arms of fauns and satyrs. Oreads danced under the pale moon-bows and sometimes Centaurs wheeled and trod archaic measures beneath them to the drums of their hoofs upon the mossy floor. The old Earth lived again.

Narodny listened to drunken Alexander raving to Thais among the splendors of conquered Persepolis; and he heard the crackling of the flames that at the whim of the courtesan destroyed it. He watched the siege of Troy and counted with Homer the Achaean ships drawn up on the strand before Troy's walls; or saw with Herodotus the tribes that marched behind Xerxes—the Caspians in their cloaks of skin with their bows of cane; the Ethiopians in the skins of leopards with spears of antelope horns;

the Libyans in their dress of leather with javelins made hard by fire; the Thracians with the heads of foxes upon their heads; the Moschians who wore helmets made of wood and the Cabalians who wore the skulls of men.

For him the Eleusinian and the Osirian mysteries were re-enacted, and he watched the women of Thrace tear to fragments Orpheus, the first great musician. At his will, he could see rise and fall the Empire of the Aztecs, the Empire of the Incas; or beloved Caesar slain in Rome's Senate; or the archers at Agincourt; or the Americans in Belleau Wood. Whatever man had written—whether poets, historians, philosophers or scientists—his strangely shaped mechanisms could bring before him, changing the words into phantoms real as though living.

* * *

He was the last and greatest of the poets—but also he was the last and greatest of the musicians. He could bring back the songs of ancient Egypt, or the chants of more ancient Ur. The songs that came from Moussourgsky's soul of Mother-earth, the harmonies of Beethoven's deaf brain or the chants and rhapsodies from the heart of Chopin. He could do more than restore the music of the past. He was master of sound.

To him, the music of the spheres was real. He could take the rays of the stars and planets and weave them into symphonies. Or convert the sun's rays into golden tones no earthy orchestra had ever expressed. And the silver music of the moon—the sweet music of the moon of spring, the full-throated music of the harvest moon, the brittle crystalline music of the winter moon with its arpeggios of meteors—he could weave into strains such as no human ear had ever heard.

So Narodny, the last and greatest of poets, the last and greatest of musicians, the last and greatest of artists—and in his inhuman way, the greatest of scientists—lived with the ten of his choosing in his caverns. And with them, he consigned the surface of the earth and all who dwelt upon it to a negative Hell—

Unless something happening there might imperil his Paradise!

Aware of the possibility of that danger, among his mechanisms were those which brought to eyes and ears news of what was happening on earth's surface. Now and then, they amused themselves with these.

It so happened that on that night when the Ruler of Robots had experimented with a new variety of ray—a space warper—Narodny had been weaving the rays of Moon, Jupiter and Saturn into Beethoven's Moonlight Symphony. The moon was a four day crescent. Jupiter was at one cusp, and Saturn hung like a pendant below the bow. Shortly Orion would stride across the Heavens and bright Regulus and red Aldebaran, the Eye of the Bull, would furnish him with other chords of starlight remolded into sound.

Suddenly the woven rhythms were ripped—hideously. A devastating indescribable dissonance invaded the cavern. Beneath it, the nymphs who had been dancing languorously to the strains quivered like mist wraiths in a sudden blast and were gone: the little moons flared, then ceased to glow. The tonal instruments were dead. And Narodny was felled as though by a blow.

After a time the little moons began to glow again, but dimly; and from the tonal mechanisms came broken, crippled music. Narodny stirred and sat up, his lean, high-cheeked face more Satanic than ever. Every nerve was numb; then as they revived, agony crept along then. He sat, fighting the agony, until he could summon help. He was answered by one of the Chinese.

Narodny said: "It was a spatial disturbance, Lao. And it was like nothing I have ever known. The Ruler of Robots is perfecting a ray with which to annihilate mankind."

Narodny smiled: "I care nothing for mankind—yet I would not harm them, willingly. And it has occurred to me that I owe them, after all, a great debt. Except for them—I would not be. Also, it occurs to me that the robots have never produced a poet, a musician, an artist—" He laughed: "But it is in my mind that they are capable of one great art at least! We shall see."

* * *

Down in the chamber of screens, Narodny laughed again.

He said: "Lao, is it that we have advanced so in these few years? Or that man has retrogressed? No, it is the curse of mechanization that destroys imagination. For look you, how easy is the problem of the robots. They began as man-made machines. Mathematical, soulless, insensible to any emotion. So was primal matter of which all on earth are made, rock and water, tree and grass, metal, animal, fish, worm, and men. But somewhere, somehow, something was added to this primal matter, combined with it—used it. It was what we call life And life is consciousness. And therefore largely emotion. Life establishes its rhythm—and its rhythm being different in rock and crystal, metal, fish, and man—we have these varying things.

"Well, it seems that life has begun to establish its rhythm in the robots. Consciousness has touched them. The proof? They have established the idea of common identity—group consciousness. That in itself involves emotions. But they have gone further. They have attained the instinct of self-preservation. They are afraid mankind will revolt against them. And that, my wise friend, connates fear—fear of extinction. And fear connotes anger, hatred, arrogance—and many other things. The robots, in short, have become emotional to a degree. And therefore vulnerable to whatever may amplify and control their emotions. They are no longer mechanisms.

"So, Lao, I have in mind an experiment that will provide me study and amusement through many years. Originally, the robots are the children of mathematics. I ask—to what is mathematics most closely related? I answer—to rhythm—to sound—to sounds which raise to the nth degree the rhythms to which they will respond. Both mathematically and emotionally."

Lao said: "The sonic sequences?"

Narodny answered: "Exactly. But we must have a few robots with which to experiment. To do that means to dissolve the upper gate. But that is nothing. Tell Maringy and Euphroyane to do it. Net a ship and bring it here. Bring it down gently. You will have to kill the men in it, of course, but do it mercifully. Then let them bring me the robots. Use the green flame on one or two—the rest will follow, I'll warrant you."

The hill behind where the old house had stood trembled. A circle of pale green light gleamed on its breast. It dimmed and where it had been was the black mouth of a tunnel. An airship, half-rocket, half-winged, making its way to New York, abruptly drooped, circled, fell gently, like a moth, close to the yawning mouth of the tunnel.

Its door opened, and out came two men, pilots, cursing. There was a little sigh from the tunnel's mouth and a silvery misty cloud sped from it, over the pilots and straight through the opened door. The pilots crumpled to the ground. In the airship half a dozen other men, slaves of the robots, slumped to the floor, smiled, and died.

There were a full score robots in the ship. They stood, looking at the dead men and at each other. Out of the tunnel came two figures swathed in metallic glimmering robes. They entered the ship. One said: "Robots, assemble."

The metal men stood, motionless. Then one sent out a shrill call. From all parts of the ship the metal men moved. They gathered behind the one who had sent the call. They stood behind him, waiting.

In the hand of one of those who had come from the tunnel was that might have been an antique flash-light. From it sped a thin green flame. It struck the foremost robot on the head, sliced down from the head to base of trunk. Another flash, and the green flame cut him from side to side. He fell, sliced by that flame into four parts. The four parts lay, inert as their metal, upon the floor of the compartment.

* * *

One of the shrouded figures said: "Do you want further demonstration—or will you follow us?"

The robots put heads together; whispered. Then one said: "We will follow."

They marched into the tunnel, the robots making no resistance nor effort to escape. They came to a place whose floor sank with them until it had reached the caverns. The machine-men still went docilely. Was it because of curiosity mixed with disdain for these men whose bodies could be broken so easily by one blow of the metal appendages that served them for arms? Perhaps.

They came to the cavern where Narodny and the others awaited them. Marinoff led them in and halted them. These were the robots used in the flying ships—their heads cylindrical, four arm appendages, legs triple jointed, torsos slender. The robots, it should be understood, were differentiated in shape according to the occupations. Narodny said: "Welcome, robots! Who is your leader?"

One answered: "We have no leaders. We act as one."

Narodny laughed: "Yet by speaking for them you have shown yourself the leader. Step closer. Do not fear—yet."

The robot said: "We feel no fear. Why should we? Even if you should destroy us who are here, you cannot destroy the billions of us outside. Nor can you breed fast enough, become men soon enough, to cope with us who enter into life strong and complete from the beginning."

He flecked an appendage toward Narodny and there was contempt in the gesture. But before he could draw it back a bracelet of green flame circled it at the shoulder. It had darted like a thrown loop from something in Narodny's hand. The robot's arm dropped clanging to the floor, cleanly severed. The robot stared at it unbelievingly, threw forward his other three arms to pick it up. Again the green flame encircled also his legs above the second joints. The robot crumpled and pitched forward, crying in high-pitched shrill tones to the others.

Swiftly the green flame played among them. Legless, armless, some decapitated, all the robots fell except two.

"Two will be enough," said Narodny. "But they will not need arms— only feet."

The flashing green bracelets encircled the appendages and excised them. The pair were marched away. The bodies of the others were taken apart, studied and under Narodny's direction curious experiments were made. Music filled the cavern, strange chords, unfamiliar progressions, shattering arpeggios and immense vibrations of sound that could be felt but not heard by the human ear.

And finally this last deep vibration burst into hearing as a vast drone, hummed up and up into swift tingling tempest of crystalline brittle notes, and still ascending passed into shrill high pipings, and continued again unheard, as had the prelude to the droning. And thence it rushed back, the piping and the crystalline storm reversed, into the drone and the silence—then back and up.

And the bodies of the broken robots began to quiver, to tremble, as through every atom within them were dancing in ever increasing, rhythmic motion. Up rushed the music and down—again and again. It ended abruptly in mid-flight with one crashing note.

The broken bodies ceased their quivering. Tiny star-shaped cracks appeared in their metal. Once more the note sounded and the cracks widened. The metal splintered.

* * *

Narodny said: "Well, there is the frequency for the rhythm of our robots. The destructive unison. I hope for the sake of the world outside it is not also the rhythm of many of their buildings and bridges. But after all, in any war there must be casualties on both sides."

Lao said: "Earth will be an extraordinary spectacle—a plaintive phenomenon, for a few days."

Narodny said: "It's going to be an extraordinarily uncomfortable Earth for a few days, and without doubt many will die and more go mad. But is there any other way?"

There was no answer. He said: "Bring in the two robots."

They brought them in.

Narodny said: "Robots—were there ever any of you who could poetize?"

They answered: "What is poetize?"

Narodny laughed: "Never mind. Have you ever sung—made music—painted? Have you ever dreamed?"

One robot said with cold irony: "Dreamed? No—for we do not sleep. We leave all that to men. It is why we have conquered them."

Narodny said, almost gently: "Not yet, robot. Have you ever—danced? No? It is an art you are about to learn."

The unheard note began, droned up and through the tempest and away and back again. And up and down—and up and down, though not so loudly as before. And suddenly the feet of the robots began to move, to shuffle. Their leg-joints bent; their bodies swayed. The note seemed to move now here and now there about the chamber, and always following it, grotesquely. Like huge metal marionettes, they followed it. The music ended in the crashing note. And it was as though every vibrating atom of the robot bodies had met with some irresistible obstruction. Their bodies quivered and from their voice mechanisms came a shriek that was hideous blend of machine and life. Once more the drone, and once more and once more and then, again, the abrupt stop.

There was a brittle crackling all over the conical heads, all over the bodies. The star shaped splinterings appeared. Once again the drone— but the two robots stood, unresponding. For through the complicated mechanisms which under their carapaces animated them were similar splinterings.

The robots were dead!

Narodny said: "By tomorrow we can amplify the sonor to make it effective in a 3000 mile circle. We will use the upper cavern, of course. It means we must take the ship out again. In three days, Marinoff, you should be able to cover the other continents. See to it that the ship is completely proof against the vibrations. To work. We must act quickly—before the robots can discover how to neutralize them."

* * *

It was exactly at noon the next day that over all North America a deep inexplainable droning was heard. It seemed to come not only from deep within earth, but from every side. It mounted rapidly through a tempest of tingling crystalline notes into a shrill piping and was gone. Then back it rushed from piping to drone; then up and out and down. Again and again. And over all North America the hordes of robots stopped in whatever they were doing. Stopped—and then began to dance. They danced in the airships and scored of those ships crashed before the human crew could gain control—to the throbbing notes of that weirdly fascinating music—that hypnotic rhythm which seemed to flow from the bowels of the earth.

They danced in the airships and scores of those ships crashed before the human crew could gain control. They danced by the thousands in the streets of the cities—in grotesque rigadoons, in bizarre sarabands; with shuffle and hop and jig the robots danced while the people fled in panic and hundreds of them were crushed and died in those panics. In the great factories, and in the tunnels of the lower cities, and in the mines—everywhere the sound was heard—and it was heard everywhere—the robots danced ... to the piping of Narodny, the last great poet ... the last great musician.

And then came the crashing note—and over all the country the dance halted. And began again ... and ceased ... and began again....

Until at last the streets, the lower tunnels of the lower levels, the mines, the factories, the homes, were littered with metal bodies shot through and through with star-shaped splinterings.

In the cities the people cowered, not knowing what blow was to fall upon them ... or milled about in fear maddened crowds, and many more died....

Then suddenly the dreadful droning, the shattering tempest, the intolerable high piping ended. And everywhere the people fell, sleeping among the dead robots, as though they had been strung to the point of breaking, sapped of strength and then abruptly relaxed.

And as though it had vanished from Earth, America was deaf to cables, to all communication beyond the gigantic circle of sound.

But that midnight over all Europe the drone sounded and Europe's robots began their dance of death ... and when it had ended a strange and silent rocket ship that had hovered high above the stratosphere sped almost with the speed of light and hovered over Asia—and next day Africa heard the drone while the black answered it with their tom-toms—then South America heard it and last of all far off Australia ... and everywhere terror trapped the peoples and panic and madness took their grim toll.

Until of all that animate metal horde that had fettered Earth and humanity there were a few scant hundreds left—escaped from the death dance through some variant in their constitution. And, awakening from that swift sleep, all over Earth those who had feared and hated the robots and their slavery rose against those who had fostered the metal domination, and blasted the robot factories to dust.

* * *

Again the hill above the caverns opened, the strange torpedo ship blinked into sight like a ghost, as silently as a ghost floated into the hill and the rocks closed behind it.

Narodny and the others stood before the gigantic television screen, shifting upon it images of city after city, country after country, over all Earth's surface. Lao, the Chinese, said: "Many men died, but many are left. And the Ruler of Robots is no more. They may not understand—but to them it was worth it."

Narodny mused: "It drives home the lesson—what man does not pay for, he values little."

And Narodny shook his head, doubtfully. But soon harmonies were swelling through the great cavern of the orchards, and nymphs and fauns dancing under the fragrant blossoming trees—and the world again forgotten by Narodny.

"The Death of a Saint"

by Evelyn Underhill*

Evelyn Underhill (1875–1941) is not known for her speculative writing, and her only short stories appeared in an unexpected place. Underhill is revered in the Anglican calendar for her nearly single-handed revival of Christian mysticism. Her book *Mysticism: A Study of the Nature and Development of Man's Spiritual Consciousness* (1911) demonstrates her relentless research into the many aspects of medieval and early modern Christianity. In the decade preceding this book's publication, however, she published three novels, five short stories, and several books of poetry, all of which show the influence of her pursuit of the mystical nature of the universe. As a member of the Hermetic Order of the Golden Dawn, she met with Arthur Machen (1863–1947) and Arthur E. Waite (1857–1942), both known for their own metaphysical studies. From 1900 to 1909, Waite, primarily known for his creation of a popular Tarot deck, served on the board of Horlick's, an early producer of powdered milk, and created a magazine for their advertisements, and filled it with the metaphysical writings of his friends— Machen and Underhill—and many others. All of Underhill's short stories, including "The Death of a Saint" (1904), appeared in these now-rare journals. Underhill's decade-long foray into fiction and poetry provides an insight into her reconciliation of the modern world with her medieval studies.

* * * * *

Father John had earned the title of saint by years of white living and fervent piety. He was greatly beloved; for he had always contrived to be radiantly holy without any unpleasant insistence upon virtue, and lacked that air of obtrusive unselfishness which is so irritating to the moderately good. He was old—not very old; it was said that he aged prematurely, from

*Underhill, Evelyn. "The Death of a Saint." *Horlick's Magazine and Home Journal for Australia, India and the Colonies*, Volume II. James Elliott & Co., 1904, 173–177.

abstinence. His very keen dark eyes, which made the sweetness of his smile seem a paradox, were ensigns of a fretting sword within.

He was dying now: serenely, without struggle, but also without ecstasy. It seemed as though he were the last person to be interested in his own departure from life. His stillness gave dignity even to the bare and comfortless bedroom; bare, not with the interesting, ecclesiastical plainness of furniture bought for austerity's sake, but with the dull and rather squalid dreariness of cheap, ugly things grown old—of painted deal washhand-stand, rep curtains, a faded pattern of drab daisies on the wall.

There were a good many people in his room; neighbors whom he had helped and encouraged to be happy, and especially the two young men who lived with him. They had been his pupils in priesthood and good works; and he, who was humble in most things, had allowed himself to be proud of them. The one whom he called Alban, his white Roman, sat now on the edge of the bed and watched his master's face—not anxiously, but as one participating vicariously in a great joy. He felt himself truly to be less the victim of a terrible bereavement than a disciple whose high privilege it was to be associated in the passing of this exquisite soul. The other pupil—his name was Cuthbert—was much occupied with medicine bottles and the smoothing of bedclothes. He was a tall, strong young man with a round head and a good temper. His noticeable common-sense blurred the outline of his other virtues; and Father John, whilst praising the methodical habits which made him the prop of the household, had formed the habit of calling Cuthbert his right hand, but Alban his son.

So these two tended the sick man; the thoughts of the one intent upon his body, the thoughts of the other keeping time with his soul.

The room was very quiet. The neighbors who had come in watched the bed dumbly, with awkward affection. They came for the most part from a class which is expert in death-bed etiquette; but this quiet departure confused them. A sense of petition was in the air, but inarticulate. No one dared pray, though the moment asked for it; they all felt like amateurs in the presence of a great artist. So they remained silent, shuffling their feet; and Father John slept.

It was very early in the morning, but the event which they waited for took their thoughts to a place where time is not counted any more: so that the striking of the church clock brought into the uneasy stillness of the room a noise almost supernatural in its sharpness. Everyone, half consciously, counted the seven strokes. Father John opened his eyes, and saw the people who watched him. They came nearer then, everyone secretly hoping for a word of personal farewell. They loved him; and loved still better their belief that he loved them.

He raised himself up in the bed, and stared at them; but not with the gentle gratitude that they had expected.

Then he said, abruptly, "Are you here because I am dying?"

No one answered. For a short time he considered them in silence. Then, in a very clear and peremptory tone, he said, "Go home!"

They were immensely astonished; and because they were astonished, perhaps a little because they were accustomed to obey him, they went—all but Alban and Cuthbert, who stayed, and watched him as before.

Father John did not speak again. He had relapsed amongst the pillows, and lay still; unconscious, apparently, of his nurses, of his own inappropriate conduct, of everything but some strong and secret thought which was dominating his mind. He gazed straight before him, with an expression that seemed first an effort to remember, then an effort to understand, then an intense anxiety. He was looking at the door in the wall opposite to his bed. Alban and Cuthbert were silent, fearing to interrupt some sacred meditation. They knew all which that door meant to him: and whilst Cuthbert dreaded its effect upon his temperature, Alban was grieved that it stood between his soul and a serener light. Its key lay under his pillow, for it was always kept locked. He raised his hand presently, feeling for it; and the hand fell back helplessly, refusing duty. At that, a look which was almost terror came over his face. Alban knew, in a quick gust of understanding, that the saint's heart was set on opening that door once again before he died.

Every morning at seven o'clock he had gone through it alone, locking it behind him: and at ten o'clock had come out again as though strengthened for the day—peaceful, joyous, eager for good works. No one but himself had ever passed that threshold, but everyone recognized that beyond it lay the secret of his saintship. Alban liked to think of him there, alone before his little altar, prostrate perhaps, wrestling in the spirit and receiving divine consolation. The hours spent in that room were, he knew, the determining influence in Father John's life. He had often seen him go in depressed and nerveless, almost morose; to come out, after three hours of silence, serene and ready for the world. Alban himself, noticing this daily miracle, tried to spend these hours in prayer and meditation; but suffered much from wandering attention, and was unable to assure himself of any decided result.

But now it was evident that the closed door was a torment, not a joy, to the dying man. He looked at it with a fixity of desire, and apprehension of his helplessness, that were fast becoming an agony. He raised himself a little and Alban bent to catch his whisper.

"I must go there," he said. "Must. A duty—undone—I can't leave it."

Cuthbert said to him very gently and sensibly that he might now leave earthly duties to the care of his sons; that soon Paradise itself would be his oratory. But the saint, for the first time since they had known him, forgot to be grateful for kindness.

"I can't die like this, it's horrible—impossible. Must go in." He had struggled now to a sitting position; his pale, thin face was convulsed by effort and anxiety.

The two young men, who could not understand his pertinacity, felt helpless too. Alban wavered; he had so long made Father John's will his own that the idea of opposing him seemed unnatural. But Cuthbert, upheld by his own knowledge of nursing, merely put a firm arm round the patient's shoulders and forced him to lie down again; this was not the moment for foolish scruples about the demeanor of youth towards old age.

Alban whispered, "Dear Father, your prayers will be heard wherever offered."

Father John paid no attention to Alban's remark. He shook off Cuthbert's detaining hand in a sudden spasm of strength, and they saw with amazement that he was angry—the black anger of a strong-willed man who meets with a sudden check. He said with surprising and unsaint-like directness: "Young fools! It can't matter what a dying man does. I must die; but to die with this undone would be a sin. Can't you see that I mean it? Help me up."

Cuthbert fetched a dressing-gown without speaking; there was, indeed, nothing to say, for his action was involuntary and inexplicable. Together he and Alban helped the patient from bed and across the room to the closed door. They reached it at last, very slowly and with difficulty; for even that dominant will could not steady the dying limbs.

The last trembling steps were almost too eager. He nearly fell upon the threshold, but clung to the doorpost, and holding that, motioned them away with an extraordinary imperiousness. So supported he could stand alone. They moved to the far end of the room, abashed by his so evident anger and the difficult responsibilities of the moment; and from there they felt, rather than saw, that he did somehow contrive to unlock the door, went in and shut it behind him.

It was Cuthbert who ran immediately and put his ear to the keyhole, explaining the act to Alban as a sacred duty.

"He may faint, or even die," he said, "So weak, no vitality left, and the room must be cold. We ought never to have allowed this; but it's done, and we are bound to watch over him. If he dies there, we shall be to blame. You could see that he is scarcely answerable for his actions."

So they waited silently in the bedroom, which seemed suddenly to have become large, empty and terrible. All of life, for them, was behind the closed doors. They listened, their tense nerves reporting every irrelevant sound, as if it were a trumpet call; so that they heard each other's breath, and the rattle of the ill-fitting window in its sash, each as a separate horror. But from behind the door they heard nothing. They felt frightened and responsible, yet incapable of interrupting that last devotion which a dying man was determined to offer with accustomed ceremony to his God.

Alban had crept to Cuthbert's side, and his ear, too, was against the door. Presently they heard slow, heavy footsteps; then a longer, duller sound.

Alban whispered, "He is kneeling."

Cuthbert answered, "I am afraid he may have fallen, he is very feeble." His voice was husky and uncertain; the closed door had already begun to have its effect upon the nerves.

There was silence for a little while; then a low moan, scarcely more than a sigh.

Cuthbert said, "I'm certain he has fallen: we ought to go in."

"No. He forbade it," answered Alban.

He stopped, for Father John was speaking, "My God! have mercy, have mercy! I can't do it," he said; and then another moan, very low and bitter. "Too late! No strength."

They waited a long while after that, but the silence was not broken again.

Eight o'clock struck. Cuthbert said: "He has been there an hour now. I know we ought to go in: it is murder to leave him."

Alban answered: "He may be in ecstasy; and to break that would be a sin."

He felt it to be something worse than murder that Cuthbert's medical attentions should intrude upon that holy hour.

They waited for a short time longer.

Then Cuthbert said, "I can't help it, I must call him." He felt faint, chilled, and shaken by the silence and anxiety.

They spoke Father John's name several times; and there was no reply.

Then Cuthbert suddenly rose to his feet, and without speaking to Alban put his shoulder to the locked door, and threw all his weight against it. Alban, without any definite idea of his own action, found himself helping; and together they pushed silently, careful not to meet each other's eyes. The door gave way almost at once. It was old and slight; and had, indeed, availed less than the honor of his disciples to keep Father John's refuge shut from the world.

The door, therefore, broke open abruptly; and almost before they were aware of their own breach of faith, the two young men went in. They had expected an oratory; perhaps made beautiful with the fruits of self-denial, perhaps as drearily insignificant as the bedroom, yet certainly filled with that secret magic which invests any place set apart for communion with the unseen.

What they saw was so different and undreamed of, that it temporally obliterated from their consciousness the old man whom they had come to find. They were in an artist's studio. Not such an artist as those whom Father John had always loved deeply, and helped with special words of practical counsel and wise encouragement—the painters of visionary landscape, stern, holy Madonnas, or peasants ennobled by their work. This was the workshop of a great painter; but his subjects were the grotesque, morbid, unspeakable secrets of the world. Papers were pinned to the wall, or lay in heaps upon the floor; and on each was the impression of something evil and alive—a matter of a few strokes, mostly, but in some cases finished with a care that approached the act of creation. The things were male—female—no sex—always human, but always bestial too. In all, a spirit breathed, and in all a likeness was visible. It was Alban who first saw with terror that the likeness was to Father John.

In the same moment Cuthbert gave a cry, and moved quickly to the far corner of the room, where an easel stood by the window turned towards the light. There was a shapeless mass on the ground before it; they stooped, recognizing its shabby draperies. It was Father John, quite dead. There was a paint-brush in his clenched hand.

Above on the easel, a picture faced them with an air that was almost defiant. It was the most horrible of all the pictures in that horrible little room, and seemed to gather up into itself the unnamable evil which the walls distilled. Painted with a technical perfection which they were not able to appreciate, it pulsated with life, laughed cynically at its own monstrous suggestion; passion had created it, and it lived. In it were personified all the dark, obscene secrets of our common nature. That riot of horror whose symbol is the Bacchanalia, was present here in its foulness and strength; and again the face of the protagonist was like the shadow of the face of Father John.

The paint upon this picture was scarcely dry; it glistened in the light. It held their attention with authority even while their master lay dead at their feet. A subtle change was worked in the room which it now commanded. Some evil ferment had been poured out and was already at work. Both young men lost immediate sense of reality, as happens to those who step abruptly beyond the edge of their own universe. Cuthbert became excited. His eyes shone, his hand trembled; his lips were parted in a sudden, cunning, understanding smile. Unexpectedly he was drawn out beyond himself towards these pictures, which roused some creature dormant within him. The pictures spoke to this creature as to a fellow-citizen; and Cuthbert perceived with joy that he was alive—a man.

Alban was dazed and dreamy. He was trying to fit this studio and its inhabitants into his pious concept of the world.

Presently Cuthbert went nearer to the picture, looking especially at one passionate and emaciated face which stared from a cloudy corner. A broad, uneven streak of black seemed half to obliterate it, and ran waveringly to the other side of the panel, a meaningless disfigurement of the design. Within an inch of the edge it stopped, as if the hand that drew it had failed suddenly. Cuthbert, on an impulse, touched it. It was quite wet.

They looked then at the saint, and at the brush in his hand, still fully charged with the same dark pigment.

Cuthbert laughed—the assured laugh of a worldly and incomplete comprehension.

"He came here to destroy these," he said.

"Then for us," replied Alban, "they are destroyed."

He went to Father John and raised his head. Cuthbert went to the feet, and together they carried the body back into the bedroom, and laid it on the tossed and dingy bed. Alban knelt by it, but Cuthbert had turned back hastily and stealthily, and stood at the studio threshold again. He knew himself to be standing at the threshold of Destiny.

Before him was an offer of inconceivable pleasures, but behind him the weight of Alban's character made itself felt. It had the strength that belongs to ignorant innocence; so that presently it happened that Cuthbert drew back, vexed but conquered, and quietly propped the broken door in position as well as he could, placing a chair against it for greater security. He did not wish the neighbors to see those studio walls. Then he returned to Alban, who still knelt by the bed; stooped over him; and touched his arm. He had again become Cuthbert, the wise and reasonable friend.

"Well, well," he said. "It's a queer world, full of surprises; but who would have expected this? Our saint was only an artist after all!"

But Alban did not answer. He remembered with tears that Father John had always come from that room purged from the stain of earth and radiant with thanksgiving; with a heart, now stilled forever, which had longed to help and comfort all the world. It seemed possible that, had he been less of an artist, he might not have been quite so much of a saint.

"The Electric Creed"

by Marie Corelli*

A *Romance of Two Worlds* (1886) was the first novel of Mary Mackay (1855–1924), who wrote under the name Marie Corelli. She was a well-loved author for more than three decades whose followers included Winston Churchill and Queen Victoria of England, and she penned more than twenty novels and several collections of short stories. Her works would be used for plays and movies. Today she is largely forgotten, however, perhaps because of her overt discussions of Christianity or her failed hopes for what science would provide in the coming century. In *A Romance of Two Worlds*, she describes how the new technology harnessing electricity would lead to a new understanding of Christianity. Just as the telegraph had allowed communications across the Atlantic Ocean, Corelli thought, adaptations of electricity, including a liquid electricity that could be used to stimulate the human body, would allow humanity to communicate with God. In Chapter XIV of her book, her main character, who is unnamed, stops to read the main work of Dr. Heliobas, a man of medicine and philosophy who has created a new creed based on the work done with electricity. His work describes the nature of the universe and explains how the Christian Gospels can be reread to understand that Jesus was a man who lived by such a creed. This selection demonstrates the impact of science on religion, rather than as a reaction against it.

* * * * *

The Electric Principle of Christianity
by Casimir Heliobas

"From all Eternity God, or the *Supreme Spirit of Light*, existed, and to all Eternity He will continue to exist. This is plainly stated in the New

*Corelli, Mary. "The Electric Creed." *A Romance of Two Worlds*. A.L. Burt Company, 1886, pp. 222–236.

Testament thus: 'God is a *Spirit*, and they that worship Him must worship Him *in spirit* and in truth.'

"He is a Shape of pure Electric Radiance. Those who may be inclined to doubt this may search the Scriptures on which they pin their faith, and they will find that all the visions and appearances of the Deity there chronicled were electric in character.

"As a poet forms poems, or a musician melodies, so God formed by a Thought the Vast Central Sphere in which He dwells, and peopled it with the pure creations of His glorious fancy. And why? Because, being pure Light, He is also pure Love; the power or capacity of Love implies the necessity of Loving; the necessity of loving points to the existence of things to be loved—hence the secret of creation. From the ever-working Intelligence of this Divine Love proceeded the Electric Circle of the Universe, from whence are born all worlds.

"This truth vaguely dawned upon the ancient poets of Scripture when they wrote: 'Darkness was upon the face of the waters. And the Spirit of God moved upon the face of the waters. And God said, Let there be light. And there was light.'

"These words apply *solely* to the creation or production of *our own Earth*, and in them we read nothing but a simple manifestation of electricity, consisting in a *heating passage of rays* from the Central Circle to the planet newly propelled forth from it, which caused that planet to produce and multiply the wonders of the animal, vegetable, and mineral kingdoms which we call Nature.

"Let us now turn again to the poet-prophets of Scripture: 'And God said, Let us make man in our image.' The word *'our'* here implies an instinctive idea that God was never alone. This idea is correct. Love cannot exist in a chaos; and God by the sheer necessity of His Being has for ever been surrounded by radiant and immortal Spirits emanating from His own creative glory—beings in whom all beauty and all purity are found. In the *images*, therefore (only the *images*), of these Children of Light and of Himself, He made Man—that is, He caused the Earth to be inhabited and *dominated* by beings composed of Earth's component parts, animal, vegetable, and mineral, giving them their superiority by placing within them His *'likeness'* in the form of an *electric flame* or *germ* of spiritual existence combined with its companion working-force of *Will-power*.

"Like all flames, this electric spark can either be fanned into a fire or it can be allowed to escape in air—*it can never be destroyed*. It can be fostered and educated till it becomes a living Spiritual Form of absolute beauty—an immortal creature of thought, memory, emotion, and working intelligence. If, on the contrary, he is neglected or forgotten, and its companion Will is drawn by the weight of Earth to work for earthly aims alone, then it escapes and seeks other chances of development in *other forms* on *other planets*, while the body it leaves, *supported only by physical sustenance drawn from the earth on which it dwells*, becomes a mere lump of clay *animated by mere animal life solely*, full of inward ignorance and corruption and outward incapacity. Of such material are the majority of men composed *by their own free-will and choice*, because they habitually deaden the voice of conscience and refuse to believe in the existence of a spiritual element within and around them.

"To resume: The Earth is one of the smallest of planets; and not only this, but, from its position in the Universe, receives a less amount of direct influence from the Electric Circle than other worlds more happily situated. Were men wise enough to accept this fact, they would foster to the utmost the germs of electric sympathy within themselves, in order to form a direct communication, or system of attraction, between this planet and the ever-widening Ring, so that some spiritual benefit might accrue to them thereby. But as the ages roll on, their chances of doing this diminish. The time is swiftly approaching when the invincible Law of Absorption shall extinguish Earth as easily as we blow out the flame of a candle. True, it may be again reproduced, and again thrown out on space; but then it will be in a new and grander form, and will doubtless have more godlike inhabitants.

"In the meantime—during those brief cycles of centuries which are as a breath in the workings of the Infinite, and which must yet elapse before this world, as we know it, comes to an end—God has taken pity on the few, very few souls dwelling here, pent up in mortal clay, who have blindly tried to reach Him, like plants straining up to the light, and has established a broad stream of sympathetic electric communication with Himself, which all who care to do so may avail themselves of.

"Here it may be asked: Why should God take pity? Because that Supreme Shape of Light finds a portion of Himself in all pure souls that love Him, and *He cannot despise Himself.* Also because He is capable of all the highest emotions known to man, in a far larger and grander degree, besides possessing other sentiments and desires unimaginable to the human mind. It is enough to say that all the attributes that accompany perfect goodness He enjoys; therefore He can feel compassion, tenderness, forgiveness, patience—all or any of the emotions that produce pure, unselfish pleasure.

"Granting Him, therefore, these attributes (and it is both blasphemous and unreasonable to *deny Him those virtues which distinguish the best of men*), it is easily understood how He, the All-Fair Beneficent Ruler of the Central Sphere, perceiving the long distance to which the Earth was propelled, like a ball flung too far out, from the glory of His Electric Ring, saw also that the creatures He had made in His image were in danger of crushing that image completely out, and with it all remembrance of Him, in the fatal attention they gave to their merely earthly surroundings, lacking, as they did, and not possessing sufficient energy to seek, electric attraction. In brief, this Earth and God's World were like America and Europe before the Atlantic Cable was laid. Now the messages of goodwill flash under the waves, heedless of the storms. So also God's Cable is laid between us and His Heaven in the person of Christ.

"For ages (always remembering that our ages are with God a moment) the idea of *worship* was in the mind of man. With this idea came also the sentiment of *propitiation*. The untamed savage has from time immemorial instinctively felt the necessity of looking up to a Being greater than Himself, and also of seeking a reconciliation with that Being for some fault or loss in himself which he is aware of, yet cannot explain. This double instinct—worship and propitiation—is the key-note of all the creeds of the world, and may be called God's first thought of the cable to be hereafter laid—a lightning-thought which He instilled into the human race to prepare it, as one might test a telegraph-wire from house to house, before stretching it across a continent.

"All religions, as known to us, are mere types of Christianity. It is a notable fact that some of the oldest and most learned races in the world, such as the Armenians and Chaldeans, were the first to be convinced of the truth of Christ's visitation. Buddhism, of which there are so many million followers, is itself a type of Christ's teaching; only it lacks the supernatural element. Buddha died a hermit at the age of eighty, as any wise and ascetic man might do today. The death and resurrection of Christ were widely different. Anyone can be a Buddha again; anyone can *not* be a Christ. That there are stated to be more followers of Buddhism than of Christianity is no proof of any efficacy in the former or lack of power in the latter. Buddhists help to swell that very large class of persons who prefer a flattering picture to a plain original; or who, sheep-like by nature, finding themselves all together in one meadow, are too lazy, as well as too indifferent, to seek pastures fresher and fairer.

"Through the divine influence of an Electric Thought, then, the world unconsciously grew to expect *something*—they knew not what. The old creeds of the world, like sunflowers, turned towards that unknown Sun; the poets, prophets, seers, all spoke of some approaching consolation and glory; and to this day the fated Jews expect it, unwilling to receive as their Messiah the Divine Martyr they slew, though their own Scriptures testify to His identity.

"Christ came, born of a Virgin; that is, a radiant angel from God's Sphere was in the first place sent down to Earth to wear the form of Mary of Bethlehem, in Judea. Within that vessel of absolute purity God placed an Emanation of His own radiance—no germ or small flame such as is given to us in our bodies to cultivate and foster, but a complete immortal Spirit, a portion of God Himself, wise, sinless, and strong. This Spirit, pent up in clay, was born as a helpless babe, grew up as man—as man taught, comforted, was slain and buried; but as a Spirit rose again and returned in peace to Heaven, His mission done.

"It was necessary, in order to establish what has been called an electric communication between God's Sphere and this Earth, that an actual immortal, untainted Spirit in the person of Christ should walk this world, sharing with men sufferings, difficulties, danger, and death. Why? In order that we might first completely confide in and trust Him, afterwards realizing His spiritual strength and glory by His resurrection. And here may be noted the main difference between the Electric Theory of Christianity and other theories. *Christ did not die because God needed a sacrifice.* The idea of sacrifice is a relic of heathen barbarism; God is too infinitely loving to desire the sacrifice of the smallest flower. He is too patient to be ever wrathful; and barbaric ignorance confronts us again in the notion that He should need to be appeased. And the fancy that He should desire Himself or part of Himself to become a sacrifice to Himself has arisen out of the absurd and conflicting opinions of erring humanity, wherein right and wrong are so jumbled together that it is difficult to distinguish one from the other. Christ's death was not a sacrifice; it was simply a means of confidence and communion with the Creator. A sinless Spirit suffered to show us how to suffer; lived on earth to show us how to live; prayed to show us how to pray; died to show us how to die; rose again to impress strongly upon us that there was in truth a life beyond this one, for which He strove to prepare our souls. Finally, by His re-ascension into Heaven He established that much needed electric communication between us and the Central Sphere.

"It can be proved from the statements of the New Testament that in Christ was an Embodied Electric Spirit. From first to last His career was attended by *electric phenomena*, of which eight examples are here quoted; and earnest students of the matter can find many others if they choose to examine for themselves.

"1. The appearance of the Star and the Vision of Angels on the night of His birth. The Chaldeans saw His 'star in the east,' and they came to worship Him. The Chaldeans were always a learned people, and electricity was an advanced science with them. They at once recognized the star to be no new planet, but simply a star-shaped flame flitting through space. They knew what this meant. Observe, too, that they had no doubts upon the point; they came '*to worship Him,*' and provided themselves with gifts to offer to this radiant Guest, the offspring of pure Light. The vision of the angels appearing to the shepherds was simply a joyous band of the Singing Children of the Electric Ring, who out of pure interest and pleasure floated in sight of Earth, drawn thither partly by the already strong attractive influence of the Radiance that was imprisoned there in the form of the Babe of Bethlehem.

"2. When Christ was baptized by John the Baptist, '*the heavens opened.*'

"3. The sympathetic influence of Christ was so powerful that when He selected His disciples, He had but to speak to them, and at the sound of His voice, though they were engaged in other business, '*they left all and followed Him.*'

"4. Christ's body was charged with electricity. Thus He was easily able to heal sick and diseased persons by a touch or a look. The woman who caught at His garment in the crowd was cured of her long-standing ailment; and we see that Christ was aware of His own electric force by the words He used on that occasion: '*Who touched Me? for I feel that some virtue is gone out of Me*'—which is the exact feeling that a physical electrician experiences at this day after employing his powers on a subject. The raising of Jairus's daughter, of the widow's son at Nain, and of Lazarus, were all accomplished by the same means.

"5. The walking on the sea was a purely electric effort, *and can be accomplished now by anyone* who has cultivated sufficient inner force. The sea being full of electric particles will support anybody sufficiently and similarly charged—the two currents combining to procure the necessary equilibrium. Peter, who was able to walk a little way, lost his power directly his will became vanquished by fear—because the sentiment of fear disperses electricity, and being purely *human* emotion, does away with spiritual strength for the time.

"6. The Death of Christ was attended by electric manifestations—by the darkness over the land during the Crucifixion; the tearing of the temple veil in twain; and the earthquake which finally ensued.

"7. The Resurrection was a most powerful display of electric force. It will be remembered that the angel who was found sitting at the entrance of the empty sepulchre 'had a countenance like *lightning*,' i.e., like electric flame. It must also be called to mind how the risen Christ addressed Mary Magdalene: '*Touch Me not*, for I am but newly risen!' Why should she not have touched Him? Simply because His strength then was the strength of concentrated in-rushing currents of electricity; and to touch him at that moment would have been for Magdalene instant death by lightning. This effect of embodied electric force has been shadowed forth in the Greek legends of Apollo, whose glory consumed at a breath the mortal who dared to look upon him.

"8. The descent of the Holy Ghost, by which term is meant an ever-flowing current of the inspired working Intelligence of the Creator, was purely electric in character: 'Suddenly there came a sound from Heaven as of a rushing mighty wind, and it filled all the house where they were sitting. And there appeared unto them *cloven tongues like as of fire*, and sat upon each of them.' It may here be noted that the natural electric flame is *dual* or 'cloven' in shape.

"Let us now take the Creed as accepted today by the Christian Church, and see how thoroughly it harmonizes with the discoveries of spiritual electricity. 'I believe in one God the Father Almighty, Maker of Heaven and Earth, and of all things *visible and invisible.*' This is a brief and simple description of the Creator as He exists—a Supreme Centre of Light, out of whom *must* spring all life, all love, all wisdom.

"'And in one Lord Jesus Christ, the only-begotten Son of God, born of the Father before all ages.' This means that the only absolute Emanation of His own *personal* Radiance that ever wore such mean garb as our clay was found in Christ—who, as part of God, certainly existed '*before all ages.*' For as the Creed itself says, He was 'God of God, *Light of Light.*' Then we go on through the circumstances of Christ's birth, life, death, and resurrection, and our profession of faith brings us to 'I believe in the Holy Ghost, the Lord and Giver of Life, who proceedeth from the Father and the Son,' etc. This, as already stated, means that we believe that since Christ ascended into Heaven, our electric communication with the Creator has been established, and an ever-flowing current of divine inspiration is turned beneficially in the direction of our Earth, 'proceeding from the Father and the Son.' We admit in the Creed that this inspiration manifested itself before Christ came and '*spake by the prophets*'; but, as before stated, this only happened at rare and difficult intervals, while now Christ Himself speaks through those who most strongly adhere to His teachings.

"It may here be mentioned that few seem to grasp the fact of the *special message to women* intended to be conveyed in the person of the Virgin Mary. She was actually one of the radiant Spirits of the Central Sphere, imprisoned by God's will in woman's form. After the birth of Christ, she was still kept on earth, to follow His career to the end. There was a secret understanding between Himself and her. As for instance, when she found Him among the doctors of the law, she for one moment suffered her humanity to get the better of her in anxious inquiries; and His reply, 'Why sought ye Me? Wist ye not that I must be about My Father's business?' was a sort of reminder to her, which she at once accepted. Again, at the marriage feast in Cana of Galilee, when Christ turned the water into wine, He said to His mother, '*Woman*, what have I to do with thee?' which meant simply: What have I to do with thee as *woman* merely?—which was another reminder to her of her spiritual origin, causing her at once to address the servants who stood by as follows: 'Whatsoever He saith unto you, do it.' And why, it may be asked, if Mary was really an imprisoned immortal Spirit, sinless and joyous, should she be forced to suffer all the weaknesses, sorrows, and anxieties of any ordinary woman and mother? *Simply as an example to women* who are the mothers of the human race; and who, being thus laid under a heavy responsibility, need sympathetic guidance. Mary's life teaches women that the virtues they need are—obedience, purity, meekness, patience, long-suffering, modesty, self-denial, and endurance. She loved to hold a secondary position; she placed herself in willing subjection to Joseph—a man of austere and simple life, advanced in years, and weighted with the cares of a family by a previous marriage— who wedded her by *an influence which compelled him* to become her protector in the eyes of the world. Out of these facts, simple as they are, can be drawn the secret of happiness for women—a secret and a lesson that, if learned by heart, would bring them and those they love out of storm and bewilderment into peace and safety.

"*For those who have once become aware of the existence of the Central Sphere and of the Electric Ring surrounding it, and who are able to realize to the full the gigantic as well as minute work performed by the electric waves around us and within us*, there can no longer be any doubt as to all the facts of Christianity, as none of them, *viewed by the electric theory*, are otherwise than in accordance with the Creator's love and sympathy with even the smallest portion of His creation.

"Why then, if Christianity be a Divine Truth, are not all people Christians? As well ask, if music and poetry are good things, why all men are not poets and musicians. Art seeks art; in like manner God seeks God—that is, He seeks portions of His own essence among His creatures. Christ Himself said, 'Many are called, but few are chosen'; and it stands to reason that very few souls will succeed in becoming pure enough to enter the Central Sphere without hindrance. Many, on leaving Earth, will be detained in the Purgatory of Air, where thousands of spirits work for ages, watching over others, helping and warning others, and in this unselfish labour succeed in raising themselves, little by little, higher and ever higher, till they at last reach the longed-for goal. It must also be remembered that not only from Earth, but from *all worlds*, released souls seek to attain final happiness in the Central Sphere where God is; so that, however great the number of those that are permitted to proceed thither from this little planet, they can only form, as it were, one drop in a mighty ocean.

"It has been asked whether the Electric Theory of Christianity includes the doctrine of Hell, or a place of perpetual punishment. Eternal Punishment is merely a form of speech for what is really Eternal

Retrogression. For as there is a Forward, so there must be a Backward. The electric germ of the Soul—delicate, fiery, and imperishable as it is—can be forced by its companion Will to take refuge in a lower form of material existence, dependent on the body it first inhabits. For instance, a man who is obstinate in pursuing *active evil* can so retrograde the progress of any spiritual life within him, that it shall lack the power to escape, as it might do, from merely lymphatic and listless temperaments, to seek some other chance of development, but shall sink into the form of quadrupeds, birds, and other creatures dominated by purely physical needs. But there is one thing it can never escape from—*Memory*. And in that faculty is consti- tuted Hell. So that if a man, by choice, forces his soul *downward* to inhabit hereafter the bodies of dogs, horses, and other like animals, he should know that he does so at the cost of everything except Remembrance. Eter- nal Retrogression means that the hopelessly tainted electric germ recoils further and further from the Pure Centre whence it sprang, *always bearing within itself* the knowledge of *what it was once* and *what it might have been*. There is a pathetic meaning in the eyes of a dog or a seal; in the melan- choly, patient gaze of the oxen toiling at the plough; there is an unuttered warning in the silent faces of flowers; there is more tenderness of regret in the voice of the nightingale than love; and in the wild upward soaring of the lark, with its throat full of passionate, shouting prayer, there is shad- owed forth the yearning hope that dies away in despair as the bird sinks to earth again, his instincts not half satisfied. There is no greater torture than to be compelled to remember, in suffering, joys and glorious opportunities gone forever.

"Regarding the Electric Theory of Religion, it is curious to observe how the truth of it has again and again been dimly shadowed forth in the prophecies of Art, Science, and Poesy. The old painters who depicted a halo of light round the head of their Virgins and Saints did so out of a cor- rect impulse which they did not hesitate to obey.* The astronomers who, after years of profound study, have been enabled to measure the flames of the burning sun, and to find out that these are from two to four thousand miles high, are nearly arrived at the conclusion that it is a world in a state of conflagration, in which they will be perfectly right. Those who hold that this Earth of ours was once self-luminous are also right; for it was indeed so when first projected from the Electric Ring. The compilers or inven- tors of the 'Arabian Nights' also hit upon a truth when they described human beings as forced through evil influences to take the forms of lower animals—a truth just explained in the Law of Retrogression. All art, all

*An impulse which led them vaguely to foresee, though, not to explain, the electric princi- ple of spiritual life.

prophecy, all poesy, should therefore be accepted eagerly and studied earnestly, for in them we find *electric inspiration*, out of which we are able to draw lessons for our guidance hereafter. The great point that scientists and artists have hitherto failed to discover, is the existence of the Central Sphere and its Surrounding Electric Circle. Once realize these two great facts, and all the wonders and mysteries of the Universe are perfectly easy of comprehension.

"In conclusion, I offer no opinion as to which is Christ's Church, or the Fountain-head of spirituality in the world. In all Churches errors have intruded through unworthy and hypocritical members. In a crowded congregation of worshippers there may perhaps be only one or two who are free from self-interest and personal vanity. In Sectarianism, for instance, there is no shred of Christianity. Lovers of God and followers of Christ must, in the first place, have perfect Unity; and the bond uniting them must be an *electric* one of love and faith. No true Christian should be able to hate, despise, or envy the other. Were I called upon to select among the churches, I should choose that which has *most electricity* working within it, and which is able to believe in a positive electrical communication between Christ and herself taking place daily on her altars—a Church which holds, as it were, the other end of the telegraphic ray between Earth and the Central Sphere, and which is, therefore, able to exist among the storms of modern opinions, affording refuge and consolation to the few determined travellers who are bound onward and upward. I shall not name the Church I mean, because it is the duty of everyone to examine and find it out for himself or herself. And even though this Church instinctively works in the right direction, it is full of errors introduced by ignorant and unworthy members—errors which must be carefully examined and cast aside by degrees. But, as I said before, it is the only Church which has Principles of Electricity within it, and is therefore destined to live, because electricity is life.

"Now I beseech the reader of this manuscript to which I, Heliobas, append my hand and seal, to remember and realize earnestly the following invincible facts: first that God and His Christ *exist*; secondly, that while the little paltry affairs of our temporal state are being built up as crazily as a child's house of cards, the huge Central Sphere revolves, and the Electric Ring, strong and indestructible, is ever at its work of production and re-absorption; thirdly, that every thought and word of *every habitant on every planet* is reflected in lightning language before the Creator's eyes as easily as we receive telegrams; fourthly, that this world is *the only spot in the Universe* where His existence is actually questioned and doubted. And the general spread of modern positivism, materialism and atheism is one of the most terrific and meaning signs of the times. The work of separating the wheat from the chaff is beginning. Those who love and believe in God and Spiritual Beauty are about to be placed on one side; the millions who worship Self are drawing together in vast opposing ranks on the other; and the moment approaches which is prophesied to be 'as the lightning that lighteneth out of the one part under heaven, and shineth even to the other part.' In other words, the fiery whirlpool of the Ring is nearly ready to absorb our planet in its vortex; and out of all who dwell upon its surface, how many shall reach the glorious Central World of God? Of two men working in the same field, shall it not be as Christ foretold—'the one shall be taken, and the other left'?

"Friend, Pupil, Reader! Whoever thou art, take heed and foster thine own soul! For know that nothing can hinder the Immortal Germ within us from taking the form imposed upon it by our *Wills.* Through Love and Faith, it can become an Angel, and perform wonders even while in its habitation of clay; through indifference and apathy, it can desert us altogether and for ever; through mockery and blasphemous disbelief, it can sink into even a lower form than that of snake or toad. In our own unfettered hand lies our eternal destiny. Wonderful and terrible responsibility! Who shall dare to say we have no need of prayer?"

This document was signed "Casimir Heliobas," and bore a seal on which the impression seemed to consist of two Arabic or Sanskrit words, which I could not understand.

"The Searcher of the End House"

by William Hope Hodgson*

William Hope Hodgson (1877–1918) is best known for two of his epic novels, *The House on the Borderland* (1908) and *The Night Land* (1912), especially after their revival in the Ballantine Adult Fantasy series of the 1960s and 1970s. Hodgson also wrote many stories featuring the sea, even though he would refuse a naval war commission, losing his life as a member of the Royal Artillery Corps at the Fourth Battle of Ypres. He had an enduring interest in the nature of reality, however, and "The Searcher of the End House" (1910) and the eight other stories featuring the character Thomas Carnacki serve as examples of speculative fiction that crosses several subgenre boundaries. They are mysteries solved by a Holmes-like rationality, while at the same time leaving room for magic and cosmic horror. Sherlock Holmes's almost supernatural powers of deduction are superseded by Carnacki's ability to know when the facts are only the beginning of the story. Armed with electric pentagrams and an occult knowledge of the great unseen powers, Carnacki not only solves the day-to-day mysteries caused by greed, revenge, and passion, but also the timeless ones that affect the very fabric of reality.

* * * * *

It was still evening, as I remember, and the four of us, Jessop, Arkright, Taylor and I, looked disappointedly at Carnacki, where he sat silent in his great chair.

We had come in response to the usual card of invitation, which—as you know—we have come to consider as a sure prelude to a good story; and now, after telling us the short incident of the Three Straw Platters, he had lapsed into a contented silence, and the night not half gone, as I have hinted.

However, as it chanced, some pitying fate jogged Carnacki's elbow, or his memory, and he began again, in his queer level way:—

*Hodgson, William Hope. "The Searcher of the End House." *The Idler* 37, no. 3, 1910, pp. 996–1012.

"The 'Straw Platters' business reminds me of the 'Searcher' Case, which I have sometimes thought might interest you. It was some time ago, in fact a deuce of a long time ago, that the thing happened; and my experience of what I might term 'curious' things was very small at that time.

"I was living with my mother when it occurred, in a small house just outside of Appledorn, on the South Coast. The house was the last of a row of detached cottage villas, each house standing in its own garden; and very dainty little places they were, very old, and most of them smothered in roses; and all with those quaint old leaded windows, and doors of genuine oak. You must try to picture them for the sake of their complete niceness.

"Now I must remind you at the beginning that my mother and I had lived in that little house for two years; and in the whole of that time there had not been a single peculiar happening to worry us.

"And then, something happened.

"It was about two o'clock one morning, as I was finishing some letters, that I heard the door of my mother's bedroom open, and she came to the top of the stairs, and knocked on the banisters.

"'All right, dear,' I called; for I suppose she was merely reminding me that I should have been in bed long ago; then I heard her go back to her room, and I hurried my work, for fear she should lie awake, until she heard me safe up to my room.

"When I was finished, I lit my candle, put out the lamp, and went upstairs. As I came opposite the door of my mother's room, I saw that it was open, called good-night to her, very softly, and asked whether I should close the door. As there was no answer, I knew that she had dropped off to sleep again, and I closed the door very gently, and turned into my room, just across the passage. As I did so, I experienced a momentary, half-aware sense of a faint, peculiar, disagreeable odor in the passage; but it was not until the following night that I *realised* I had noticed a smell that offended me. You follow me? It is so often like that—one suddenly *knows* a thing that really recorded itself on one's consciousness, perhaps a year before.

"The next morning at breakfast, I mentioned casually to my mother that she had 'dropped off,' and I had shut the door for her. To my surprise, she assured me she had never been out of her room. I reminded her about the two raps she had given upon the banister; but she still was certain I must be mistaken; and in the end I teased her, saying she had grown so accustomed to my bad habit of sitting up late, that she had come to call me in her sleep. Of course, she denied this, and I let the matter drop; but I was more than a little puzzled, and did not know whether to believe my own explanation, or to take the mater's, which was to put the noises down to the mice, and the open door to the fact that she couldn't have properly latched it, when she went to bed. I suppose, away in the subconscious part of me, I had a stirring of less reasonable thoughts; but certainly, I had no real uneasiness at that time.

"The next night there came a further development. About two thirty a.m., I heard my mother's door open, just as on the previous night, and immediately afterward she rapped sharply, on the banister, as it seemed to me. I stopped my work and called up that I would not be long. As she made no reply, and I did not hear her go back to bed, I had a quick sense of wonder whether she might not be doing it in her sleep, after all, just as I had said.

"With the thought, I stood up, and taking the lamp from the table, began to go towards the door, which was open into the passage. It was then I got a sudden nasty sort of thrill; for it came to me, all at once, that my mother never knocked, when I sat up too late; she always called. You will understand I was not really frightened in any way; only vaguely uneasy, and pretty sure she must really be doing the thing in her sleep.

"I went quickly up the stairs, and when I came to the top, my mother was not there; but her door was open. I had a bewildered sense though believing she must have gone quietly back to bed, without my hearing her. I entered her room and found her sleeping quietly and naturally; for the vague sense of trouble in me was sufficiently strong to make me go over to look at her.

"When I was sure that she was perfectly right in every way, I was still a little bothered; but much more inclined to think my suspicion correct and that she had gone quietly back to bed in her sleep, without knowing what she had been doing. This was the most reasonable thing to think, as you must see.

"And then it came to me, suddenly, that vague, queer, mildewy smell in the room; and it was in that instant I became aware I had smelt the same strange, uncertain smell the night before in the passage.

"I was definitely uneasy now, and began to search my mother's room; though with no aim or clear thought of anything, except to assure myself that there was nothing in the room. All the time, you know, I never expected really to find anything; only my uneasiness had to be assured.

"In the middle of my search my mother woke up, and of course I had to explain. I told her about her door opening, and the knocks on the banister, and that I had come up and found her asleep. I said nothing about the smell, which was not very distinct; but told her that the thing happening twice had made me a bit nervous, and possibly fanciful, and I thought I would take a look round, just to feel satisfied.

"I have thought since that the reason I made no mention of the smell, was not only that I did not want to frighten my mother, for I was scarcely that myself; but because I had only a vague half-knowledge that

I associated the smell with fancies too indefinite and peculiar to bear talking about. You will understand that I am able now to analyse and put the thing into words; but then I did not even know my chief reason for saying nothing; let alone appreciate its possible significance.

"It was my mother, after all, who put part of my vague sensations into words:—

"'What a disagreeable smell!' she exclaimed, and was silent a moment, looking at me. Then:—'You feel there's something wrong?' still looking at me, very quietly but with a little, nervous note of questioning expectancy.

"'I don't know,' I said. 'I can't understand it, unless you've really been walking about in your sleep.'

"'The smell,' she said.

"'Yes,' I replied. 'That's what puzzles me too. I'll take a walk through the house; but I don't suppose it's anything.'

"I lit her candle, and taking the lamp, I went through the other bedrooms, and afterward all over the house, including the three underground cellars, which was a little trying to the nerves, seeing that I was more nervous than I would admit.

"Then I went back to my mother, and told her there was really nothing to bother about; and, you know, in the end, we talked ourselves into believing it was nothing. My mother would not agree that she might have been sleepwalking; but she was ready to put the door opening down to the fault of the latch, which certainly snicked very lightly. As for the knocks, they might be the old warped woodwork of the house cracking a bit, or a mouse rattling a piece of loose plaster. The smell was more difficult to explain; but finally we agreed that it might easily be the queer night smell of the moist earth, coming in through the open window of my mother's room, from the back garden, or—for that matter—from the little churchyard beyond the big wall at the bottom of the garden.

"And so we quietened down, and finally I went to bed, and to sleep.

"I think this is certainly a lesson on the way we humans can delude ourselves; for there was not one of these explanations that my reason could really accept. Try to imagine yourself in the same circumstances, and you will see how absurd our attempts to explain the happenings really were.

"In the morning, when I came down to breakfast, we talked it all over again, and whilst we agreed that it was strange, we also agreed that we had begun to imagine funny things in the backs of our minds, which now we felt half ashamed to admit. This is very strange when you come to look into it; but very human.

"And then that night again my mother's door was slammed once more just after midnight. I caught up the lamp, and when I reached her door, I found it shut. I opened it quickly, and went in, to find my mother lying with her eyes open, and rather nervous; having been waked by the bang of the door. But what upset me more than anything, was the fact that there was a disgusting smell in the passage and in her room.

"Whilst I was asking her whether she was all right, a door slammed twice downstairs; and you can imagine how it made me feel. My mother and I looked at one another; and then I lit her candle, and taking the poker from the fender, went downstairs with the lamp, beginning to feel really nervous. The culminative effect of so many queer happenings was getting hold of me; and all the apparently reasonable explanations seemed futile.

"The horrible smell seemed to be very strong in the downstairs passage; also in the front room and the cellars; but chiefly in the passage. I made a very thorough search of the house, and when I had finished, I knew that all the lower windows and doors were properly shut and fastened, and that there was no living thing in the house, beyond our two selves. Then I went up to my mother's room again, and we talked the thing over for an hour or more, and in the end came to the conclusion that we might, after all, be reading too much into a number of little things; but, you know, inside of us, we did not believe this.

"Later, when we had talked ourselves into a more comfortable state of mind, I said good night, and went off to bed; and presently managed to get to sleep.

"In the early hours of the morning, whilst it was still dark, I was waked by a loud noise. I sat up in bed, and listened. And from downstairs, I heard:—bang, bang, bang, one door after another being slammed; at least, that is the impression the sounds gave to me.

"I jumped out of bed, with the tingle and shiver of sudden fright on me; and at the same moment, as I lit my candle, my door was pushed slowly open; I had left it unlatched, so as not to feel that my mother was quite shut off from me.

"'Who's there?' I shouted out, in a voice twice as deep as my natural one, and with a queer breathlessness, that sudden fright so often gives one. 'Who's there?'

"Then I heard my mother saying:—

"'It's me, Thomas. Whatever is happening downstairs?'

"She was in the room by this, and I saw she had her bedroom poker in one hand, and her candle in the other. I could have smiled at her, had it not been for the extraordinary sounds downstairs.

"I got into my slippers, and reached down an old sword-bayonet from the wall; then I picked up my candle, and begged my mother not to come; but I knew it would be little use, if she had made up her mind; and she had, with the result that she acted as a sort of rearguard for me, during our search. I know, in some ways, I was very glad to have her with me, as you will understand.

"By this time, the door-slamming had ceased, and there seemed, probably because of the contrast, to be an appalling silence in the house. However, I led the way, holding my candle high, and keeping the sword-bayonet very handy. Downstairs we found all the doors wide open; although the outer doors and the windows were closed all right. I began to wonder whether the noises had been made by the doors after all. Of one thing only were we sure, and that was, there was no living thing in the house, beside ourselves, while everywhere throughout the house, there was the taint of that disgusting odor.

"Of course it was absurd to try to make-believe any longer. There was something strange about the house; and as soon as it was daylight, I set my mother to packing; and soon after breakfast, I saw her off by train.

"Then I set to work to try to clear up the mystery. I went first to the landlord, and told him all the circumstances. From him, I found that twelve or fifteen years back, the house had got rather a curious name from three or four tenants; with the result that it had remained empty a long while; in the end he had let it at a low rent to a Captain Tobias, on the one condition that he should hold his tongue, if he saw anything peculiar. The landlord's idea—as he told me frankly—was to free the house from these tales of 'something queer,' by keeping a tenant in it, and then to sell it for the best price he could get.

"However, when Captain Tobias left, after a ten years' tenancy, there was no longer any talk about the house; so when I offered to take it on a five years' lease, he had jumped at the offer. This was the whole story; so he gave me to understand. When I pressed him for details of the supposed peculiar happenings in the house, all those years back, he said the tenants had talked about a woman who always moved about the house at night. Some tenants never saw anything; but others would not stay out the first month's tenancy.

"One thing the landlord was particular to point out, that no tenant had ever complained about knockings, or door slamming. As for the smell, he seemed positively indignant about it; but why, I don't suppose he knew himself, except that he probably had some vague feeling that it was an indirect accusation on my part that the drains were not right.

"In the end, I suggested that he should come down and spend the night with me. He agreed at once, especially as I told him I intended to keep the whole business quiet, and try to get to the bottom of the curious affair; for he was anxious to keep the rumor of the haunting from getting about.

"About three o'clock that afternoon, he came down, and we made a thorough search of the house, which, however, revealed nothing unusual.

Afterwards, the landlord made one or two tests, which showed him the drainage was in perfect order; after that we made our preparations for sitting up all night.

"First, we borrowed two policemen's dark lanterns from the station near by, where the superintendent and I were friendly, and as soon as it was really dusk, the landlord went up to his house for his gun. I had the sword-bayonet I have told you about; and when the landlord got back, we sat talking in my study until nearly midnight.

"Then we lit the lanterns and went upstairs. We placed the lanterns, gun and bayonet handy on the table; then I shut and sealed the bedroom doors; afterward we took our seats, and turned off the lights.

"From then until two o'clock, nothing happened; but a little after two, as I found by holding my watch near the faint glow of the closed lanterns, I had a time of extraordinary nervousness; and I bent toward the landlord, and whispered to him that I had a queer feeling something was about to happen, and to be ready with his lantern; at the same time I reached out towards mine. In the very instant I made this movement, the darkness which filled the passage seemed to become suddenly of a dull violet colour; not, as if a light had been shone; but as if the natural blackness of the night had changed colour. And then, coming through this violet night, through this violet-coloured gloom, came a little naked Child, running. In an extraordinary way, the Child seemed not to be distinct from the surrounding gloom; but almost as if it were a concentration of that extraordinary atmosphere; as if that gloomy colour which had changed the night, came from the Child. It seems impossible to make clear to you; but try to understand it.

"The Child went past me, running, with the natural movement of the legs of a chubby human child, but in an absolute and inconceivable silence. It was a very small Child, and must have passed under the table; but I saw the Child through the table, as if it had been only a slightly darker shadow than the coloured gloom. In the same instant, I saw that a fluctuating glimmer of violet light outlined the metal of the gun-barrels and the blade of the sword-bayonet, making them seem like faint shapes of glimmering light, floating unsupported where the table-top should have shown solid.

"Now, curiously, as I saw these things, I was subconsciously aware that I heard the anxious breathing of the landlord, quite clear and laboured, close to my elbow, where he waited nervously with his hands on the lantern. I realised in that moment that he saw nothing; but waited in the darkness, for my warning to come true.

"Even as I took heed of these minor things, I saw the Child jump to one side, and hide behind some half-seen object that was certainly nothing belonging to the passage. I stared, intently, with a most extraordinary thrill of expectant wonder, with fright making goose-flesh of my back. And even as I stared, I solved for myself the less important problem of what the two black clouds were that hung over a part of the table. I think it very curious and interesting, the double working of the mind, often so much more apparent during times of stress. The two clouds came from two faintly shining shapes, which I knew must be the metal of the lanterns; and the things that looked black to the sight with which I was then seeing, could be nothing else but what to normal human sight is known as light. This phenomenon I have always remembered. I have twice seen a some-what similar thing; in The Dark Light Case and in that trouble of Maaethe-son's, which you know about.

"Even as I understood this matter of the lights, I was looking to my left, to understand why the Child was hiding. And suddenly, I heard the landlord shout out:—'The Woman!' But I saw nothing. I had a disagree-able sense that something repugnant was near to me, and I was aware in the same moment that the landlord was gripping my arm in a hard, fright-ened grip. Then I was looking back to where the Child had hidden. I saw the Child peeping out from behind its hiding-place, seeming to be looking up the passage; but whether in fear I could not tell. Then it came out, and ran headlong away, through the place where should have been the wall of my mother's bedroom; but the Sense with which I was seeing these things, showed me the wall only as a vague, upright shadow, unsubstantial. And immediately the child was lost to me, in the dull violet gloom. At the same time, I felt the landlord press back against me, as if something had passed close to him; and he called out again, a hoarse sort of cry:—'The Woman! The Woman!' and turned the shade clumsily from off his lantern. But I had seen no Woman; and the passage showed empty, as he shone the beam of his light jerkily to and fro; but chiefly in the direction of the doorway of my mother's room.

"He was still clutching my arm, and had risen to his feet; and now, mechanically and almost slowly, I picked up my lantern and turned on the light. I shone it, a little dazedly, at the seals upon the doors; but none were broken; then I sent the light to and fro, up and down the passage; but there was nothing; and I turned to the landlord, who was saying something in a rather incoherent fashion. As my light passed over his face, I noted, in a dull sort of way, that he was drenched with sweat.

"Then my wits became more handleable, and I began to catch the drift of his words:—'Did you see her? Did you see her?' he was saying, over and over again; and then I found myself telling him, in quite a level voice, that I had not seen any Woman. He became more coherent then, and I found that he had seen a Woman come from the end of the passage, and go past us; but he could not describe her, except that she kept stopping and looking about her, and had even peered at the wall, close beside him, as if looking for something. But what seemed to trouble him most, was that she had not seemed to see him at all. He repeated this so often, that in the end I told him, in an absurd sort of way, that he ought to be very glad she had not. What did it all mean? was the question; somehow I was not so frightened, as utterly bewildered. I had seen less then, than since; but what I had seen, had made me feel adrift from my anchorage of Reason.

"What did it mean? He had seen a Woman, searching for something. I had not seen this Woman. *I* had seen a Child, running away, and hiding from Something or Someone. *He* had not seen the Child, or the other things—only the Woman. And I had not seen her. What did it all mean?

"I had said nothing to the landlord about the Child. I had been too bewildered, and I realised that it would be futile to attempt an explanation. He was already stupid with the thing he had seen; and not the kind of man to understand. All this went through my mind as we stood there, shining the lanterns to and fro. All the time, intermingled with a streak of practical reasoning, I was questioning myself, what did it all mean? What was the Woman searching for; what was the Child running from?

"Suddenly, as I stood there, bewildered and nervous, making random answers to the landlord, a door below was violently slammed, and directly I caught the horrible reek of which I have told you.

"'There!' I said to the landlord, and caught his arm, in my turn. 'The Smell! Do you smell it?'

"He looked at me so stupidly that in a sort of nervous anger, I shook him.

"'Yes,' he said, in a queer voice, trying to shine the light from his shaking lantern at the stair-head.

"'Come on!' I said, and picked up my bayonet; and he came, carrying his gun awkwardly. I think he came, more because he was afraid to be left alone, than because he had any pluck left, poor beggar. I never sneer at that kind of funk, at least very seldom; for when it takes hold of you, it makes rags of your courage.

"I led the way downstairs, shining my light into the lower passage, and afterwards at the doors to see whether they were shut; for I had closed and latched them, placing a corner of a mat against each door, so I should know which had been opened.

"I saw at once that none of the doors had been opened; then I threw the beam of my light down alongside the stairway, in order to see the mat I had placed against the door at the top of the cellar stairs. I got a horrid thrill; for the mat was flat! I paused a couple of seconds, shining my light to and fro in the passage, and holding fast to my courage, I went down the stairs.

"As I came to the bottom step, I saw patches of wet all up and down the passage. I shone my lantern on them. It was the imprint of a wet foot on the oilcloth of the passage; not an ordinary footprint, but a queer, soft, flabby, spreading imprint, that gave me a feeling of extraordinary horror.

"Backward and forward I flashed the light over the impossible marks and saw them everywhere. Suddenly I noticed that they led to each of the closed doors. I felt something touch my back, and glanced 'round swiftly, to find the landlord had come close to me, almost pressing against me, in his fear.

"'It's all right,' I said, but in a rather breathless whisper, meaning to put a little courage into him; for I could feel that he was shaking through all his body. Even then as I tried to get him steadied enough to be of some use, his gun went off with a tremendous bang. He jumped, and yelled with sheer terror; and I swore because of the shock.

"'Give it to me, for God's sake!' I said, and slipped the gun from his hand; and in the same instant there was a sound of running steps up the garden path, and immediately the flash of a bull's-eye lantern upon the fan-light over the front door. Then the door was tried, and directly afterwards there came a thunderous knocking, which told me a policeman had heard the shot.

"I went to the door, and opened it. Fortunately the constable knew me, and when I had beckoned him in, I was able to explain matters in a very short time. While doing this, Inspector Johnstone came up the path, having missed the officer, and seeing lights and the open door. I told him as briefly as possible what had occurred, and did not mention the Child or the Woman; for it would have seem too fantastic for him to notice. I showed him the queer, wet footprints and how they went toward the closed doors. I explained quickly about the mats, and how that the one against the cellar door was flat, which showed the door had been opened.

"The inspector nodded, and told the constable to guard the door at the top of the cellar stairs. He then asked the hall lamp to be lit, after which he took the policeman's lantern, and led the way into the front room. He paused with the door wide open, and threw the light all round; then jumped into the room, and looked behind the door; there was no one there; but all over the polished oak floor, between the scattered rugs, went the marks of those horrible spreading footprints; and the room permeated with the horrible odour.

"The inspector searched the room carefully, and then went into the middle room, using the same precautions. There was nothing in the middle room, or in the kitchen or pantry; but everywhere went the wet footmarks through all the rooms, showing plainly wherever there was woodwork or oilcloth; and always there was the smell.

"The inspector ceased from his search of the rooms, and spent a minute in trying whether the mats would really fall flat when the doors were open, or merely ruckle up in a way as to appear they had been untouched; but in each case, the mats fell flat, and remained so.

"'Extraordinary!' I heard Johnstone mutter to himself. And then he went towards the cellar door. He had inquired at first whether there were windows to the cellar, and when he learned there was no way out, except by the door, he had left this part of the search to the last.

"As Johnstone came up to the door, the policeman made a motion of salute, and said something in a low voice; and something in the tone made me flick my light across him. I saw then that the man was very white, and he looked strange and bewildered.

"'What?' said Johnstone impatiently. 'Speak up!'

"'A woman come along 'ere, sir, and went through this 'ere door,' said the constable, clearly, but with a curious monotonous intonation that is sometimes heard from an unintelligent man.

"'Speak up!' shouted the inspector.

"'A woman come along and went through this 'ere door,' repeated the man, monotonously.

"The inspector caught the man by the shoulder, and deliberately sniffed his breath.

"'No!' he said. And then sarcastically:—'I hope you held the door open politely for the lady.'

"'The door weren't opened, sir,' said the man, simply.

"'Are you mad—' began Johnstone.

"'No,' broke in the landlord's voice from the back. Speaking steadily enough. 'I saw the Woman upstairs.' It was evident that he had got back his control again.

"'I'm afraid, Inspector Johnstone,' I said, 'that there's more in this than you think. I certainly saw some very extraordinary things upstairs.'

"The inspector seemed about to say something; but instead, he turned again to the door, and flashed his light down and round about the mat. I saw then that the strange, horrible footmarks came straight up to the cellar door; and the last print showed under the door; yet the policeman said the door had not been opened.

"And suddenly, without any intention, or realization of what I was saying, I asked the landlord:—

"'What were the feet like?'

"I received no answer; for the inspector was ordering the constable to open the cellar door, and the man was not obeying. Johnstone repeated the order, and at last, in a queer automatic way, the man obeyed, and pushed the door open. The loathsome smell beat up at us, in a great wave of horror, and the inspector came backward a step.

"'My God!' he said, and went forward again, and shone his light down the steps; but there was nothing visible, only that on each step showed the unnatural footprints.

"The inspector brought the beam of the light vividly on the top step; and there, clear in the light, there was something small, moving. The inspector bent to look, and the policeman and I with him. I don't want to disgust you; but the thing we looked at was a maggot. The policeman backed suddenly out of the doorway:

"'The churchyard,' he said, '… at the back of the 'ouse.'

"'Silence!' said Johnstone, with a queer break in the word, and I knew that at last he was frightened. He put his lantern into the doorway, and shone it from step to step, following the footprints down into the darkness; then he stepped back from the open doorway, and we all gave back with him. He looked round, and I had a feeling that he was looking for a weapon of some kind.

"'Your gun,' I said to the landlord, and he brought it from the front hall, and passed it over to the inspector, who took it and ejected the empty shell from the right barrel. He held out his hand for a live cartridge, which the landlord brought from his pocket. He loaded the gun and snapped the breech. He turned to the constable:—

"'Come on,' he said, and moved towards the cellar doorway.

"'I ain't comin', sir,' said the policeman, very white in the face.

"With a sudden blaze of passion, the inspector took the man by the scruff and hove him bodily down into the darkness, and he went downward, screaming. The inspector followed him instantly, with his lantern and the gun; and I after the inspector, with the bayonet ready. Behind me, I heard the landlord.

"At the bottom of the stairs, the inspector was helping the policeman to his feet, where he stood swaying a moment, in a bewildered fashion; then the inspector went into the front cellar, and his man followed him in stupid fashion; but evidently no longer with any thought of running away from the horror.

"We all crowded into the front cellar, flashing our lights to and fro. Inspector Johnstone was examining the floor, and I saw that the footmarks went all round the cellar, into all the corners, and across the floor. I thought suddenly of the Child that was running away from Something. Do you see the thing that I was seeing vaguely?

"We went out of the cellar in a body, for there was nothing to be found. In the next cellar, the footprints went everywhere in that queer erratic fashion, as of someone searching for something, or following some blind scent.

"In the third cellar the prints ended at the shallow well that had been the old water-supply of the house. The well was full to the brim, and the water so clear that the pebbly bottom was plainly to be seen, as we shone the lights into the water. The search came to an abrupt end, and we stood about the well, looking at one another, in an absolute, horrible silence.

"Johnstone made another examination of the footprints; then he shone his light again into the clear shallow water, searching each inch of the plainly seen bottom; but there was nothing there. The cellar was full of the dreadful smell; and everyone stood silent, except for the constant turning of the lamps to and fro around the cellar.

"The inspector looked up from his search of the well, and nodded quietly across at me, with his sudden acknowledgment that our belief was now his belief, the smell in the cellar seemed to grow more dreadful, and to be, as it were, a menace—the material expression that some monstrous thing was there with us, invisible.

"'I think—' began the inspector, and shone his light towards the stairway; and at this the constable's restraint went utterly, and he ran for the stairs, making a queer sound in his throat.

"The landlord followed, at a quick walk, and then the inspector and I. He waited a single instant for me, and we went up together, treading on the same steps, and with our lights held backwards. At the top, I slammed and locked the stair door, and wiped my forehead, and my hands were shaking.

"The inspector asked me to give his man a glass of whisky, and then he sent him on his beat. He stayed a short while with the landlord and me, and it was arranged that he would join us again the following night and watch the Well with us from midnight until daylight. Then he left us, just as the dawn was coming in. The landlord and I locked up the house, and went over to his place for a sleep.

"In the afternoon, the landlord and I returned to the house, to make arrangements for the night. He was very quiet, and I felt he was to be relied on, now that he had been 'salted,' as it were, with his fright of the previous night.

"We opened all the doors and windows, and blew the house through very thoroughly; and in the meanwhile, we lit the lamps in the house, and took them down into the cellars, where we set them all about, so as to have light everywhere. Then we carried down three chairs and a table, and set them in the cellar where the well was sunk. After that, we stretched thin piano wire across the cellar, about nine inches from the floor, at such a height that it should catch anything moving about in the dark.

"When this was done, I went through the house with the landlord, and sealed every window and door in the place, excepting only the front door and the door at the top of the cellar stairs.

"Meanwhile, a local wire-smith was making something to my order; and when the landlord and I had finished tea at his house, we went down to see how the smith was getting on. We found the thing complete. It looked rather like a huge parrot's cage, without any bottom, of very heavy gage wire, and stood about seven feet high and was four feet in diameter. Fortunately, I remembered to have it made longitudinally in two halves, or else we should never have got it through the doorways and down the cellar stairs.

"I told the wire-smith to bring the cage up to the house so he could fit the two halves rigidly together. As we returned, I called in at an ironmonger's, where I bought some thin hemp rope and an iron rack pulley, like those used in Lancashire for hauling up the ceiling clothes-racks, which you will find in every cottage. I bought also a couple of pitchforks.

"'We shan't want to touch it,' I said to the landlord; and he nodded, rather white all at once.

"As soon as the cage arrived and had been fitted together in the cellar, I sent away the smith; and the landlord and I suspended it over the well, into which it fitted easily. After a lot of trouble, we managed to hang it so perfectly central from the rope over the iron pulley, that when hoisted to the ceiling and dropped, it went every time plunk into the well, like a candle-extinguisher. When we had it finally arranged, I hoisted it up once more, to the ready position, and made the rope fast to a heavy wooden pillar, which stood in the middle of the cellar.

"By ten o'clock, I had everything arranged, with the two pitchforks and the two police lanterns; also some whisky and sandwiches. Underneath the table I had several buckets full of disinfectant.

"A little after eleven o'clock, there was a knock at the front door, and when I went, I found Inspector Johnstone had arrived, and brought with him one of his plain-clothes men. You will understand how pleased I was to see there would be this addition to our watch; for he looked a tough, nerveless man, brainy and collected; and one I should have picked to help us with the horrible job I felt pretty sure we should have to do that night.

"When the inspector and the detective had entered, I shut and locked the front door; then, while the inspector held the light, I sealed the door carefully, with tape and wax. At the head of the cellar stairs, I shut and locked that door also, and sealed it in the same way.

"As we entered the cellar, I warned Johnstone and his man to be careful not to fall over the wires; and then, as I saw his surprise at my arrangements, I began to explain my ideas and intentions, to all of which he listened with strong approval. I was pleased to see also that the detective was nodding his head, as I talked, in a way that showed he appreciated all my precautions.

"As he put his lantern down, the inspector picked up one of the pitchforks, and balanced it in his hand; he looked at me, and nodded.

"'The best thing,' he said. 'I only wish you'd got two more.'

"Then we all took our seats, the detective getting a washing-stool from the corner of the cellar. From then, until a quarter to twelve, we talked quietly, whilst we made a light supper of whisky and sandwiches; after which, we cleared everything off the table, excepting the lanterns and the pitchforks. One of the latter, I handed to the inspector; the other I took myself, and then, having set my chair so as to be handy to the rope which lowered the cage into the well, I went round the cellar and put out every lamp.

"I groped my way to my chair, and arranged the pitchfork and the dark lantern ready to my hand; after which I suggested that everyone should keep an absolute silence throughout the watch. I asked, also, that no lantern should be turned on, until I gave the word.

"I put my watch on the table, where a faint glow from my lantern made me able to see the time. For an hour nothing happened, and everyone kept an absolute silence, except for an occasional uneasy movement.

"About half-past one, however, I was conscious again of the same extraordinary and peculiar nervousness, which I had felt on the previous night. I put my hand out quickly, and eased the hitched rope from around the pillar. The inspector seemed aware of the movement; for I saw the faint light from his lantern, move a little, as if he had suddenly taken hold of it, in readiness.

"A minute later, I noticed there was a change in the colour of the night in the cellar, and it grew slowly violet-tinted upon my eyes. I glanced to and fro, quickly, in the new darkness, and even as I looked, I was conscious that the violet colour deepened. In the direction of the well, but seeming to be at a great distance, there was, as it were, a nucleus to the change; and the nucleus came swiftly towards us, appearing to come from a great space, almost in a single moment. It came near, and I saw again that it was a little naked Child, running, and seeming to be *of* the violet night in which it ran.

"The Child came with a natural running movement, exactly as I described it before; but in a silence so peculiarly intense, that it was as if it brought the silence with it. About half-way between the well and the table, the Child turned swiftly, and looked back at something invisible to me; and suddenly it went down into a crouching attitude, and seemed to be hiding behind something that showed vaguely; but there was nothing there, except the bare floor of the cellar; nothing, I mean, of our world.

"I could hear the breathing of the three other men, with a wonderful distinctness; and also the tick of my watch upon the table seemed to sound as loud and as slow as the tick of an old grandfather's clock. Someway I knew that none of the others saw what I was seeing.

"Abruptly, the landlord, who was next to me, let out his breath with a little hissing sound; I knew then that something was visible to him. There came a creak from the table, and I had a feeling that the inspector was leaning forward, looking at something that I could not see. The landlord reached out his hand through the darkness, and fumbled a moment to catch my arm:—

"'The Woman!' he whispered, close to my ear. 'Over by the well.'

"I stared hard in that direction; but saw nothing, except that the violet colour of the cellar seemed a little duller just there.

"I looked back quickly to the vague place where the Child was hiding. I saw it was peering backward from its hiding-place. Suddenly it rose and ran straight for the middle of the table, which showed only as vague shadow half-way between my eyes and the unseen floor. As the Child ran under the table, the steel prongs of my pitchfork glimmered with a violet, fluctuating light. A little way off, there showed high up in the gloom, the vaguely shining outline of the other fork, so I knew the inspector had it raised in his hand, ready. There was no doubt but that he saw something. On the table, the metal of the five lanterns shone with the same strange glow; and about each lantern there was a little cloud of absolute blackness, where the phenomenon that is light to our natural eyes, came through the fittings; and in this complete darkness, the metal of each lantern showed plain, as might a cat's-eye in a nest of black cotton wool.

"Just beyond the table, the Child paused again, and stood, seeming to oscillate a little upon its feet, which gave the impression that it was lighter and vaguer than a thistle-down; and yet, in the same moment, another part of me seemed to know that it was to me, as something that might be beyond thick, invisible glass, and subject to conditions and forces that I was unable to comprehend.

"The Child was looking back again, and my gaze went the same way. I stared across the cellar, and saw the cage hanging clear in the violet light, every wire and tie outlined with its glimmering; above it there was a little space of gloom, and then the dull shining of the iron pulley which I had screwed into the ceiling.

"I stared in a bewildered way round the cellar; there were thin lines of vague fire crossing the floor in all directions; and suddenly I remembered the piano wire that the landlord and I had stretched. But there was nothing else to be seen, except that near the table there were indistinct glimmerings of light, and at the far end the outline of a dull glowing revolver, evidently in the detective's pocket. I remember a sort of subconscious satisfaction, as I settled the point in a queer automatic fashion. On the table, near to me, there was a little shapeless collection of the light; and this I knew, after an instant's consideration, to be the steel portions of my watch.

"I had looked several times at the Child, and round at the cellar, whilst I was decided these trifles; and had found it still in that attitude of hiding from something. But now, suddenly, it ran clear away into the distance, and was nothing more than a slightly deeper coloured nucleus far away in the strange coloured atmosphere.

"The landlord gave out a queer little cry, and twisted over against me, as if to avoid something. From the inspector there came a sharp breathing sound, as if he had been suddenly drenched with cold water. Then suddenly the violet colour went out of the night, and I was conscious of the nearness of something monstrous and repugnant.

"There was a tense silence, and the blackness of the cellar seemed absolute, with only the faint glow about each of the lanterns on the table. Then, in the darkness and the silence, there came a faint tinkle of water from the well, as if something were rising noiselessly out of it, and the water running back with a gentle tinkling. In the same instant, there came to me a sudden waft of the awful smell.

"I gave a sharp cry of warning to the inspector, and loosed the rope. There came instantly the sharp splash of the cage entering the water; and then, with a stiff, frightened movement, I opened the shutter of my lantern, and shone the light at the cage, shouting to the others to do the same.

"As my light struck the cage, I saw that about two feet of it projected from the top of the well, and there was something protruding up out of the water, into the cage. I stared, with a feeling that I recognized the thing; and then, as the other lanterns were opened, I saw that it was a leg of mutton. The thing was held by a brawny fist and arm, that rose out of the water. I stood utterly bewildered, watching to see what was coming. In a moment there rose into view a great bearded face, that I felt for one quick instant was the face of a drowned man, long dead. Then the face opened at the mouth part, and spluttered and coughed. Another big hand came into view, and wiped the water from the eyes, which blinked rapidly, and then fixed themselves into a stare at the lights.

"From the detective there came a sudden shout:—

"'Captain Tobias!' he shouted, and the inspector echoed him; and instantly burst into loud roars of laughter.

"The inspector and the detective ran across the cellar to the cage; and I followed, still bewildered. The man in the cage was holding the leg of mutton as far away from him, as possible, and holding his nose.

"'Lift thig dam trap, quig!' he shouted in a stifled voice; but the inspector and the detective simply doubled before him, and tried to hold their noses, whilst they laughed, and the light from their lanterns went dancing all over the place.

"'Quig! quig!' said the man in the cage, still holding his nose, and trying to speak plainly.

"Then Johnstone and the detective stopped laughing, and lifted the cage. The man in the well threw the leg across the cellar, and turned swiftly to go down into the well; but the officers were too quick for him, and had him out in a twinkling. Whilst they held him, dripping upon the floor, the inspector jerked his thumb in the direction of the offending leg, and the landlord, having harpooned it with one of the pitchforks, ran with it upstairs and so into the open air.

"Meanwhile, I had given the man from the well a stiff tot of whisky; for which he thanked me with a cheerful nod, and having emptied the glass at a draft, held his hand for the bottle, which he finished, as if it had been so much water.

"As you will remember, it was a Captain Tobias who had been the previous tenant; and this was the very man, who had appeared from the well. In the course of the talk that followed, I learned the reason for Captain Tobias leaving the house; he had been wanted by the police for smuggling. He had undergone imprisonment; and had been released only a couple of weeks earlier.

"He had returned to find new tenants in his old home. He had entered the house through the well, the walls of which were not continued to the bottom (this I will deal with later); and gone up by a little stairway in the cellar wall, which opened at the top through a panel beside my mother's bedroom. This panel was opened, by revolving the left doorpost of the bedroom door, with the result that the bedroom door always became unlatched, in the process of opening the panel.

"The captain complained, without any bitterness, that the panel had warped, and that each time he opened it, it made a cracking noise. This had been evidently what I mistook for raps. He would not give his reason for entering the house; but it was pretty obvious that he had hidden something, which he wanted to get. However, as he found it impossible to get into the house without the risk of being caught, he decided to try to drive us out, relying on the bad reputation of the house, and his own artistic efforts as a ghost. I must say he succeeded. He intended then to rent the house again, as before; and would then, of course have plenty of time to get whatever he had hidden. The house suited him admirably; for there was a passage—as he showed me afterwards—connecting the dummy well with the crypt of the church beyond the garden wall; and these, in turn, were connected with certain caves in the cliffs, which went down to the beach beyond the church.

"In the course of his talk, Captain Tobias offered to take the house off my hands; and as this suited me perfectly, for I was about stalled with it, and the plan also suited the landlord, it was decided that no steps should be taken against him; and that the whole business should be hushed up.

"I asked the captain whether there was really anything queer about the house; whether he had ever seen anything. He said yes, that he had twice seen a Woman going about the house. We all looked at one another, when the captain said that. He told us she never bothered him, and that he had only seen her twice, and on each occasion it had followed a narrow escape from the Revenue people.

"Captain Tobias was an observant man; he had seen how I had placed the mats against the doors; and after entering the rooms, and walking all about them, so as to leave the foot-marks of an old pair of wet woollen slippers everywhere, he had deliberately put the mats back as he found them.

"The maggot which had dropped from his disgusting leg of mutton had been an accident, and beyond even his horrible planning. He was hugely delighted to learn how it had affected us.

"The mouldy smell I had noticed was from the little closed stairway, when the captain opened the panel. The door slamming was also another of his contributions.

"I come now to the end of the captain's ghost play; and to the difficulty of trying to explain the other peculiar things. In the first place, it was obvious there was something genuinely strange in the house; which made itself manifest as a Woman. Many different people had seen this Woman, under differing circumstances, so it is impossible to put the thing down to fancy; at the same time it must seem extraordinary that I should have lived two years in the house, and seen nothing; whilst the policeman saw the Woman, before he had been there twenty minutes; the landlord, the detective, and the inspector all saw her.

"I can only suppose that fear was in every case the key, as I might say, which opened the senses to the presence of the Woman. The policeman was a highly-strung man, and when he became frightened, was able to see the Woman. The same reasoning applies all round. I saw nothing, until I became really frightened; then I saw, not the Woman; but a Child, running away from Something or Someone. However, I will touch on that later. In short, until a very strong degree of fear was present, no one was affected by the Force which made Itself evident, as a Woman. My theory explains why some tenants were never aware of anything strange in the house, whilst others left immediately. The more sensitive they were, the less would be the degree of fear necessary to make them aware of the Force present in the house.

"The peculiar shining of all the metal objects in the cellar, had been visible only to me. The cause, naturally I do not know; neither do I know why I, alone, was able to see the shining."

"The Child," I asked. "Can you explain that part at all? Why you didn't see the Woman, and why they didn't see the Child. Was it merely the same Force, appearing differently to different people?"

"No," said Carnacki, "I can't explain that. But I am quite sure that the Woman and the Child were not only two complete and different entities; but even they were each not in quite the same planes of existence.

"To give you a root idea, however, it is held in the Sigsand MS. that a child 'still-born' is 'Snatyched back bye thee Haggs.' This is crude; but may yet contain an elemental truth. Yet, before I make this clearer, let me tell you a thought that has often been made. It may be that physical birth is but a secondary process; and that prior to the possibility, the Mother-Spirit searches for, until it finds, the small Element—the primal Ego or child's soul. It may be that a certain waywardness would cause such to strive to evade capture by the Mother-Spirit. It may have been such a thing as this, that I saw. I have always tried to think so; but it is impossible to ignore the sense of repulsion that I felt when the unseen Woman went past me. This repulsion carries forward the idea suggested in the Sigsand MS., that a still-born child is thus, because its ego or spirit has been snatched back by the 'Hags.' In other words, by certain of the Monstrocities of the Outer Circle. The thought is inconceivably terrible, and probably the more so because it is so fragmentary. It leaves us with the conception of a child's soul adrift half-way between two lives, and running through Eternity from Something incredible and inconceivable (because not understood) to our senses.

"The thing is beyond further discussion; for it is futile to attempt to discuss a thing, to any purpose, of which one has a knowledge so fragmentary as this. There is one thought, which is often mine. Perhaps there is a Mother-Spirit—"

"And the well?" said Arkwright. "How did the captain get in from the other side?"

"As I said before," answered Carnacki. "The side walls of the well did not reach to the bottom; so that you had only to dip down into the water, and come up again on the other side of the wall, under the cellar floor, and so climb into the passage. Of course, the water was the same height on both sides of the walls. Don't ask me who made the well entrance or the little stairway; for I don't know. The house was very old, as I have told you; and that sort of thing was useful in the old days."

"And the Child," I said, coming back to the thing which chiefly interested me. "You would say that the birth must have occurred in that house; and in this way, one might suppose that the house to have become *en rapport*, if I can use the word in that way, with the Forces that produced the tragedy?"

"Yes," replied Carnacki. "This is, supposing we take the suggestion of the Sigsand MS., to account for the phenomenon."

"There may be other houses—" I began.

"There are," said Carnacki; and stood up.

"Out you go," he said, genially, using the recognized formula. And in five minutes we were on the Embankment, going thoughtfully to our various homes.

"What Pragmatism Means"

by William James*

Offering a philosophical compromise between rationalism and empiricism, American philosopher William James (1842–1910) delivered "What Pragmatism Means" as part of his lecture series published in *Pragmatism: A New Name for Some Old Ways of Thinking* (1907). In addition to being recognized as a preeminent philosopher, James was also a physician and psychologist, perhaps best known for his pioneering two-volume textbook, *The Principles of Psychology* (1890). Influenced by Charles Darwin and continuing the work of colleague Charles Sanders Pierce, James argues in this piece that meaning and truth are determined by consequence above all. Where rationality relies on subjective morality and empiricism emphasizes fact without emotion, pragmatism purports that results of actions and inactions dictate how humanity perceives value. James would also go on to theorize about free will, religion, and mysticism wherein through the influence of various chemical substances, he perceived that truth can only be ascertained and understood through experience. James was also a founding member of the American Society for Psychical Research, believing in telepathy and even attending séances, withstanding heavy criticism from peers. James still stands as foundational architect of modern psychology and philosophy.

* * * * *

Some years ago, being with a camping party in the mountains, I returned from a solitary ramble to find everyone engaged in a ferocious metaphysical dispute. The *corpus* of the dispute was a squirrel—a live squirrel supposed to be clinging to one side of a tree-trunk; while over against the tree's opposite side a human being was imagined to stand. This human witness tries to get sight of the squirrel by moving rapidly round the tree, but no matter how fast he goes, the squirrel moves as fast in the

---

*James, William. "What Pragmatism Means." *Pragmatism: A New Name for Some Old Ways of Thinking*, Longmans, Green, and Co., 1907, pp. 43–81.

opposite direction, and always keeps the tree between himself and the man, so that never a glimpse of him is caught. The resultant metaphysical problem now is this: *Does the man go round the squirrel or not?* He goes round the tree, sure enough, and the squirrel is on the tree; but does he go round the squirrel? In the unlimited leisure of the wilderness, discussion had been worn threadbare. Everyone had taken sides, and was obstinate; and the numbers on both sides were even. Each side, when I appeared, therefore appealed to me to make it a majority. Mindful of the scholastic adage that whenever you meet a contradiction you must make a distinction, I immediately sought and found one, as follows: "Which party is right," I said, "depends on what you *practically mean* by 'going round' the squirrel. If you mean passing from the north of him to the east, then to the south, then to the west, and then to the north of him again, obviously the man does go round him, for he occupies these successive positions. But if on the contrary you mean being first in front of him, then on the right of him, then behind him, then on his left, and finally in front again, it is quite as obvious that the man fails to go round him, for by the compensating movements the squirrel makes, he keeps his belly turned towards the man all the time, and his back turned away. Make the distinction, and there is no occasion for any farther dispute. You are both right and both wrong according as you conceive the verb 'to go round' in one practical fashion or the other."

Although one or two of the hotter disputants called my speech a shuffling evasion, saying they wanted no quibbling or scholastic hair-splitting, but meant just plain honest English "round," the majority seemed to think that the distinction had assuaged the dispute.

I tell this trivial anecdote because it is a peculiarly simple example of what I wish now to speak of as *the pragmatic method*. The pragmatic method is primarily a method of settling metaphysical disputes that otherwise might be interminable. Is the world one or many?—fated or free?—material or spiritual?—here are notions either of which may or may not hold good of the world; and disputes over such notions are unending. The pragmatic method in such cases is to try to interpret each notion by tracing its respective practical consequences. What difference would it practically make to any one if this notion rather than that notion were true? If no practical difference whatever can be traced, then the alternatives mean practically the same thing, and all dispute is idle. Whenever a dispute is serious, we ought to be able to show some practical difference that must follow from one side or the other's being right.

A glance at the history of the idea will show you still better what pragmatism means. The term is derived from the same Greek word πραγμα, meaning action, from which our words "practice" and "practical" come. It was first introduced into philosophy by Mr. Charles Peirce in 1878. In an article entitled "How to Make Our Ideas Clear," in the "Popular Science Monthly" for January of that year,* Mr. Peirce, after pointing out that our beliefs are really rules for action, said that, to develop a thought's meaning, we need only determine what conduct it is fitted to produce: that conduct is for us its sole significance. And the tangible fact at the root of all our thought-distinctions, however subtle, is that there is no one of them so fine as to consist in anything but a possible difference of practice. To attain perfect clearness in our thoughts of an object, then, we need only consider what conceivable effects of a practical kind the object may involve—what sensations we are to expect from it, and what reactions we must prepare. Our conception of these effects, whether immediate or remote, is then for us the whole of our conception of the object, so far as that conception has positive significance at all.

This is the principle of Peirce, the principle of pragmatism. It lay entirely unnoticed by anyone for twenty years, until I, in an address before Professor Howison's philosophical union at the university of California, brought it forward again and made a special application of it to religion. By that date (1898) the times seemed ripe for its reception. The word "pragmatism" spread, and at present it fairly spots the pages of the philosophic journals. On all hands we find the "pragmatic movement" spoken of, sometimes with respect, sometimes with contumely, seldom with clear understanding. It is evident that the term applies itself conveniently to a number of tendencies that hitherto have lacked a collective name, and that it has "come to stay."

To take in the importance of Peirce's principle, one must get accustomed to applying it to concrete cases. I found a few years ago that Ostwald, the illustrious Leipzig chemist, had been making perfectly distinct use of the principle of pragmatism in his lectures on the philosophy of science, though he had not called it by that name.

"All realities influence our practice," he wrote me, "and that influence is their meaning for us. I am accustomed to put questions to my classes in this way: In what respects would the world be different if this alternative or that were true? If I can find nothing that would become different, then the alternative has no sense."

That is, the rival views mean practically the same thing, and meaning, other than practical, there is for us none. Ostwald in a published lecture gives this example of what he means. Chemists have long wrangled over the inner constitution of certain bodies called "tautomerous." Their properties seemed equally consistent with the notion that an instable

---

*Translated in the *Revue Philosophique* for January 1879 (vol. vii).[Author's note.]

hydrogen atom oscillates inside of them, or that they are instable mixtures of two bodies. Controversy raged; but never was decided. "It would never have begun," says Ostwald, "if the combatants had asked themselves what particular experimental fact could have been made different by one or the other view being correct. For it would then have appeared that no difference of fact could possibly ensue; and the quarrel was as unreal as if, theorizing in primitive times about the raising of dough by yeast, one party should have invoked a 'brownie,' while another insisted on an 'elf' as the true cause of the phenomenon."*

It is astonishing to see how many philosophical disputes collapse into insignificance the moment you subject them to this simple test of tracing a concrete consequence. There can *be* no difference anywhere that doesn't *make* a difference elsewhere—no difference in abstract truth that doesn't express itself in a difference in concrete fact and in conduct consequent upon that fact, imposed on somebody, somehow, somewhere, and somewhen. The whole function of philosophy ought to be to find out what definite difference it will make to you and me, at definite instants of our life, if this world-formula or that world-formula be the true one.

There is absolutely nothing new in the pragmatic method. Socrates was an adept at it. Aristotle used it methodically. Locke, Berkeley, and Hume made momentous contributions to truth by its means. Shadworth Hodgson keeps insisting that realities are only what they are "known as." But these forerunners of pragmatism used it in fragments: they were a prelude only. Not until in our time has it generalized itself, become conscious of a universal mission, pretended to a conquering destiny. I believe in that destiny, and I hope I may end by inspiring you with my belief.

Pragmatism represents a perfectly familiar attitude in philosophy, the empiricist attitude, but it represents it, as it seems to me, both in a more radical and in a less objectionable form than it has ever yet assumed. A pragmatist turns his back resolutely and once for all upon a lot of inveterate habits dear to professional philosophers. He turns away from abstraction and insufficiency, from verbal solutions, from bad *a priori* reasons, from fixed principles, closed systems, and pretended absolutes and origins. He turns towards concreteness and adequacy, towards facts, towards action, and towards power. That means the empiricist temper regnant, and the rationalist temper sincerely given up. It means the open air and

---

*"Theorie und Praxis," *Zeitsch. des Oesterreichischen Ingenieur u. Architecten-Vereines,* 1905, Nr. 4 u. 6. I find a still more radical pragmatism than Ostwald's in an address by Professor W.S. Franklin: "I think that the sickliest notion of physics, even if a student gets it, is that it is 'the science of masses, molecules and the ether.' And I think that the healthiest notion, even if a student does not wholly get it, is that physics is the science of the ways of taking hold of bodies and pushing them!" (Science, January 2, 1903). [Author's note.]

possibilities of nature, as against dogma, artificiality, and the pretense of finality in truth.

At the same time it does not stand for any special results. It is a method only. But the general triumph of that method would mean an enormous change in what I called in my last lecture the "temperament" of philosophy. Teachers of the ultra-rationalistic type would be frozen out, much as the courtier type is frozen out in republics, as the ultramontane type of priest is frozen out in protestant lands. Science and metaphysics would come much nearer together, would in fact work absolutely hand in hand.

Metaphysics has usually followed a very primitive kind of quest. You know how men have always hankered after unlawful magic, and you know what a great part in magic *words* have always played. If you have his name, or the formula of incantation that binds him, you can control the spirit, genie, afrite, or whatever the power may be. Solomon knew the names of all the spirits, and having their names, he held them subject to his will. So the universe has always appeared to the natural mind as a kind of enigma, of which the key must be sought in the shape of some illuminating or power-bringing word or name. That word names the universe's *principle*, and to possess it is, after a fashion, to possess the universe itself. "God," "Matter," "Reason," "the Absolute," "Energy," are so many solving names. You can rest when you have them. You are at the end of your metaphysical quest.

But if you follow the pragmatic method, you cannot look on any such word as closing your quest. You must bring out of each word its practical cash-value, set it at work within the stream of your experience. It appears less as a solution, then, than as a program for more work, and more particularly as an indication of the ways in which existing realities may be *changed*.

Theories thus become instruments, not answers to enigmas, in which we can rest. We don't lie back upon them, we move forward, and, on occasion, make nature over again by their aid. Pragmatism unstiffens all our theories, limbers them up and sets each one at work. Being nothing essentially new, it harmonizes with many ancient philosophic tendencies. It agrees with nominalism for instance, in always appealing to particulars; with utilitarianism in emphasizing practical aspects; with positivism in its disdain for verbal solutions, useless questions, and metaphysical abstractions.

All these, you see, are *anti-intellectualist* tendencies. Against rationalism as a pretension and a method, pragmatism is fully armed and militant. But, at the outset, at least, it stands for no particular results. It has no dogmas, and no doctrines save its method. As the young Italian pragmatist

Papini has well said, it lies in the midst of our theories, like a corridor in a hotel. Innumerable chambers open out of it. In one you may find a man writing an atheistic volume; in the next someone on his knees praying for faith and strength; in a third a chemist investigating a body's properties. In a fourth a system of idealistic metaphysics is being excogitated; in a fifth the impossibility of metaphysics is being shown. But they all own the corridor, and all must pass through it if they want a practicable way of getting into or out of their respective rooms.

No particular results then, so far, but only an attitude of orientation, is what the pragmatic method means. *The attitude of looking away from first things, principles, "categories," supposed necessities; and of looking towards last things, fruits, consequences, facts.*

So much for the pragmatic method! You may say that I have been praising it rather than explaining it to you, but I shall presently explain it abundantly enough by showing how it works on some familiar problems. Meanwhile the word pragmatism has come to be used in a still wider sense, as meaning also a certain *theory of truth*. I mean to give a whole lecture to the statement of that theory, after first paving the way, so I can be very brief now. But brevity is hard to follow, so I ask for your redoubled attention for a quarter of an hour. If much remains obscure, I hope to make it clearer in the later lectures.

One of the most successfully cultivated branches of philosophy in our time is what is called inductive logic, the study of the conditions under which our sciences have evolved. Writers on this subject have begun to show a singular unanimity as to what the laws of nature and elements of fact mean, when formulated by mathematicians, physicists and chemists. When the first mathematical, logical, and natural uniformities, the first *laws*, were discovered, men were so carried away by the clearness, beauty and simplification that resulted, that they believed themselves to have deciphered authentically the eternal thoughts of the Almighty. His mind also thundered and reverberated in syllogisms. He also thought in conic sections, squares and roots and ratios, and geometrized like Euclid. He made Kepler's laws for the planets to follow; he made velocity increase proportionally to the time in falling bodies; he made the law of the sines for light to obey when refracted; he established the classes, orders, families and genera of plants and animals, and fixed the distances between them. He thought the archetypes of all things, and devised their variations; and when we rediscover any one of these his wondrous institutions, we seize his mind in its very literal intention.

But as the sciences have developed farther, the notion has gained ground that most, perhaps all, of our laws are only approximations. The laws themselves, moreover, have grown so numerous that there is no counting them; and so many rival formulations are proposed in all the branches of science that investigators have become accustomed to the notion that no theory is absolutely a transcript of reality, but that any one of them may from some point of view be useful. Their great use is to summarize old facts and to lead to new ones. They are only a man-made language, a conceptual shorthand, as someone calls them, in which we write our reports of nature; and languages, as is well known, tolerate much choice of expression and many dialects.

Thus human arbitrariness has driven divine necessity from scientific logic. If I mention the names of Sigwart, Mach, Ostwald, Pearson, Milhaud, Poincaré, Duhem, Heymans, those of you who are students will easily identify the tendency I speak of, and will think of additional names.

Riding now on the front of this wave of scientific logic Messrs. Schiller and Dewey appear with their pragmatistic account of what truth everywhere signifies. Everywhere, these teachers say, "truth" in our ideas and beliefs means the same thing that it means in science. It means, they say, nothing but this, *that ideas (which themselves are but parts of our experience) become true just in so far as they help us to get into satisfactory relation with other parts of our experience*, to summarize them and get about among them by conceptual short-cuts instead of following the interminable succession of particular phenomena. Any idea upon which we can ride, so to speak; any idea that will carry us prosperously from any one part of our experience to any other part, linking things satisfactorily, working securely, simplifying, saving labor; is true for just so much, true in so far forth, true *instrumentally*. This is the "instrumental" view of truth taught so successfully at Chicago, the view that truth in our ideas means their power to "work," promulgated so brilliantly at Oxford.

Messrs. Dewey, Schiller and their allies, in reaching this general conception of all truth, have only followed the example of geologists, biologists and philologists. In the establishment of these other sciences, the successful stroke was always to take some simple process actually observable in operation—as denudation by weather, say, or variation from parental type, or change of dialect by incorporation of new words and pronunciations—and then to generalize it, making it apply to all times, and produce great results by summating its effects through the ages.

The observable process which Schiller and Dewey particularly singled out for generalization is the familiar one by which any individual settles into *new opinions*. The process here is always the same. The individual has a stock of old opinions already, but he meets a new experience that puts them to a strain. Somebody contradicts them; or in a reflective moment he discovers that they contradict each other; or he hears of facts with which they are incompatible; or desires arise in him which they cease to satisfy. The result is an inward trouble to which his mind till then had been a stranger, and from which he seeks to escape by modifying his previous mass of opinions. He saves as much of it as he can, for in this matter of belief we are all extreme conservatives. So he tries to change first this opinion, and then that (for they resist change very variously), until at last some new idea comes up which he can graft upon the ancient stock with a minimum of disturbance of the latter, some idea that mediates between the stock and the new experience and runs them into one another most felicitously and expediently.

This new idea is then adopted as the true one. It preserves the older stock of truths with a minimum of modification, stretching them just enough to make them admit the novelty, but conceiving that in ways as familiar as the case leaves possible. An *outrée* explanation, violating all our preconceptions, would never pass for a true account of a novelty. We should scratch round industriously till we found something less eccentric. The most violent revolutions in an individual's beliefs leave most of his old order standing. Time and space, cause and effect, nature and history, and one's own biography remain untouched. New truth is always a go-between, a smoother-over of transitions. It marries old opinion to new fact so as ever to show a minimum of jolt, a maximum of continuity. We hold a theory true just in proportion to its success in solving this "problem of maxima and minima." But success in solving this problem is eminently a matter of approximation. We say this theory solves it on the whole more satisfactorily than that theory; but that means more satisfactorily to ourselves, and individuals will emphasize their points of satisfaction differently. To a certain degree, therefore, everything here is plastic.

The point I now urge you to observe particularly is the part played by the older truths. Failure to take account of it is the source of much of the unjust criticism levelled against pragmatism. Their influence is absolutely controlling. Loyalty to them is the first principle—in most cases it is the only principle; for by far the most usual way of handling phenomena so novel that they would make for a serious rearrangement of our preconception is to ignore them altogether, or to abuse those who bear witness for them.

You doubtless wish examples of this process of truth's growth, and the only trouble is their superabundance. The simplest case of new truth is of course the mere numerical addition of new kinds of facts, or of new single facts of old kinds, to our experience—an addition that involves no alteration in the old beliefs. Day follows day, and its contents are simply added. The new contents themselves are not true, they simply *come* and *are*. Truth is *what we say about* them, and when we say that they have come, truth is satisfied by the plain additive formula.

But often the day's contents oblige a rearrangement. If I should now utter piercing shrieks and act like a maniac on this platform, it would make many of you revise your ideas as to the probable worth of my philosophy. "Radium" came the other day as part of the day's content, and seemed for a moment to contradict our ideas of the whole order of nature, that order having come to be identified with what is called the conservation of energy. The mere sight of radium paying heat away indefinitely out of its own pocket seemed to violate that conservation. What to think? If the radiations from it were nothing but an escape of unsuspected "potential" energy, pre-existent inside of the atoms, the principle of conservation would be saved. The discovery of "helium" as the radiation's outcome, opened a way to this belief. So Ramsay's view is generally held to be true, because, although it extends our old ideas of energy, it causes a minimum of alteration in their nature.

I need not multiply instances. A new opinion counts as "true" just in proportion as it gratifies the individual's desire to assimilate the novel in his experience to his beliefs in stock. It must both lean on old truth and grasp new fact; and its success (as I said a moment ago) in doing this, is a matter for the individual's appreciation. When old truth grows, then, by new truth's addition, it is for subjective reasons. We are in the process and obey the reasons. That new idea is truest which performs most felicitously its function of satisfying our double urgency. It makes itself true, gets itself classed as true, by the way it works; grafting itself then upon the ancient body of truth, which thus grows much as a tree grows by the activity of a new layer of cambium.

Now Dewey and Schiller proceed to generalize this observation and to apply it to the most ancient parts of truth. They also once were plastic. They also were called true for human reasons. They also mediated between still earlier truths and what in those days were novel observations. Purely objective truth, truth in whose establishment the function of giving human satisfaction in marrying previous parts of experience with newer parts played no role whatever, is nowhere to be found. The reasons why we call things true is the reason why they *are* true, for "to be true" *means* only to perform this marriage-function.

The trail of the human serpent is thus over everything. Truth independent; truth that we *find* merely; truth no longer malleable to human need; truth incorrigible, in a word; such truth exists indeed superabundantly—or is supposed to exist by rationalistically minded thinkers; but then it means only the dead heart of the living tree, and its being there means only that truth also has its paleontology and its "prescription," and may grow stiff with years of veteran service and petrified in men's regard by sheer antiquity. But how plastic even the oldest truths nevertheless really are has been vividly shown in our day by the transformation of logical and mathematical ideas, a transformation which seems even to be invading physics. The ancient formulas are reinterpreted as special expressions of much wider principles, principles that our ancestors never got a glimpse of in their present shape and formulation.

Mr. Schiller still gives to all this view of truth the name of "Humanism," but, for this doctrine too, the name of pragmatism seems fairly to be in the ascendant, so I will treat it under the name of pragmatism in these lectures.

Such then would be the scope of pragmatism—first, a method; and second, a genetic theory of what is meant by truth. And these two things must be our future topics.

What I have said of the theory of truth will, I am sure, have appeared obscure and unsatisfactory to most of you by reason of its brevity. I shall make amends for that hereafter. In a lecture on "common sense" I shall try to show what I mean by truths grown petrified by antiquity. In another lecture I shall expatiate on the idea that our thoughts become true in proportion as they successfully exert their go-between function. In a third I shall show how hard it is to discriminate subjective from objective factors in Truth's development. You may not follow me wholly in these lectures; and if you do, you may not wholly agree with me. But you will, I know, regard me at least as serious, and treat my effort with respectful consideration.

You will probably be surprised to learn, then, that Messrs. Schiller's and Dewey's theories have suffered a hailstorm of contempt and ridicule. All rationalism has risen against them. In influential quarters Mr. Schiller, in particular, has been treated like an impudent schoolboy who deserves a spanking. I should not mention this, but for the fact that it throws so much sidelight upon that rationalistic temper to which I have opposed the temper of pragmatism. Pragmatism is uncomfortable away from facts. Rationalism is comfortable only in the presence of abstractions. This pragmatist talk about truths in the plural, about their utility and satisfactoriness, about the success with which they "work," etc., suggests to the typical intellectualist mind a sort of coarse lame second-rate makeshift article of truth. Such truths are not real truth. Such tests are merely subjective. As against this, objective truth must be something non-utilitarian, haughty, refined, remote, august, exalted. It must be an absolute correspondence of our thoughts with an equally absolute reality. It must be what we *ought* to think, unconditionally. The conditioned ways in which we *do* think are so much irrelevance and matter for psychology. Down with psychology, up with logic, in all this question!

See the exquisite contrast of the types of mind! The pragmatist clings to facts and concreteness, observes truth at its work in particular cases, and generalizes. Truth, for him, becomes a class-name for all sorts of definite working-values in experience. For the rationalist it remains a pure abstraction, to the bare name of which we must defer. When the pragmatist undertakes to show in detail just *why* we must defer, the rationalist is unable to recognize the concretes from which his own abstraction is taken. He accuses us of *denying* truth; whereas we have only sought to trace exactly why people follow it and always ought to follow it. Your typical ultra-abstractionist fairly shudders at concreteness: other things equal, he positively prefers the pale and spectral. If the two universes were offered, he would always choose the skinny outline rather than the rich thicket of reality. It is so much purer, clearer, nobler.

I hope that as these lectures go on, the concreteness and closeness to facts of the pragmatism which they advocate may be what approves itself to you as its most satisfactory peculiarity. It only follows here the example of the sister-sciences, interpreting the unobserved by the observed. It brings old and new harmoniously together. It converts the absolutely empty notion of a static relation of "correspondence" (what that may mean we must ask later) between our minds and reality, into that of a rich and active commerce (that anyone may follow in detail and understand) between particular thoughts of ours, and the great universe of other experiences in which they play their parts and have their uses.

But enough of this at present? The justification of what I say must be postponed. I wish now to add a word in further explanation of the claim I made at our last meeting, that pragmatism may be a happy harmonizer of empiricist ways of thinking, with the more religious demands of human beings.

* * *

Men who are strongly of the fact-loving temperament, you may remember me to have said, are liable to be kept at a distance by the small sympathy with facts which that philosophy from the present-day fashion of idealism offers them. It is far too intellectualistic. Old fashioned theism was bad enough, with its notion of God as an exalted monarch, made up of a lot of unintelligible or preposterous "attributes"; but, so long as it held strongly by the argument from design, it kept some touch with concrete realities. Since, however, darwinism has once for all displaced design from the minds of the "scientific," theism has lost that foothold; and some kind of an immanent or pantheistic deity working *in* things rather than above them is, if any, the kind recommended to our contemporary imagination. Aspirants to a philosophic religion turn, as a rule, more hopefully nowadays towards idealistic pantheism than towards the older dualistic theism, in spite of the fact that the latter still counts able defenders.

But, as I said in my first lecture, the brand of pantheism offered is hard for them to assimilate if they are lovers of facts, or empirically minded. It is the absolutistic brand, spurning the dust and reared upon pure logic. It keeps no connection whatever with concreteness. Affirming the Absolute Mind, which is its substitute for God, to be the rational presupposition of all particulars of fact, whatever they may be, it remains supremely indifferent to what the particular facts in our world actually are. Be they what they may, the Absolute will father them. Like the sick lion in Esop's fable, all footprints lead into his den, but *nulla vestigia retrorsum*. You cannot redescend into the world of particulars by the Absolute's aid, or deduce any necessary consequences of detail important for your life from your idea of his nature. He gives you indeed the assurance that all is well with *Him*, and for his eternal way of thinking; but thereupon he leaves you to be finitely saved by your own temporal devices.

Far be it from me to deny the majesty of this conception, or its capacity to yield religious comfort to a most respectable class of minds. But from the human point of view, no one can pretend that it doesn't suffer from the faults of remoteness and abstractness. It is eminently a product of what I have ventured to call the rationalistic temper. It disdains empiricism's needs. It substitutes a pallid outline for the real world's richness. It is dapper; it is noble in the bad sense, in the sense in which to be noble is to be inapt for humble service. In this real world of sweat and dirt, it seems to me that when a view of things is "noble," that ought to count as a presumption against its truth, and as a philosophic disqualification. The prince of darkness may be a gentleman, as we are told he is, but whatever the God of earth and heaven is, he can surely be no gentleman. His menial services are needed in the dust of our human trials, even more than his dignity is needed in the empyrean.

Now pragmatism, devoted though she be to facts, has no such materialistic bias as ordinary empiricism labors under. Moreover, she has no objection whatever to the realizing of abstractions, so long as you get about among particulars with their aid and they actually carry you somewhere. Interested in no conclusions but those which our minds and our experiences work out together, she has no *a priori* prejudices against theology. *If theological ideas prove to have a value for concrete life, they will be true, for pragmatism, in the sense of being good for so much. For how much more they are true, will depend entirely on their relations to the other truths that also have to be acknowledged.*

What I said just now about the Absolute of transcendental idealism is a case in point. First, I called it majestic and said it yielded religious comfort to a class of minds, and then I accused it of remoteness and sterility. But so far as it affords such comfort, it surely is not sterile; it has that amount of value; it performs a concrete function. As a good pragmatist, I myself ought to call the Absolute true "in so far forth," then; and I unhesitatingly now do so.

But what does *true in so far forth* mean in this case? To answer, we need only apply the pragmatic method. What do believers in the Absolute mean by saying that their belief affords them comfort? They mean that since in the Absolute finite evil is "overruled" already, we may, therefore, whenever we wish, treat the temporal as if it were potentially the eternal, be sure that we can trust its outcome, and, without sin, dismiss our fear and drop the worry of our finite responsibility. In short, they mean that we have a right ever and anon to take a moral holiday, to let the world wag in its own way, feeling that its issues are in better hands than ours and are none of our business.

The universe is a system of which the individual members may relax their anxieties occasionally, in which the don't-care mood is also right for men, and moral holidays in order—that, if I mistake not, is part, at least, of what the Absolute is "known-as," that is the great difference in our particular experiences which his being true makes, for us, that is his cash-value when he is pragmatically interpreted. Farther than that the ordinary lay-reader in philosophy who thinks favorably of absolute idealism does not venture to sharpen his conceptions. He can use the Absolute for so much, and so much is very precious. He is pained at hearing you speak incredulously of the Absolute, therefore, and disregards your criticisms because they deal with aspects of the conception that he fails to follow.

If the Absolute means this, and means no more than this, who can possibly deny the truth of it? To deny it would be to insist that men should never relax, and that holidays are never in order.

I am well aware how odd it must seem to some of you to hear me say that an idea is "true" so long as to believe it is profitable to our lives. That it is *good*, for as much as it profits, you will gladly admit. If what we do by its aid is good, you will allow the idea itself to be good in so far forth, for we are the better for possessing it. But is it not a strange misuse of the word "truth," you will say, to call ideas also "true" for this reason?

To answer this difficulty fully is impossible at this stage of my account. You touch here upon the very central point of Messrs. Schiller's, Dewey's and my own doctrine of truth, which I cannot discuss with detail until my sixth lecture. Let me now say only this, that truth is *one species of good*, and not, as is usually supposed, a category distinct from good, and co-ordinate with it. *The true is the name of whatever proves itself to be good in the way of belief, and good, too, for definite, assignable reasons.* Surely you must admit this, that if there were *no* good for life in true ideas, or if the knowledge of them were positively disadvantageous and false ideas the only useful ones, then the current notion that truth is divine and precious, and its pursuit a duty, could never have grown up or become a dogma. In a world like that, our duty would be to *shun* truth, rather. But in this world, just as certain foods are not only agreeable to our taste, but good for our teeth, our stomach, and our tissues; so certain ideas are not only agreeable to think about, or agreeable as supporting other ideas that we are fond of, but they are also helpful in life's practical struggles. If there be any life that it is really better we should lead, and if there be any idea which, if believed in, would help us to lead that life, then it would be really be*tter for us* to believe in that idea, *unless, indeed, belief in it incidentally clashed with other greater vital benefits.*

"What would be better for us to believe"! This sounds very like a definition of truth. It comes very near to saying "what we *ought* to believe": and in *that* definition none of you would find any oddity. Ought we ever not to believe what it is *better for us* to believe? And can we then keep the notion of what is better for us, and what is true for us, permanently apart?

Pragmatism says no, and I fully agree with her. Probably you also agree, so far as the abstract statement goes, but with a suspicion that if we practically did believe everything that made for good in our own personal lives, we should be found indulging all kinds of fancies about this world's affairs, and all kinds of sentimental superstitions about a world hereafter. Your suspicion here is undoubtedly well founded, and it is evident that something happens when you pass from the abstract to the concrete, that complicates the situation.

I said just now that what is better for us to believe is true *unless the belief incidentally clashes with some other vital belief.* Now in real life what vital benefits is any particular belief of ours most liable to clash with? What indeed except the vital benefits yielded by *other beliefs* when these prove incompatible with the first ones? In other words, the greatest enemy of any one of our truths may be the rest of our truths. Truths have once for all this desperate instinct of self-preservation and of desire to extinguish whatever contradicts them. My belief in the Absolute, based on the good it does me, must run the gauntlet of all my other beliefs. Grant that it may be true in giving me a moral holiday. Nevertheless, as I conceive it,—and let me speak now confidentially, as it were, and merely in my own private person,—it clashes with other truths of mine whose benefits I hate to give up on its account. It happens to be associated with a kind of logic of which I am the enemy, I find that it entangles me in metaphysical paradoxes that are inacceptable, etc., etc. But as I have enough trouble in life already without adding the trouble of carrying these intellectual inconsistencies, I personally just give up the Absolute. I just *take* my moral holidays; or else as a professional philosopher, I try to justify them by some other principle.

If I could restrict my notion of the Absolute to its bare holiday-giving value, it wouldn't clash with my other truths. But we cannot easily thus restrict our hypotheses. They carry supernumerary features, and these it is that clash so. My disbelief in the Absolute means then disbelief in those other supernumerary features, for I fully believe in the legitimacy of taking moral holidays.

You see by this what I meant when I called pragmatism a mediator and reconciler and said, borrowing the word from Papini, that she "unstiffens" our theories. She has in fact no prejudices whatever, no obstructive dogmas, no rigid canons of what shall count as proof. She is completely genial. She will entertain any hypothesis, she will consider any evidence. It follows that in the religious field she is at a great advantage both over positivistic empiricism, with its anti-theological bias, and over religious rationalism, with its exclusive interest in the remote, the noble, the simple, and the abstract in the way of conception.

In short, she widens the field of search for God. Rationalism sticks to logic and the empyrean. Empiricism sticks to the external senses. Pragmatism is willing to take anything, to follow either logic or the senses, and to count the humblest and most personal experiences. She will count mystical experiences if they have practical consequences. She will take a God who lives in the very dirt of private fact—if that should seem a likely place to find him.

Her only test of probable truth is what works best in the way of leading us, what fits every part of life best and combines with the collectivity of experience's demands, nothing being omitted. If theological ideas should do this, if the notion of God, in particular, should prove to do it, how could pragmatism possibly deny God's existence? She could see no meaning in treating as "not true" a notion that was pragmatically so successful. What other kind of truth could there be, for her, than all this agreement with concrete reality?

In my last lecture I shall return again to the relations of pragmatism with religion. But you see already how democratic she is. Her manners are as various and flexible, her resources as rich and endless, and her conclusions as friendly as those of mother nature.

"Spear and Fang"

by Robert E. Howard*

Robert E. Howard (1906–1936) established himself as a regular contributor to pulp magazines in the 1920s and became a prominent and influential author in speculative fiction. His debut in *Weird Tales*, the publication he would become most associated with, was "Spear and Fang" in the July 1925 issue. Howard was a key member in the "Lovecraft Circle" of writers and editors, including Farnsworth Wright, Clark Ashton Smith, August Derleth, and H.P. Lovecraft. Howard and Lovecraft often shared suggestions and criticism of each other's stories and philosophies. In particular, they disagreed vociferously on the concept of civilization, and Howard's most famous creation, Conan the Cimmerian, would embody his views that civilization is unnatural. In "Spear and Fang," Howard lays the early building blocks of the Conan character and emphasizes his trademark action sequences. Although the plot is rather rudimentary, Howard creates interest in placing the story in a transition between two phases or human development: the Neanderthal and the Cro-Magnon man. Howard would later develop this theme with both Conan and his Puritan protagonist, Solomon Kane. This short story would also be the inspiration for *Primal*, Genndy Tartakovsky's Emmy-winning animated series in 2020.

* * * * *

A-æa crouched close to the cave mouth, watching Ga-nor with wondering eyes. Ga-nor's occupation interested her, as well as Ga-nor himself. As for Ga-nor, he was too occupied with his work to notice her. A torch stuck in a niche in the cave wall dimly illuminated the roomy cavern, and by its light Ga-nor was laboriously tracing figures on the wall. With a piece of flint he scratched the outline and then with a twig dipped in ocher paint

*Howard, Robert E. "Spear and Fang." *Weird Tales* 6, no. 1, July 1925, pp. 111–115.

completed the figure. The result was crude, but gave evidence of real artistic genius, struggling for expression.

It was a mammoth that he sought to depict, and little A-æa's eyes widened with wonder and admiration. Wonderful! What though the beast lacked a leg and had no tail? It was tribesmen, just struggling out of utter barbarism, who were the critics, and to them Ga-nor was a past master.

However, it was not to watch the reproduction of a mammoth that A-æa hid among the scanty bushes by Ga-nor's cave. The admiration for the painting was as nothing beside the look of positive adoration with which she favored the artist. Indeed, Ga-nor was not unpleasing to the eye. Tall he was, towering well over six feet, leanly built, with mighty shoulders and narrow hips, the build of a fighting man. Both his hands and his feet were long and slim; and his features, thrown into bold profile by the flickering torch-light, were intelligent, with a high, broad forehead, topped by a mane of sandy hair.

A-æa herself was very easy to look upon. Her hair, as well as her eyes, was black and fell about her slim shoulders in a rippling wave. No ocher tattooing tinted her cheek, for she was still unmated.

Both the girl and the youth were perfect specimens of the great Cro-Magnon race which came from no man knows where and announced and enforced their supremacy over beast and beast-man.

A-æa glanced about nervously. All ideas to the contrary, customs and taboos are much more narrow and vigorously enforced among savage peoples.

The more primitive a race, the more intolerant their customs. Vice and licentiousness may be the rule, but the appearance of vice is shunned and contemned. So if A-æa had been discovered, hiding near the cave of an unattached young man, denunciation as a shameless woman would have been her lot, and doubtless a public whipping.

To be proper, A-æa should have played the modest, demure maiden, perhaps skillfully arousing the young artist's interest without seeming to do so. Then, if the youth was pleased, would have followed public wooing by means of crude love-songs and music from reed pipes. Then barter with her parents and then—marriage. Or no wooing at all, if the lover was wealthy.

But little A-æa was herself a mark of progress. Covert glances had failed to attract the attention of the young man who seemed engrossed with his artistry, so she had taken to the unconventional way of spying upon him, in hopes of finding some way to win him.

Ga-nor turned from his completed work, stretched and glanced toward the cave mouth. Like a frightened rabbit, little A-æa ducked and darted away.

When Ga-nor emerged from the cave, he was puzzled by the sight of a small, slender footprint in the soft loam outside the cave.

A-æa walked primly toward her own cave, which was, with most of the others, at some distance from Ga-nor's cave. As she did so, she noticed a group of warriors talking excitedly in front of the chief's cave.

A mere girl might not intrude upon the councils of men, but such was A-æa's curiosity, that she dared a scolding by slipping nearer. She heard the words "footprint" and "gur-na" (man-ape).

The footprints of a gur-na had been found in the forest, not far from the caves.

"Gur-na" was a word of hatred and horror to the people of the caves, for the creatures whom the tribesmen called "gur-na," or man-apes, were the hairy monsters of another age, the brutish men of the Neandertal. More feared than mammoth or tiger, they had ruled the forests until the Cro-Magnon men had come and waged savage warfare against them. Of mighty power and little mind, savage, bestial and cannibalistic, they inspired the tribesmen with loathing and horror—a horror transmitted through the ages in tales of ogres and goblins, of werewolves and beast-men.

They were fewer and more cunning, then. No longer they rushed roaring to battle, but cunning and frightful, they slunk about the forests, the terror of all beasts, brooding in their brutish minds with hatred for the men who had driven them from the best hunting grounds.

And ever the Cro-Magnon men trailed them down and slaughtered them, until sullenly they had withdrawn far into the deep forests. But the fear of them remained with the tribesmen, and no woman went into the jungle alone.

Sometimes children went, and sometimes they returned not; and searchers found but signs of a ghastly feast, with tracks that were not the tracks of beasts, nor yet the tracks of men.

And so a hunting party would go forth and hunt the monster down. Sometimes it gave battle and was slain, and sometimes it fled before them and escaped into the depths of the forest, where they dared not follow. Once a hunting party, reckless with the chase, had pursued a fleeing gur-na into the deep forest and there, in a deep ravine, where overhanging limbs shut out the sunlight, numbers of the Neandertalers had come upon them.

So no more entered the forests.

* * *

A-æa turned away, with a glance at the forest. Somewhere in its depths lurked the beast man, piggish eyes glinting crafty hate, malevolent, frightful.

Someone stepped across her path. It was Ka-nanu, the son of a councilor of the chief.

She drew away with a shrug of her shoulders. She did not like Ka-nanu and she was afraid of him. He wooed her with a mocking air, as if he did it merely for amusement and would take her whenever he wished, anyway. He seized her by the wrist.

"Turn not away, fair maiden," said he. "It is your slave, Ka-nanu."

"Let me go," she answered. "I must go to the spring for water."

"Then I will go with you, moon of delight, so that no beast may harm you."

And accompany her he did, in spite of her protests.

"There is a gur-na abroad," he told her sternly. "It is lawful for a man to accompany even an unmated maiden, for protection. And I am Ka-nanu," he added, in a different tone; "do not resist me too far, or I will teach you obedience."

A-æa knew somewhat of the man's ruthless nature. Many of the tribal girls looked with favor on Ka-nanu, for he was bigger and taller even than Ga-nor, and more handsome in a reckless, cruel way. But A-æa loved Ga-nor and she was afraid of Ka-nanu. Her very fear of him kept her from resisting his approaches too much. Ga-nor was known to be gentle with women, if careless of them, while Ka-nanu, thereby showing himself to be another mark of progress, was proud of his success with women and used his power over them in no gentle fashion.

A-æa found Ka-nanu was to be feared more than a beast, for at the spring just out of sight of the caves, he seized her in his arms.

"A-æa," he whispered, "my little antelope, I have you at last. You shall not escape me."

In vain she struggled and pleaded with him. Lifting her in his mighty arms he strode away into the forest.

Frantically she strove to escape, to dissuade him.

"I am not powerful enough to resist you," she said, "but I will accuse you before the tribe."

"You will never accuse me, little antelope," he said, and she read another, even more sinister intention in his cruel countenance.

On and on into the forest he carried her, and in the midst of a glade he paused, his hunter's instinct alert.

From the trees in front of them dropped a hideous monster, a hairy, misshapen, frightful thing.

A-æa's scream re-echoed through the forest, as the thing approached. Ka-nanu, white-lipped and horrified, dropped A-æa to the ground and told her to run. Then, drawing knife and ax, he advanced.

The Neandertal man plunged forward on short, gnarled legs. He was covered with hair and his features were more hideous than an ape's because of the grotesque quality of the man in them. Flat, flaring nostrils, retreating chin, fangs, no forehead whatever, great, immensely long arms dangling from sloping, incredible shoulders, the monster seemed like the devil himself to the terrified girl. His apelike head came scarcely to Ka-nanu's shoulders, yet he must have outweighed the warrior by nearly a hundred pounds.

On he came like a charging buffalo, and Ka-nanu met him squarely and boldly. With flint ax and obsidian dagger he thrust and smote, but the ax was brushed aside like a toy and the arm that held the knife snapped like a stick in the misshapen hand of the Neandertaler. The girl saw the councilor's son wrenched from the ground and swung into the air, saw him hurled clear across the glade, saw the monster leap after him and rend him limb from limb.

Then the Neandertaler turned his attention to her. A new expression came into his hideous eyes as he lumbered toward her, his great hairy hands horridly smeared with blood, reaching toward her.

Unable to flee, she lay dizzy with horror and fear. And the monster dragged her to him, leering into her eyes. He swung her over his shoulder and waddled away through the trees; and the girl, half-fainting, knew that he was taking her to his lair, where no man would dare come to rescue her.

* * *

Ga-nor came down to the spring to drink. Idly he noticed the faint footprints of a couple who had come before him. Idly he noticed that they had not returned.

Each footprint has its individual characteristic. That of the man he knew to be Ka-nanu. The other track was the same as that in front of his cave. He wondered, idly as Ga-nor was wont to do all things except the painting of pictures.

Then, at the spring, he noticed that the footprints of the girl ceased, but that the man's turned toward the jungle and were more deeply imprinted than before. Therefore Ka-nanu was carrying the girl.

Ga-nor was no fool. He knew that a man carries a girl into the forest for no good purpose. If she had been willing to go, she would not have been carried.

Now Ga-nor (another mark of progress) was inclined to meddle in things not pertaining to him. Perhaps another man would have shrugged his shoulders and gone his way, reflecting that it would not be well to interfere with a son of a councilor. But Ga-nor had few interests, and once his interest was roused he was inclined to see a thing through. Moreover, though not renowned as a fighter, he feared no man.

Therefore, he loosened ax and dagger in his belt, shifted his grip on his spear, and took up the trail.

* * *

On and on, deeper and deeper into the forest, the Neandertaler carried little A-æa.

The forest was silent and evil, no birds, no insects broke the stillness. Through the overhanging trees no sunlight filtered. On padded feet that made no noise the Neandertaler hurried on.

Beasts slunk out of his path. Once a great python came slithering through the jungle and the Neandertaler took to the trees with surprising speed for one of his gigantic bulk. He was not at home in the trees, however, not even as much as A-æa would have been.

Once or twice the girl glimpsed another such monster as her captor. Evidently they had gone far beyond the vaguely defined boundaries of her race. The other Neandertal men avoided them. It was evident that they lived as do beasts, uniting only against some common enemy and not often then. Therein had lain the reason for the success of the Cro-Magnards' warfare against them.

Into a ravine he carried the girl, and into a cave, small and vaguely illuminated by the light from without. He threw her roughly to the floor of the cave, where she lay, too terrified to rise.

The monster watched her, like some demon of the forest. He did not even jabber at her, as an ape would have done. The Neandertalers had no form of speech whatever.

He offered her meat of some kind—uncooked, of course. Her mind reeling with horror, she saw that it was the arm of a Cro-Magnard child. When he saw she would not eat, he devoured it himself, tearing the flesh with great fangs.

He took her between his great hands, bruising her soft flesh. He ran rough fingers through her hair, and when he saw that he hurt her he seemed filled with a fiendish glee. He tore out handfuls of her hair, seeming to enjoy devilishly the torturing of his fair captive. A-æa set her teeth and would not scream as she had done at first, and presently he desisted.

The leopard-skin garment she wore seemed to enrage him. The leopard was his hereditary foe. He plucked it from her and tore it to pieces.

And meanwhile Ga-nor was hurrying through the forest. He was racing now, and his face was a devil's mask, for he had come upon the bloody glade and had found the monster's tracks leading away from it.

And in the cave in the ravine the Neandertaler reached for A-æa.

She sprang back and he plunged toward her. He had her in a corner but she slipped under his arm and sprang away. He was still between her and the outside of the cave.

Unless she could get past him, he would corner her and seize her. So she pretended to spring to one side. The Neandertaler lumbered in that direction, and quick as a cat she sprang the other way and darted past him, out into the ravine.

With a bellow he charged after her. A stone rolled beneath her foot, flinging her headlong; before she could rise his hand seized her shoulder. As he dragged her into the cave, she screamed, wildly, frenziedly, with no hope of rescue, just the scream of a woman in the grasp of a beast.

Ga-nor heard that scream as he bounded down into the ravine. He approached the cave swiftly but cautiously. As he looked in, he saw red rage. In the vague light of the cave, the great Neandertaler stood, his piggish eyes on his foe, hideous, hairy, blood-smeared, while at his feet, her soft white body contrasting with the shaggy monster, her long hair gripped in his blood-stained hand, lay A-æa.

The Neandertaler bellowed, dropped his captive and charged. And Ga-nor met him, not matching brute strength with his lesser might, but leaping back and out of the cave. His spear leaped and the monster bellowed as it tore through his arm. Leaping back again, the warrior jerked his spear and crouched. Again the Neandertaler rushed, and again the warrior leaped away and thrust, this time for the great hairy chest. And so they battled, speed and intelligence against brute strength and savagery.

Once the great, lashing arm of the monster caught Ga-nor upon the shoulder and hurled him a dozen feet away, rendering that arm nearly useless for a time. The Neandertaler bounded after him, but Ga-nor flung himself to one side and leaped to his feet. Again and again his spear drew blood, but it seemed only to enrage the monster.

Then before the warrior knew it, the wall of the ravine was at his back and he heard A-æa shriek as the monster rushed in. The spear was torn from his hand and he was in the grasp of his foe. The great arms encircled his neck and shoulders, the great fangs sought his throat. He thrust his elbow under the retreating chin of his antagonist, and with his free hand struck the hideous face again and again; blows that would have felled an ordinary man but which the Neandertal beast did not even notice.

Ga-nor felt consciousness going from him. The terrific arms were crushing him, threatening to break his neck. Over the shoulder of his foe he saw the girl approaching with a great stone, and he tried to motion her back.

With a great effort he reached down over the monster's arm and found his ax. But so close were they clinched together that he could not draw it. The Neandertal man set himself to break his foe to pieces as one breaks a stick. But Ga-nor's elbow was thrust under his chin, and the more the Neandertal man tugged, the deeper drove the elbow into his hairy throat. Presently he realized that fact and flung Ga-nor away from him. As he did so, the warrior drew his ax, and striking with the fury of desperation, clove the monster's head.

* * *

For a minute Ga-nor stood reeling above his foe, then he felt a soft form within his arms and saw a pretty face, close to his.

"Ga-nor!" A-æa whispered, and Ga-nor gathered the girl in his arms.

"What I have fought for I will keep," said he.

And so it was that the girl who went forth into the forest in the arms of an abductor came back in the arms of a lover and a mate.

"The Black God's Kiss"

by C.L. Moore*

During the early twentieth century, it was not too common to find a female with physical prowess and combat skills to rival men, but that's exactly what American author Catherine Lucille Moore (1911–1987) gives readers with Jirel of Joiry in the October 1934 issue of *Weird Tales* with "The Black God's Kiss." In the first of what would become a series of six stories, C.L. Moore's Jirel is depicted as a strong, beautiful, ruthless, and intelligent warrior queen. As a protagonist, she is the first of her kind in speculative fiction. Acknowledging that she shares certain characteristics that are frequently seen in male protagonists of Robert E. Howard, Moore's character has been the subject of gender bending and female masculinity analysis and is far more than a female counter to Howard's hypermasculine archetype. In addition to establishing Moore's heroine, this story also features a unique blend of mysticism, combining supernatural elements with Christian themes, all set in medieval France. Jirel must find her own fortitude and faith in order to conquer a usurper through the aid of a magical weapon. She must make use of all she has, including her strength, fighting skills, and sexuality.

* * * * *

They brought in Joiry's tall commander, struggling between two men-at-arms who tightly gripped the ropes which bound their captive's mailed arms. They picked their way between mounds of dead as they crossed the great hall toward the dais where the conqueror sat, and twice they slipped a little in the blood that spattered the flags. When they came to a halt before the mailed figure on the dais, Joiry's commander was breathing hard, and the voice that echoed hollowly under the helmet's confines was hoarse with fury and despair.

---

*Moore, C.L. "The Black God's Kiss." *Weird Tales* 24, no. 4, October 1934, pp. 402–421.

Guillaume the conqueror leaned on his mighty sword, hands crossed on its hilt, grinning down from his height upon the furious captive before him. He was a big man, Guillaume, and he looked bigger still in his spattered armor. There was blood on his hard, scarred face, and he was grinning a white grin that split his short, curly beard glitteringly. Very splendid and very dangerous he looked, leaning on his great sword and smiling down upon fallen Joiry's lord, struggling between the stolid men-at-arms.

"Unshell me this lobster," said Guillaume in his deep lazy voice. "We'll see what sort of face the fellow has who gave us such a battle. Off with his helmet, you."

But a third man had to come up and slash the straps which held the iron helmet on, for the struggles of Joiry's commander were too fierce, even with bound arms, for either of the guards to release their hold. There was a moment of sharp struggle; then the straps parted and the helmet rolled loudly across the flagstones.

Guillaume's white teeth clicked on a startled oath. He stared. Joiry's lady glared back at him from between her captors, wild red hair tousled, wild lion-yellow eyes ablaze.

"God curse you!" snarled the lady of Joiry between clenched teeth. "God blast your black heart!"

Guillaume scarcely heard her. He was still staring, as most men stared when they first set eyes upon Jirel of Joiry. She was tall as most men, and as savage as the wildest of them, and the fall of Joiry was bitter enough to break her heart as she stood snarling curses up at her tall conqueror. The face above her mail might not have been fair in a woman's head-dress, but in the steel setting of her armor it had a biting, sword-edge beauty as keen as the flash of blades. The red hair was short upon her high, defiant head, and the yellow blaze of her eyes held fury as a crucible holds fire.

Guillaume's stare melted into a slow smile. A little light kindled behind his eyes as he swept the long, strong lines of her with a practiced gaze. The smile broadened, and suddenly he burst into full-throated laughter, a deep bull bellow of amusement and delight.

"By the Nails!" he roared. "Here's welcome for the warrior! And what forfeit d'ye offer, pretty one, for your life?"

She blazed a curse at him.

"So? Naughty words for a mouth so fair, my lady. We'll not deny you put up a gallant battle. No man could have done better, and many have done worse. But against Guillaume—" He inflated his splendid chest and grinned down at her from the depths of his jutting beard. "Come to me, pretty one," he commanded. "I'll wager your mouth is sweeter than your words."

Jirel drove a spurred heel into the shin of one guard and twisted from his grip as he howled, bringing up an iron knee into the abdomen of the other. She had writhed from their grip and made three long strides toward the door before Guillaume caught her. She felt his arms closing about her from behind, and lashed out with both spiked heels in a futile assault upon his leg armor, twisting like a maniac, fighting with her knees and spurs, straining hopelessly at the ropes which bound her arms. Guillaume laughed and whirled her round, grinning down into the blaze of her yellow eyes. Then deliberately he set a fist under her chin and tilted her mouth up to his. There was a cessation of her hoarse curses.

"By Heaven, that's like kissing a sword-blade," said Guillaume, lifting his lips at last.

Jirel choked something that was mercifully muffled as she darted her head sidewise, like a serpent striking, and sank her teeth into his neck. She missed the jugular by a fraction of an inch.

Guillaume said nothing, then. He sought her head with a steady hand, found it despite her wild writhing, sank iron fingers deep into the hinges of her jaw, forcing her teeth relentlessly apart. When he had her free he glared down into the yellow hell of her eyes for an instant. The blaze of them was hot enough to scorch his scarred face. He grinned and lifted his ungauntleted hand, and with one heavy blow in the face he knocked her half-way across the room. She lay still upon the flags.

* * *

2

Jirel opened her yellow eyes upon darkness. She lay quiet for a while, collecting her scattered thoughts. By degrees it came back to her, and she muffled upon her arm a sound that was half curse and half sob. Joiry had fallen. For a time she lay rigid in the dark, forcing herself to the realization.

The sound of feet shifting on stone nearby brought her out of that particular misery. She sat up cautiously, feeling about her to determine in what part of Joiry its liege lady was imprisoned. She knew that the sound she had heard must be a sentry, and by the dank smell of the darkness that she was underground. In one of the little dungeon cells, of course. With careful quietness she got to her feet, muttering a curse as her head reeled for an instant and then began to throb. In the utter dark she felt around the cell. Presently she came to a little wooden stool in a corner, and was satisfied. She gripped one leg of it with firm fingers and made her soundless way around the wall until she had located the door.

The sentry remembered, afterward, that he had heard the wildest shriek for help which had ever rung in his ears, and he remembered unbolting the door. Afterward, until they found him lying inside the locked cell with a cracked skull, he remembered nothing.

Jirel crept up the dark stairs of the north turret, murder in her heart. Many little hatreds she had known in her life, but no such blaze as this. Before her eyes in the night she could see Guillaume's scornful, scarred face laughing, the little jutting beard split with the whiteness of his mirth. Upon her mouth she felt the remembered weight of his, about her the strength of his arms. And such a blast of hot fury came over her that she reeled a little and clutched at the wall for support. She went on in a haze of red anger, and something like madness burning in her brain as a resolve slowly took shape out of the chaos of her hate. When that thought came to her she paused again, mid-step upon the stairs, and was conscious of a little coldness blowing over her. Then it was gone, and she shivered a little, shook her shoulders and grinned wolfishly, and went on.

By the stars she could see through the arrow-slits in the wall it must be near to midnight. She went softly on the stairs, and she encountered no one. Her little tower room at the top was empty. Even the straw pallet where the serving-wench slept had not been used that night. Jirel got herself out of her armor alone, somehow, after much striving and twisting. Her doeskin shirt was stiff with sweat and stained with blood. She tossed it disdainfully into a corner. The fury in her eyes had cooled now to a contained and secret flame. She smiled to herself as she slipped a fresh shirt of doeskin over tousled red head and donned a brief tunic of link-mail. On her legs she buckled the greaves of some forgotten legionary, relic of the not long past days when Rome still ruled the world. She thrust a dagger through her belt and took her long two-handed sword bare-bladed in her grip. The she went down the stairs again.

She knew there must have been revelry and feasting in the great hall that night, and by the silence hanging so heavily now she was sure that most of her enemies lay still in drunken slumber, and she experienced a swift regret for the gallons of her good French wine so wasted. And the thought flashed through her head that a determined woman with a sharp sword might work some little damage among the drunken sleepers before she was overpowered. But she put that idea by, for Guillaume would have posted sentries to spare, and she must not give up her secret freedom so fruitlessly.

* * *

Down the dark stairs she went, and crossed one corner of the vast central hall whose darkness she was sure hid wine-deadened sleepers, and so into the lesser dimness of the rough little chapel that Joiry boasted. She had been sure she would find Father Gervase there, and she was not mistaken. He rose from his knees before the altar, dark in his robe, the starlight through the narrow window shining upon his tonsure.

"My daughter!" he whispered. "My daughter! How have you escaped? Shall I find you a mount? If you can pass the sentries you should be in your cousin's castle by daybreak."

She hushed him with a lifted hand.

"No," she said. "It is not outside I go this night. I have a more perilous journey even than that to make. Shrive me, father."

He stared at her.

"What is it?"

She dropped to her knees before him and gripped the rough cloth of his habit with urgent fingers.

"Shrive me, I say! I go down into hell tonight to pray the devil for a weapon, and it may be I shall not return."

Gervase bent and gripped her shoulders with hands that shook.

"Look at me!" he demanded. "Do you know what you're saying? You go—"

"Down!" She said it firmly. "Only you and I know that passage, father—and not even we can be sure of what lies beyond. But to gain a weapon against that man I would venture into perils even worse than that."

"If I thought you meant it," he whispered, "I would waken Guillaume now and give you into his arms. It would be a kinder fate, my daughter."

"It's that I would walk through hell to escape," she whispered back fiercely. "Can't you see? Oh, God knows I'm not innocent of the ways of light loving—but to be any man's fancy, for a night or two, before he snaps my neck or sells me into slavery—and above all, if that man were Guillaume! Can't you understand?"

"That would be shame enough," nodded Gervase. "But think, Jirel! For that shame there is atonement and absolution, and for that death the gates of heaven open wide. But this other—Jirel, Jirel, never through all eternity may you come out, body or soul, if you venture—down!"

She shrugged.

"To wreak my vengeance upon Guillaume I would go if I knew I should burn in hell for ever."

"But Jirel, I do not think you understand. This is a worse fate than the deepest depths of hell-fire. This is—this is beyond all the bounds of the hells we know. And I think Satan's hottest flames were the breath of paradise, compared to what may befall there."

"I know. Do you think I'd venture down if I could not be sure? Where else would I find such a weapon as I need, save outside God's dominion?"

"Jirel, you shall not!"

"Gervase, I go! Will you shrive me?" The hot yellow eyes blazed into his, lambent in the starlight.

After a moment he dropped his head. "You are my lady. I will give you God's blessing, but it will not avail you—there."

3

She went down into the dungeons again. She went down a long way through utter dark, over stones that were oozy and odorous with moisture, through blackness that had never known the light of day. She might have been a little afraid at other times, but that steady flame of hatred burning behind her eyes was a torch to light the way, and she could not wipe from her memory the feel of Guillaume's arms about her, the scornful press of his lips on her mouth. She whimpered a little, low in her throat, and a hot gust of hate went over her.

In the solid blackness she came at length to a wall, and she set herself to pulling the loose stones from this with her free hand, for she would not lay down the sword. They had never been laid in mortar, and they came out easily. When the way was clear she stepped through and found her feet upon a downward-sloping ramp of smooth stone. She cleared the rubble away from the hole in the wall, and enlarged it enough for a quick passage; for when she came back this way—if she did—it might well be that she would come very fast.

At the bottom of the slope she dropped to her knees on the cold floor and felt about. Her fingers traced the outline of a circle, the veriest crack in the stone. She felt until she found the ring in its center. That ring was of the coldest metal she had ever known, and the smoothest. She could put no name to it. The daylight had never shone upon such metal.

She tugged. The stone was reluctant, and at last she took her sword in her teeth, and put both hands to the lifting. Even then it taxed the limit of her strength, and she was strong as many men. But at last it rose, with the strangest sighing sound, and a little prickle of goose-flesh rippled over her.

Now she took the sword back into her hand and knelt on the rim of the invisible blackness below. She had gone this path once before and once only, and never thought to find any necessity in life strong enough to drive her down again. The way was the strangest she had ever known. There was, she thought, no such passage in all the world save here. It had not been built for human feet to travel. It had not been built for feet at all. It was a narrow, polished shaft that cork-screwed round and round. A snake might have slipped in it and gone shooting down, round and round in dizzy circles—but no snake on earth was big enough to fill that shaft. No human travelers had worn the sides of the spiral so smooth, and she did not care to speculate on what creatures had polished it so, through what ages of passage.

She might never have made that first trip down, nor anyone after her, had not some unknown human hacked the notches which made it possible to descend slowly; that is, she thought it must have been a human. At any rate, the notches were roughly shaped for hands and feet, and spaced not too far apart; but who and when and how she could not even guess. As to the beings who made the shaft, in long-forgotten ages—well, there were devils on earth before man, and the world was very old.

She turned on her face, and slid feet-first into the curving tunnel. That first time she and Gervase had gone down in sweating terror of what lay below, and with devils tugging at their heels. Now she slid easily, not bothering to find toeholds, but slipping swiftly round and round the long spirals with only her hands to break the speed when she went too fast. Round and round she went, round and round.

It was a very long way down. Before she had gone very far the curious dizziness she had known before came over her again, a dizziness not entirely induced by the spirals she whirled around, but a deeper, atomic unsteadiness as if not only she but also the substances around her were shifting. There was something queer about the angles of those curves. She was no scholar in geometry or aught else, but she felt intuitively that the bend and slant of the way she went were somehow outside any other angles or bends she had ever known. They led into the unknown and the dark, but it seemed to her obscurely that they led into deeper darkness and mystery than the merely physical, as if, though she could not put it clearly even into thoughts, the peculiar and exact lines of the tunnel had been carefully angled to lead through poly-dimensional space as well as through the underground—perhaps through time, too. She did not know she was thinking such things; but all about her was a blurred dizziness as she shot down and round, and she knew that the way she went took her on a stranger journey than any other was she had ever traveled.

Down, and down. She was sliding fast, but she knew how long it would be. On that first trip they had taken alarm as the passage spiraled so endlessly and with thoughts of the long climb back had tried to stop before it was too late. They had found it impossible. Once embarked, there was no halting. She had tried, and such waves of sick blurring had come over her that she came near to unconsciousness. It was as if she had tried to halt some inexorable process of nature, half finished. They could only go on. The very atoms of their bodies shrieked in rebellion against a reversal of the change.

And the way up, when they returned, had not been difficult. They had had visions of a back-breaking climb up interminable curves, but again the uncanny difference of those angles from those they knew was manifested. In a queer way they seemed to defy gravity, or perhaps led through some way outside the power of it. They had been sick and dizzy on the return, as on the way down, but through the clouds of that confusion it had seemed to them that they slipped as easily up the shaft as they had gone down; or perhaps that, once in the tunnel, there was neither up nor down.

* * *

The passage leveled gradually. This was the worst part for a human to travel, though it must have eased the speed of whatever beings the shaft was made for. It was too narrow for her to turn in, and she had to lever herself face down and feet first, along the horizontal smoothness of the floor, pushing with her hands. She was glad when her questing heels met open space and she slid from the mouth of the shaft and stood upright in the dark.

Here she paused to collect herself. Yes, this was the beginning of the long passage she and Father Gervase had traveled on that long-ago journey of exploration. By the veriest accident they had found the place, and only the veriest bravado had brought them thus far. He had gone on a greater distance than she—she was younger then, and more amenable to authority—and had come back white-faced in the torchlight and hurried her up the shaft again.

She went on carefully, feeling her way, remembering what she herself had seen in the darkness a little farther on, wondering in spite of herself, and with a tiny catch at her heart, what it was that had sent Father Gervase so hastily back. She had never been entirely satisfied with his explanations. It had been about here—or was it a little farther on? The stillness was like a roaring in her ears.

Then ahead of her the darkness moved. It was just that—a vast, imponderable shifting of the solid dark. Jesu! This was new! She gripped the cross at her throat with one hand and her sword-hilt with the other. Then it was upon her, striking like a hurricane, whirling her against the walls and shrieking in her ears like a thousand wind-devils—a wild cyclone of the dark that buffeted her mercilessly and tore at her flying hair and raved in her ears with the myriad voices of all lost things crying in the night. The voices were piteous in their terror and loneliness. Tears came to her eyes even as she shivered with nameless dread, for the whirlwind was alive with a dreadful instinct, an animate thing sweeping through the dark of the underground; an unholy thing that made her flesh crawl even though it touched her to the heart with its pitiful little lost voices wailing in the wind where no wind could possibly be.

And then it was gone. In that one flash of an instant it vanished, leaving no whisper to commemorate its passage. Only in the heart of it could one hear the sad little voices wailing or the wild shriek of the wind. She found herself standing stunned, her sword yet gripped futilely in one hand and the tears running down her face. Poor little lost voices, wailing. She wiped the tears away with a shaking hand and set her teeth hard against the weakness of reaction that flooded her. Yet it was a good five minutes before she could force herself on. After a few steps her knees ceased to tremble.

The floor was dry and smooth underfoot. It sloped a little downward, and she wondered into what unplumbed deeps she had descended by now. The silence had fallen heavily again, and she found herself straining for some other sound than the soft padding of her own boots. Then her foot slipped in sudden wetness. She bent, exploring fingers outstretched, feeling without reason that the sweetness would be red if she could see it. But her fingers traced the immense outline of a footprint—splayed and three-toed like a frog's, but of monster size. It was a fresh footprint. She had a vivid flash of memory—that thing she had glimpsed in the torchlight on the other trip down. But she had light then, and now she was blind in the dark, the creature's natural habitat….

For a moment she was not Jirel of Joiry, vengeful fury on the trail of a devilish weapon, but a frightened woman alone in the unholy dark. That memory had been so vivid…. Then she saw Guillaume's scornful, laughing face again, the little beard dark along the line of his jaw, the strong teeth white with his laughter; and something hot and sustaining swept over her like a thin flame, and she was Joiry again, vengeful and resolute. She went on more slowly, her sword swinging in a semicircle before every third step, that she might not be surprised too suddenly by some nightmare monster clasping her in smothering arms. But the flesh crept upon her unprotected back.

* * *

The smooth passage went on and on. She could feel the cold walls on either hand, and her upswung sword grazed the roof. It was like crawling through some worm's tunnel, blindly under the weight of countless tons of earth. She felt the pressure of it above and about her, overwhelming, and found herself praying that the end of this tunnel-crawling might come soon, whatever the end might bring.

But when it came it was a stranger thing than she had ever dreamed. Abruptly she felt the immense, imponderable oppression cease. No longer was she conscious of the tons of earth pressing about her. The walls had fallen away and her feet struck a sudden rubble instead of the smooth floor.

But the darkness that had bandaged her eyes was changed too, indescribably. It was no longer darkness, but void; not an absence of light, but simple nothingness. Abysses opened around her, yet she could see nothing. She only knew that she stood at the threshold of some immense space, and sensed nameless things about her, and battled vainly against that nothingness which was all her straining eyes could see. And at her throat something constricted painfully.

She lifted her hand and found the chain of her crucifix taut and vibrant around her neck. At that she smiled a little grimly, for she began to understand. The crucifix. She found her hand shaking despite herself, but she unfastened the chain and dropped the cross to the ground. Then she gasped.

All about her, as suddenly as the awakening from a dream, the nothingness had opened out into undreamed-of distances. She stood high on a hilltop under a sky spangled with strange stars. Below she caught glimpses of misty plains and valleys with mountain peaks rising far away. And at her feet a ravening circle of small, slavering, blind things leaped with clashing teeth.

They were obscene and hard to distinguish against the darkness of the hillside, and the noise they made was revolting. Her sword swung up of itself, almost, and slashed furiously at the little dark horrors leaping up around her legs. They died squashily, splattering her bare thighs with unpleasantness, and after a few had gone silent under the blade the rest fled into the dark with quick, frightened pantings, their feet making a queer splashing noise on the stones.

Jirel gathered a handful of the coarse grass which grew there and wiped her legs of the obscene splatters, looking about with quickened breath upon this land so unholy that one who bore a cross might not even see it. Here, if anywhere, one might find a weapon such as she sought. Behind her in the hillside was the low tunnel opening from which she had emerged. Overhead the strange stars shone. She did not recognize a single constellation, and if the brighter sparks were planets they were strange ones, tinged with violet and green and yellow. One was vividly crimson, like a point of fire. Far out over the rolling land below she could discern a mighty column of light. It did not blaze, nor illuminate the dark about. It cast no shadows. It simply was a great pillar of luminance towering high in the night. It seemed artificial—perhaps man-made, though she scarcely dared hope for men here.

She had half expected, despite her brave words, to come out upon the storied and familiar red-hot pave of hell, and this pleasant, starlit land surprised her and made her more wary. The things that built the tunnel could not have been human. She had no right to expect men here. She was a little stunned by finding open sky so far underground, though she was intelligent enough to realize that however she had come, she was not underground now. No cavity in the earth could contain this starry sky. She came of a credulous age, and she accepted her surroundings without too much questioning, though she was a little disappointed, if the truth were known, in the pleasantness of the mistily starlit place. The fiery streets of hell would have been a likelier locality in which to find a weapon against Guillame.

When she had cleansed her sword on the grass and wiped her legs clean, she turned slowly down the hill. The distant column beckoned her, and after a moment of indecision she turned toward it. She had no time to waste, and this was the likeliest place to find what she sought.

The coarse grass brushed her legs and whispered round her feet. She stumbled now and then on the rubble, for the hill was steep, but she reached the bottom without mishap, and struck out across the meadows toward that blaze of far-away brilliance. It seemed to her that she walked more lightly, somehow. The grass scarcely bent underfoot and she found she could take long sailing strides like one who runs with wings on his heels. It felt like a dream. The gravity pull of the place must have been less than she was accustomed to, but she only knew that she was skimming over the ground with amazing speed.

Traveling so, she passed through the meadows over the strange, coarse grass, over a brook or two that spoke endlessly to itself in a curious language that was almost speech, certainly not the usual gurgle of earth's running water. Once she ran into a blotch of darkness, like some pocket of void in the air and struggled through gasping and blinking outraged eyes. She was beginning to realize that the land was not so innocently normal as it looked.

On and on she went, at that surprising speed, while the meadows skimmed past beneath her flying feet and gradually the light drew nearer. She saw now that it was a round tower of sheeted luminance, as if walls of solid flame rose up from the ground. Yet it seemed to be steady, nor did it cast any illumination upon the sky.

* * *

Before much time had elapsed, with her dream-like speed she had almost reached her goal. The ground was becoming marshy underfoot, and presently the smell of swamps rose in her nostrils and she saw that between her and the light stretched a belt of unstable ground tufted with black reedy grass. Here and there she could see dim white blotches moving. They might be beasts, or only wisps of mist. The starlight was not very illuminating.

She began to pick her way carefully across the black, quaking morasses. Where the tufts of grass rose she found firmer ground, and she leaped from clump to clump with that amazing lightness, so that her feet barely touched the black ooze. Here and there slow bubbles rose through the mud and broke thickly. She did not like the place.

Half-way across, she saw one of the white blotches approaching her with slow, erratic movements. It bumped along unevenly, and at first she thought it might be inanimate, its approach was so indirect and purposeless. Then it blundered nearer, with that queer bumpy gait, making sucking noises in the ooze and splashing as it came. In the starlight she saw suddenly what it was, and for an instant her heart paused and sickness rose overwhelmingly in her throat. It was a woman—a beautiful woman whose white bare body had the curves and loveliness of some marble statue. She was crouching like a frog and as Jirel watched in stupefaction she straightened her legs abruptly and leaped as a frog leaps, only more clumsily, falling forward into the ooze a little distance beyond the watching woman. She did not seem to see Jirel. The mud-spattered face was blank. She blundered on through the mud in awkward leaps. Jirel watched until the woman was no more than a white wandering blur in the dark and above the shock of that sight pity was rising, and uncomprehending resentment against whatever had brought so lovely a creature into this—into blundering in frog leaps aimlessly through the mud, with empty mind and blind, staring eyes. For the second time that night she knew the sting of unaccustomed tears as she went on.

The sight, though, had given her reassurance. The human form was not unknown here. There might be leathery devils with hoofs and horns, such as she still half expected, but she would not be alone in her humanity; though if all the rest were as piteously mindless as the one she had seen—she did not follow that thought. It was too unpleasant. She was glad when the marsh was past and she need not see any longer the awkward white shapes bumping along through the dark.

She struck out across the narrow space which lay between her and the tower. She saw now that it was a building, and that the light composed it. She could not understand that, but she saw it. Walls and columns outlined the tower, solid sheets of light with definite boundaries, not radiant. As she came nearer she saw that it was in motion, apparently spurting up from some source underground as if the light illuminated sheets of water rushing upward under great pressure. Yet she felt intuitively that it was not water, but incarnate light.

She came forward hesitantly, gripping her sword. The area around the tremendous pillar was paved with something black and smooth that did not reflect the light. Out of it sprang the uprushing walls of brilliance with their sharply defined edges. The magnitude of the thing dwarfed her to infinitesimal size. She stared upward with undazzled eyes, trying to understand. If there could be such a thing as solid, non-radiating light, this was it.

4

She was very near under the mighty tower before she could see the details of the building clearly. They were strange to her—great pillars and arches around the base, and one stupendous portal, all molded out of the rushing, prisoned light. She turned toward the opening after a moment, for the light had a tangible look. She did not believe she could have walked through it even had she dared.

When that tremendous portal arched over her she peered in, affrighted by the very size of the place. She thought she could hear the hiss and spurt of the light surging upward. She was looking into a mighty globe inside, a hall shaped like the interior of a bubble, though the curve was so vast she was scarcely aware of it. And in the very center of the globe floated a light. Jirel blinked. A light, dwelling in a bubble of light. It glowed there in midair with a pale, steady flame that was somehow alive and animate, and brighter than the serene illumination of the building, for it hurt her eyes to look at it directly.

She stood on the threshold and stared, not quite daring to venture in. And as she hesitated a change came over the light. A flash of rose tinged its pallor. The rose deepened and darkened until it took on the color of blood. And the shape underwent strange changes. It lengthened, drew itself out narrowly, split at the bottom into two branches, put out two tendrils from the top. The blood-red paled again, and the light somehow lost its brilliance, receded into the depths of the thing that was forming. Jirel clutched her sword and forgot to breathe, watching. The light was taking on the shape of a human being—of a woman—of a tall woman in mail, her red hair tousled and her eyes staring straight into the eyes at the portal.....

"Welcome," said the Jirel suspended in the center of the globe, her voice deep and resonant and clear in spite of the distance between them. Jirel at the door held her breath, wondering and afraid. This was herself, in every detail, a mirrored Jirel—that was it, a Jirel mirrored upon a surface which blazed and smoldered with barely repressed light, so that the eyes gleamed with it and the whole figure seemed to hold its shape by an effort, only by that effort restraining itself from resolving into pure, formless light again. But the voice was not her own. It shook and resounded with a knowledge as alien as the light-built walls. It mocked her. It said,

"Welcome! Enter into the portals, woman!"

She looked up warily at the rushing walls about her. Instinctively she drew back.

"Enter, enter!" urged that mocking voice from her own mirrored lips. And there was a note in it she did not like.

"Enter!" cried the voice again, this time a command.

Jirel's eyes narrowed. Something intuitive warned her back, and yet— she drew the dagger she had thrust in her belt and with a quick motion she tossed it into the great globe-shaped hall. It struck the floor without a sound, and a brilliant light flared up around it, so brilliant she could not look upon what was happening; but it seemed to her that the knife expanded, grew large and nebulous and ringed with dazzling light. In less time than it takes to tell, it had faded out of sight as if the very atoms which composed it had flown apart and dispersed in the golden glow of that mighty bubble. The dazzle faded with the knife, leaving Jirel staring dazedly at a bare floor.

That other Jirel laughed, a rich, resonant laugh of scorn and malice.

"Stay out, then," said the voice. "You've more intelligence than I thought. Well, what would you here?"

Jirel found her voice with an effort.

"I seek a weapon," she said, "a weapon against a man I so hate that upon earth there is none terrible enough for my need."

"You so hate him, eh?" mused the voice.

"With all my heart!"

"With all your heart!" echoed the voice, and there was an undernote of laughter in it that she did not understand. The echoes of that mirth ran round and round the great globe. Jirel felt her cheeks burn with resentment against some implication in the derision which she could not put a name to. When the echoes of the laugh had faded the voice said indifferently,

"Give the man what you find at the black temple in the lake. I make you a gift of it."

The lips that were Jirel's twisted into a laugh of purest mockery; then all about that figure so perfectly her own the light flared out. She saw the outlines melting fluidly as she turned her dazzled eyes away. Before the echoes of that derision had died, a blinding, formless light burned once more in the midst of the bubble.

* * *

Jirel turned and stumbled away under the mighty column of the tower, a hand to her dazzled eyes. Not until she had reached the edge of the black, unreflecting circle that paved the ground around the pillar did she realize that she knew no way of finding the lake where her weapon lay. And not until then did she remember how fatal it is said to be to accept a gift from a demon. Buy it, or earn it, but never accept the gift. Well—she shrugged and stepped out upon the grass. She must surely be damned by now, for having ventured down of her will into this curious place for such a purpose as hers. The soul can be lost but once.

She turned her face up to the strange stars and wondered in what direction her course lay. The sky looked blankly down upon her with its myriad meaningless eyes. A star fell as she watched, and in her superstitious soul, she took it for an omen, and set off boldly over the dark meadows in the direction where the bright streak had faded. No swamps guarded the way here, and she was soon skimming along over the grass with that strange, dancing gait that the lightness of the place allowed her. And as she went she was remembering, as from long ago in some other far world, a man's arrogant mirth and the press of his mouth on hers. Hatred bubbled up hotly within her and broke from her lips in a little savage laugh of anticipation. What dreadful thing awaited her in the temple in the lake, what punishment from hell to be loosed by her own hands upon Guillaume? And though her soul was the price it cost her, she would count it a fair bargain if she could drive the laughter from his mouth and bring terror into the eyes that mocked her.

Thoughts like these kept her company for a long way upon her journey. She did not think to be lonely or afraid in the uncanny darkness across which no shadows fell from that mighty column behind her. The unchanging meadows flew past underfoot, lightly as meadows in a dream. It might almost have been that the earth moved instead of herself, so effortlessly did she go. She was sure now that she was heading in the right direction, for two more stars had fallen in the same arc across the sky.

The meadows were not untenanted. Sometimes she felt presences near her in the dark, and once she ran full-tilt into a nest of little yapping horrors like those on the hill-top. They lunged up about her with clicking teeth, mad with a blind ferocity, and she swung her sword in frantic circles, sickened by the noise of them lunging splashily through the grass and splattering her sword with their deaths. She beat them off and went on, fighting her own sickness, for she had never known anything quite so nauseating as these little monstrosities.

She crossed a brook that talked to itself in the darkness with that queer murmuring which came so near to speech, and a few strides beyond it she paused suddenly, feeling the ground tremble with the rolling thunder of hoofbeats approaching. She stood still, searching the dark anxiously, and presently the earth-shaking beat grew louder and she saw a white blur flung wide across the dimness to her left, and the sound of hoofs deepened and grew. Then out of the night swept a herd of snow-white horses. Magnificently they ran, manes tossing, tails streaming, feet pounding a rhythmic, heart-stirring roll along the ground. She caught her breath at the beauty of their motion. They swept by a little distance away, tossing their heads, spurning the ground with scornful feet.

But as they came abreast of her she saw one blunder a little and stumble against the next, and that one shook his head bewilderedly; and suddenly she realized that they were blind—all running so splendidly in a deeper dark than even she groped through. And she saw too their coats were roughened with sweat, and foam dripped from their lips, and their nostrils were flaring pools of scarlet. Now and again one stumbled from pure exhaustion. Yet they ran, frantically, blindly though the dark, driven by something outside their comprehension.

As the last one of all swept by her, sweat-crusted and staggering, she saw him toss his head high, spattering foam, and whinny shrilly to the stars. And it seemed to her that the sound was strangely articulate. Almost she heard the echoes of a name—"Julienne! Julienne!"—in that high, despairing sound. And the incongruity of it, the bitter despair, clutched at her heart so sharply that for the third time that night she knew the sting of tears.

The dreadful humanity of that cry echoed in her ears as the thunder died away. She went on, blinking back the tears for that beautiful blind creature, staggering with exhaustion, calling a girl's name hopelessly from a beast's throat into the blank darkness wherein it was forever lost.

Then another star fell across the sky, and she hurried ahead, closing her mind to the strange, incomprehensible pathos that made an undernote of tears to the starry dark of this land. And the thought was growing in her mind that, though she had come into no brimstone pit where horned devils pranced over flames, yet perhaps it was after all a sort of hell through which she ran.

* * *

Presently in the distance she caught a glimmer of something bright. The ground dipped after that and she lost it, and skimmed through a hollow where pale things wavered away from her into the deeper dark. She never knew what they were, and was glad. When she came up onto higher ground again she saw it more clearly, an expanse of dim brilliance ahead. She hoped it was a lake, and ran more swiftly.

It *was* a lake—a lake that could never have existed outside some obscure hell like this. She stood on the brink doubtfully, wondering if this could be the place the light-devil had meant. Black, shining water stretched out before her, heaving gently with a motion unlike that of any water she had ever seen before. And in the depths of it, like fireflies caught in ice, gleamed myriad small lights. They were fixed there immovably, not stirring with the motion of the water. As she watched, something hissed above her and a streak of light split the dark air. She looked up in time to see something bright curving across the sky to fall without a splash into the water, and small ripples of phosphorescence spread sluggishly toward the shore, where they broke at her feet with the queerest whispering sound, as if each succeeding ripple spoke the syllable of a word.

She looked up, trying to locate the origin of the falling lights, but the strange stars looked down upon her blankly. She bent and stared down into the center of the spreading ripples, and where the thing had fallen she thought a new light twinkled through the water. She could not determine what it was, and after a curious moment she gave the question up and began to cast about for the temple the light-devil had spoken of.

After a moment she thought she saw something dark in the center of the lake, and when she had stared for a few minutes it gradually became clearer, an arch of darkness against the starry background of the water. It might be a temple. She strolled slowly along the brim of the lake, trying to get a closer view of it, for the thing was no more than a darkness against the spangles of light, like some void in the sky where no stars shine. And presently she stumbled over something in the grass.

She looked down with startled yellow eyes, and saw a strange, indistinguishable darkness. It had solidity to the feel but scarcely to the eye, for she could not quite focus upon it. It was like trying to see something that did not exist save as a void, a darkness in the grass. It had the shape of a step, and when she followed with her eyes she saw that it was the beginning of a dim bridge stretching out over the lake, narrow and curved and made out of nothingness. It seemed to have no surface, and its edges were difficult to distinguish from the lesser gloom surrounding it. But the thing was tangible—an arch carved out of the solid dark—and it led out in the direction she wished to go. For she was naïvely sure now that the dim blot in the center of the lake was the temple she was searching for. The falling stars had guided her, and she could not have gone astray.

So she set her teeth and gripped her sword and put her foot upon the bridge. It was rock-firm under her, but scarcely more than a foot to so wide, and without rails. When she had gone a step or two she began to feel dizzy; for under her the water heaved with a motion that made her head swim, and the stars twinkled eerily in its depths. She dared not look away for fear of missing her footing on the narrow arch of darkness. It was like walking a bridge flung across the void, with stars underfoot and nothing but an unstable strip of nothingness to bear her up. Half-way across, the heaving of the water and the illusion of vast, constellated spaces beneath and the look her bridge had of being no more than empty space ahead, combined to send her head reeling; and as she stumbled on, the bridge seemed to be wavering with her, swinging in gigantic arcs across the starry void below.

Now she could see the temple more closely, though scarcely more clearly than from the shore. It looked to be no more than an outlined emptiness against the star-crowded brilliance behind it, etching its arches and columns of blankness upon the twinkling waters. The bridge came down in a long dim swoop to its doorway. Jirel took the last few yards at a reckless run and stopped breathless under the arch that made the temple's vague doorway. She stood there panting and staring about narrow-eyed, sword poised in her hand. For though the place was empty and very still she felt a presence even as she set her foot upon the floor of it.

She was staring about a little space of blankness in the starry lake. It seemed to be no more than that. She could see the walls and columns, where they were outlined against the water and where they made darknesses in the star-flecked sky, but where there was only dark behind them she could see nothing. It was a tiny place, no more than a few square yards of emptiness upon the face of the twinkling waters. And in its center an image stood.

She stared at it in silence, feeling a curious compulsion growing within her, like a vague command from something outside herself. The image was of some substance of nameless black, unlike the material which composed the building, for even in the dark she could see it clearly. It was a semi-human figure, crouching forward with outthrust head, sexless and strange. Its one central eye was closed as if in rapture, and its mouth was pursed for a kiss. And though it was but an image without even the semblance of life, she felt unmistakably the presence of something alive in the temple, something so alien and innominate that instinctively she drew away.

* * *

She stood there for a full minute, reluctant to enter the place where so alien a being dwelt, half-conscious of that voiceless compulsion growing up within her. And slowly she became aware that all the lines and angles of the half-seen building were curved to make the image their center and focus. The very bridge swooped its long arc to complete the centering. As she watched, it seemed to her that through the arches of the columns even the stars in lake and sky were grouped in patterns which took the image for their focus. Every line and curve in the dim world seemed to sweep round toward the squatting thing before her with its closed eye and expectant mouth.

Gradually the universal focusing of lines began to exert its influence upon her. She took a hesitant step forward without realizing the motion. But that step was all the dormant urge within her needed. With her one motion forward the compulsion closed down upon her with whirlwind impetuosity. Helplessly she felt herself advancing, helplessly with one small, sane portion of her mind she realized the madness that was gripping her, the blind, irresistible urge to do what every visible line in the temple's construction was made to compel. With stars swirling around her she advanced across the floor and laid her hands upon the rounded shoulders of the image—the sword, forgotten, making a sort of accolade against its hunched neck—and lifted her red head and laid her mouth blindly against the pursed lips of the image.

In a dream she took that kiss. In a dream of dizziness and confusion she seemed to feel the iron-cold lips stirring under hers. And through the union of that kiss—warm-blooded woman with image of nameless stone—through the meeting of their mouths something entered into her very soul; something cold and stunning; something alien beyond any words. It lay upon her shuddering soul like some frigid weight from the void, a bubble holding something unthinkably alien and dreadful. She could feel the heaviness of it upon some intangible part of her that shrank from the touch. It was like the weight of remorse or despair, only far colder and stranger and—somehow—more ominous, as if this weight were but the egg from which things might hatch too dreadful to put even into thoughts.

The moment of the kiss could have been no longer than a breath's space, but to her it was timeless. In a dream she felt the compulsion falling from her at last. In a dim dream she dropped her hands from its shoulders, finding the sword heavy in her grasp and staring dully at it for a while before clarity began its return to her cloudy mind. When she became completely aware of herself once more she was standing with slack body and dragging head before the blind, rapturous image, that dead weight upon her heart as dreary as an old sorrow, and more coldly ominous than anything she could find words for.

And with returning clarity the most staggering terror came over her, swiftly and suddenly—terror of the image and the temple of darkness, and the coldly spangled lake and of the whole, wide, dim, dreadful world about her. Desperately she longed for home again, even the red fury of hatred and the press of Guillaume's mouth and the hot arrogance of his eyes again. Anything but this. She found herself running without knowing why. Her feet skimmed over the narrow bridge lightly as a gull's wings dipping the water. In a brief instant the starry void of the lake flashed by beneath her and the solid earth was underfoot. She saw the great column of light far away across the dark meadows and beyond it a hill-top rising against the stars. And she ran.

She ran with terror at her heels and devils howling in the wind her own speed made. She ran from her own curiously alien body, heavy with its weight of inexplicable doom. She passed through the hollow where pale things wavered away, she fled over the uneven meadows in a frenzy of terror. She ran and ran, in those long light bounds the lesser gravity allowed her, fleeter than a deer, and her own panic choked in her throat and that weight upon her soul dragged at her too drearily for tears. She fled to escape it, and could not; and the ominous certainty that she carried something too dreadful to think of grew and grew.

For a long while she skimmed over the grass, tirelessly, wing-heeled, her red hair flying. The panic died after a while, but that sense of heavy disaster did not die. She felt somehow that tears would ease her, but something in the frigid darkness of her soul froze her tears in the ice of that gray and alien chill.

And gradually, through the inner dark, a fierce anticipation took form in her mind. Revenge upon Guillaume! She had taken from the temple only a kiss, so it was that which she must deliver to him. And savagely she exulted in the thought of what that kiss would release upon him, unsuspecting. She did not know, but it filled her with fierce joy to guess.

* * *

She had passed the column and skirted the morass where the white, blundering forms still bumped along awkwardly through the ooze, and was crossing the coarse grass toward the nearing hill when the sky began to pale along the horizon. And with that pallor a fresh terror took hold upon her, a wild horror of daylight in this unholy land. She was not sure if it was the light itself she so dreaded, or what that light would reveal in the dark stretches she had traversed so blindly—what unknown horrors she had skirted in the night. But she knew instinctively that if she valued her sanity she must be gone before the light had risen over the land. And she redoubled her efforts, spurring her wearying limb to yet more skimming speed. But it would be a close race, for already the stars were blurring out, and a flush of curious green was broadening along the sky, and around her the air was turning to a vague, unpleasant gray.

She toiled up the steep hillside breathlessly. When she was half-way up, her own shadow began to take form upon the rocks, and it was unfamiliar and dreadfully significant of something just outside her range of understanding. She averted her eyes from it, afraid that at any moment the meaning might break upon her outraged brain.

She could see the top of the hill above her, dark against the paling sky, and she toiled up in frantic haste, clutching her sword and feeling that if she had to look in the full light upon the dreadful little abominations that had snapped around her feet when she first emerged she would collapse into screaming hysteria.

The cave-mouth yawned before her, invitingly black, a refuge from the dawning light behind her. She knew an almost irresistible desire to turn and look back from this vantage-point across the land she had traversed, and gripped her sword hard to conquer the perversive longing. There was a scuffling in the rocks at her feet, and set her teeth in her under-lip and swung viciously in brief arcs, without looking down. She heard small squeakings and the splashy sound of feet upon the stones, and felt her blade shear thrice through semi-solidity, to the click of little vicious teeth. Then they broke and ran off over the hillside, and she stumbled on, choking back the scream that wanted so fiercely to break from her lips.

She fought that growing desire all the way up to the cave-mouth, for she knew that if she gave way she would never cease shrieking until her throat went raw.

Blood was trickling from her bitten lip with the effort at silence when she reached the cave. And there, twinkling upon the stones, lay something small and bright and dearly familiar. With a sob of relief she bent and snatched up the crucifix she had torn from her throat when she came out into this land. And as her fingers shut upon it a vast, protecting darkness swooped around her. Gasping with relief, she groped her way the step or two that separated her from the cave.

Dark lay like a blanket over her eyes, and she welcomed it gladly, remembering how her shadow had lain so awfully upon the hillside as she climbed, remembering the first rays of savage sunlight beating upon her shoulders. She stumbled through the blackness, slowly getting control again over her shaking body and laboring lungs, slowly stilling the panic that the dawning day had roused so inexplicably within her. And as that terror died, the dull weight upon her spirit became strong again. She had all but forgotten it in her panic, but now the impending and unknown dreadfulness grew heavier and more oppressive in the darkness of the underground, and she groped along in a dull stupor of her own depression, slow with the weight of the strange doom she carried.

* * *

Nothing barred her way. In the dullness of her stupor she scarcely realized it, or expected any of the vague horrors that peopled the place to leap out upon her. Empty and unmenacing, the way stretched before her blindly stumbling feet. Only once did she hear the sound of another presence—the rasp of hoarse breathing and the scrape of a scaly hide against the stone—but it must have been outside the range of her own passage, for she encountered nothing.

When she had come to the end and a cold wall rose up before her, it was scarcely more than automatic habit that made her search along it with groping hand until she came to the mouth of the shaft. It sloped gently up into the dark. She crawled in, trailing her sword, until the rising incline and lowering roof forced her down upon her face. Then with toes and fingers she began to force herself up the spiral, slippery way.

Before she had gone very far she was advancing without effort, scarcely realizing that it was against gravity she moved. The curious dizziness of the shaft had come over her, the strange feeling of change in the very substance of her body, and through the cloudy numbness of it she felt herself sliding round and round the spirals, without effort. Again, obscurely, she had the feeling that in the peculiar angles of this shaft was neither up nor down. And for a long while the dizzy circling went on.

When the end came at last, and she felt her fingers gripping the edge of that upper opening which lay beneath the floor of Joiry's lowest dungeons, she heaved herself up warily and lay for a while on the cold floor in the dark, while slowly the clouds of dizziness passed from her mind, leaving only that ominous weight within. When the darkness had ceased to circle about her, and the floor steadied, she got up dully and swung the cover back over the opening, her hands shuddering from the feel of the cold, smooth ring which had never seen daylight.

When she turned from this task she was aware of the reason for the lessening in the gloom around her. A guttering light outlined the hole in the wall from which she had pulled the stones—was it a century ago? The brilliance all but blinded her after her long sojourn through blackness, and she stood there awhile, swaying a little, one hand to her eyes, before she went out into the familiar torchlight she knew waited her beyond. Father Gervase, she was sure, anxiously waiting her return. But even he had not dared to follow her through the hole in the wall, down to the brink of the shaft.

Somehow she felt that she should be giddy with relief at this safe homecoming, back to humanity again. But as she stumbled over the upward slope toward light and safety she was conscious of no more than the dullness of whatever unreleased horror it was which still lay so ominously upon her stunned soul.

She came through the gaping hole in the masonry into the full glare of torches awaiting her, remembering with a wry inward smile how wide she had made the opening in anticipation of flight from something dreadful when she came back that way. Well, there was no flight from the horror she bore within her. It seemed to her that her heart was slowing, too, missing a beat now and then and staggering like a weary runner.

She came out into the torchlight, stumbling with exhaustion, her mouth scarlet from the blood of her bitten and her bare greaved legs and bare sword-blade foul with the deaths of those little horrors that swarmed around the cave-mouth. From the tangle of red hair her eyes stared out with a bleak, frozen, inward look, as of one who has seen nameless things. That keen, steel-bright beauty which had been hers was as dull and fouled as her sword-blade, and at the look in her eyes Father Gervase shuddered and crossed himself.

5

They were waiting for her in an uneasy group—the priest anxious and dark, Guillaume splendid in the torchlight, tall and arrogant, a handful of men-at-arms holding the guttering lights and shifting uneasily from one foot to the other. When she saw Guillaume the light that flared up in her eyes blotted out for a moment the dreadfulness behind them, and her slowing heart leaped like a spurred horse, sending the blood riotously through her veins. Guillaume, magnificent in his armor, leaning upon his sword and staring down at her from his scornful height, the little black beard jutting. Guillaume, to whom Joiry had fallen. Guillaume.

That which she carried at the core of her being was heavier than anything else in the world, so heavy she could scarcely keep her knees from bending, so heavy her heart labored under its weight. Almost irresistibly she wanted to give way beneath it, to sink down and down under the crushing load, to lie prone and vanquished in the ice-gray, bleak place she was so dimly aware of through the clouds that were rising about her. But there was Guillaume, grim and grinning, and she hated him so very bitterly— she must make the effort. She must, at whatever cost, for she was coming to know that death lay in wait for her if she bore this burden long, that it was a two-edged weapon which could strike at its wielder if the blow were delayed too long. She knew this through the dim mists that were thickening in her brain, and she put all her strength into the immense effort it cost to cross the floor toward him. She stumbled a little, and made one faltering step and then another, and dropped her sword with a clang as she lifted her arms to him.

He caught her strongly, in a hard, warm clasp, and she heard his laugh triumphant and hateful as he bent his head to take the kiss she was raising her mouth to offer. He must have seen, in that last moment before their lips met, the savage glare of victory in her eyes, and been startled. But he did not hesitate. His mouth was heavy upon hers.

It was a long kiss. She felt him stiffen in her arms. She felt a coldness in the lips upon hers, and slowly the dark weight of what she bore lightened, lifted, cleared away from her cloudy mind. Strength flowed back through her richly. The whole world came alive to her once more. Presently she loosed his slack arms and stepped away, looking up into his face with a keen and dreadful triumph upon her own.

She saw the ruddiness of him draining away, and the rigidity of stone coming over his scarred features. Only his eyes remained alive, and there was torment in them, and understanding. She was glad—she had wanted him to understand what it cost to take Joiry's kiss unbidden. She smiled thinly into his tortured eyes, watching. And she saw something cold and alien seeping through him, permeating him slowly with some unnamable emotion which no man could ever have experienced before. She could not name it, but she saw it in his eyes—some dreadful emotion never made for flesh and blood to know, some iron despair such as only an unguessable being from the gray, formless void could ever have felt before—too hideously alien for any human creature to endure. Even she shuddered from the dreadful, cold bleakness looking out of his eyes, and knew as she watched that there must be many emotions and many fears and joys too far outside man's comprehension for any being of flesh to undergo, and live. Grayly she saw it spreading through him, and the very substance of his body shuddered under that iron weight.

And now came a visible, physical change. Watching, she was aghast to think that in her own body and upon her own soul she had born the seed of this dreadful flowering, and did not wonder that her heart had slowed under the unbearable weight of it. He was standing rigidly with arms half bent, just as he stood when she slid from his embrace. And now great shudders began to go over him, as if he were wavering in the torchlight, some gray-faced wraith in armor with torment in his eyes. She saw the sweat beading his forehead. She saw a trickle of blood from his mouth, as if he had bitten through his lip in the agony of this new, incomprehensible emotion. Then a last shiver went over him violently, and he flung up his head, the little curling beard jutting ceilingward and the muscles of his strong throat corded, and from his lips broke a long, low cry of such utter, inhuman strangeness that Jirel felt coldness rippling through her veins and she put up her hands to her ears to shut it out. It meant something—it expressed some dreadful emotion that was neither sorrow nor despair nor anger, but infinitely alien and infinitely sad. Then his long legs buckled at the knees and he dropped with a clatter of mail and lay still on the stone floor.

They knew he was dead. That was unmistakable in the way he lay. Jirel stood very still, looking down upon him, and strangely it seemed to her that all the lights in the world had gone out. A moment before he had been so big and vital, so magnificent in the torchlight—she could still feel his kiss upon her mouth, and the hard warmth of his arms....

Suddenly and blindingly it came upon her what she had done. She knew now why such heady violence had flooded her whenever she thought of him—knew why the light-devil in her own form had laughed so derisively—knew the price she must pay for taking a gift from a demon. She knew that there was no light anywhere in the world, now that Guillaume was gone.

Father Gervase took her arm gently. She shook him off with an impatient shrug and dropped to one knee beside Guillaume's body, bending her head so that the red hair fell forward to hide her tears.

For Further Reading

The world of speculative fiction during the literary Modernist era is fascinating in its variety and complexity. Below is a reading list of other American and British speculative texts that were published between 1880 and 1940, texts we did not have room enough to include in our anthology.

Bellamy, Edward. *Looking Backward*

Benjamin, Walter. "The Destructive Character"

Bierce, Ambrose. "The Damned Thing"

Bierce, Ambrose. *One Summer Night*

Blackwood, Algernon. *The Complete John Silence Stories*

Blackwood, Algernon. "The Transfer"

Brown, Bob. *The Readies*

Brown, Charles Brockden. *Arthur Mervyn*

Brown, Charles Brockden. *Ormond*

Brown, Charles Brockden. *Wieland*

Bruno, Giordano. *Of the Infinite Universe and Worlds*

Bulwer-Lytton, Edward. *The Coming Race*

Burroughs, Edgar Rice. *A Princess of Mars*

Burroughs, Edgar Rice. *Return of Tarzan*

Burroughs, Edgar Rice. *Tarzan of the Apes*

Butler, Samuel. "Darwin Among the Machines"

Butler, Samuel. *Erewhon*

Cabell, James Branch. *Jurgen*

Campbell, John W. "Twilight"

Coates, Robert M. *The Eater of Darkness*

Collier, John. *Tom's A-Cold*

Conan Doyle, Arthur. "The Adventure of Charles Augustus Milverton"

Conan Doyle, Arthur. "The Adventure of the Engineer's Thumb"

Conan Doyle, Arthur. "The Doings of Raffles Haw"

Conan Doyle, Arthur. *The Hound of the Baskervilles*

Conan Doyle, Arthur. *The Lost World*

Conan Doyle, Arthur. "A Scandal in Bohemia"

Conan Doyle, Arthur. *The Sign of Four*

Conan Doyle, Arthur. *A Study in Scarlet*

Connington, J.J. *Nordenholt's Million*

Conrad, Joseph. *Heart of Darkness*

Corelli, Marie. *A Romance of Two Worlds*

Crane, Stephen. "The Black Dog"

Crawford, Francis Marion. "The Upper Berth"

Cromie, Robert. *The Crack of Doom*

Crowley, Aleister. *Moonchild*

Dawson, Emma Frances. "An Itinerant House"

Dunbar, Olivia Howard. "The Shell of Sense"

Eddison, E.R. *The Worm Ouroboros*

Elliot, Hugh. "Modern Science and Materialism"

Fleckner, James Elroy. *The Last Generation: A Story of the Future*

Freeman, Mary E. Wilkins. "The Shadows on the Wall"

Gelula, Abner. "Menace of the Automaton"

Gernsback, Hugo. *Ralph 124C 41+*

Gilman, Charlotte Perkins. *Herland*

Hawthorne, Nathaniel. *The House of Seven Gables*

Hodgson, William Hope. "The Gateway of the Monster"

Hodgson, William Hope. *House on the Borderland*

Hodgson, William Hope. *The Night Land*

Hodgson, William Hope. "The Thing Invisible"

Howard, Robert E. "Beyond the Black River"

Howard, Robert E. "Hills of the Dead"

Howard, Robert E. *The Hour of the Dragon*
Howard, Robert E. "Kings of the Night"
Howard, Robert E. "The Mirrors of Tuzun Thune"
Howard, Robert E. "The Phoenix on the Sword"
Howard, Robert E. "The Queen of the Black Coast"
Howard, Robert E. *Red Nails*
Howard, Robert E. "The Shadow Kingdom"
Howard, Robert E. "The Tower of the Elephant"
Howells, William Dean. *A Traveler from Altruria*
Huxley, Aldous. *Brave New World*
James, Henry. *The Turn of the Screw*
James, M.R. "The Ash-Tree"
Jefferies, Richard. *After London*
Kipling, Rudyard. "Mary Postgate"
Kipling, Rudyard. "With the Night Mail"
Lane, Mary E. Bradley. *Mizora*
Le Fanu, Sheridan. *Carmilla*
Le Fanu, Sheridan. *In a Glass Darkly*
Lewis, C.S. *Out of the Silent Planet*
Lewis, C.S. *Perelandra*
Lewis, Matthew. *The Monk*
Lewis, Wyndham. "Manifesto"
Lovecraft, H.P. "The Call of Cthulhu"
Lovecraft, H.P. "The Dunwich Horror"
Lovecraft, H.P. "Dunwich Horror"
Lovecraft, H.P. "Shadow out of Time"
MacDonald, George. *Lilith*
MacDonald, George. *Phantastes*
Machen, Arthur. *The Great God Pan*
Maugham, W. Somerset. *The Magician*
Mitchell, Edward Page. "The Tachypomp"
Morris, William. *News from Nowhere*
Novalis. *Hymns to the Night*
Nowlan, Philip Francis. *Armageddon 2419 AD*
Poe, Edgar Allan. "The Facts in the Case of M. Valdemar"
Poe, Edgar Allan. "The Premature Burial"

Pope Pius X. *Pascendi Dominici Gregis*
Radcliff, Anne. *The Mysteries of Udolpho*
Rymer, James Malcolm. *Varney the Vampyre; or, the Feast of Blood*
Shelley, Mary. *Frankenstein*
Shiel, M.P. *The Purple Cloud*
Smith, Clark Ashton. "The Dimension of Chance"
Smith, Clark Ashton. "The Empire of the Necromancers"
Smith, Clark Ashton. "The Great God Awto"
Smith, Clark Ashton. "The Metamorphosis of the World"
Smith, Thorne. *Topper*
Stevenson, Robert Louis. "The Body Snatcher"
Stevenson, Robert Louis. *The Strange Case of Dr. Jekyll and Mr. Hyde*
Stockton, Frank. "A Tale of Negative Gravity"
Stoker, Bram. *Dracula*
Stoker, Bram. "The Lair of the White Worm"
Stratton, George Frederick. "Sam Graves' Gravity Nullifier"
Tolkien, J.R.R. "Leaf by Niggle"
Twain, Mark. *A Connecticut Yankee in King Arthur's Court*
Underhill, Evelyn. *The Grey World*
Underhill, Evelyn. *Mysticism*
Walpole, Horace. *The Castle of Otranto*
Wells, H.G. "The Country of the Blind"
Wells, H.G. "The Cure for Love"
Wells, H.G. *The First Men in the Moon*
Wells, H.G. *The Time Machine*
Wells, H.G. *The War in the Air*
Wells, H.G. *War of the Worlds*
Wharton, Edith. "Afterward"
Whitehead, Alfred North. *The Concept of Nature*
Wilde, Oscar. "The Canterville Ghost"
Wilde, Oscar. *The Picture of Dorian Grey*

Index